DATE DUE			

BRITANNIA MEWS

MARGERY SHARP

Britannia Mews

Little, Brown and Company · Boston
1946

PRINTED IN THE UNITED STATES OF AMERICA
BY H. WOLFF, NEW YORK

TO

GEOFFREY CASTLE

PART ONE

CHAPTER I

BRITANNIA MEWS was built in 1865 to accommodate the carriage-horses, coachmen, and other respectable dependents of the ten houses in Albion Place. The Place, facing directly upon Hyde Park, and forming in fact a section of the Bayswater Road, was bounded by the north-and-south perpendiculars of Chester Street and Bedford Street; its back doors opened on Albion Alley, which also debouched on these streets; and Britannia Mews opened off the opposite side of the Alley, through a wide and rather handsome arch. The Mews, too, ran north-and-south, squeezed up in the shape of a gin-bottle between the backs of the Chester and Bedford Street houses. Carriages passed in or out by the archway only, and to reach their appropriate front-doors in Albion Place went round, in the current phrase, by either Chester or Bedford. This gave rise to a topographical joke very popular among the young fry of the Place—"James is late again, what can be amiss?" "You know he has to come round by Chester, Mamma!" Many families thought it good enough for *Punch*.

The Mews contained ten sets of stables, each with a three-roomed flat above reached by a steep iron stairway outside. From the head of the stair a narrow iron balcony was carried across the width of the coach-house below, with the door of the flat opening in the middle. As for the interiors, they were rightly considered luxurious. Each separate coach-house boasted its own water-tap, so that housewives had to carry their pails up only one flight of stairs, while in the apartments above were sinks with waste-pipes. Fuel also was carried up, and the combined ovens and hearths necessitated fires all the year round—but it was a great convenience to be able to keep one's half-sack of coals out of the way below. On an average

(3)

the women made no more than six or seven such trips a day; and a good housekeeper, like Mrs. Benson at Number 2 (her husband coachman to the Culvers in Albion Place), could show a spotless establishment by twelve and go out sewing in the afternoon.

There was naturally a manure-heap. It was neatly confined within a low brick wall, and wholesomely redolent not only of itself but also of coachmen's perquisites—being drawn on at regular intervals by local gardeners. The cobbles, scoured by the water of perpetual carriage-washings, rang cleanly under the horses' hoofs; and the horses themselves shone with good grooming like chestnuts, or rosewood, or polished iron.

Such was Britannia Mews in its too brief prime; but besides the archway a second exit, at its northern end, pointed towards the more dubious neighbourhood of the Edgware Road. This "slype" or foot-passage emerged between a public convenience and the Cock public-house, whose side-door ("jug and bottle") actually opened in it; moralists anxious for the good standing of the Mews perceived a perpetual tug of war, pull-Devil-pull-Baker, between the Cock at one end and Albion Place at the other. Their worst fears, alas, were swiftly realized: within but a decade the Cock gained the upper hand and it was apparent that Britannia Mews would soon go, so to speak, entirely native.

In this catastrophe Albion Place was not guiltless; and here a word must be said as to the character, both architectural and moral, of the Albion Place houses. They were tall and porticoed, but less roomy than their elevation promised; they copied the bad Mayfair example of sacrificing too much space to a handsome drawing-room, cramped the entrance hall with a couple of hollow pillars that supported nothing, and relegated the servants to box-rooms above and cellars below. The nurseries were in the attics—for the denizens of Albion Place, unlike their genuinely fashionable ex-emplars, lived in London all the year round and reared their families on the spot; nurseries there had to be. In short, the dominant characteristic of these houses was falseness; as a direct result, the tenants tended to live beyond their means. For they had to keep up appearances. The large drawing-rooms demanded to be filled, the pillars in the hall postulated six-course dinners in the dining-rooms. Not for Albion Place the Bloomsbury saddle of lamb, the Baker Street pair of fowls—and not for Albion Place, either, the liberal supply of butcher's meat below-stairs. One had to economize somewhere; though living above one's income, one didn't (in Albion Place) go the whole hog and ruin oneself. But one economized where one could; one subscribed with particular alacrity to the new convention (discovered about 1870) that it was just as smart to "job" a brougham (got up of course to look like a private carriage) as to keep one's own cattle. Horses were sold, coachmen dismissed, the last locks of hay mouldered in the empty cribs; by 1875 only four sets of stables, all at the Albion or anti-Cock end, retained their proper tenants. In these flats, the windows were clean and curtained; Number 2 still showed pots of geranium on the sills; but the rest of the Mews had long been "squatted" by a low-class colony of private traders—flower girls, step women, knife-grinders, a chimney-sweep, a Punch-and-Judy man, their numerous progeny often unlicensed shoeblacks—whose iniquity blackened all about them. Here windows were often broken and always dirty; washing was left to hang till the dust from beaten mats grimed it afresh; slatternly women gossiped and quarrelled, debated the affairs of their petty Alsatia, and shouted ribald abuse at the men round the door of the Cock. If it were asked *What was the landlord about?* the answer was that he had found out the value of slum property. Britannia Mews cost him not a penny, and let at three shillings a week per fourth part of a room.

At half-past ten on a May morning, in the year 1875, Adelaide Culver, aged ten and a half, issued from the back-door of Number 8 Albion Place, and slipped across the Alley, and entered the Mews.

2

SHE HAD no business there. The Mews was strictly forbidden territory to both the Culver children, though Treff, as a boy, could always escape blame by lisping that he had gone to look at

(5)

the pretty horses. But he rarely went. He was not an enterprising child. Even then, from where she stood just under the archway, Adelaide could see him waiting patiently, ready, dressed to go out, at the back-window of the nursery upstairs. Adelaide flashed him a look of contempt. About four years younger than herself, Treff appeared to her the merest baby, unworthy of any serious consideration. ("What a dear little brother you have!" ladies used to say, at Mrs. Culver's tea-parties; and though Adelaide had early learned the proper answer, she frequently gave it in so off-hand a tone that the ladies were quite disconcerted.)

Adelaide too was dressed for Kensington Gardens, her short jacket buttoned, her beaver muff hanging on its cord round her neck; it was long past the muff season, but Adelaide had a passion for muffs and a stronger will than her governess's. In conjunction with the bunched-up rear of her fishwife skirt this muff gave her upper part a very solid, almost matronly appearance, whereas her legs in their striped stockings were unmistakably the legs of an active and wiry little girl. On her head she wore a pork-pie hat, maroon felt trimmed with a quill, and round her neck a sort of lace cravat—the costume, in fact, destined to be preserved for at least three more generations in the popular art of the scrap-book and Christmas cracker. It suited Adelaide well enough, and perhaps better than any prettier or freer style, for she was a plain child, with features already strongly marked—aquiline nose, black brows, and stubborn chin. Her mother hoped she would grow up to look distinguished; Adelaide for her part secretly considered her appearance interesting, and was almost too satisfied with it.

She now took a step forward, under the arch. At that morning hour the Mews was quiet enough, placid in the spring sunshine; for a moment the child was seeing it as the complacent builder saw it ten years before—neat, cosy, a model dwelling. No one now remembered the builder's name, but perhaps he had been country-bred, for in one corner he had spared a triangle of soil, brick-bordered, about the roots of a lime-tree.

Adelaide turned round, and so discovered that she was now *in* the Mews, looking out. On the other side of the cobbled Alley rose the tall backs of the houses in Albion Place; they had no gardens, only yards, bounded by a wall with spikes on top. The ten back-doors were all painted green, and showed up nicely against the brick; the house next to the Culvers', however, had its wall white-washed, and this, together with a lilac appearing over its top, made it the most attractive in the row. The Culvers' house had nothing remarkable about it at all; it simply looked, like all the rest, solid, rather ugly, and very difficult to burgle. Noting that Treff was no longer at the window, Adelaide gave a last glance into the Mews; and at that moment the side-door of the Cock was pushed open and out came a little girl carrying a jug.

No neat pork-pie crowned the tangle of red hair, no striped stockings clothed her dirty legs. She wasn't barefoot; she wore a pair of old boots, many sizes too large. A ragged shawl was tied over a ragged tartan dress, of which the skirt was far too short. At the sight of Adelaide she stopped dead, like an animal in its form, clasping the jug to her flat bosom. Adelaide felt slightly unsure of herself. She knew only one mode of approach to a "ragged-child" (they were a definite species, like "gun-dogs"), and that was to give it a penny. She had occasionally done so, in company with her mother or Miss Bryant, and the ragged child (similarly accompanied by a ragged adult) gave a grateful snivel. But now no adults were at hand: the two young female creatures met without any social buffer. There was of course no reason why Adelaide should not simply walk off, but such was not Adelaide's way.

The purse inside her muff contained five coppers. She fumbled one of them out and held it up.

"Little girl, would you like a penny?"

The child merely stared.

"Here's a penny for you," persisted Adelaide.

The child set down her jug and stealthily advanced. Then she took the last few steps at a run, seized the coin, and fled back. She had not uttered a single word, she hadn't even smiled, and Adelaide was naturally annoyed.

"You should say thank you!" she called angrily.

Instead, the child did an astonishing, a wicked thing. As she stooped to her jug she also picked up a small pebble and threw it hard and straight at her benefactress's legs. Adelaide uttered a cry of pain; immediately the door of Number 2 opened, and down rushed Mrs. Benson. The ragged child made off.

"Miss Addie!" cried Mrs. Benson. "Whatever's amiss?"

"A little girl threw a stone at me!" wailed Adelaide. "A little girl with red hair!"

"And what were you doing playing with her?" retorted Mrs. Benson unsympathetically. "You've no business in the Mews, as well you know! I never heard of such a thing!"

"I wasn't playing with her!" protested Adelaide. "I only—"

"She's a bad child," raged Mrs. Benson, "and you're to have no truck with her. I've a good mind to tell your mamma."

Adelaide ignored this, long experience having taught her that servants never did tell Mamma, for fear of the consequences to themselves.

"How is she bad?" she asked curiously.

"She's a thief," said Mrs. Benson.

Instinctively Adelaide clutched her muff more tightly. Instinctively she glanced over her shoulder at that comfortable row of spikes. For the word "thief"—a sly, secret word, like the *whish* of a knife—produced in her the same shiver that the word "gipsy" produced in a country child of the same age and standing. London, Adelaide knew, was full of thieves: they crept behind you in a crowd and stole your purse: they lurked in the area to steal your table silver; they stole your dog, sometimes holding him to ransom, sending—oh, horror!—his tail in a brown-paper parcel through the letter-box. It was dreadful to think that a person of this stamp lived so close to Albion Place.

"Does—does Papa know?" stammered Adelaide.

"If he don't, it's no business of yours to tell him," retorted Mrs. Benson illogically. "You go straight back to the house, Miss, and never let me see you here again."

With as much dignity as she could muster Adelaide turned and walked away. But luck was against her. Just as she reached the back-door it opened in her face, and there stood Miss Bryant, white with anger, all save her nose, which remained red.

"*There* you are!" cried Miss Bryant. "How often have you been *told* not to go into the Mews! You are a very naughty, disobedient little girl."

Adelaide took this calmly enough, for she was rather out of the current fashion in that she neither loved nor hated her good governess. She tolerated her. Miss Bryant, without being consciously aware of this, nevertheless felt something amiss in their relations. It made her over-emphatic.

"And there's poor Treff waiting and waiting!" she elaborated feverishly. "We shall be late for our walk, and we mustn't be late back, for you're going visiting with your mamma this afternoon, and Treff must get his rest—"

"Treff isn't coming visiting," said Adelaide calmly.

"Oh, isn't he?" said Miss Bryant.

"No," said Adelaide.

3

EVERY MORNING the Culver children met their cousins, the Hambro children, in Kensington Gardens: on this occasion, owing to Adelaide's disobedience, the little Hambros were there first. There were four of them, Alice and the twins and the baby Milly, so that they had a nurse as well as a governess. Her name was Miss Grigson. Alice was more than a year older than Adelaide, and far prettier: she had pink cheeks, a rosebud mouth, the upper lip slightly lifted over little white teeth, and quantities of naturally curling light brown hair. Even her fringe curled neatly above her fair eyebrows, and when she ran her thick mane flew out in a picturesque cloud. She was living for the day when she would be able to sit on its ends, and with this object let the twins, James and John, pull her hair whenever they wished.

"Why have you got a muff?" asked Alice at once.

"I like muffs," said Adelaide.

"But people don't carry muffs in May."

"I do," said Adelaide.

Treff meanwhile had run off to join the Black Watch. This famous regiment, composed of a dozen children whose nurses, if not their mothers, all knew each other, mustered every morning opposite the new Albert Memorial. He was just in time to answer to his name—"William Trefusis Culver?" "Here!" piped Treff—and to take part in the opening ceremony, which consisted of the following chant:—

The Black Watch will go night and day.
The Black Watch can be depended upon in any climate.
The Black Watch always keeps time.
The Black Watch never needs winding.
The Black Watch can be depended upon for any period.

They were then inspected by Sir Garnet Wolseley.

Adelaide and her cousin watched these proceedings with matronly tolerance. (No girls were allowed in the regiment, and no girl would have admitted to such an ambition.) Then they strolled off towards the Round Pond, for they were permitted to walk, together, wherever they liked in the Gardens. Alice was very fond of her little brothers and sister, but she really saw quite enough of them at home.

"Mamma says," she told Adelaide, "if you and Treff would like to come to tea this afternoon, we can make toffee."

"*I* can't," said Adelaide at once. "My mamma is taking me calling."

Alice regarded her with envy. To be taken calling was one of the major pleasures of her life.

"Just one call, or a whole lot?"

"Just one. I don't suppose it will be much of a call. It's on a very poor person."

"Then it isn't a call at all," said Alice firmly.

Adelaide hesitated. She was more than a little dubious herself, for there was something about the afternoon's engagement which she would in later years have described as fishy. From scraps of conversation overheard between her parents she had gathered that this particular visit was one Mrs. Culver wished to avoid. "After all," said Mrs. Culver, "I suppose it's a duty"; and then they had both glanced uneasily at Adelaide. "I suppose it is," said Mr. Culver. "After all, at *that* age—" said Mrs. Culver; and then, very firmly, "Poor thing, one mustn't be uncharitable. . . ."

So Adelaide thought they were probably going to visit one of the poor—not the wicked poor, like the little girl who was a thief, but the deserving poor, a different class altogether—recruited from ex-housekeepers, old nurses, governesses fallen upon hard times. Such calls were never very enjoyable; there was usually too much food, of inferior quality, which had to be eaten for fear of giving offence. However—

"I suppose it's a duty," quoted Adelaide. "Will Auntie Ham let us come to-morrow?"

"Of course. And if we've had the toffee, I'll make Mamma let us try on all her hats."

Adelaide never ceased to wonder at the freedom with which the young Hambros treated their parents. They seemed to have not the least fear even of their papa, and swarmed over their mother even when she was dressed to go out. But Adelaide was saved from envy by the knowledge that she herself was being much better brought up.

They wandered on. Presently Treff ran up after them, already tired of military discipline and wanted to play I Spy. Alice good-naturedly did so while Adelaide went on thinking about her adventure in the Mews and the afternoon's engagement. (It seemed to be a day when things happened.) Now and then they saw someone they knew, a lady from Bayswater or Kensington, who smiled and waved to them; ladies were beginning to come into the gardens after their shopping. Some still wore ulsters, some smart cloth jackets, cut very short and cocked up over their bustles. Not one carried a muff. Adelaide's hands were growing quite sticky

(11)

with the warmth of her own, but she wouldn't take them out.

"Look at that funny dog!" exclaimed Treff suddenly.

Alice and Adelaide looked, and saw a big Airedale running round in a wide circle, of which they were the centre. Every few yards he paused, threw up his head, and uttered a queer little sniggering whine. There was something clownish about him, and the children laughed.

"He's playing," said Alice. "He's chasing his tail, like a kitten."

Treff ran after the animal, who hesitated, seemed to scrutinize him, and then set off again. The two girls joined in, racing at Treff's heels. "It's the Caucus Race!" cried Alice. "We'll all win and all get prizes!" They were enjoying the sport immensely, when all at once a most dreadful thing happened. The dog stopped, uttered a last cry of despair, and fell down in a fit. His body jerked all over, white foam was forming on his muzzle: the three children drew back in horror.

"He wasn't playing," breathed Alice. "He's *mad*. . . ."

Adelaide took an uncertain step towards him, but her cousin held her. Treff burst into tears. They looked desperately round for adult aid, but Miss Bryant and Miss Grigson and the nurse were far from view, and it was extraordinary how the Gardens, a moment ago thronged, had suddenly emptied.

"Suppose he isn't mad at all, only ill?" said Adelaide.

"I don't care. If he bites us, we'll all go mad too," said Alice.

Adelaide shivered. *Mad dog, mad dog!* An anguished sympathy filled her heart, but Alice held her fast. The animal's whimperings were now dreadful to hear, but they could not tear themselves away; impotent, they could not quite desert him. All around the Gardens stretched away in the sunshine, filled with the peculiar emptiness of London out-of-doors when no one is about.

It was Treff who broke the stricken silence with his famous railway-engine shriek. He had seen a young man walking swiftly up from the Serpentine; at the ear-splitting sound the man began to hurry, then to run. He ran faster than any grown-up they had ever seen, straight to where the dog lay, whipping off his jacket as he came. The children soon saw why: dropping on his knees the young man swiftly muffled the animal's head, then began to rub his hand along its heaving flanks, talking all the while in kind admonishing tones. The Airedale's name was Bob. Quite soon the heaving subsided and Bob lay still, whimpering no more.

"Is he—dead?" whispered Alice.

"No," said the young man, over his shoulder. "He's had a fit. He ran off when he felt it coming."

"If I hadn't whistled, you'd never have found him," said Treff importantly.

But the dog's master was not interested in them, and with a sense of being in the way (as so often happened in cases of illness) the three children walked slowly and silently off. It was not until they were in sight of Miss Bryant and the others that Alice spoke again.

"He knew he was going to have a fit, and we laughed at him," she said remorsefully. "He must have thought we were beasts . . ."

They all felt rather uncomfortable. By common consent, because the incident was of importance and deeply felt, they did not mention it to their elders.

4

SITTING beside her mother in the carriage, Adelaide gazed superiorly down on the foot-traffic of the Bayswater Road. They were driving towards Mayfair. Adelaide had on her best blue velvet coat. Mrs. Culver wore a velvet jacket over her new magenta moire. Though thirty-five, and therefore middle-aged, Mrs. Culver was still a handsome woman, and Adelaide at that moment admired her mother very much. But she couldn't understand why they were both so grandly dressed—as for a call of the first water—when they were really on an errand of mercy. "Aren't we going to take a basket?" Adelaide had asked, as they got into the carriage; but Mrs. Culver either did not, or decided not to, hear. The children were used to these parental deafnesses, and Adelaide realized she had made a mistake. She was disappointed, however; she enjoyed taking out the tea or the jellies, pressing them into thankful hands, and listening to the expressions of gratitude they always evoked. (Or nearly always: there was an ex-housemaid with a Radical brother-in-law whose name could no longer be mentioned.)

"Addie, put your hat forward," said Mrs. Culver.

Adelaide tilted her blue velvet toque, with the ermine's head in front, till she could feel its hard rim pressing on her eyebrows. Mrs. Culver nodded absently. Adelaide never expected much notice from her mother, which was odd, since Mrs. Culver considered that she devoted her life to her children. She did in fact devote herself to the work of making nine hundred pounds a year do the work, or at least produce the effect, of twelve, and so from one point of view was possibly right.

The carriage turned into Park Lane. The tension—it was now nothing less—increased. They drove on and turned into Curzon Street, turned again into a smaller but still very elegant thoroughfare, where the narrow houses had each a tiny balcony along the first floor. (As in Britannia Mews.) The carriage stopped. "Half an hour, Benson," said Mrs. Culver. She rang the bell and the door was opened to them by the smartest page Adelaide had ever seen.

Mrs. Burnett was at home.

5

ADELAIDE's immediate thought, as they entered Mrs. Burnett's drawing-room, was that she would like to be left there a long time, by herself, so that she could look at everything thoroughly. It was a wonderful room: the walls, hung with very pale yellow damask, were covered with sketches and paintings: two cabinets, and three or four little tables, offered the most fascinating array of luxurious bric-à-brac; a stand in the window overflowed with flowers. Adelaide was so occupied with all this that she missed the first greetings between her mother and their hostess; she was still agape when the former's hand descended firmly on her shoulder.

"And this," said Mrs. Culver, "is Adelaide."

Adelaide automatically advanced her cheek for the usual kiss—and felt Mrs. Culver's hand tighten. But Mrs. Burnett evidently wasn't a "kissing-lady," she merely stooped gracefully forward, disengaging a faint but very sweet perfume. Adelaide stared up at a beautiful white throat, all the whiter for a sapphire cross, at a pale, pretty face under an enormous chignon of auburn hair.

"And this is Adelaide," repeated Mrs. Burnett. "Sit down, *chérie,* and take off your hat."

Adelaide sat down, but kept her hat on. Her Culver blood, always socially suspicious, reminded her that she didn't yet know the lady as well as that. She folded her hands in her lap and continued to gaze. Mrs. Burnett wore a gown of pale bluish-green silk, the bustle looped by an enormous bow of black velvet: she had heavy gold bracelets, and sparkling rings, and in her ears the most beautiful earrings like bunches of grapes. She wasn't poor at all: she looked richer than the richest person the Culvers knew. Adelaide shifted her gaze to her mother, now seated opposite Mrs. Burnett by the fire, and for the first time felt dissatisfied with her appearance.

"Adelaide, look at the dear little houses!" said Mrs. Culver rather sharply.

Adelaide obediently turned her attention to the table at her side, which was quite covered with small wooden objects—chalets, gondolas, bears, windmills. They were charming, but she still kept an ear cocked for the conversation by the fire; to her extreme disappointment it was now proceeding in French—which Mrs. Burnett spoke much better than Mrs. Culver: her pretty voice rippled lightly and fluently, never hesitating for a word, while Mrs. Culver's plodded after. Adelaide could understand hardly anything, but she did pick up the rather surprising fact that the two ladies addressed each other by their Christian names. She distinctly heard Mrs. Burnett call Mrs. Culver "Bertha"; and Mrs. Burnett's name was "Isabel." It was interesting, but baffling; Adelaide soon began to look about again and examine the room in more detail.

The mantelpiece alone was as good as a bazaar. On either side of the enormous mirror rose a tier of little brackets and ledges, each containing some small object of art—porcelain, ivory, or coloured glass. The marble shelf bore a golden clock topped by a female figure; and there were also two china monkeys entirely covered with tiny china forget-me-nots instead of fur. Adelaide thought Mrs. Burnett must be particularly fond of monkeys, for in the cabinet between the fireplace and the door was a whole orchestra of them, each playing a different instrument. Her eye travelled on, noting a picture made of needlework, a trophy of Japanese fans, another cabinet containing blue-and-white china and a collection of tropic shells, and so—Adelaide wriggled round—came back to the stand of flowers behind her and the "wooden-table" at her side.

There, on the lower shelf, she now observed something that took her fancy more than anything else, something one would hardly have expected to see there at all, or indeed anywhere in a lady's drawing-room. This object was a cigar box, and within the open lid was one of the loveliest pictures Adelaide had ever seen. In the richest and most glowing hues, embossed and gilt, it depicted Romeo and Juliet on their balcony against a sky unimaginably blue.

The page brought in tea. It was so splendid a tea, with so many little French cakes, that Adelaide again had the feeling that she would like to be left alone with it; far too soon Mrs. Culver set down her cup—and rose, billowing her magenta silk, settling her jacket, with an air that was very nearly one of relief. Mrs. Burnett did not press her to stay longer; instead, she said kindly:—

"Adelaide must take a little present. Walk round, child, and see what you would like."

With a pretty gesture of her tiny hands, she put the whole room at Adelaide's disposal. Adelaide glanced quickly at her mother and saw that the offer was acceptable. Then what should she choose? Not the forget-me-not monkeys, much as she desired them; a budding social consciousness warned her that they were too valuable. Indeed, as she circled the room under the eyes of the two ladies, she began to feel as though she were playing Hunt the Thimble, getting now colder, now warmer, as she approached the blue china or the stand of flowers. She was warmest of all by the table with the wooden houses on it, and this suited Adelaide very well. But her mind was on no chalet, or gondola; it was on the cigar box. She had actually put out her hand to it when all at once—*colder, colder!* —something in the atmosphere warned her again. Mrs. Culver had moved; so had Mrs. Burnett, who with a swift rustle of silk swooped upon a cabinet and whipped out a tropic shell.

"There, isn't that pretty?" she exclaimed. "It came all the way from the Indian Ocean!"

"Adelaide shall look it out on the map," chimed in Mrs. Culver. "Isn't it pretty, Adelaide? Say thank you, dear."

"Thank you very much," said Adelaide.

6

THE DRIVE home proceeded rather silently. Adelaide sat with the shell between her hands. It was really odd rather than beautiful—pink and smooth within, but outside roughened by a sort of white tracery, like worm-casts. It was about the size of a small teapot, and had four blunt spines.

"What shall I do with it, Mamma?"

"You may put it on the nursery mantelpiece," said Mrs. Culver, without looking at it.

"Am I to share it with Treff?"

"I don't suppose he'd care for it," said Mrs. Culver.

Adelaide thought he probably would, for Treff always wanted to go shares in anything that belonged to her. However, she let the subject drop, nor did she ask any other questions.

But when they reached home, and Benson had driven round to the Mews, she said suddenly, "Mamma, I've left my handkerchief in the carriage."

"Then run and get it," said Mrs. Culver impatiently. "What a careless child you are!"

Adelaide ran through the house, and out at the back-door, and found Benson just backing the carriage into the coach-house; his wife was there too, which was annoying, because she still looked cross with Adelaide after the morning's encounter. (In some households, at the Hambros' for example, the servants and the children lived on terms of alliance; at the Culvers' they were foes.) Adelaide jumped into the carriage and pretended to rummage under the cushions, and Benson rather crossly told her to get out.

"I've lost my handkerchief," explained Adelaide. "Look, here it is! Benson, who is Mrs. Burnett?"

"How would I know?" grumbled the coachman. "You get off that seat."

"Well, I just thought you might," said Adelaide. It was her experience that servants knew most things. "I liked her."

"Did you, now?" said Benson ironically.

"Yes, I did. She isn't a kissing-lady."

The coachman and his wife exchanged a peculiar glance. So they did know, thought Adelaide triumphantly. But whatever information they possessed, they were not going to share it; and in fact nearly ten years were to elapse before Adelaide discovered that Mrs. Burnett, born a Culver, was actually her own aunt.

7

THE LONG twelvemonths of childhood passed uneventfully. No more little Culvers appeared, and Adelaide's and Treff's most intimate friends were still the Hambro children. This was not from any similarity of temperament, but simply on account of the relationship: their parents expected them to be intimate, so intimate they were. Alice, indeed, whose family feeling was very strong, could easily love any cousin, and Adelaide, submitting to be loved, was warmed to a reciprocal affection; but they did not influence one another, for the character of each was formed at home.

There was no doubt that the little Culvers were much better brought up. Mrs. Culver's theory of child-management was entirely rational, and confirmed by success. She never forgot, for instance (nor did Adelaide forget either) how Adelaide at seven had been cured of fearing the dark. This was shortly after the child began to sleep alone: and she had a nightmare. Twice in one night did Adelaide flee wailing to her parents' room, and twice did Mrs.

Culver kindly but firmly make her return and conquer her fears by facing them. The second time Adelaide stayed; she was rather white next morning, and sick after breakfast, but never again showed the least fear of the dark. No wonder that Mrs. Culver was complacent; and how foolish of Miss Bryant to suggest a night-light! The latter had no theory of child-management, she was simply used to children, and noticed that Addie's stomach had become very easily upset. "But why a night-light?" asked Mrs. Culver, much amused; and Miss Bryant could not say. (Treff subsequently had a night-light till the age of ten; but then Treff shrieked till he got it.) No similar crisis could arise at the Hambros', because Alice shared a room with one little sister, the two others slept together, and the twins from a shockingly early age kept boxes of matches under their pillows; but there was little doubt that they could all have had what illumination they desired.

Besides meeting daily in the Gardens the children went to tea with each other at least once a week. At Albion Place they did transfers; in Kensington, where the Hambros lived, they played on "the Redan." (This was a derelict lounge of the type commonly found in hotels—the seat circular about a truncated cone, the whole covered in red leather. Mr. Hambro had seen it in an auction-room, and with really remarkable intelligence had bought it as a present for his children. He never gave them anything they loved more.) The young Culvers enjoyed going to Kensington more than the young Hambros enjoyed coming to Bayswater; indeed, as the twins grew older they sometimes balked at the "treat" altogether. "It's their arithmetic!" Alice used to apologize—until one day Adelaide took her up rather sharply by observing that whenever they played Sums in Your Head (a game cunningly introduced by Miss Grigson) the twins always won. They were not bad at arithmetic, they were good at it. Alice flushed. She knew perfectly well that James and John weren't doing lessons, they were probably Redanning.

"I expect they're sliding down the Redan," said Adelaide unsparingly.

She slid down it herself whenever she had the opportunity, and made Treff do so too. But Treff was timid and had to be pushed; he preferred playing with Milly and the new baby, Sybil; and then with Milly and Sybil and the new baby, Ellen. He also allowed Alice to hug him, which her own brothers would not, and which Adelaide never attempted. "I can't understand it!" Alice once exclaimed. "With only two of you, you ought to be so fond of each other!" "Of course we're fond of each other," said Adelaide impatiently.

She felt the comment as a slur, because brothers and sisters were expected to love each other, just as children were expected to love their parents and parents their children: anything else would be very shocking. She might also have retorted that the Hambros went too far in reciprocal indulgence: even at dinner parties the twins came in, if they felt like it, to recite "Lays of Ancient Rome." One result of Adelaide's upbringing was that she genuinely reprobated, in the jolly commotion of her cousins' home, a certain disorderliness; she could echo her mother's criticism that the children were all over the place.

"You simply make no attempt at control," said Mrs. Culver to Mrs. Hambro. "Alice is naturally obedient, and so gives no trouble; but the boys have got completely out of hand. Their father should whip them."

"We don't believe in whipping," said Mrs. Hambro.

"You mean you don't *like* whipping. I suppose no one does. But what would become of the world if we none of us did our duty just because it was unpleasant? When Addie didn't want to have her ears pierced, it would have been much *pleasanter* for me to give way to her; but it had to be done, and it was done, and no nonsense. As for the twins—"

"Don't tell me, dear, I know it," begged Mrs. Hambro. "They're a plague, and the Porters will never dine with us again. But if you had six children instead of two—"

"I should know how to keep them in order," said Mrs. Culver positively.

The sisters were not much alike, and their husbands remarkably dissimilar. Mr. Hambro was a silk merchant, and though this was practically being in trade, never tried to conceal the fact; he made a habit of bringing home City friends, and freely, if dryly, advised lady guests on the respective qualities of moire and surah. But Mr. Culver associated himself with the publishing house of Culver, Blore and Masterman merely because it was a family business. Old Mr. Culver had founded it, and done well out of evangelical pamphlets; Masterman brought in scholastic text-books, and Blore a series of didactic Lives. Should any misguided author submit a novel, it was returned unread: Culver, Blore and Masterman were not interested in fiction. Few commercial ventures were accompanied by so little risk, or brought in such steady profits; but William Culver found it necessary to buttress a naturally cautious spirit by cultivating detachment. He refused all contact with printers (a notoriously turbulent set) and rarely saw even a hack author; but he was great on Latin primers, and popularly supposed to work out every problem in every fresh edition of the *Algebra for Lower Forms*. At home he left the direction of the household entirely to his wife, and when the children had measles went to stay at his Club. Mrs. Culver's social activity rather irked him than otherwise, but she told him so often it was necessary to keep up appearances that he had come to believe her.

Adelaide and Treff did not see much of their father. Neither parent, indeed, played so large a part in their lives as either Miss Bryant or their cousins. But everyone knew Treff was Mrs. Culver's favourite, and Adelaide early accepted the fact. As she grew older she naturally spent more time in her mother's company; but it might fairly be said that the acquaintance did not ripen.

8

In 1880 occurred the major event of this period: the Culvers moved from Albion Place to Kensington. Albion Place was going down. The proximity of the Mews, perhaps of the Edgware Road, infected its gentility; trade, in the person of a wine merchant, moved in to Number 5; and for all these reasons, or perhaps for none, the shifting sunlight of fashion passed on. The house in Kensington, near the Hambros', was smarter though smaller; there was no stabling, so Mrs. Culver at last gave up her carriage and jobbed a brougham instead. But one link with Albion Place remained, or was rather reforged: Adelaide's twenty-first birthday present from her father was a series of drawing-lessons from a Mr. Lambert, who taught at a near-by school for girls. He was looking for a lodging—a very cheap lodging, said Mr. Lambert unashamedly, a couple of rooms in a central slum—and asked Mrs. Culver's advice. With a certain irony she recommended Britannia Mews; she had not, she said, a very wide experience of slums. The young man, however, not only went to look at the Mews, but found there just what he wanted. Number 2, once occupied by the Bensons, was empty, and he moved in on the first of October, 1885.

CHAPTER II

ADELAIDE, are you coming calling with me?" asked Mrs. Culver.

"I can't, Mamma. It's my drawing-lesson."

Mrs. Culver looked at her daughter with a frown. It was of course quite proper that Adelaide should remember the lesson that her father had so kindly paid for, but at the same time she ought to have shown more regret at not going out with her mother. It was a sort of remissness to which Adelaide was particularly prone.

"I sometimes think," said Mrs. Culver, "that you don't care whether you come with me or not."

"Of course I do, Mamma. I don't much care for the calls; they're so boring."

"You girls talk far too much about being bored," said Mrs. Culver severely. "What is there boring, pray, about going to see Mrs. Orton?"

Adelaide was silent. Silence was one of her outstanding characteristics—and how unfortunately, since she had turned out only moderately good-looking. If you were beautiful and silent you could pass for statuesque; the average girl was expected to be bright. But Adelaide couldn't produce brightness at Mrs. Orton's: as she had once tried to explain to Alice, she couldn't possibly say anything when no one said anything to her. . . .

"But they do!" protested Alice. Bright herself, as well as pretty, she was always an immense success at the tea-table. "I often see people talking to you!"

"But they don't *say* anything," explained Adelaide glumly. "They just ask me if I've seen *The Mikado.*"

"Well, what do you want them to talk about?"

"I don't know," said Adelaide.

If she couldn't explain to Alice, she certainly couldn't explain to her mother: the desire to get below the surface of things, to discover what life was really about, was apparently unknown in Culver circles. Adelaide sometimes wondered whether all their acquaintances were not suffering from the same unacknowledged hunger—whether their polite chit-chat did not mask a universal desire for some more genuine communion; on the whole she thought it unlikely. Only once had she glimpsed any sign of such an attitude, and that was in a girl called Agatha Yates, who had been to Queen's College. Adelaide saw Miss Yates, at an At Home, collar a middle-aged gentleman and begin talking to him about rent collection: they were soon deep in argument, impervious to the ironic glances of all the other ladies present, and as she left Miss Yates said loudly, "Well, *this* has been worth while!" Very rude, of course, but Adelaide could not help envying her. She wished she had been clever enough to go to Queen's College herself—though it probably wouldn't have been allowed. . . .

"Well, I suppose I must make your excuses," said Mrs. Culver. "I shall give Mrs. Orton your love."

"Yes, do," said Adelaide. She was so used to having bits of her love left here and there, like a card with the corner turned down, that the word had lost all significance.

2

THE TWO cousins took drawing-lessons together—and indeed Alice's father paid half. When they began, a few months earlier, the Hambros still had their Miss Grigson, and she acted as chaperone; when she left it was decided that the girls could chaperone each other. Alice always arrived before Mr. Lambert and stayed to tea afterwards. To-day Adelaide hoped she would come early, for Mrs. Culver had a lunch engagement, and announced that after it she would do a little shopping in the West End (see what Adelaide was missing!) and go straight on to her calls. Adelaide saw her mother off and sat down to solitary cold mutton with a pleasing sensation of independence. She determined that if Alice came in time, they would have black coffee.

But two o'clock struck, and quarter-past, and still no Alice. Mr. Lambert was due at two-thirty. At twenty minutes past, there was a ring at the door; Adelaide flew from the dining-room to open it, and there stood a Hambro twin.

"Oh, dear!" cried Adelaide, at once scenting disaster. "Can't Alice come?"

"She's sorry, she's got her autumn cold," announced Jimmy Hambro stolidly. "She's streaming."

"Oh, dear!" cried Adelaide again. "Poor thing! But—oh, *dear!*— what about Mr. Lambert?"

"Johnny's gone with a note to put him off. We tossed up."

The twins were a great convenience to the Hambro family. At twelve, and of the male sex, they were considered competent to penetrate London in almost any direction: they carried notes and messages, fetched parcels, ran for cabs. They were much more useful than Treff had ever been, and Adelaide as a rule was quite fond of them; but now in her deep disappointment she did not even ask James if he would like to come in. It was all she could do to send Alice her best love.

"She sent hers," agreed Jimmy, and paused. He, too, seemed to have his preoccupations. He said, "Are you going to write to Treff?"

"I expect so," said Adelaide. Treff was at Harrow; during term-time she was supposed to write to him once a week, and did so about once a fortnight.

"You might tell him we've got the Prince Albert working."

Adelaide vaguely remembered that this was an elaborate model steamboat bought by Treff for two pounds, and subsequently sold to the twins as a derelict for seven and six.

"Of course I will, dear. I'm sure he'll be very glad."

"We think he'll be sick as mud," said Jimmy dispassionately—and stumped off down the steps.

Adelaide closed the door and stood there in the hall feeling extraordinarily flat. How long, how empty, an afternoon now stretched before her! How steep was the drop from expectancy to disappointment! And how unreasonable! For what had she missed? A drawing-lesson, and Alice's company; shopping and calls with Mrs. Culver; the merest recurrent commonplaces. Yet she felt life ebbing away; the very house, at that moment, felt uninhabited, like a house one comes back to after the holidays. Too depressed even to walk upstairs, Adelaide sat down on the oak chest—it held winter blankets; open the lid an inch and you released a strong smell of moth-balls—and gave herself up to a mood which during the past year had become more and more familiar. She thought of it as "the Hollows," because when she slipped into it she felt completely empty, undirected and purposeless: a dumb creature awaiting unimagined assuagement. At first she had put it down to lack of Faith: she had tried to acquire Faith by going every morning to early service at St. Mark's. Apart from annoying the maids, who had to call her specially early, it produced no result. Adelaide was left with an alarm clock. Would higher education have helped? Possibly, thought Adelaide, remembering Miss Yates; but it was too late for that now. Family affection, then? Alas, when Adelaide followed this line she discovered only a feeling of guilt; it was so evident that she did not love Papa and Mamma and Treff nearly so much as she ought. Sometimes, from the depths of her mind, there even rose the shocking cry *I don't love them at all*—but that Adelaide hastily stifled. It was wicked. She thought: I love Alice. I love Alice dearly. . . .

Unconsciously she pressed her hands tightly to her breast. Through the slate-blue merino she could feel a light movement: the beating of her heart.

3

When the door-bell rang again Adelaide started as though from sleep—back to full consciousness, back to the thought, What will Rose think if she sees me sitting here? But Rose the parlour-maid did not appear, she was probably changing her dress, and after a brief hesitation Adelaide opened the door herself. The person outside was Mr. Lambert.

For a moment she could only stare speechlessly. To her horror, because she was startled and confused, she felt the blood rise to her cheeks. The drawing-master looked at her in surprise.

"Mayn't I come in?" he asked.

"Of course," said Adelaide quickly, and stepping back. "Only I thought—I wasn't expecting—didn't Johnny Hambro bring you a note?"

"What note?" asked Mr. Lambert. He was still looking at her with peculiar intentness, as though she were a drawing to be corrected; he had remarkably bright brown eyes under rather arched eyebrows.

"Oh, dear!" said Adelaide. At that moment she heard the service-door open; over her shoulder she saw Rose bounce into the hall and bounce back; most unfortunate. "A note from my aunt," she went on hastily, "from Mrs. Hambro. Alice has a bad cold."

"I'm sorry to hear that," said Mr. Lambert obtusely.

"So you see, there isn't a drawing-lesson. I can't think how Johnny missed you."

"I had probably started before he got there. I walked across the Gardens."

"Mamma's out too," said Adelaide.

"Well, haven't you any drawings for me to see?" asked Mr. Lambert—and calmly stepping into the hall, hung up his hat.

The coolness of this action—but it wasn't cool, it was simply matter-of-fact—put Adelaide in a most awkward position. Should she explain again that there was no drawing-lesson because Alice couldn't come, and she was therefore unchaperoned? In the face of his extremely businesslike air this seemed absurd—indeed the whole matter of being chaperoned was absurd, girls like Agatha Yates never gave it a thought. So swiftly reflected Adelaide (to whom a moment before Mrs. Hambro's note seemed the most natural thing in the world) and with a calmness equalling (she hoped) his own, she led Mr. Lambert upstairs into the back drawing-room.

Her portfolio was there ready; Adelaide untied it and took out her week's work: a neatly executed copy of a Landseer dog, and an original still-life, of pears. Mr. Lambert sat down to examine them; Adelaide stood docile at his shoulder. The back drawing-room, overlooking a small paved yard, was always very quiet, and to-day seemed quieter than usual—though in fact the only sound missing was Alice's breathing. It was strange what a difference her absence made. If anyone had asked Adelaide whether she had ever been alone with a young man before, she would at once have replied Yes, of course, dozens of times; but all these occasions had been at dances, at picnics, in public and liable to interruption. Even in a conservatory there was always another couple on the other side of the palm. Adelaide, however, was peculiarly conscious of being alone with Mr. Lambert. She looked down at the top of his head—he had very thick, springy hair—and was more aware of male proximity than even in the arms of a dancing-partner. It was inexplicable. . . . I do hope I haven't got Alice's cold! thought Adelaide—for she really felt slightly feverish.

Mr. Lambert meanwhile continued to examine the drawings. He looked at the pears so long, without speaking, that Adelaide now began to wonder whether she had accidentally achieved a masterpiece; but his expression, as he suddenly pushed the paper aside, was inscrutable. No criticism apparently was forthcoming. Adelaide rather uncertainly came from behind his chair and sat down as usual with her sketch-book before her. It opened at a half-finished pastel of Alice; the girls had been using each other as models.

"I can't go on with this, Alice isn't here."

"No," said Mr. Lambert vaguely. He picked up a crayon and gave Alice a more convincing eye; eyes were always the difficulty. Then he let the crayon drop, let his hand drop; and it dropped upon Adelaide's.

Adelaide's course was perfectly clear; she should have removed her hand at once. But Mr. Lambert (though he was pressing it so firmly as to make removal difficult) seemed unaware of what he had done. Moreover, his next words were at least as startling as his action.

"You can't *want* to go on with that awful thing. . . ."

"Awful?" repeated Adelaide blankly. The shock was now double; but she couldn't deal with both aspects at once. "Oh, Mr. Lambert, do you really think it's awful?"

"It's terrible," said Mr. Lambert.

"But you said last week—you said last week it was good!"

"I was lying," said Mr. Lambert simply.

Adelaide flushed. Even with her hand so astonishingly in his, she retained her strong sense of commercial morality.

"If you don't think I've any talent, you shouldn't have gone on teaching me. You told Mamma I *had* talent. If that was untrue and—and it's all just a waste of time, I shall tell Papa and he can stop paying for my lessons."

She was pleased to see Mr. Lambert look really startled. He let go her hand, and took up the chalk again, but still kept his eyes on her face. Adelaide felt a pleasing sense of power.

"Whether Alice has more talent than I have," she went on angrily, "of course I can't judge. And as *your* judgment seems hardly to be trusted, I shouldn't think she'd want to go on with her lessons either. If we've simply been made fools of—."

"Adelaide," said Mr. Lambert softly.

She paused. Her indignant glance wavered. She felt she had perhaps gone too far.

"I'd rather die than hurt your feelings," said Mr. Lambert earnestly. "I've hated to deceive you—"

"But you have!" cried Adelaide.

"Can't you guess why?"

Long afterwards, Adelaide was astonished at the rapidity with which she did guess. Only half an hour before she could honestly have sworn that the idea of Mr. Lambert as a lover had never entered her mind; now, in a moment, as though he had thrown off a cloak of invisibility—there he was. She had a lover, and he was Mr. Lambert. Mr. Lambert was in love with her. As her face showed, Adelaide was astounded, electrified, but not for one instant incredulous.

"I may have told a few lies," went on the drawing-master, more confidently, "but if I didn't how the deuce was I to see you? I'm not the sort of man Mrs. Culver asks to dinner. Whereas by giving you lessons I was certain of once a week . . . Are you still angry?"

Adelaide shook her head. These revelations were too delicious to interrupt.

"Thank heaven for that." Mr. Lambert sighed deeply and picked up her hand again with great naturalness. "Has any one ever told you you're very beautiful?"

"No," said Adelaide. "And I'm not."

"To an artist you are," said Mr. Lambert firmly. "You're like a Holbein. You're also rather like the Sleeping Princess."

This should have been warning enough, but Adelaide was unused to love-making. When Mr. Lambert drew her gently to her feet and stood looking at her in the moment before he kissed her, she perceived neither his intent nor his hesitation. It was the moment to give a rebuff; but Adelaide stood passive and he kissed her on the mouth. When he let her go she knew that she was in love with him.

"Now what are you going to do with me?" asked Mr. Lambert lightly.

He sounded—how odd!—genuinely puzzled. Adelaide almost laughed aloud. For it was obvious what she was going to do with him: she was going to marry him. Her upbringing had at least freed her from all perplexities as to conduct: if one did certain things, certain other things followed; if you let a man kiss you, you subsequently married him—which was why girls had to be so careful. But if Mr. Lambert did not know this, if he were still in doubt, so much the better—Adelaide did not wish him to be too sure of her.

With equal lightness she said gaily:—

"Shall I expose you to Mamma?"

"No, don't do that," said Mr. Lambert hastily. But he looked relieved.

"Then talk to me," said Adelaide. "Tell me all you've ever done. Tell me all I don't know about you."

"Or you tell me?" suggested Mr. Lambert hopefully.

"Oh, I've nothing to tell!" cried Adelaide. "Girls never have. Even Treff, going away to school, has a more exciting time than I do. Where were you at school?"

"Rugby."

Her instant of relief was so brief that she hardly noticed it; but her subconscious mind docketed the fact under the heading *Information for Papa*.

"Where was your home?"

"In Cornwall."

"Why, Mamma comes from Cornwall!" exclaimed Adelaide. "She was a Trefusis. Do you know Bude?"

But Mr. Lambert, it seemed, did not wish to talk about his childhood—naturally enough, for he had been orphaned very young, and his early memories were all sad ones. With sympathetic tact Adelaide changed the subject, hurrying him on to Paris and the beginning of his artistic career; and in Paris Mr. Lambert was perfectly at ease. What a fascinating picture he drew of hard work and frugal living, innocent gaiety and idyllic friendships! Adelaide could have listened for ever. An hour passed in a flash; when the clock struck four she could hardly credit it.

"Damn, I've got to go," said Mr. Lambert. "I've another lesson at half-past. It won't be so enjoyable as this one."

Adelaide laughed back. She loved his conscientiousness, and the lightness with which he wore it.

"I've enjoyed it too," she said demurely.

Mr. Lambert put his arm round her and kissed her again.

"Aren't you glad I didn't pay any attention to that note?"

She stared. They were so close that she could look straight into his eyes—brown eyes, flecked round the pupil with tiny motes of amber.

"But you didn't get the note!"

"I did. There's another confession. Johnny caught me just as I was starting. When I knew Miss Hambro wouldn't be here, and I thought you might—nothing would have kept me away. Do you forgive me?"

Of course Adelaide forgave him. Indeed, nothing could have been more welcome than this evidence that Mr. Lambert had fallen in love with her before she fell in love with Mr. Lambert: it made it all so much more proper. But her practical brain saw certain difficulties.

"But we can't go on pretending you didn't get it," she pointed out, "because Johnny will have told Mrs. Hambro, and she'll tell Mamma."

"Then don't tell Mrs. Culver I came."

"Rose saw you in the hall."

Already they were accomplices. Without even considering the matter, Adelaide realised that the time was not yet come for Mr. Lambert to declare himself. He hadn't even proposed. . . . She stood looking at him enquiringly; and Mr. Lambert suddenly grinned.

"You can say I insisted on coming because I didn't want to lose my fee. I'll leave you some evidence. . . ."

He seized chalk and paper, and with incredible rapidity, within ten minutes, executed two sketches of the drawing-room, one competent and almost detailed, the other in Adelaide's wavering amateurish style; and they were taken from opposite sides of the room.

"Now show those to Mamma!" said Mr. Lambert.

He kissed her again, and was gone.

4

For some time afterwards Adelaide stood just as he left her, the two sketches still in her hand; presently she sank down on the nearest chair, and there for half an hour gave herself up to delicious reverie. At last she had something to think about—moments to live over, memories to sort and examine, glimpses of the future as yet scarcely formed but promising inexhaustible pleasures. A whole panorama of bliss seemed to burst on her at once: her thoughts swung between the minutest details, like the smear of chalk left on her hand by Mr. Lambert's, and plans for the future embracing tens of years. Her body shared in her happiness; she sighed, and the breath rose gently, enjoyably to her parted lips—moved a little in the chair, and felt the plush caress her shoulders. "Henry," she said aloud; and on that name the needle of her spirit at last found its north.

While it might fairly be said that Nature abhors a vacuum, therefore Adelaide fell in love with the drawing-master, her love was none the less true, complete—making her happy, making her vulnerable; and altering for ever the whole course of her life.

CHAPTER III

ALICE HAMBRO ran down the top flight of stairs from the night-nursery, looked over the banisters, and saw Johnny eating an orange on the landing below.

"Johnny!" she called. (The Hambros were always calling to each other up and down stairs. It was a family habit.) "Johnny, is Mamma ready?"

"She's ready, but she's tying up Jimmy's knee."

"What's Jimmy done to his knee?"

"Fell down the cellar steps."

"You boys!" wailed Alice, picking up her blue tulle skirts and running down to join him. "You always pick the most inconvenient times. . . . Where did you get that orange?"

"Off the sideboard."

"Well, don't leave peel on the stairs. Is Papa ready?"

"He's been ready. Now he's taken his coat off again."

"What I suffer in this house!" complained Alice desperately. "What I *suffer—!*"

She flew down the last flight, across the hall, into her father's study. She wasn't really suffering: she was extremely happy. This was the first party she had been to since her cold of the month before, her new dress suited her perfectly, the troublesomeness of the children simply added to the excitement. She couldn't keep still, she had to run, so she ran into her father's study.

"Papa, we shan't be a minute!"

"Don't hurry on my account," said Mr. Hambro calmly. "I'm just settling down again."

"Papa, you mustn't! Do you like my frock? Jimmy has just hurt his knee," reported Alice rapidly; and flew off again up to her mother's room. Jimmy was seated on the edge of the big bed, his right leg extended stiffly before him, while Mrs. Hambro bathed it. She had a bath towel spread over her evening dress but was otherwise quite ready, even to the jet butterfly on top of her elaborate coiffure.

"Is it bad, and what was he *doing* in the cellar?" demanded Alice.

"He was looking for a hammer, dear."

"A hammer! At this time of night!" Alice sat down on the opposite side of the bed and automatically (as she always did in any spare moments before a party) waved her hands above her head so that the blood should run down and leave them lily-white. "Really, Mamma, if I'd been spoiled as they are—"

"You look like a beetle," observed James.

"Hold the bandage, dear," said Mrs. Hambro.

Alice leaned over and laid a finger on the lint while her mother safety-pinned it in place. Nurse ought to be doing this, thought Alice; and then remembered that the twins were having a feud with her—something about putty in their beds. Jimmy hoisted himself to his feet and hobbled from the room; they heard him limp upstairs till he reached the second landing, where a fight broke out, presumably with Johnny over the orange.

"Goodness," said Alice. But she had already forgotten him as she watched Mrs. Hambro sit before the dressing-table and apply a light film of violet powder. To see her mother do this gave Alice a pleasant feeling of eldest-daughter intimacy: she herself was allowed no more aid to beauty than a piece of chamois leather rubbed over the nose. It was believed to take the shine off. Alice looked at the big glass powder-bowl, and thought that when she was married she would have one exactly the same.

"I suppose Adelaide will be there?" said Mrs. Hambro.

"Oh, I hope so. I want to see her particularly."

"She's been looking brighter these last weeks."

"She's been going regular walks, in the Gardens. Mamma, when the Culvers moved, didn't they take a big box of toys out of the nursery—things Treff wouldn't give up?"

"They may have. I remember your father saying he'd seen the Crystal Palace dismantled with less fuss."

"Because I want them for the Sunday-school party. I shall ask Adelaide if I can go round and look to-morrow. Mamma, will there be dancing?"

"Not at a musical, dear."

"Oh, well," said Alice. She stretched out her feet in their blue satin slippers and danced a few steps in the air. She had pretty feet. She was pretty Alice Hambro, going to a party; she began to bounce gently up and down on her mother's bed.

2

Mrs. Orton's musical evenings were not calculated to produce such excitement generally. The majority of her guests came from old habit, and because the claret-cup was reliable, and because one didn't have to sit in a draught; they were mostly matrons with daughters. Mrs. Orton often lamented that young men were no longer musical, by which she meant uncritical; she had come to harbour a vague, resentful suspicion that a pianist at a guinea and a soprano at two somehow corresponded to female lunch on a tray, as opposed to male joint and vegetables; men always expected more. However, as she often said, her musicals had quite a character of their own.

"Adelaide," said Alice softly. She felt as though she had fizzed over too soon and now gone rather flat. She wanted to whisper, to draw her cousin's attention to an old lady opposite, an old lady whose nodding head, at first keeping time to the music, now followed a gentle rhythm of its own. But Adelaide did not hear; for once she was behaving better than her cousin—she sat utterly absorbed, wearing an expression of dreamy happiness. It was so perfect that Alice wondered if she had been practising.

The song ended, the last song before the interval; the noise of chairs and rout-seats being pushed back almost drowned the applause. One went downstairs to the buffet-supper, and this movement and the resulting buzz of talk brought the party to life. Alice looked for Mrs. Hambro and began working towards her, pulling Adelaide by the hand; but Alice could squeeze where Adelaide could, or would, not; the cousins were separated, and in the end Adelaide was the last person to go through the door. A girl just ahead waited for her, and Adelaide recognized Miss Yates.

"How I admire you for not crowding!" exclaimed Agatha Yates. "And how hard it is not to!"

Adelaide smiled back. She had at that moment a curious, fleeting, but quite definite sensation of regret: she regretted that this offer of friendship—for such it was, most frankly expressed in look and tone—was no longer worth the acceptance.

"Do you like parties?" continued Miss Yates, as they went downstairs. "I don't, they seem such a waste of time. But Miss Hill says the more we go about and lead normal social lives, the more useful we'll be."

Adelaide smiled again. All around people were offering and accepting plates of food, raising and setting down glasses, looking for somewhere to sit, chattering about the music; Adelaide stood quite still, her hands lightly clasped before her. It was the conventional attitude of the well-bred young woman—except that a supper-room called for more animation.

"You must surely," Miss Yates was saying, "have heard of Miss Octavia Hill?"

"Oh, yes, slums," said Adelaide.

Agatha Yates groaned.

"*Please* don't call them that. They're Courts, or Mews, or Alleys. It's like calling people 'the poor' instead of by their names. That's the whole point of our method—dealing with people individually. And it's working." Miss Yates's rather plain face suddenly flushed. "You can't imagine how glorious it is to see an idea actually work!"

As all her friends knew, once she was embarked on a panegyric of rent collecting, nothing would stop her, and she did not stop now. But she was aware of a lack of response, and of an increasing disappointment; for she had noticed Adelaide before (at the very tea-party when Adelaide watched her with such admiration) and thought her rather intelligent and capable-looking; had actually formed the idea of inviting her to a tenants' social. But now Miss Culver's attention was so barely polite that Agatha began to feel rather foolish. She said abruptly:—

"I'm keeping you from your friends. Are you staying for the rest of the concert?"

"Oh, yes," said Adelaide.

"I don't think I shall. I must find Mrs. Orton."

Adelaide nodded. The implications of this remark—that Miss Yates was leaving, and presumably going home, unaccompanied—did not even strike her. She was simply glad to be left alone; for even in a room containing fifty people, Adelaide at this time could easily find space to be alone with her thoughts.

3

It was just three weeks since her first secret rendezvous with Mr. Lambert in Kensington Gardens. Nothing could have been simpler to arrange: "I'm going to walk as far as the Serpentine every morning after breakfast," announced Adelaide—sitting beside Alice over their sketch-books, Mr. Lambert standing behind them—"Mamma says I need more exercise"; and next morning there was Mr. Lambert waiting for her. This happened the week after the faked drawing-lesson; Adelaide was a little surprised not to have heard from Mr. Lambert in the meantime, but she understood his delicacy; she thought he was waiting for a sign from herself. Even when she stepped quickly up to him, her face glowing, her hands (concealed in her muff) clasped over her heart, his greeting remained formal. . . .

"Good morning, Miss Culver."

Adelaide glanced round. There was no one within earshot: her look of surprise and disappointment was so explicit that he at once corrected himself.

"Adelaide . . ."

"Henry!" cried Adelaide.

As though something had been settled, they turned and began to walk along the Serpentine, towards the bridge. Their situation was not easy, however, and Adelaide for want of something better to say remarked that Alice's cold was clearing up.

"Does she often get them?" asked Mr. Lambert politely.

"Oh, yes. At least, not very often. Henry—"

"Adelaide?"

She felt slightly impatient. Delicious as it was to be walking along calling each other Adelaide and Henry, it wasn't leading anywhere. There was so much that needed clarification. She wanted their relationship to be properly established.

"Henry," she began tentatively, "last week—"

"Don't talk about it if you don't want to," said Mr. Lambert hastily.

"What *do* you mean?" cried Adelaide.

"Well, I didn't know." He paused and looked at the water. "I thought perhaps you might want to forget all about it."

"But I couldn't!"

"To ignore it, then. I mean, when you came to think it over—"

(37)

"I've thought of nothing else ever since!" cried Adelaide, passionately. "It's changed my whole life! Henry, if you mean you regret—"

"No, no, no," said Mr. Lambert. He laid his hand on her wrist where it disappeared inside the muff; thrust in his fingers so that they met her own in the close warmth. "I only meant, my dear, that if *you* had any regrets, if you were in any way angry with me, I'd behave as though it had never happened. I don't want to take advantage of—of an hour's light-heartedness."

All at once Adelaide saw what he meant: he had thought she might be simply flirting with him—though he was too much of a gentleman to say so outright. She hastened to relieve him.

"No, Henry, no," she said anxiously. "You mustn't think that. Though it was so—so sudden. I suppose it always is sudden. You mustn't think I'm that sort of girl."

"I don't know what sort of a girl you are," said Mr. Lambert, almost uneasily. "I've never met anyone like you before."

This was exquisite, but Adelaide had to finish making her position plain.

"I do know that some girls, quite nice girls, sometimes flirt with young men and don't think anything of it. In fact," said Adelaide honestly, "Alice says I ought to learn *how* to flirt, because the men expect it. At dances, you know. And indeed Alice gets on much better at dances than I do. But you mustn't think I was just flirting with you, Henry, because I couldn't bear it."

Inside the muff his fingers tightened on hers.

"I'm sure you've never flirted in your life."

"No, I haven't. Have you?"

"Dozens of times."

Adelaide laughed.

"I don't mind that a bit. No girl minds how many other women a man's admired before. In fact it makes it more flattering. Henry, when did you first begin to—to think about me?"

Mr. Lambert reflected.

"I believe it was the second time I saw you, when you wore a brown dress with trimming on it—"

"Green," corrected Adelaide. "Oh, Henry, was it as long ago as that?"

"And when did you begin to think about me?"

"I don't know," said Adelaide, apologetically. "At least, I always looked forward to the drawing-lessons, but I didn't know why. It must have been there all the time, Henry, waiting till you—" she broke off and looked at him, smiling, delightfully sure of herself. "May I say, until you made me a declaration? And then of course I knew. But Henry, when you speak to Papa—"

"What about?" asked Mr. Lambert.

"About us, of course."

"My dear Adelaide," said Mr. Lambert, withdrawing his hand and beginning to walk on again, "if I speak to your father, you will immediately be taken to Switzerland, or at any rate Torquay."

This was so true that Adelaide could not deny it. She did not actually fear a removal to the Alps, the expense and upheaval would be far too great; but Mr. Culver would undoubtedly make himself unpleasant. Adelaide did not pause to ask herself why: the fact was obvious.

"We must do nothing in a hurry," said Mr. Lambert.

"No," said Adelaide.

"Until my future is more assured."

Adelaide felt it wonderful to be dependent upon the future of an artist. And what a future it would be! She thought of Sir John Millais, and her heart swelled.

"Shall you have a picture in the Academy?" she asked longingly.

"If I've time to paint one," said Mr. Lambert, with great carelessness.

"But you must! You must make time!" cried Adelaide—and thought how glorious it would be if she could only help him to make it, arrange his still-necessary drawing-lessons, serve him nourishing meals, guard his scanty hours of unremitting toil. For she read what was in his mind: he wished to wait until he could bring her his success as a wedding gift, give her the pride of overwhelming Culvers and Hambros alike with the splendour of her match.

(39)

. . . As if I cared for that! thought Adelaide. Indeed she desired not only love but work, a life-work: the proper life-work of the woman, ancillary to the male. . . .

The rest of their brief interview was passed in making plans for Henry Lambert's Academy picture. They decided that it should have a religious but non-sectarian subject, and contain a great many life-sized figures. Adelaide suggested the finding of Moses in the bulrushes, and Mr. Lambert agreed that the combination of an infant (Moses) and a semi-nude (Pharaoh's daughter) had definite possibilities. Adelaide had never before heard even a semi-nude actually referred to in conversation; to use the term herself produced a wonderful sense of emancipation. Neither referred again to the prospective interview with Mr. Culver. There was no need, for Adelaide had instantly accepted her lover's decision that the time was not yet ripe. After all, they had only to wait until May, when Henry's genius would burst upon the world with the opening of the Academy; for the meanwhile Adelaide felt quite as strongly as he did—and without even seeking a reason—the necessity of concealment.

With the greatest ease, without a pang, she slipped into the ways of deceit.

A hundred feminine shifts, long-used, long-tried, lay ready to her hand; Adelaide found she knew them all, as if by instinct. To take the matter of letters: Mrs. Culver sometimes opened her daughter's correspondence, but she never opened a letter from Mr. Lambert, because they came addressed to—James Seeley. He was the previous occupier of the house, and genuine letters still came for him occasionally; it was anyone's duty to forward them to his bank, but often they lay about for days, and Adelaide had no difficulty in making off with them. This was her own contrivance—its elaborateness perhaps betrayed the 'prentice hand, and Mr. Lambert made use of it rather warily. (Adelaide wrote often.) Her walks in the Gardens had become an accepted routine: still, cunningly, for greater security, Adelaide sometimes complained of a bleak day, was a little late (with what curbings of impatience!) in setting out,

so that her mother sharply reminded her of the time. How intoxi-
catingly sweet, spiced with secrecy, were the half-hours that followed,
in the autumnal Gardens, under the falling leaves, under the bare
branches! How delicious the weekly drawing-lessons, spiced with
danger as eyes met, hands touched, behind Alice's back! What
wonder that Adelaide, standing in Mrs. Orton's supper-room, had
so much to think about that Miss Yates's talk was as the babble of
a brook; or that her cousin Alice, with two plates of chicken salad,
at last ate both herself?

CHAPTER IV

ALICE CAME ROUND early the next afternoon to go through
the old Culver toys; there was, as she remembered, quite a quantity
of them, packed away in a battered tin trunk. The two girls hauled
it from the box-room and sat down on the top landing to pull out
china dolls, jumping-jacks, wooden soldiers and a sheaf of scrap-
books; and right at the bottom found a large shell, faintly pink
under a tracery of white, with four blunt spines. Adelaide rubbed her
finger along the smooth inside of the lip and looked at it thoughtfully.

"Where did that come from?" asked Alice.

"Do you remember, ages ago, Mamma took me to call on a
Mrs. Burnett—and never again? I wonder who she was. . . ."

"Why, don't you know?" exclaimed Alice. "She's your aunt!"

It was typical of Adelaide that she did not burst into ejaculations.
She looked at her cousin, looked at the shell, and waited.

"*I* know," went on Alice, rather importantly, "because your Miss
Bryant told our Miss Grigson (isn't it astonishing how governesses

find out *everything?*) and one day Grigs told me. Mrs. Burnett was Isabel Culver, she's your Papa's sister, and she married a Mr. Thompson. *And,* my dear . . . perhaps I shouldn't tell you this . . . but if I know, I don't see why you shouldn't—"

"Good gracious, I don't suppose she murdered any one," said Adelaide, at last impatient.

"No, of course not. But, my dear"—Alice dropped her voice—"she's been *divorced.*"

For a moment Adelaide was too startled to speak. She was thoroughly shocked. For to have a divorce in the family was little better than having insanity, and indeed not so respectable. She felt at once repelled and extraordinarily curious.

"When did it happen?" she asked nervously.

"Oh, years and years ago—quite soon after she married. And she went to Paris with—with Mr. Burnett. Wasn't it awful!"

Adelaide nodded. She did feel it to be awful, but curiosity gained over horror. There was so much she didn't understand. She firmly believed, as her education had taught her, that the wages of sin was death; and all she could remember of her aunt pointed to some suspension of this law. The luxury of that drawing-room off Curzon Street; the extreme smartness of the page; even the lavish garland of velvet adorning Mrs. Burnett's gown, gradually reappeared to her memory in the most precise detail. Even more bewildering was the fact that she herself, as a child, had been allowed the opportunity of observing them. She had been taken to call on the sinner. . . .

"Mamma can't have known," said Adelaide suddenly.

"My dear, she must have!"

"Then why did she take me? You'd have thought—"

"Yes, wouldn't you?" agreed Alice.

"I don't believe it."

Alice put on a worldly and very grown-up air.

"Well, Mr. Burnett left her an immense deal of money, and I suppose she's got to leave it to some one."

"I think that's perfectly horrid," said Adelaide coldly.

She stooped again over the trunk and pulled out another doll, part of a toy theatre, a bundle of old Christmas-cards that had evidently been saved for scrap-books. There was a short silence, while Alice looked injured.

"I'm sorry I told you, Addie, if you're going to be upset."

"I'm not upset. At least, not about that. But I do think it's horrid to suggest that Mamma was thinking about Mrs. Burnett's money."

"I'm sure I don't know what else she could have been thinking about!" cried Alice.

It was very distasteful—but at the back of her mind Adelaide began to think that her cousin might be right. She remembered the peculiar atmosphere of the whole visit: her mother's nervousness, her own childish impression that they were doing something unusual, something that needed explaining. Or was it possible that Mrs. Culver, by the production of the infant Adelaide, was making a tacit offer to readmit a penitent sister-in-law to the respectable family circle? Did she hope by the spectacle of such innocence to soften a sin-hardened heart? If so, the attempt had failed. Either Mrs. Burnett didn't care for family life, or she had failed to repent.

"Oh, never mind," said Adelaide. "It's over and finished with; I'm sorry I snapped. Alice, do you really want *all* this rubbish?"

"All of it," said Alice good-humouredly. She easily forgave Adelaide's touchiness, because after all Mrs. Burnett was *her* aunt, it wasn't the Hambros who had a divorce in the family. "Look, Addie, let's tie a Christmas card to each thing, and put who it's from!"

Overriding Adelaide's objection that it wasn't yet Christmas, and the gifts weren't from anyone in particular, Alice swept up a lapful of toys, seized the cards, and carried them to the old schoolroom table; and the idea turned out to be quite amusing. *From Santa Claus,* wrote Alice, *From Mr. Pickwick . . . From Mother Goose.* . . . Adelaide wrote cards from Robinson Crusoe, Hans Andersen, and the Sleeping Beauty. They exhausted fairy-tale characters, they went on to Sir Garnet Wolseley—"Do you remember the Black Watch?" asked Alice; and Lord George Sanger—"Do you remember going to the circus?" cried Adelaide—"Oh, dear, do you remember sliding down the Redan?" They had all their youthful memories in common; even their present occupation was familiar, for the young Culvers and Hambros always bought their Christmas cards and Valentines together, and addressed them together, so that they shouldn't send the same one to a common friend. Adelaide actually found a card with Alice's name on it: frost and robins, for Alice always went in for robins, as the twins always went in for coaches: it must have been the last card to come to the house in Albion Place. . . .

For perhaps half an hour, in the old schoolroom, Adelaide slipped into a mood very rare with her: a mood in which family ties seemed the solid basis of life, their detail absorbing, their continuity a promise of stability for the future; perhaps she caught it from Alice, to whom such an attitude was so accepted, such a commonplace, that she took it for granted. But it had no real hold over Adelaide; it was as though she had walked by accident into someone else's room, into someone else's garden—and watched children playing there, and then walked out again.

Already, as they went downstairs to tea, leaving a great parcel for the twins to fetch, she was considering how she should break the news about Mrs. Burnett to Henry Lambert.

2

FOR OF COURSE she had to tell him. On that point Adelaide never had the least doubt. She could conceal nothing from the man who was to be her husband. She hoped Henry would be broadminded enough to realize that it wasn't her fault, and saw no incongruity in seeking forgiveness for something she hadn't done. As Alice had silently pointed out, Mrs. Burnett was her aunt, her blood-relation; reason as she might, Adelaide could not quite free herself from a sense of guilt.

When Adelaide had to do anything unpleasant, it was her instinct to rush at it. As soon as she saw Mr. Lambert next morning she rushed into confession.

"Henry, there's something I have to tell you. Something dreadful. I only found out yesterday or I'd have told you before."

Mr. Lambert, who had taken her arm, gave it a reassuring squeeze. He was in a very good humour—poor Henry! He said:—

"You look like a little girl who's been stealing jam."

Adelaide drew a deep breath.

"I'm serious, Henry. It *is* serious. Henry, there—there's a divorce in our family."

Watching him closely, she observed with relief that though startled, he was not overwhelmed. He didn't even drop her arm. She hurried on.

"It happened years and years ago, and I don't think many people know, but it was papa's sister, my aunt Isabel. Her husband divorced her and she went to live in Paris."

"With her lover?" asked Mr. Lambert calmly.

Adelaide flushed.

"With Mr. Burnett. Of course they got married. Now he's dead." (Adelaide felt that Mr. Burnett's death slightly improved matters.) "Henry, I'm so sorry. . . ."

But Mr. Lambert now appeared rather interested than in any way shocked—and also slightly incredulous. His raised, arched eyebrows gave him the air of a dog with its ears cocked.

He said, "Look here, are you possibly talking about Belle Burnett?"

"Belle?" repeated Adelaide. "Her name's Isabel—I suppose it might be. I dare say she'd very likely change it . . ."

"And she lived in Paris? Do you mean to say Belle Burnett's your aunt?"

"Why, do you mean you knew her?" cried Adelaide, startled in turn.

"I didn't exactly know her, I wasn't grand enough," said Mr. Lambert, more startlingly still. "But everyone knew who she was. She was one of the smartest women in Paris. I'm damned."

Adelaide felt slightly annoyed, both at his swearing in her presence and at the peculiar angle from which he seemed to regard the whole subject. She also, more obscurely, resented his way of referring to Mrs. Burnett without any prefix—though indeed that unfortunate woman had so nearly forfeited her right to it that perhaps this was natural.

"I suppose Paris is different," she said severely. "I dare say a few people *would* call on her there; but as for your not being grand enough—"

"My dear child, of course I wasn't. Belle Burnett went in for politicians and the Embassies; she said she left artists to the cocottes. She had the most elegant salon—"

"Then why did she come back to England?" demanded Adelaide sharply.

"Because the Austrian minister was transferred here— At least, I've no doubt she had good reasons. If you'd ever seen her—"

"But I have. Mamma took me to call on her once, when I was a little girl."

Mr. Lambert whistled.

"Your mother took you . . . ? Why on earth did she do that?"

"Because she was sorry for her. She felt it her duty. I think she was perfectly right."

"Oh, so do I," agreed Mr. Lambert. "Still, it's surprising."

For a moment his expression was rather like Alice's; then he looked into Adelaide's earnest face and let the thought go. "And what did you," he asked, "think of your aunt?"

Adelaide paused. Annoyed and disturbed as she was, she could not deny the memory of that white throat, those white hands, that silky rustle and faint sweet scent.

"I thought she was the most beautiful person I'd ever seen," she said honestly.

There in the Gardens, Mr. Lambert swiftly put his arm round her and kissed her on the cheek.

"You're a darling," he said. "Thank God you're not prejudiced like the rest of them. Adelaide, I adore you."

There was now no point in asking him whether he minded her having Mrs. Burnett for an aunt, since he plainly did not; and as

Adelaide walked home alone she found that her own attitude was already changing: she could think of Mrs. Burnett without shame.

3

SOMETHING else was changed too. From that conversation dated a subtle alteration in her relations with Henry Lambert. He gained assurance with her; his love-making became bolder. A prejudiced observer might have said that he treated her with slightly less respect. Adelaide however saw only a delightful increase in intimacy, and followed wherever he led.

A day or two later, going up to the box-room with a broken lamp, she noticed the lid of the tin trunk still open. Before closing it she glanced inside: it was almost empty, but in one corner lay the Indian shell. Either through delicacy, or because she saw no use in it, Alice had left it behind. After a moment's hesitation Adelaide picked it up and carried it downstairs and set it on her bedroom mantelpiece. Then she hesitated again; and at last put it out of sight in her bureau drawer.

CHAPTER V

IT WAS too much to hope that these daily meetings would never attract notice. The Gardens were frequented by Mrs. Culver's friends, who, while they praised her broad-mindedness in permitting Adelaide to walk there unchaperoned, were not at all averse to letting her know its consequences.

"Mrs. Orton saw you in the Gardens this morning, Adelaide."

Adelaide thought swiftly.

"Did she, Mamma? I didn't see her. But I saw Mr. Lambert."

Mrs. Culver waited. There was no telling whether Adelaide's tone had deceived her or not. In any case, she waited.

"He walked as far as the bridge with me," went on Adelaide. "He said he hoped we should go and see his picture in next year's Academy."

"Will he have one there?" Mrs. Culver looked very slightly pleased; a picture in the Academy, unlike most manifestations of art, was something she could recognize as a definite achievement. Not sufficient, of course, to alter Mr. Lambert's standing, but creditable in one's drawing-master.

"I said we always went anyway," finished Adelaide carelessly. "Mamma, have you any message? I'm writing to Treff."

The dangerous moment passed. Now and then it would recur. Alice was observant; she began to notice that Mr. Lambert spent more time at her cousin's shoulder than at her own, and fortunately remarked on it to Adelaide, who was able to give Henry warning. But they were in greater danger from Alice than from anyone, and it was particularly lucky that during that winter she was unusually occupied with her own concerns.

For Alice was about to have an offer. Like everything to do with the Hambros, it was a thoroughly family affair; even the twins, when Freddy Baker came to call on Sundays, regarded him with interested and speculative eyes. He came so regularly, and stayed so long; he listened so attentively to Mr. Hambro's political views. He went to all the dances Alice went to, and put her in the proud position of being able to book three waltzes as soon as she received her programme. Before matters reached this point Mr. Hambro naturally made a few enquiries: Mr. Baker's income (he was in Lloyd's), connections, and character were all satisfactory. When at last, on the third of January, he actually proposed, all the Hambros were pleased, and all advised Alice to accept him.

"Any one would think my family wanted to be rid of me," Alice told her cousin indignantly. "The children want to be bridesmaids, and the twins say they don't want me to be an old maid, and Mamma and Papa keep saying how sad it is to part with a daughter

—but they're quite prepared to part, they say they'll resign them-selves. I suppose it's the first time Papa has resigned himself in his life!"

Adelaide watched her cousin curiously. Alice, looking prettier than usual, was walking briskly about the Culver drawing-room as though she were out of doors. She was too full of energy to sit down. Adelaide thought that probably no one at the Hambros' had sat down for days.

"But what about you?" she asked. "Are you in love with Mr. Baker?"

"Well, I don't know," explained Alice. "I *like* him. I like him better than any man I know. It *is* such a comfort always to have one's programme filled. Do you like him, Addie?"

With a slight effort Adelaide fixed the image of a sleek-haired, high-collared, altogether average young man. If she liked him, it was because there was nothing to dislike.

"Yes, of course," she said. "Though I don't see what that has to do with it."

"Well, you're my cousin. And I must say he's awfully sweet with the children. The twins like him. We're all going on Sunday to sail their steamer on the Round Pond."

"Then if you're marrying to suit your family—I should say you'd better take Mr. Baker."

Alice stopped walking about and looked at Adelaide suspiciously.

"If you *don't* like him, Addie, I wish you'd say so outright."

"Good heavens!" cried Adelaide. "Of course I like him! Only it does seem to me that if you're thinking so much about the twins and the children and your cousins and all your other relatives—you can't be in love with Mr. Baker at all. And if you're not in love with him, you oughtn't to marry him."

"But I think I am."

"You know perfectly well you aren't!"

"Anyway," said Alice, rather offendedly, "I don't see how you can judge. I'm not saying this to be unkind, dear, but you've never had an offer at all—unless you count the Matthews boy, and I don't see how you can count him, when he hadn't a penny. I know just as much about being in love as you do."

Adelaide nearly laughed aloud. She had been walking that morning with Mr. Lambert in the snowy Gardens—only for ten minutes, but every one of them brimmed with exquisite emotion, spiced with danger. She felt she had already lived more intensely in those ten minutes than Alice would ever do in her whole married life. She was filled with kindness, and a sort of pity; almost the feeling of the married woman for the virgin.

She slipped her arm round her cousin's waist and said gently, "I'm sure you'll do whatever's right, dear. In fact, you're so good and sweet, I don't believe you could do wrong."

Alice looked gratified.

"Anyway, if I do marry Freddy, I'll try and make him a good wife. Adelaide . . ."

"Yes, dear?"

"I am in love with him," said Alice firmly.

2

THE HAMBROS were all delighted to hear this, and so, naturally, was Mr. Baker. The engagement was announced, and Alice immediately went off to pay a visit to his family in Somerset. Her letters thence were ecstatic: Freddy Baker also had brothers and sisters, Alice loved them all and they loved Alice. The little girls were to be bridesmaids along with Milly and Sybil and Ellen. Alice's wedding, observed her father thoughtfully, was evidently going to look like a school-treat.

Adelaide welcomed these events because her cousin's absence left her freer. Mrs. Culver was so used to thinking of the two girls together that she did not realize how much of the time Adelaide was now on her own. The question of the drawing-lessons did of course arise, but Alice's share in them was already promised, and Mrs. Hambro resourcefully sent the twins along instead (on the railway principle that two children equalled one adult). Mr. Lambert, equally resourceful, set them to copying sailing-vessels in the front part of the drawing-room, so that he and Adelaide had the back to themselves. Before this comfortable solution was reached, however, something occurred which made Adelaide so angry that she nearly wrecked the whole plan.

The twins, as has been said, got about a lot. Arriving ten minutes early for their first lesson, they informed their cousin that they had seen Mr. Lambert the day before, coming out of the Café Royal.

"He was squiffy," added James casually.

"James!" cried Adelaide. "How dare you say such a thing!"

"But he was," corroborated John stolidly. "He nearly fell down."

"I don't believe you!" cried Adelaide. "You horrid boys! Mr. Lambert will be here in five minutes, and I shall tell him what you've said!"

The five minutes passed in furious silence. As they heard Mr. Lambert run upstairs they all three turned and faced the door. He paused and looked at them enquiringly, as well he might; for they had rather the air of a reception committee at odds with itself.

Adelaide at once said:—

"James, repeat to Mr. Lambert what you've just told me."

James remained obstinately silent.

"Or confess that you were lying. Or you shan't have any drawing-lesson!"

"We weren't," muttered John.

"If you've been lying to Miss Culver," said Mr. Lambert sternly, "you must apologize at once."

"We weren't lying," repeated John; and he looked Mr. Lambert in the eye. "We only told her we'd seen you outside the Café Royal."

Mr. Lambert stooped and rubbed his ankle.

"Then you saw me take a nasty spill," he said cheerfully. "I went down on a piece of ice, Miss Culver, and nearly broke my leg."

Adelaide was glad to find that her young cousins weren't liars, but she read them a long lecture on the wickedness of jumping to conclusions, especially slanderous ones. They didn't answer her. They got about so much, they already knew when it was best to hold their peace.

3

ADELAIDE never referred to this incident again, nor did Mr. Lambert; it was beneath their notice. They talked about his picture for the Academy, often about his other pupils; for Adelaide was eager to inform herself on every part of her lover's life. He gave lessons almost every day—to the Misses Pomfret and the Misses Drew in Bayswater, to a Miss Ocock in Knightsbridge, besides his girls' school. Adelaide made him describe them to her in detail, and it was a secret pleasure to learn that every one of these young ladies was exceptionally plain. "But they can't all be plain!" she once protested insincerely. "They are," said Mr. Lambert, with a grin, "otherwise they wouldn't be taking drawing-lessons." He added hastily, "It's only a very rare person like you, dear, who's clever as well as beautiful." No wonder Adelaide liked hearing about Enid Pomfret, who was freckled, and Florence Ocock, who looked like a dumpling; and on the one occasion when she actually met Miss Ocock, at an At Home, Adelaide was hardly disconcerted to find her, though plump, exceedingly pretty. She had curly brown hair and a bright colour; some men would have admired her very much; and Adelaide saw it as a further proof of his devotion to herself that Mr. Lambert did not. Out of sheer gay-heartedness she led the conversation round to art.

"Do you sketch?" asked Adelaide.

"Oh, yes," said Miss Ocock. "At least, my mamma makes me take drawing-lessons. They're a fearful bore."

Adelaide smiled. How indifferent, how preoccupied, must Mr. Lambert be, that anyone should find him boring!

"I think accomplishments are such nonsense," went on Miss Ocock ingenuously. "Except dancing, of course. I can't sing, and I can't play a note, and I certainly can't draw, and dear me, what does it matter?"

Adelaide could see it didn't matter at all, to a girl who even at an At Home had just been talking to three young men at once—a circumstance all the more striking because there were only three young men present, all the rest being middle-aged or old. The next time she saw Mr. Lambert she told him of the encounter, and made a loving joke of his insensibility.

"I've met your Miss Ocock, Henry. I think she's quite fascinating."

"She's an empty-headed little bundle of conceit."

"Other men don't seem to think so. . . . I don't believe you can have paid her proper attention."

"I've had no attention to spare," said he.

Adelaide's own looks at this time began to improve. She had always possessed a good, though rather thin figure; now her complexion and her eyes brightened, her mouth took a softer curve. It annoyed Mrs. Culver that with these improvements went an increased absent-mindedness, an unsuitable aloofness; more young men asked to be introduced to Adelaide, but she seemed unable to hold their interest. She didn't try to. "She stands there like a duchess," complained Mrs. Culver to her husband, "saying 'Yes' and 'No' till they go away again!" "You'd better speak to her about it," said Mr. Culver.

This was his usual answer to all domestic problems, for he was still cultivating detachment. Like Adelaide, he was aloof—or Adelaide was like her father: she had inherited an acquired characteristic. Mrs. Culver herself had never been either impulsive or emotional, but as she grew older a belated desire for affection was altering her character—whereas the characters of both Adelaide and Mr. Culver remained, in this direction at least, unchanged. As a result Mrs. Culver's heart turned more and more towards her impulsive and amiable son.

Treff was now nearly eighteen, on the point of leaving Harrow and going up to Cambridge. His scholastic career had been undistinguished, but he possessed a knack of scraping through examinations. Most people liked him. He was tall, like Adelaide, his straight dark hair fell untidily over his forehead, giving him a rather ro-

mantic look, and his manners were often charming. Most people
liked Treff, but especially women. Even in adolescence he showed
no awkwardness with them, he approached them with ingenuous
confidence. Tea-parties had no terrors for Treff, he handed cups
neatly and easily—and, as Adelaide observed, always got a good tea.
None of these qualities however pointed to any definite career, and
in moments of clear-sightedness Mrs. Culver felt it fortunate that
he was destined for his father's firm.

Or so she had always assumed. As her husband left the house to
her, so she left the office to him; if she ever thought about it, she
fixed the age of his retirement at about sixty, or sixty-five—after
Treff was firmly established. But now, at fifty-three, Mr. Culver
suddenly announced that the firm of Culver, Blore and Masterman
was about to become Masterman, Masterman and Blore.

He was in fact being bought out. Masterman and Blore also had
sons; they were unluckily two of the people who did not think much
of Treff Culver. It was possible that in his heart of hearts Mr. Culver
didn't either. When a handsome offer was made, he accepted it—
and found his technique of detachment perfectly equal to this new
task.

"But what about Treff?" cried his wife.

"Treff will go to Cambridge as arranged."

"But after?"

"Three years will give him time to consider. I think I'll go round
to the Club."

"No, William," said Mrs. Culver firmly. "You must tell me more.
Are we to stay here, for instance? Should we move again, into a
smaller house? Are we to stay in London at all? William, what will
our income be?"

Mr. Culver hesitated. Even at this crisis of their fortunes, he could
not quite bring himself to give her the precise figure. He never
had. The only precise figures Mrs. Culver knew were those of her
housekeeping and dress allowances.

"You'll have to manage on about half. Adelaide has the hundred
a year her grandmother left her, which I suppose amply covers her

expenses, and when Treff finishes at Cambridge things will be easier. But no doubt there must be changes."

"No doubt," said Mrs. Culver.

She tried not to speak bitterly. They had been married twenty-five years, an emotion never very rapturous had long settled into habit; they were used to each other, they got on as well as most couples. If Mrs. Culver ever felt disappointed—if she had had to put aside secret dreams of Mayfair or Belgravia—she did so in silence. They were married, for better or worse, and it might have been a great deal worse. Already she was beginning to disguise from herself the fact that her husband had been dropped from his own firm at the age of fifty-three. That he had been paid, in fact, to get out . . .

The great thing was to keep up appearances.

"Will, I'm quite glad," she said thoughtfully. "I believe it's a good thing. You haven't been looking at all well lately, and I don't think that in any case you could have gone on much longer. So many men have to retire for reasons of health—and then find they've left it too late."

Mr. Culver nodded seriously. He was perfectly willing to retire for reasons of health, he thought it a very good notion. And soon it was no longer a notion, but an accepted fact. He began to take care of himself. He told people—or Mrs. Culver told them for him—that he had to avoid any strain on the heart. "My dear, why don't you move out of London?" said Mrs. Orton; and Mrs. Culver, anxious and sensible, agreed that this might be the wisest plan.

4

ADELAIDE was aghast.

"Move into the country!" she repeated. "Mamma, we can't!"

There was fortunately so very natural a reason for her looks of dismay that Mrs. Culver did not even rebuke her.

"I know you'll miss your friends, dear; but you'll soon make others. Indeed, I sometimes think a girl has better chances in the country than in town; one gets more intimate with people."

Adelaide realized at once what sort of chances her mother referred to; it was the uncomfortable fact that in the three years she had been out only one man had proposed to her, and he the Matthews boy.

"Besides," went on Mrs. Culver, "you'll always be able to visit the Hambros—and when Alice is married you can stay with her. That will be really nice." Mrs. Culver brightened; she knew she could rely on Alice's co-operation, and a young married woman was the very person to get Adelaide off—Adelaide, who was too old now to be taken about like a girl in her first season . . . The more she thought of this the more hopeful Mrs. Culver became; until she began to see it as almost worth while moving into the country, simply to be able to send Adelaide back to town . . .

But Adelaide still struggled.

"What about Treff? He'll hate the country!"

"Treff will be going to Cambridge next year. Besides, I'm sure it will be much nicer for him to bring his friends home to a pleasant country house, than to Kensington."

"Mamma, do you mean it's *decided?*"

"Practically, dear. Mrs. Orton knows of a place in Surrey."

CHAPTER VI

THIS NEWS Adelaide did not immediately report to her lover. She could not quite believe it herself; moreover, she hoped for delay. The move from Albion Place—only across the Park—had been talked of for at least six months in advance; an exodus from London altogether was a much greater undertaking. They had to find a house; they had to get rid of the lease of their present one; and surely, persisted Adelaide, they ought to consult Treff? She wrote to him herself, painting an almost macabre picture of rural life, urging him to protest; Treff wrote back, to his mother, saying he thought the country would be rather jolly. Treff was a broken reed. So (from Adelaide's point of view) were the house-agents. With unique efficiency they produced a retired Anglo-Indian who was seeking just such a house as the Culvers', and who wished to move in as soon as the Culvers could move out. Mrs. Culver took Adelaide down to Farnham to look at a house belonging to Mrs. Orton's second cousin; it was the very thing. Even Adelaide had to admit its charm: medium-sized, two-storied, facing south; a white, bow-windowed villa, with a garden before and an orchard behind; within, plenty of cupboards and a modern hot-water system. Mrs. Culver also saw at a glance that it was a house of good standing, carrying the right to a prominent pew in church and a place on flower-show committees: no struggling, if one lived at Platt's End, to keep up one's position. The very name, in its plainness and lack of pretence, guaranteed a minor but solid importance. Mrs. Culver felt she could be happy there; for a moment, standing in the sun-shine of the empty drawing-room, she had an almost poetic vision of herself, in the right sort of hat, hobnobbing with nice people after morning service. . . .

"Don't you think it's very nice, dear?" she asked almost persua-sively. She felt so expansive that she wanted Adelaide to share her pleasure.

"Oh, very nice," said Adelaide.

"You can have the pretty room at the back. Or you could have the corner one. . . . I do think you might show a little enthusiasm."

"It won't make any difference whether I do or not," said Adelaide resentfully.

But still, looking through the wide light bow of the window, at the pretty garden, at the chestnut-trees in the lane and the roofs of Farnham rising picturesquely beyond, she felt the charm of the place. It was rustic, but civilized: the good proportions of the room behind her matched the cultivation and neatness of the view; a gentlefolk's house in a gentle landscape. Something in Adelaide stirred; as she had once been ready to respond to Miss Yates, so she could once have responded to this. For it is rarely that life offers no alternative: there were two other possible Adelaides—a social worker, and a country gentlewoman—each with a fair chance of happiness. But now it was too late, her course was already set; and being what she was, she could not alter it.

"I shall tell your father we like it very much," said Mrs. Culver.

They walked back to the station in silence. For once it was the elder lady who day-dreamed, while Adelaide was absorbed in the most practical considerations. They led her, as soon as she got home, to slip into Mr. Culver's study and borrow *Whitaker's Almanac*.

2

THE FOLLOWING DAY, Adelaide visited Mr. Lambert at his rooms in Britannia Mews. She was fully aware of the impropriety of this step—or rather that it would have been improper, in other circumstances. Now it was simply necessary. Mrs. Culver went out early to see Mrs. Hambro, she longed to pour into more sympathetic ears a description of Platt's End; and as soon as she had gone Adelaide went out too. She walked swiftly across the Gardens, across the Bayswater Road, past the old house in Albion Place, down the turning that led to the Alley beyond. There for a moment she paused. On one side rose the familiar wall, spiked on top, with the lilac hanging over; on the other opened the archway into the Mews.

The morning was bright and sunny, but even in that favourable light it was obvious that the Mews had reached its nadir. Anxious and hurried as she was, Adelaide could not fail to notice it; the respectable portion had shrunk, only two windows showed clean curtains: the brick enclosure round the lime-tree had become a sort of communal dust-bin, from which refuse of all sorts, much of it organic, overflowed and was blown about the cobbles. Dirty clouts hung here and there over the balcony railings, in one place bedding; such was the general squalor that the Cock at the far end no longer repelled but drew the eye. It looked at least solid, in good repair; the glass in the side-door was clean, the brass rim of the step moderately bright. Britannia Mews, re-orienting itself, now found its bulwark of respectability in a public-house.

Without giving herself time to think, Adelaide walked under the arch, to the stable where Benson had once groomed his horses. The great doors were shut. She ran up the steep iron staircase and knocked sharply on the door above. She had to knock several times before it was cautiously opened; then she pushed at it and almost fell through, into Mr. Lambert's arms.

"Adelaide!" he exclaimed. "Adelaide—good God!—what are you doing here?"

"I had to see you. We've got to talk."

"But I was just coming to meet you, in the Gardens!"

"We've got to talk," repeated Adelaide stubbornly. "Not in the Gardens. This is the only place. . . ."

But looking round, she gave an involuntary gasp. She had seen the room before, in the days of the Bensons; Mrs. Benson had kept it like a new pin; Adelaide distinctly remembered a clean red-and-white tablecloth, a row of plants in the window, and an extraordinarily brilliant array of brass. Now it matched the scene without. Old canvases, originally stacked against the wall, had collapsed upon the floor; the hearth was stuffed with oil- and paint-rags; dirty brushes protruded from among the unwashed crockery in the sink. An enormous wicker basket cumbered the floor, one of the two chairs was broken and the other heaped with old newspapers. Everywhere there were empty bottles. Through the inner door, wedged ajar by a soiled towel, she glimpsed an equally chaotic bedroom. Adelaide looked at it all, and parenthetically felt a great longing to clean it up.

"Sit down," said Mr. Lambert, pushing the papers from the sound chair. "Adelaide, my dearest girl, you shouldn't have come here."

"I know. But what does it matter? I've got to talk to you," repeated Adelaide. She sat down and pulled off her gloves. "Henry, the most dreadful thing has happened. We're leaving town."

"You mean you're going to move? When?"

"Next month. Papa's had an offer for the rest of the lease, and Mamma's found a house in Farnham. But I won't go. I can't! Henry, you'll simply have to speak to Papa."

Mr. Lambert sat down opposite her, on the wicker basket.

"Of course I will, if you think it'll do any good. But it won't, my darling. We've been into all that before. I've no money and no prospects—"

"You have prospects! You're going to be a great artist!"

"Do you think your father will believe that? He'll just throw me out."

In spite of all her dreams, Adelaide knew this to be true. Of all professions, that of art was least calculated to inspire confidence in Mr. Culver. Show him a struggling barrister and a wealthy Q.C., and he could at least perceive a connection between them, they stood at different points on a well-defined road; but show him Mr. Lambert and Sir John Millais, and he would see no connection at all, simply because the latter had never been his daughter's drawing-master.

"It's no use," said Mr. Lambert abruptly. "Adelaide: I must give you up."

Adelaide looked at him fondly. She was not surprised, she had expected him to say this; but of course she wasn't going to accept it.

"Don't you love me, Henry?"

"You know I do."

"Then that's all that matters. We'll be married."

"Your parents will never consent."

"I don't care. And it can't be wrong, Henry; doesn't it say in the Bible that a woman must leave her parents and cleave to her husband?"

For a moment Mr. Lambert met her earnest, loving gaze; then he stood up and walked to the window, and spoke to her over his shoulder.

"I don't like telling you this, dear, but I must. I'm not a fit husband for you. Apart from having no income—"

"I've a hundred a year," said Adelaide.

"Have you?" asked Mr. Lambert, momentarily distracted. "Have you control of it?"

"Yes, now I'm twenty-one. My grandmother left it me."

"That doesn't make any difference," said Mr. Lambert resolutely. "I'm not talking about money now. You don't know me, Adelaide: you bring out the best in me and never see the worst. I've . . . vices you've never dreamed of."

"I'm sure you haven't!" cried Adelaide. She looked round the room and laughed. "I can see you're dreadfully untidy—"

"Exactly. And you think that's the worst that can be said of me. Go down into the Mews, Adelaide, and see what they'll tell you there. They'll tell you I drink like a fish."

3

For a minute she hardly understood him. The vice of drunkenness was not only outside her experience, but also outside her comprehension. Her mental picture of a drunkard was taken from *Punch*: an uncouth trampish navvy, a half-gorilla—unchecked against reality, for though there was drunkenness in the London streets, a well-bred woman averted her eyes from it. Adelaide looked at Mr. Lambert therefore with perplexity, but without real alarm.

"I don't know what you mean," she said blankly.

"I mean that I drink too much wine—or gin, or spirits, or anything I can get hold of—and become intoxicated. I can't walk properly—as your young cousins have observed. I can't speak properly. I become maudlin and quarrelsome. I have no control over my actions. That's what being drunk is."

"But you'd never be like that!"

"I have been, frequently. And I shall be drunk again. Look here, Adelaide," said Mr. Lambert roughly, "I'm trying to play straight with you. I'm no good. If you can't get that into your innocent mind, you'll just have to take my word for it."

Adelaide stood up. His roughness, which to her was exciting masculinity, did not repel but drew her. With great plainness she said:—

"You don't have to get drunk. There's nothing to make you. Why don't you stop?"

"I can't."

"Then I'll stop you," said Adelaide confidently.

For now she breathed confidence; and energy, and resolution. Instead of alarming or disgusting, Mr. Lambert's unfortunate weakness simply made her all the more eager to marry and save him. The love of a good woman was notoriously omnipotent. Home influences, too, refining society, regular meals—how Adelaide yearned to deploy one after the other in a brief victorious campaign over Mr. Lambert's thirst!

"You don't know what you're talking about," said he gloomily.

"Yes, I do." Adelaide took his hand between her own and held it fast. "I quite understand, my dearest, I'm not a bit narrow-minded, I do see how sometimes when you're all alone in the evenings you sometimes take a glass too much. I'm sure many bachelors do. But when you have me with you all the time, it just won't happen. Why should it?"

"Because the dog," said Mr. Lambert slowly, "returns to its vomit."

Adelaide let his hand drop. The brutality of the words momentarily shocked her. But almost at once she saw why he had used them: out of the tenderness of his heart, fighting against his great desire, he was trying to frighten her away. Adelaide smiled.

"You don't know what a very strong character I have," she told him.

Mr. Lambert looked at her uneasily. Her youth and vigour, the unused force of her will, made her at that moment almost formidable. His artist's eye marked the extreme erectness of her back and shoulders, the confident lift of her chin. She looked like a moral principle made flesh, beautiful with the beauty of righteousness: she looked in fact rather like an angel; and as Mr. Lambert's thoughts found issue in this most conventional simile, he too smiled.

"There!" cried Adelaide. "Now you're happy again!"

Softening, melted, laughing, she threw her arms round his neck and kissed him, for the first time with passion. Her smooth un-powdered cheek pressed close against his, he breathed the clean youthful scent of her hair. Adelaide had won.

"We'll be married," she murmured.

"We'll be married," echoed Mr. Lambert.

"By special licence," added Adelaide.

"Is that the best way?"

"Much," said Adelaide practically. "I've looked it up in Whitaker. You get it at the Vicar-General's Office, in Doctor's Commons, be-tween ten and four."

Mr. Lambert, now completely subjugated, released her in order to give these particulars his full attention; he felt Adelaide would not expect him to need telling twice. She continued.

"Then we can be married one clear day after, any time within the next three months, at the Registrar's Office in either of our dis-tricts. It costs three pounds seven and six. Oh, Henry, doesn't it seem little?"

As a matter of fact it did not, at that moment, seem little to Henry Lambert; but he could hardly tell her so. He was too fasci-nated, too touched, by her absolute confidence; yet it was this second emotion that made him suddenly take her by the shoulders and turn her round to face the squalid room.

"Look at it, Adelaide," he adjured her, almost desperately. "Could you stand living in a place like this? Look at it. Here, or anywhere else, this is how I live. I've found my level. Neither you nor any one else is going to be able to raise me. Can you stand it?"

"Why, of course, my darling," said Adelaide, with great eager-ness. "I've been longing, ever since I came in, to clear it all up."

4

THEY AGREED, before she left, to an elopement, its exact date to be fixed by Adelaide; but Mr. Lambert was to procure the licence immediately. They would get married, and tell the Culvers afterwards. This decision, however, and the knowledge that her parents could by no means prevent her carrying it out, calmed Ade-

(63)

laide's spirits to such an extent, and filled her with such confidence, that she began to reconsider the position. Her recent behaviour notwithstanding, she had no love of deceit for deceit's sake. She still desired her parents' approval. Was it so certain, after all, that they would refuse it? Was not Henry Lambert's diffidence perhaps exaggerated? "He thinks so little of himself!" mused Adelaide fondly; for she had soon discounted the bulk of his confession; the self-portrait he had drawn was too unlike all she knew of him to convince. After reflecting on all these points for a couple of days Adelaide decided to tell the truth and give her parents a chance to display magnanimity and understanding. If they did not, her conscience would be clear; if they did—"We can be married in church!" thought Adelaide.

She waited till they were all together, in the drawing-room after dinner. Rose had taken away the coffee-cups, Mr. and Mrs. Culver were reading, Adelaide sat with embroidery in her hands; they made a family group such as might have been found, at that hour, in half the drawing-rooms of Kensington. But in how many young female breasts surged the emotion that filled Adelaide's? Others might be as loving, few so resolute. The clock struck nine; Adelaide put aside her work and stood up.

"Mamma, Papa, I've something to tell you."

Mr. Culver hardly lowered his book; but Adelaide saw instantly that her mother, by some sort of telepathic communication, already knew part at least of what she was about to say. Adelaide rushed at it.

"I want to get married," she stated baldly.

That brought Mr. Culver's book down with a bang. He looked, however, not at his daughter but at his wife; he naturally expected her to know all about it. Mrs. Culver smiled at him reassuringly: she was indeed as ignorant as himself, but she did not doubt her ability to handle the situation. She began first of all by re-establishing his male supremacy.

"Adelaide, my dear!" she said smoothly. "Is a young man coming to see Papa?"

"Yes," said Adelaide. "At least he will if it's necessary. . . . It's Mr. Lambert."

"Good God!" exclaimed Mr. Culver.

Again his wife's glance reassured and restrained him. With rising anger Adelaide saw that her mother did not even consider it worth while to release Mr. Culver's wrath.

"If you mean that Mr. Lambert has made you an offer, Adelaide, then it was a piece of impertinence which I hope you were not silly enough to allow. You are quite right to tell us—"

Adelaide perceived vaguely that she was being given a chance to rat; to gloss over her original statement, to slide from an impossible position, rejoin as it were her proper party. The blood beat in her cheeks.

"But I didn't consider it impertinent, Mamma. Why should I?"

"Because he is a young man without means, and probably without character. No young man of good character would dream of such a thing. I'm afraid you must have been a little foolish; but as of course he won't come here any more, and indeed we shall very soon have left town, the best thing we can do is to forget all about it."

This was unendurable. Adelaide's hands shook as she deliberately turned her back on her mother and addressed herself to Mr. Culver.

"Papa!" she said loudly.

"And don't bother your father, dear; he has quite enough on his mind as it is."

"Papa," repeated Adelaide, "I am twenty-one, and I love Mr. Lambert, and I am going to marry him."

For the third time Mr. Culver looked at his wife, and for the third time received the assurance that he need not lose his temper.

"Nonsense," said Mr. Culver firmly.

He picked up his book and began looking for his place. Mrs. Culver swiftly rose, passed her arm through Adelaide's, and led her from the room. Outside, in the hall, she said coldly:—

"You will not see Mr. Lambert again, Adelaide, and you will not mention him again. Your father's heart won't stand it. But you had better tell me at once how far this has gone."

Adelaide released herself. Nothing in all her life had made her angrier than this contemptuous ease with which her mother thought to dominate her.

"You treat me like a child," she said bitterly.

"Because you behave like a child. Most girls have these fits of silliness—and the drawing-master is the usual object."

"But this is different!" cried Adelaide.

Mrs. Culver uttered a short, harsh laugh.

"My dear, in a year or two's time, when, we'll hope, you are properly married, you'll see that it's extraordinarily commonplace. One might almost say vulgar. . . . And you'll be very grateful to me for not allowing you to give it undue importance by making sentimental scenes."

Adelaide looked at her steadily. Over the wound to her pride, to her love, there was already forming a defensive scar: the barrier between herself and her mother which nothing would ever break down.

"Very well," she said steadily. "I'll tell you nothing, except that I love Mr. Lambert, and he loves me, and we're going to be married. Good night, Mamma."

Such was the force of habit that she instinctively put up her cheek for her mother's kiss; Mrs. Culver as automatically gave it. Immediately after this display of affection they drew away from each other.

"You have heard what your father and I say. I hope we shall not have to mention the matter again."

Adelaide said nothing.

5

THE NEXT day was Thursday; neither Mr. Lambert nor the twins appeared. Adelaide still said nothing. She had expected this. Nor was she able to go out in the morning, for her mother kept her to make an inventory of linen. It was evidently Mrs. Culver's design to leave Adelaide no moment to herself (except when sleeping) until the move to Farnham had taken place. True to her word, she never mentioned Mr. Lambert's name; it seemed she was not even going to punish her daughter. And Adelaide, her plans laid, her name already on a marriage licence, could afford to accept the situation with ironical meekness. She could afford to appear obedient, and help with the move.

For it was the peculiar fact that Adelaide still saw this as duty. She was about to wound her parents to the heart, and leave them, possibly for ever; but she couldn't leave in the middle of packing. Her mother genuinely needed her at every moment; it was Adelaide who supervised the crating of the glass, Adelaide who saw to all Treff's clothes, Adelaide who accompanied Mrs. Culver to Platt's End and took measurements for the curtains. Some of the old ones would do, some would not: Adelaide sat in the schoolroom and machined yards of casement-cloth. She advised, assisted, with as much energy as if Platt's End were to be her own future home.

On the one occasion when she saw Mr. Lambert during this period—Adelaide had slipped a letter into the box conjuring him to be by the second lamp-post at nine P.M.—this attitude rather astonished him.

"But, my dearest girl, what are we waiting for? Wherever your people are won't make any difference—"

"I've got to get this house clear," said Adelaide. "If you could see it, Henry, you'd understand."

Henry Lambert did not understand at all. There was no orderliness in him—certainly none of that feminine sense of order which would attempt to leave a house clean in the path of an invasion. Adelaide had it very strongly. When she thought of the dwelling in Britannia Mews, she thought of a spring-cleaning. Standing under the lamp-post, in the circle of his arm—like a maid-servant run out to meet her sweetheart—she was still ruled by the instinct of order.

"So I come after the removal-man?" said Mr. Lambert.

"You come the same day," corrected Adelaide. "I'm supposed to be going by the early train, while Mamma sees the things off here and comes down with Papa in the afternoon. So you see I shall have my bags, and I shall just tell the cab to drive to Britannia Mews. And you'll be waiting for me. Oh, Henry!"

"My darling?"

"It is an adventure, isn't it?"

"It is indeed. Adelaide—if you change your mind—if you tell the cab to drive to the station—"

"I shan't," said she. "Dearest, I must run back, or they'll miss me. Till Wednesday!"

"Till Wednesday," repeated Mr. Lambert.

They kissed—in the street, under the lamp-post—and she hurried away.

CHAPTER VII

THEY WERE MARRIED on the first Wednesday in May, at half-past eleven, before the Paddington Registrar, their witnesses being two respectable elderly women brought in from the next room, which they had apparently been cleaning—they whipped off their aprons as they came in. The ceremony itself struck Adelaide as uncommonly short: she and Mr. Lambert in turn declared that they knew no lawful impediment why they should not be joined in matrimony, and called on the two charwomen to witness that they took each other as husband and wife; and that was all. They were married—even before Henry put the ring on her finger. For a moment it seemed so unlikely that Adelaide stood waiting—waiting, unconsciously, for the loud thump of the Mendelssohn march, without which no wedding in her experience had ever been legalized. But there was no music, naturally. . . . She felt Henry's hand slip under her arm, and saw the Registrar waiting for them to go away.

"I trust you will be very happy together," he said courteously. "Never less happy than you are to-day."

They shook hands with him. Henry paid, and shook hands again. The two charwomen re-tied their aprons. That was all, it was over.

2

"Well, Mrs. Lambert?" said Henry, as they emerged onto the pavement. "How do you feel?"

"Rather queer," confessed Adelaide.

"That's all right, all brides feel queer. We'll go and have lunch at the Café Royal."

Divining, from his brusqueness, that Henry was feeling rather queer also, Adelaide made no demur, though she would not have chosen the Café Royal herself. They went there in a cab, and Henry ordered champagne; even so they found a peculiar difficulty in talking to each other. There ought to have been a train to catch; perhaps no part of a honeymoon is more helpful than the preliminary journey, of which the incidents naturally supply material for light conversation. What were they to do after lunch? Adelaide knew quite well what she wanted to do: she wanted to get back to Britannia Mews and start turning out. But this was hardly a suitable occupation for one's wedding-day, and when Henry suggested that they should take a hansom and drive down to Richmond she gladly agreed. The brisk motion, the fresh air, the dash of the whole proceeding, raised their spirits; walking on the terrace above the river as the evening fell they captured for the first time a proper loving intimacy. Adelaide felt her hand pressed closer within Henry's arm; they began to walk more slowly, to pause and glance at each other; as speech came more freely they had less need of it. Below them swans still showed white on the darkening water, but night had begun to be imminent, and still they lingered; presently the paths were quite deserted save for themselves and one very old man, stooped like Time over a book he could not see to read.

"Adelaide," said Henry, "don't let's go back. We can't go back to that place. Not to-night."

"But . . . Henry! Where can we stay?"

"Let's go to the Star and Garter."

"With no luggage? Won't they think it very queer?"

"Damn it, I've our marriage lines in my pocket. You can borrow from the chambermaid. Don't let's spoil it, my darling."

Adelaide had no wish to. She would have wished to stay there for ever, in the enchantment of the river. The Star and Garter was the next best thing—and the chambermaid was very obliging. Almost too obliging, thought Adelaide; and as though by chance, when Henry emptied his pockets, she picked up her marriage certificate and dropped it on the dressing-table in a prominent place.

3

OWING to this accidental circumstance Mr. Culver, hastening up from Farnham, did not find his daughter in Britannia Mews. For there was a letter from Adelaide at Platt's End, posted the day before; the information it contained was enough to make both him and his wife forget all about his heart and send him back to London by the next train. Finding his errand fruitless, Mr. Culver spent the night at his Club and returned to Farnham in the morning; he could think of nothing else to do. And there was, after the lapse of that night, fundamentally nothing to be done; Adelaide was married. A telegram from her which arrived about lunch-time was signed ADELAIDE LAMBERT. SO VERY HAPPY, it said. PLEASE FORGIVE US. YOUR AFFECTIONATE DAUGHTER—and then that signature. Mrs. Culver looked at it for a long time, and at last said:—

"At any rate, William, no one here knows. They don't know the circumstances . . ."

For if Adelaide were starting on a new life, so was her mother. The move had come at a most opportune moment.

"Are you prepared to leave your daughter living with a scoundrel in squalor?" demanded Mr. Culver violently; for it was he who had gone hurrying up to London. "I must say you take the whole thing with remarkable calm. I do my best, I go up to town after them, while you stay calmly here—"

(70)

"That is not true," said Mrs. Culver. And it wasn't true: she had spent most of the night in tears—and alone, in a strange house, the furniture not even properly arranged, which somehow made everything much more painful. But she knew how to face facts. "Adelaide has married Mr. Lambert, I feel it just as much as you do, only I must set about mending matters in my own way. This telegram was handed in at Richmond; they are evidently spending their honeymoon there; I shall go to Richmond myself this afternoon."

"And where will you look for them in Richmond?"

"At the Star and Garter," said Mrs. Culver confidently. "It's the only place."

"And what do you propose to say when you find them?"

"I shall tell Adelaide that she always has a home here. Married daughters often come to stay without their husbands," said Mrs. Culver.

She went to Richmond, and she found them: Adelaide in the first flush of happiness, Henry Lambert lover-like and debonair. Mrs. Culver observed the pretty picture, but was not touched by it. She had been deeply hurt, and even more deeply offended, and the young people's light-heartedness annoyed her. Even Adelaide's eager apologies showed no real sense of shame.

"Henry's so good, Mamma," she said earnestly; "he's hated to deceive you even more than I have. But you know Papa would never have given his consent, so what else could we do?"

Mrs. Culver looked at her son-in-law's back as he tactfully strolled apart on the terrace, and felt no more confidence in his goodness than in his ability to support a wife.

"Where are you going to live, Adelaide? And what on?"

"To begin with, in Henry's old place in the Mews. And we shall live on his earnings."

"And on your hundred a year."

"Henry says I'm to keep that as a dress allowance, till he can give me more."

Mrs. Culver opened her bag and took out four five-pound notes.

"This is a present from your father and myself. I expect you'll need it."

"Thank you very much, Mamma. But I don't in the least mind being poor—until Henry makes his name."

"I hope he will make his name, as you call it. Though I believe many artists make a name without making an income. However, you are married." Mrs. Culver paused. "I must say, Adelaide, it surprises me that you don't seem to realize what grief you have caused your parents."

"I really am sorry, Mamma."

"You have always put yourself first—"

"Doesn't everyone?" asked Adelaide, a trifle restlessly.

"Certainly not. *I* have devoted my whole life to you and to Treff and to your father."

Adelaide looked at her mother thoughtfully.

"What did you really want to do?"

Instead of answering, however, Mrs. Culver rather abruptly rose. It had occurred to her that Adelaide would probably be in a better frame of mind for such a conversation after a month or two in Britannia Mews.

"I shall come and see you again in a month's time," she said. "I suppose you will still be in the Mews then?"

"If not, of course, I'll let you know. Would—would Papa like Henry and me to come to Platt's End?"

"No," said Mrs. Culver; and went quickly on to talk about the new house, so that Adelaide had not time to grasp all the implications of that refusal, so that they could part with a decent appearance of affection. Mrs. Culver said nothing about Adelaide's coming to Platt's End alone. She thought, "In a month's time . . ."

4

"YOUR MOTHER doesn't like me," remarked Henry, as they stood in the station after seeing Mrs. Culver on her train.

"What nonsense, Henry! Of course she 'does. It's been a great shock to her, that's all. And I must say," added Adelaide, "considering everything, she's been nicer than we had any right to expect."

"Do you realize that we ought to be taking a train ourselves? I've cut a drawing-lesson to-day, and I've two to-morrow."

Adelaide began to laugh.

"Do you realize which one you've cut? It was mine. . . . But we must go back, dearest, as you say."

"Of course, your mother saw us here," said Henry reflectively. "It's going to be rather different in the Mews."

"It's going to be better," said Adelaide.

PART TWO

CHAPTER 1

THE FIRST social duty of a bride is to establish relations with her neighbours. Adelaide was thoroughly aware of the procedure, which to begin with was largely passive: after the first fortnight one sat at home every afternoon, wearing a trousseau gown and one's best jewellery, and waited for calls. These spread over about a fortnight more, and then one called back; after which a gradual sorting-out process took place, till at the end of six months the young couple had found their feet in their proper set. In Kensington, in Bayswater, in any nice neighbourhood, this was what would have happened; only Britannia Mews was not a nice neighbourhood.

Adelaide was very little of a fool: she had gone into the Mews as she thought with her eyes open, prepared for the worst, she would have laughed as much as Henry at the idea of calling or being called on; but she had expected to be able to ignore her surroundings. They were to live in a little world of their own, in a bubble of love and hope, whose elastic, iridescent walls no squalor could penetrate. Within a week she discovered that, while she could see or hear, such isolation was impossible.

Within a week, she had seen sights she had never dreamed of—and they were dreamlike. At night, in the Mews: two figures, male and female, blotted in the shadow under a stair, then the woman breaking away, her bodice open on a bosom that gleamed suddenly white. Adelaide pressed her forehead against Henry's shoulder, but she heard a door open and a voice railing. She witnessed, for the first time in her life, an exchange of blows; this was by day, outside the public-house; and a woman suckling her child at an open window leaned out to shriek abuse. Against her will she came to know her neighbours by sight and name—and by their by-names, which were more commonly employed. There was the Punch and Judy man, called "Old Bert," or "the Old 'Un," his lean scarecrow figure bent into a hoop from years of pushing at a booth; a wretched flea-ridden Dog Toby shivered at his heels, or slunk to piss against a door and was kicked back to his master. There was the young woman Harriet O'Keefe, whose flaming head gave her the name of "the Blazer"; she sometimes lent a hand at the Cock, and sometimes went flower-selling, but more often her trade took her out late at night. She had a daughter, a thin alley-cat of a five-year-old, in whom the mother's fiery colouring was diluted to sandy fairness; this child Adelaide used to see long after nightfall, huddled at the foot of the iron steps that led to the Blazer's door; but Henry told her not to pay any attention, and presently, without quite understanding how the knowledge came, Adelaide like everyone else took the child's presence as a signal that the Blazer had a man with her.

The Blazer and the Old 'Un were loathed by Adelaide, but not feared; there was however one woman whom she had feared at sight. This was Mrs. Mounsey, who lived directly opposite. Her person was obscene: beneath layers of dirty clothing great pendulous breasts rolled as she walked, for she sagged with fat; her features were almost Mongolian, flat, smooth and expressionless save for the malice in her tiny eyes. There was something sow-like about her, and that indeed was her name in the Mews: "the Sow." She dealt in rags and old clothes; and the dwellers in the Mews sometimes gave her small sums of money, because they were afraid of her. "Every village has its witch," said Henry Lambert. "The Sow is ours." And Adelaide, as though indeed fearing the evil eye, would not descend her own steps while Mrs. Mounsey was at her window; the contact of even so much as a glance was too repugnant to her. Once, when they met squarely across the Mews, Adelaide turned back and went indoors again, and stood at the window and spied until she saw the Sow waddle away, trailing the filthy sack in which she stored her rags.

If she spied, Adelaide was also spied upon; of all she had to endure almost the worst was the sensation of being continually watched. Whenever she walked through the Mews, eyes followed her. Women's faces appeared in the windows, dim and pale behind the unwashed panes like fish rising against the glass of an aquarium; round the side-door of the Cock loiterers stared. Children hung over the iron railings, or ran before her, looking over their shoulders, the Old 'Un peered round his booth and ducked back again. No one addressed her, but Adelaide knew that as soon as she had passed under the archway the women would be out on their steps and the whispering would begin. She knew that she too had a name in the Mews: it was "Poker-back."

2

Not all at once, of course, did this complete picture present itself. Adelaide absorbed its details swiftly enough, but still gradually. Her first great disillusionment, which occurred on the very day after their installation, had to do with something quite different.

She had spent the morning throwing out a great quantity of rubbish (upon which the children in the Mews swooped like hawks) and in the afternoon felt she deserved a reward. There was moreover something she very much wanted to do.

"Henry, dear, aren't we going to the Academy?"

"The Academy?" repeated Henry—so vaguely that Adelaide laughed.

"My darling, it opened on Monday, and we both forgot! There's your picture in it! 'Moses and Pharaoh's Daughter.'"

For a moment he stared at her blankly; then grinned.

"My dear, you're a year too soon. To get a picture into the Academy it would have had to be submitted a month ago. What a little ignoramus you are!"

"But you talked about it—" began Adelaide; and paused. In matters of art she was indeed an ignoramus; perhaps Henry had in fact been talking about the Academy of next year. Concealing her disappointment, she said, "At any rate, can't *I* see it?"

"There's nothing to see. I haven't started."

"Oh," said Adelaide. "I thought you had . . ."

"I've nowhere to work," explained Henry. "You can see for yourself."

Of course that was the explanation. Adelaide looked round the living-room, now comparatively tidy, but certainly not large enough for the production of a picture containing several life-sized figures. (One of them to be a semi-nude.)

"You could use the coach-house below. You could use it as a studio. Henry, isn't that a very good idea?"

"It's a good idea, but it's six shillings a week extra."

"Then I'll pay," said Adelaide joyfully.

She did so; she saw the landlord herself, and nothing had ever given her greater pleasure than this first assistance rendered to her husband's genius. She cleaned and scrubbed the place out, at first with Henry's assistance, then single-handed, for he suddenly remembered a drawing-lesson; and though her back ached and her hands grew sore Adelaide rejected other help. "Get in one of the women," advised Henry, as he put on his coat. "I don't know who to ask," said Adelaide. (A week later she would simply have said nothing.) "Ask at the Cock," called Henry, running down the stairs; but Adelaide had never entered a public-house in her life, and could not bring herself to do so. Indeed, she was at this time so filled with love and energy that the work seemed light.

They were happy days spent scrubbing, and in their results almost miraculous. Adelaide did not stop at mere cleanliness, she painted all the furniture with white enamel, and stained the floors mahogany-colour, and hung blue casement-cloth curtains, and set her Indian shell on the mantelpiece, and a fern on the window-sill. This was in the front or living-room; of the two rooms behind one was of course the bed-chamber, and the other Adelaide converted into a bath-room. Its furniture was primitive: a hip-bath, a couple of buckets to fill it, and a dipper to bail it out. There was also a nightstool. The odious task of emptying slops called for all Adelaide's heroism; heroically she performed it—after dark. She was indeed heroic altogether in her resolute application of Kensington standards to Britannia Mews; and fortunate in a constitution no less sound than her principles.

The effect on the inhabitants of the Mews was nil. No fresh paint appeared in emulation. On the other hand, the stone through the Lamberts' window was probably an accident. Fortunately Adelaide did not expect to regenerate the Mews by her example. Her cynicism was developing rapidly.

One great advantage was the acquisition of the coach-house. It took all Henry's artistic paraphernalia and left Adelaide a clear field—except, that is, for the big wicker basket. She tried to carry it down herself one morning when Henry was out, but on the steep iron steps it was too much for her; she couldn't empty it first, because it was stapled and locked, and her husband returned to find her still regarding it with an air of annoyance.

"Henry, this must go in the coach-house," she said at once.

To her surprise, he objected that it would not be safe.

"What is in it that's so valuable, Henry?"

"Relics," said he curtly. "Leave it alone, dear."

"You make me feel like Bluebeard's wife!" said Adelaide, laughing; and for the moment let the matter drop. She felt she was being immensely understanding and tactful, enjoyed the sensation, and at the same time planned to make him move it next day, after showing her what was inside. But next day seemed to offer no opportunity, nor the day after, and the basket stayed where it was, continually getting in Adelaide's way. It took up so much room: its corners, even when she pushed it under the table, stuck out, and once she caught and tore her dress on a broken withy. However, it would have taken up just as much room in the coach-house, where Henry needed space. The coach-house was Adelaide's pride, and when Henry had set up his easel there she went to Liberty's and bought a large Turkish lamp to hang from the beam. "What the deuce is that for?" demanded Henry. "To make it look like a studio," explained Adelaide simply. She would have bought some draperies as well, but though she still had quite a large part left of her last year's allowance, the draperies at Liberty's were so very expensive. For food she had already learned to shop in Paddington, where everything struck her as remarkably cheap.

The studio being completed, the next step was obviously for Henry to paint a picture in it—his Academy picture, in fact. Adelaide knew that pictures in the Academy often sold for hundreds of pounds; if Henry's fetched only two or three, that would enable them to move. When she broached this plan to Henry, however, he looked grave.

"Big pictures take time, my dear girl. Also daylight."

Adelaide waited. It seemed to her that he had plenty of time, and the month was still May.

"My damned drawing-lessons," explained Henry.

"Only four afternoons a week, darling!"

He explained further. A big picture, a masterpiece (for why mince words?), absorbed all a man's energies. He had to live with it, brood over it, think of nothing else. How could he do this when his thoughts were continually interrupted and his time broken in upon by lessons to silly girls? "You don't know what a nuisance they are," said Henry Lambert sincerely. "They put me out for the whole day."

"Very well," said Adelaide. "Give them up."

She spoke the more readily because the lessons were an object of mild jealousy to her; however slightingly her husband talked of Miss Drew and Miss Pomfret and Miss Ocock, Adelaide still disliked thinking of the hours he spent at their sides. But she was also certain that the step would be justified by its results. She was pleased to see Henry look at her with flattering surprise.

"My dearest girl, what should we live on?"

"My hundred a year," replied Adelaide promptly. "We can easily live on that—here. How long would the picture take?"

"Perhaps six months. Adelaide, do you really mean that?"

"Why not? I haven't married a great artist to have him waste his time on schoolgirls. Why do you look at me so?"

"I'm just realizing what a bold woman you are."

Her boldness won. Henry gave up all his pupils except Miss Ocock; he said he did not wish to have to ask his wife for tobacco-

(82)

money—though as Adelaide pointed out, her money was now his. She still kept control of it, however, going each month to the bank to cash a cheque for eight pounds, and thus sparing Henry all financial worries. The sum proved ample, moreover, for there was at least this to be said for life in Britannia Mews: it was dirt cheap. A family of four might spend on food and firing perhaps fourteen shillings a week; a penny paper of fish made a supper, milk was fourpence a quart, potatoes a halfpenny a pound, pickles and jam sold by the ha'porth; and yet these piecemeal dealings were in themselves an extravagance. Adelaide, buying her commodities by the pound, kept house for less than the women who ran out twice and thrice a day for a three-farthing pinch of tea; and found forty shillings a week to be wealth, in Britannia Mews.

Her boldness won. It never occurred to her that she might be not only bold, but rash, in taking from a man of Henry's temperament his only regular employment; as always at this time, Adelaide believed all her actions to be dictated by pure reason. They spent a wonderful morning buying an enormous canvas and a great new collection of paints: Adelaide would have bought new brushes and a new palette as well, but Henry preferred his old ones. In any case, he said, there were preliminary studies to be made, a month's hard work before he even prepared his canvas; and he completed the happiest day of Adelaide's life by making a sketch of her smiling profile, and scribbling below, "Head of Pharaoh's Daughter."

CHAPTER II

THIS WAS the period of their honeymoon; and as their married life arranged itself it began to seem as though Adelaide's programme of regular meals and refined companionship was indeed what Henry Lambert required. Sober, industrious, he worked at the studies of his masterpiece, destroying almost as many as he made, but still working, while Adelaide cleaned her house above, ran down to pose for him, and ran up again to cook the dinner. It was the *Vie de Bohème* of romance, marred only by two things: the squalid background of the Mews, and the fact that a *Vie de Bohème* did not really suit Adelaide's temperament.

She had married her husband for love, but her love was not physically passionate: the amorous relation, which may dominate a woman's life and put her wholly in the power of husband or lover, had almost no influence upon Adelaide. She remained in her own possession—desiring above all things stability, social standing, a settled future; she was businesslike and economical; she had in fact gambled on Henry Lambert's future as a man of her own class might gamble on the Stock Exchange. Debt was particularly abhorrent to her. All these traits made up a character as alien from Bohemianism as it was possible to be; and so long as the opposite traits continued to appear in her husband, she could not be perfectly content.

Henry was always ready, for example, to take her to a theatre or music-hall after the day's work; but though Adelaide enjoyed these outings, she felt they could not afford them. Where did the money come from? She suspected that Henry was simply spending Mrs. Culver's twenty pounds, which she had at once handed over to him. He was spending it on both of them; but to go to a music-hall four times in one week was more than Adelaide desired. Henry, on the other hand, appeared to need constant entertainment, a quiet evening at home simply made him restless: he would neither read nor be read to, and when Adelaide suggested that he should read aloud to her, while she did some sewing, inexplicably remarked that he hadn't come to that yet. He was restless even in his love-making—often being more demonstrative in public than Adelaide liked (he would put his arm round her in the theatre, or even kiss her) and then relapsing into casualness at home. It never struck Adelaide that they were perhaps too much together, for she had been brought up in the belief that a husband and wife should be self-sufficient; she was glad Henry didn't go to work because it meant she could keep a constant eye on him. Constantly, steadily, remorselessly, she applied her wifely pressure, striving to mould him to her own standards; she knew instinctively that one of them had to change ways, and she, Adelaide, obviously could not, since hers were the right ones.

On one point at least Adelaide soon decided that she had humoured Henry long enough: the big wicker basket was a continual nuisance, and she still did not know what was inside it. One day immediately after breakfast, therefore, before Henry went down to the studio, she dragged it out and with a mixture of playfulness and severity announced that if he didn't open it then and there, she would break in with a poker.

To her surprise, he turned and grasped her wrist.

"If you do any damage, Adelaide—"

"Damage to what?" she demanded impatiently. "Is it full of Crown Jewels? I warn you, Henry, I'm going to open it, because otherwise I can't move it, and it's in my way."

"You mean you're simply inquisitive."

"I'm not. Though I admit I should like to know what's inside. And if it's anything you value, Henry, I should have thought you'd like to show me. . . ."

For a moment he looked at her with a curious expression; then taking a key from his pocket, knelt and unfastened the staples. Adelaide, now strung to a high pitch of expectation, waited eagerly while the lid was thrown back; below lay a packing-layer of faded cotton, and under that a row of narrow bundles, each rolled in the same faded stuff. Henry picked a couple out, shook off the wrappings, and revealed a pair of large—dolls. One was dressed like a Harlequin, one like a Sorcerer: from their hands and feet, from their heads, depended long threads; they were so jointed that they fell this way and that in Henry's hands.

"*Dolls!*" cried Adelaide disgustedly. "My dear boy, is *that* all you've been making such a fuss about?"

"They are not dolls, they're puppets," corrected Henry Lambert. He lifted out a long, slender court lady, elaborately dressed in the style of Louis XIV: her carved face was a mask of the most sophisticated and exquisite vice. He let her flexible waist droop back over his hand: she appeared to abandon herself, still coldly, to a lover. "They are also works of art," said Mr. Lambert, "created by your husband. Like 'em?"

"Not particularly," said Adelaide.

"They are, perhaps, caviare to the general. Here's her Abbé."

The Abbé, also long and slim, in black, seemed to throw a knowing glance as Henry twitched his strings. Adelaide was forced to admit that they were wonderfully lifelike: however carelessly laid down they at once fell into the most natural positions; they ogled each other, or sulked apart. But for some reason she did not like them. She did not like even La Camargo, in a froth of white ballet-skirts, nor the fresh-faced ingénue in pink chintz. They formed a little world, an elegant and artificial little world, which she instinctively repudiated. Moreover, they represented such a shocking waste of time.

"They must have taken months," she said rebukingly.

"Two years, if you want to know. The best years of my life."

"Oh, nonsense," cried Adelaide, really annoyed. "A man doesn't spend the best years of his life making wooden dolls!"

"His best years are when he's doing his best work. These, my dear Adelaide, are my claim to fame. They have been much praised."

"In Paris, I suppose, where people admire such foolishness." (Where people call on a divorced woman, thought Adelaide, on a sudden memory.) "What are they good for?"

"Well, when I die, they ought to go to a museum," said Henry.

Adelaide looked at him to see whether he were serious, decided that he couldn't be, and then, another thought striking her, picked up the Camargo. The tulle dress, garlanded with tiny roses, was too exquisitely sewn to be the work of any male hands.

"Henry, who dressed them for you?"

"The daughter of my master. *La fille de mon maître—dans le jardin de sa tante.*"

Adelaide threw the puppet down—Camargo doubling at the waist in a magnificent curtsey—and thrust the Abbé aside with her foot.

She thought she was being mocked; yet, as he sometimes did, Henry had told her the exact truth. . . .

2

In a garden outside Paris, a French garden planted with a quincunx of lime-trees, how many hours had not he sat watching while Angélique stitched! The daughter of an old man who made puppets, as his father before him, and his grandfather before that: half-craftsman, half-artist, of whom young Henry Lambert, for the sake of the daughter's eyes, took lessons in puppet-making. But if he came for the sake of Angélique, he remained for the sake of M. Théodore's surpassing skill; he made her his mistress almost absent-mindedly, because she seemed to wish it. What was important was that he became M. Théodore's apprentice, and in the art and craft of puppetry found the release of his talent. "The pupil surpasses his teacher," said old M. Théodore. All morning the two men worked together—and Angélique never asked why, nor what their elaborate productions were good for; she adored her lover for making her father so happy. Was not that a good in itself? But they did not work aimlessly, they had an end in view, which was to complete a set of all Molière's characters; and they achieved it. "And now?" said M. Théodore. "Now we give an exhibition," said Henry Lambert, "so that you may win the fame you deserve"; and they packed all the puppets into a *fiacre* (Henry riding on the box) and drove into Paris to the studio of a fashionable artist whom neither of them knew. But when he saw what they brought, when he looked into the old man's eyes, he put his studio at their disposal, for that was how things happened, in Paris, in those days. Moreover, the *guignol* has a long and honourable French history. *Tout Paris* came to admire—*tout Paris,* in those days, as small as a village—and Mme. la Comtesse de Noailles, addressing M. Théodore as *"mon ami,"* told him he had carried into their materialistic age the traditions of a finer epoch. She would have bought La Camargo; but both Henry and M. Théodore, flown with glory, announced that none of the puppets was for sale. They were to be a gift to the

French nation. This admirable sentiment set the crown on their success; and they had their hour.

Henry afterwards wondered whether the excitement had not been too much for the old man; he died very soon after. "At least he died happy," said Angélique, walking with Henry between the trees of the quincunx. "But what will you do without him?"

Henry looked at her as fondly as he could, but now that her father was dead, now that the idyll between workshop and garden was over, he saw her too clearly for what she was: a little, not very young *bourgeoise*, with rather fine eyes. Angélique met his glance and read it.

"You will go back to England, *mon cher . . .*"

"And you?"

"I shall remain with my aunt. We have enough."

"Your father's work is of value."

"I know. But I do not think we shall sell. And I think the nation may wait until I too am not here to take pleasure in them?"

"Angélique," said Henry—for his heart was still capable of a good movement—"if you will be my wife—"

"No, no, no," said she quickly. "I am seven years the older. You have made us both happy, my dear; but it is time for you to go. And the figures that you have made you must of course take with you."

It was for this reason that the set of Molière characters, in the basket in Britannia Mews, was not complete. And sometimes Henry Lambert felt that his heart was not quite complete either. Calm, almost casual, as his feeling for Angélique had been, it had also been sweet and untroubled. When he looked back to that French garden, he sometimes thought he had been a fool ever to leave it.

3

ADELAIDE rose. Among the puppets lounging round her feet—lounging in such easy, such lifelike attitudes—she looked for a moment out of proportion, a female Gulliver. The Abbé, leaning on his elbow, stared impertinently at her: Camargo and the Marquise put their heads together. Adelaide thrust them aside with her foot in an instinctive gesture of dislike.

"Don't ill-treat the *piccoli*," said Henry Lambert.

"The what?"

"The little people."

"Nonsense!" said Adelaide again. She turned and went into the bedroom and began to tidy it. Though she had had her way, she did not feel pleased: the basket's contents were so foolish and disappointing, and Henry had behaved so foolishly about them. The best work of his life, indeed! The best years of his life! It was enough to make any wife angry. "I suppose I must take it as a joke," thought Adelaide, "for it's simply childish!"

When she came back Henry had disappeared. But the room was not empty. It was full of little people. In her absence he had taken them all out, more than a dozen of them, and set them about the room, on the chairs, on the table, on the mantelshelf, so that she was ringed by their curious, staring eyes. In a fury Adelaide seized them one after the other and bundled them back into the basket, and banged down the lid.

The hamper remained where it was, and neither Adelaide nor Henry spoke of it again. Adelaide unwillingly recognized that she would have done better to leave it alone. The thought of the unknown seamstress disturbed her, and this had the effect of making her do violence to her own character by falling in more readily with Henry's plans, and relaxing her training of him. They went out almost every night, and got up later in the morning; they took hansoms, and were festive. Against every instinct Adelaide forced herself to draw out ten pounds and give them to Henry to spend. She told herself that his extravagance would not matter, once they were rich—that indeed it was the foreshadowing of riches that made him extravagant. His conduct was simply a little in advance of his circumstances.

"Happy?" asked Henry one night, as they jingled home in a hansom.

Adelaide pressed her head against his shoulder. She was almost in his arms; the swiftly moving cab, dark and smelling of leather, enclosed them in a romantic intimacy. But Adelaide could not help thinking how absurd it was to take a hansom to Britannia Mews, when they could have walked in twenty minutes.

"Perfectly happy, dear. . . ."

"So am I," said Henry contentedly.

So they were both happy. But a day or two later they were at odds again, and the reason for this was Adelaide's discovery that she was not her husband's only model.

4

COMING BACK from her morning's shopping, Adelaide heard voices through the coach-house door: as she looked in they fell silent. Henry was standing before his easel, and over the bundle representing Moses in his basket stooped the red-haired slattern from Number 8.

"Come in," said Henry at once. "This is your lady-in-waiting, who attends on Pharaoh's daughter. My wife, Miss . . ."

He paused, evidently trying to remember the Blazer's real name; in a husky, drawling voice she supplied it.

"Harriet O'Keefe."

The two women looked at each other. Adelaide took in the buxom figure, the satiny skin, the flood of brazen hair. She said coldly, in the tone her mother used to a kitchen-maid, "How good of you, Harriet. I hope you won't get tired, standing so still."

The Blazer straightened her shoulders. There was something showy in the movement, a thrust forward of the bosom, that answered Adelaide's tone. The latter turned away and mounted the steep iron steps and went indoors. It was an hour before Henry followed her; he came in with the virtuous air of a man who has put in a hard morning's work.

"How much do you pay that woman?" asked Adelaide immediately.

"I don't pay her. Modelling flatters her vanity, she does it for love."

(90)

"I think she should be paid," said Adelaide.

"Have we so much money to give away?"

"Otherwise we are accepting a favour from her."

Henry grinned.

"Harriet's favours aren't expensive. I'll stand her a drink at the Cock."

"I would rather pay her myself. I will pay her, at the usual rate."

"Then you owe her three and sixpence."

Adelaide took her purse and went down into the Mews again. The Blazer was strolling towards the public-house; as she reached its door she turned; she was looking back at the Lamberts' windows, and when she saw Adelaide she paused. So did Adelaide. For the moment, the incident was suddenly familiar; she suddenly remembered a morning, over ten years ago, when she had run out into the Mews while Treff and Miss Bryant waited for her, and she had given a little girl a penny. Then, as now, she was fumbling in her purse; then, as now, she felt a wave of hostility that seemed to emanate not only from another human being, but from the whole Mews. Was the woman Harriet that same child? It was quite possible; it was even likely. Did she too remember? Adelaide could not tell; the hostile gaze revealed no more than hostility. Adelaide took out a shilling and a half-crown.

"Harriet, here is your money."

(*"Little girl, here's a penny for you."*)

This time Harriet answered.

"I've done nothing for you."

"You have been modelling for my husband," explained Adelaide coldly.

"Then let your husband pay me."

This time it was Adelaide who traversed the distance between them. She walked swiftly up to the other woman and thrust the coins into her hand. But she knew better now than to expect thanks.

"Take it," she said curtly, and turned her back.

This time no pebble flew after. With a certain bitter satisfaction

Adelaide reflected that her married life had at least taught her something: it had taught her how to deal with a slut.

5

Henry Lambert had not been drinking for nearly a month. The novelty of being married, the restraint imposed by Adelaide's constant presence, had restrained him; for nearly a month her confidence was justified. Then on the Saturday night he disappeared after supper and did not return until the Cock had closed its doors.

For the first few seconds Adelaide did not realize what was the matter. She had been sitting up, in a state of great anxiety, and when he stumbled in ran to meet him fully expecting to hear of some accident. When he fended her off she looked for blood on his coat, when he swayed on his feet she forcibly thrust him into a chair. At that she smelt his breath and recoiled.

"Henry, you've been drinking!"

"Sa'urday night," murmured Henry apologetically.

Adelaide stared at him in horror. He looked like another man. All the lines of his face were slackened, his eyes held an expression she did not recognize. Another man had got into Henry's skin, a man who looked back at her dispassionately, curiously, as though he wondered what she were doing there. He began to laugh.

"Li'l' wife, li'l' home," he explained. "You don' see the joke. They do in the old Cock . . ."

"You've been talking about me in the Cock!" cried Adelaide, outraged.

"Jus' tol' them you're bes' wife in the world. Told 'em you're going to keep me straight. Less go to bed, Addie."

Only anger kept her from tears; and it was to be important to their future relations that anger was her first reaction. Had she wept then, she would have gone on weeping. Anger pulled her together; she saw that it was not of the least use to reproach or plead with him, all that would have to wait till morning. In the meantime he simply had to be secured. She walked to the outer door, locked it, and put the key in her pocket.

"Fas'n up for night," said Henry approvingly. "I'll wind clock. All householders wind clocks. . . ."

He looked round for one, but it was in their bedroom. As Adelaide saw him remember this she slipped ahead and shut the door in his face. This door had no lock, but she pulled up a chair and jammed its back under the knob. Henry beat on the panel.

"Wass matter, Addie? Le' me in!"

"No," said Adelaide. "You can sleep there."

"Wife's got no right to keep out her husband! Wass a man come home for? Le' me in, I say!"

He beat again. The chair-back quivered, but his condition was lethargic rather than violent. Adelaide assured herself that the door would hold and began to undress. She heard Henry move away, try the outer door, and stumble back towards the sink: water was splashed noisily, and the pail let fall; but if by this means he hoped to bring her out again, he failed. At last all sounds subsided except for a heavy snoring; somehow, on the floor, or in a chair, Henry Lambert slept.

6

His CONDITION next morning was all that could be desired. He looked himself again, rather shabby indeed, but like the Henry Adelaide knew; and was so ashamed of himself that she let him off more lightly than she had intended. All she asked was a promise that it should never happen again, and this Henry eagerly gave. He helped her tidy the flat, and afterwards accompanied her to morning service. This was the first time they had ever been to church together, and Adelaide did manage to feel a certain married-woman importance: she stepped into the porch before her husband instead of behind her mother. They sat of course at the back: not for them the prominent pew occupied, at St. Mark's, by Culvers or Hambros. Looking up the aisle Adelaide saw the front pews in this church too filling with people who were Culvers or Hambros in all but name—women as richly dressed, men as high-collared, carrying top-hats: her own humble place was a forcible illustration of her drop in the social scale. For Adelaide, at bottom, had no illusions about all being equal in the house of God: the best people naturally sat in front. The thought made her hold her head higher than before. If not now, then quite soon, thought Adelaide, we shall take one of those pews ourselves . . . for I haven't married a nobody, I have married a man of genius. She glanced sideways at Henry's face, almost sheepish with good intentions, and thought that she could handle him. She had handled him last night. And then another and a more sardonic thought struck her: who now, looking at herself and Henry, would imagine that only a few hours before she had been forced to keep him out with a chair-back at the bed-room door?

Automatically sitting, standing or kneeling as the service required, Adelaide meditated on the deceitfulness, and importance, of appearances. At all costs they must be kept up. This could hardly be done, in a conventional sense, in Britannia Mews, but she believed that the appearance, the *persona* of a great artist, could well include a short period of indigence. It was picturesque. It was, in fact, conventional. . . . One year, thought Adelaide. Until after the next Academy. Then we will move quickly as people begin to take us up, and the Mews will be a picturesque, entertaining story. . . .

All at once she saw herself at a dinner-table: the other guests were all vague, a mere blur of ribbons and tiaras, but Henry (on the right of his hostess) was in white tie and tails, with some sort of Order round his neck, and she herself (on the right of her host) wore dark blue velvet and diamond stars. (*"What an amazing career your husband's has been, Lady Lambert! What unbroken success!" "Ah, but we had our struggles, Duke; we began our married life in an old coach-house." His Grace looked at her admiringly. "Astonishing!" he murmured. "No doubt that is why all our young artists to-day make their studios out of stables. You set the fashion . . ."*)

Adelaide sighed with pleasure. From a religious point of view the

(94)

service did not do much for her; but she came out from it considerably strengthened, and in a mood which considerably affected her meeting, next day, with Mrs. Culver.

CHAPTER III

NOW MRS. CULVER, visualizing her daughter's new home, saw Britannia Mews as she had seen it about ten years before; and indeed she had not seen it since. Her clearest recollection was of the Benson interior, humble enough to be sure, but cheerful and spotless; she remembered that it was at the right end, and quite respectable. Mrs. Culver thought it would do Adelaide no harm to spend a month in such surroundings, under the protection of her husband; she also thought that at the end of such a month Adelaide would be only too ready to come away. "We must be cruel to be kind, Will," said Mrs. Culver. "You speak as though we had any option," retorted Mr. Culver grimly. "Adelaide's married to the man, isn't she?"

Mrs. Culver did not argue with him. Her designs were so vague, so instinctive, that she could hardly have put them into words. She had seen her daughter and Henry Lambert together, and the sight had convinced her of two things: that nothing would induce Adelaide to leave him at that moment, and that very soon she would be glad to. Mrs. Culver's judgment of her son-in-law was harsh, immediate and instinctive: the very good reasons for mistrusting him, such as his lack of income and prospects (also certain comments let fall by the twins, and a visit from Mrs. Ocock), weighed less than her simple conviction that he was a bad sort of man. She felt his very charm to be against him; a man should have no need to be charming. (Treff indeed was charming too, but then Treff was her son.) Adelaide had married a wastrel; other women had done the same thing. Their case was common enough to have a common solution: they learned their lesson and came home to their families, and settled down to a useful if frustrated life performing the duties that fell to the lot of unmarried daughters or aunts. Divorces were exceptional, almost unheard-of. The husbands remained in the background, and were often said to be abroad. If there were children, of course, the case was altered; but Mrs. Culver hoped that Adelaide would be back before these had to be thought about.

She paid her visit to Britannia Mews, therefore, in a fairly collected state of mind. Whether Adelaide would be ready to admit her mistake so soon was a matter for doubt; Mrs. Culver recognized her daughter's stubbornness. But the way of retreat could be indicated, the road back to Platt's End shown to be open and not too humiliating: Mrs. Culver meant to lay great stress on her own loneliness. To invite Adelaide for a visit was the most natural thing in the world; and once the first break was made, Mrs. Culver had no fears for the issue.

"I must be discreet," she told herself, "I must be discreet, and very nice to Mr. Lambert. There shall be no hurry, and no reproaches. . . ."

But when she got out of her cab at the entrance to the Mews, and looked under the archway, and saw the changes brought about by the years, all these resolutions left her. For a moment she could hardly believe her eyes. It was a slum. Where were now the bright windows and clean curtains of her recollection? The clean carriages, the respectable coachmen hissing over their well-fed horses? For it was the horses, as Mrs. Culver unconsciously recognized, that had given Britannia Mews its countrified comfortable air, as of the stables of a big house. Now the town had swamped all, thrown up an engulfing wave of squalor; the few loungers round the Cock were its human jetsam.

As Mrs. Culver stood aghast, Adelaide came out of her door. Her first movement was one of amazement rather than pleasure, for her mother's visit was unheralded. Then (as always when she had been taken by surprise) Adelaide straightened her back; and came slowly down the iron stair.

"Well, Mamma!" she said cheerfully. "So you've paid us a visit! It's lucky I wasn't out."

They kissed. To Adelaide's still greater astonishment she saw that her mother's eyes were filled with tears, and this display of emotion, so unusual among the Culvers, thoroughly alarmed her.

"Is Papa ill?" she asked sharply. "Is that why you've come?"

Mrs. Culver shook her head. She said, "My dear, I've come to fetch you home."

As soon as the words were out of her mouth she regretted them: but they had spoken themselves. At once Adelaide stiffened again.

"Indeed you have not, Mamma; and if that is how you have come to talk—"

"No, no," said Mrs. Culver hastily. "It was a foolish thing to say. I've just come to see how you're getting on. . . ."

"Splendidly," said Adelaide.

"Won't you ask me into your home?"

Adelaide turned and led the way back up the steps. She was not ashamed of her housewifery, she knew the room to be immaculate. What she did not realize was the extent to which she herself, in becoming used to it, had lowered her standard of domestic convenience. Mrs. Culver sat down in the basket chair (now repaired) and looked round without a word.

"I do it all myself," said Adelaide.

"Is that necessary?"

Adelaide laughed.

"No, of course not. In fact, Henry objected very strongly, he wanted me to have a woman. But it's so small and convenient, it just takes up enough of my time."

"Oh," said Mrs. Culver. The monosyllable fell rather bleakly. She made haste to add, "How is Henry?"

"Very well. He's out at the moment. He's gone to see an art-dealer who is interested in his work." (Adelaide had not in fact the least idea where Henry had gone; she was surprised herself at the fluency with which these statements flowed out.) "He's working rather too hard, of course, but that is because he has several commissions."

"I'm very glad to hear it," said Mrs. Culver.

Her eye, travelling round the room, came to rest on the mantelpiece, on the Indian shell. If she recognized it, she made no comment. The silence grew. All freedom of speech had been made impossible by those first unforgivable words: mother and daughter, they sat like strangers.

"Would you like a cup of tea?" asked Adelaide politely.

"No, thank you. I hoped you might come and have lunch with me, at Fuller's."

"I'm afraid I have my shopping to do. And of course Henry will be back."

"Your father sends his love."

"Please give him mine, Mamma."

"He hopes—" by putting the words into her husband's mouth Mrs. Culver at last found a line of approach—"he hopes you will soon come and pay us a visit. The garden is looking very pretty."

"Of course we should enjoy it immensely," said Adelaide. "But just now, while Henry is so busy . . . Do you like Platt's End?"

"Oh, very much," said Mrs. Culver, quite jumping at the topic; which indeed was so suitable and fruitful that each wondered why she had not thought of it sooner. About her new house and new neighbours Mrs. Culver could talk without constraint and with real enthusiasm. (It was an odd situation: she talked, in fact, as Adelaide should have been talking.) A quarter of an hour passed quite pleasantly as she described the distribution of the furniture, the aspect of the garden, the variety of callers, and the friendliness of the Vicar. Adelaide was really interested: these things were after all a great part of her life, they made up a world from which she had only temporarily absented herself. Sir Henry and Lady Lambert might well live in the country—in a rather grander house of course than Platt's End—and come up to town only for important functions. But till then no visits would be paid. Adelaide knew well enough what her mother's invitation meant, she knew it did not include Henry, and that she was being offered the conventional asylum of the daughter whose marriage fails. She rejected it. But the talk about Platt's End produced a certain ease and amiability, and Adelaide ended it with an invitation of her own.

"Mamma, I must go out," she said, "I really must. But come again soon, and let me know, so that I can have lunch for you."

"No, you must lunch with me," said Mrs. Culver.

It was her second mistake. Adelaide looked round the room and smiled bitterly.

"Then wait until we have moved into our own house, Mamma. That will be more suitable. Have you kept your cab?"

"I can pick one up in the Bayswater Road."

Adelaide laughed.

"Take a hansom, Mamma; Henry and I always take hansoms. Good-bye, Mamma, my love to Papa and Treff!"

Had it been possible for Mrs. Culver to be wafted straight from the room on to the Bayswater Road, she would have gone home a happier woman, at least partly deluded; but it was not possible. She had to pass through Britannia Mews, and the sights and sounds —to say nothing of the smells—encountered on that brief passage undid all Adelaide's work. Adelaide could not be happy there, no one could be happy there; she could not be allowed to remain. I'll send Alice, thought Mrs. Culver suddenly; she was always Adelaide's friend. . . . Or if Alice could not be sent to the Mews, she should ask Adelaide to tea, in a shop, by themselves, the sort of thing girls always enjoyed. For a moment Mrs. Culver wondered whether she should go at once to Kensington; then she remembered that Alice was again in Somerset; and moreover, though it was early in the day, she felt very tired; and in the end she went home.

2

ADELAIDE reported this visit only briefly to her husband, and he showed little interest in it. "I suppose she didn't leave another twenty quid?" he asked. He spoke jokingly, of course, but the remark jarred, and Adelaide did not even reply.

Their conversation was increasingly liable to these sudden breaks; for Henry's chastened mood did not endure. He kept his promise not to get drunk, but Adelaide sometimes suspected that he was not quite sober; in her inexperience she couldn't tell whether he were or not, and feared to attack on what might be mistaken grounds. Men could be irritable, or morose, without being intoxicated; possibly Henry was irritable and morose for the very reason that he was reforming. So Adelaide ignored her husband's ill-humour; but her own temper became strained, she found she had a sharp tongue which needed constant control if peace were to be kept; and Henry gave her no assistance. He ceased to praise her looks, or her housewifery, and went down each morning to the studio with the dogged air of a man under compulsion. Once or twice he went out to a music hall by himself, and once or twice, seized by a malicious humour, spent the evening at home reading aloud to Adelaide in French, so rapidly that she could not follow. "Enjoy our domestic evening?" enquired Henry, at the end; "Very much," replied Adelaide calmly.

They were heading for an open quarrel, which all Adelaide's efforts could no more than postpone, and it occurred about a fortnight after Mrs. Culver's visit. The occasion was slight enough: Adelaide went in to the studio and found Henry not at his easel, but adding the last touches, in paint, to a puppet's head. It was not made of composition, like those of the puppets in the basket: it was carved out of wood, and very skilfully: one saw the bones of a long narrow skull, lantern jaws, lips drawn back over a gap-toothed mouth; the complexion was yellowish. Mr. Lambert was regarding it with complacency.

"What a hateful thing!" said Adelaide at once.

"It's meant to be. It's a Hangman," said Henry Lambert. "And don't despise it, my love, for it's a commission."

She stared incredulously.

"Do you expect me to believe that?"

"As you like. The fact remains that it's a commission from the Old 'Un, who is paying me a shilling for it. His old Hangman was chewed up by Dog Toby."

Adelaide sat down on the stool and laughed.

"A commission from a Punch and Judy man!" she exclaimed bitterly. "We're going up in the world!"

"With a little persuasion he might even offer me regular employ. He needs an assistant to push the barrow. On a profit-sharing basis, of course: I should insist on at least forty per cent."

"You're impossible," said Adelaide.

She spoke without thinking; and in the same instant realized that what she said was true. It meant the collapse of all her hopes, the failure of her life; but it was true. He was impossible. It was impossible that she should ever make anything of him. What had begun as a trifling bicker became all at once a crisis of the most fundamental importance. Adelaide looked at her husband—aware that she was seeing him at his best, sober, a job of work almost completed—and admitted defeat. She said:—

"I wish to God I'd never married you."

Henry picked up a brush and slightly thickened the Hangman's eyebrows. He seemed quite unmoved.

"You would do it," he pointed out. "I tried hard enough to stop you."

"I must have been mad."

"That's what I thought. I was never so astonished in my life."

It took Adelaide a few seconds to realize the implications of this remark. The buffet to her pride and love, so rude, so unexpected, left her momentarily shaken. Her voice trembled slightly as she said:—

"Henry, do you mean—didn't you expect me to marry you?"

"Of course not. Good God, if every girl I kissed expected to marry me—"

"Every girl!" A wave of colour rose over Adelaide's throat. "Does that mean you made love to all your pupils?"

"Unless they were positively repulsive."

(101)

"Did you—did you make love to Miss Ocock?"

He grinned.

"I tried to. *She* saw through me soon enough. It was only you, my little innocent, who took me seriously."

Adelaide began to cry. It was the first time she had cried since her marriage, and the tears surprised even herself, for she had thought she was beyond them; now they flowed uncontrollably, washing away all her pride. Henry at once walked towards the door, but she put out her hand and caught him. She began to plead.

"Henry, how can you talk so heartlessly to me? Henry, don't go! How can you go and leave me with—with such thoughts? I won't mind about the other women, they're nothing, if you'll only tell me it was me you really loved!"

Henry groaned impatiently.

"My God, of course it's you I really love! Haven't I married you?"

"But that first afternoon," persisted Adelaide, "when Alice had a cold and you came although you'd been put off—that was because you were in love with me? I want the truth, Henry!"

"All right, you shall have it. You had it then, it was what you told your mother: I came because I didn't see why I should lose my fee."

Staring at him in the blankest dismay, Adelaide was silent. In an irritated voice Mr. Lambert added abruptly:—

"I told too much truth that afternoon. I told the truth about your horrible drawings. My gorge suddenly rose, and what little honesty I had came out in me. Then I had to smoothe you down somehow, I couldn't afford to lose two pupils, and this is what came of it. There you are, my girl: if you find truth bitter, don't ask for it."

He was standing close to her, speaking into her face: Adelaide suddenly realized—realized actually with hope and relief—that he was not quite sober after all.

"Why, you've been drinking . . . ," she said thankfully.

"*In vino veritas,*" said Henry Lambert.

CHAPTER IV

THE RESULTS of this crisis were deep rather than apparent. That same evening Henry was remorseful again, told Adelaide he could not remember a word he had said, and asked her forgiveness. She forgave him—what else could she do?—and they drifted back into their old ways. But truth, that dangerous commodity, has a way of sticking: Adelaide never again cherished any illusion as to the basis of her marriage. Truth had not blinded her; on the contrary, as her spirit grew accustomed to this new and penetrating light she saw very plainly that it was she, and not Henry, who was responsible for their present pass. What she had taken for diffidence, or chivalry, had been the wriggling of a hooked fish; she even saw that she had in a sense blackmailed him into marrying her, that innocence and trust can blackmail as ruthlessly as greed or hate. She saw that she had made an enormous mistake. But trying to disentangle its root, Adelaide came back again to a fault not of her own, but of Henry's: his love-making had been not only irresponsible, but mercenary. This she could not forgive. She did not try to; she simply ceased to love him. At the same time, taking their marriage as a fact, and pride, not love, for the base of existence, Adelaide determined to make of it the best she could, and at least to keep up appearances.

With great common sense, she at once lowered her standards. Perhaps naturally, as soon as she lost her love for her husband she also lost her belief in his genius, and no longer saw in him a future P.R.A. What she now aimed at was some sort of permanent mastership, in a school or at one of the London Polytechnics. (No private pupils.) She forced Henry to visit, and leave his name with, several scholastic agencies; and it was about this time that she answered an advertisement in the paper, enclosing a postal order for half a crown. A day or two later there arrived a small package containing a bottle of colourless, odourless liquid (as guaranteed) described simply on the label as Drinknomor. She managed to slip a teaspoonful in her husband's coffee for three mornings in succession, without appreciable effect; then Henry found the bottle.

Adelaide looked at him defiantly. There was no need for words: the situation was obvious.

"How much have you given me?" he asked.

"You can see for yourself."

"Well, is this the first bottle?"

"Yes," said Adelaide, and could not suppress a flicker of hope. "Henry, have you—have you noticed anything?"

"I've noticed the coffee was rather worse than usual. I suppose this is the answer." He uncorked the bottle and sniffed. "Colourless and odourless," he agreed, quite amiably. "My dear girl, if you'd only told me in advance, I could have saved you half a crown."

"Do you mean, Henry, you've tried it before?"

"It has been tried on me. Without, I assure you, the least result. So I'll get rid of it for you."

He was standing by the sink; Adelaide fully expected to see him pour it away; but instead Henry raised the bottle to his lips and swallowed the lot—at least nine doses of Drinknomor at one draught. He wiped his moustache and grinned at her.

"We'll try an experiment, my dear: I shall now pay a visit to the Cock. . . ."

At least Adelaide wasted no more half-crowns, and she was glad to save the expense. She was becoming very economical, and even encouraged Henry to neglect his painting in order to make a Black Baby and a Crocodile for Old Bert. This ancient was the only creature in the Mews for whom Adelaide felt the least trace of liking, because he always treated her with respect. For Old Bert was indeed old: too old to wonder, or judge, or criticize. He recognized only two classes of people, those good for a tanner, and those who weren't. Adelaide's dress and bearing were those of a lady good for a tanner; had he seen her before his booth he would have elaborated his squeakings, put new life into his Hangman. That she actually lived in Britannia Mews, the wife of a man who carved him a head for a bob, was to the Old 'Un neither here nor there. She was a lady, one of the gentry; when he saw her he touched his forehead, and Adelaide as instinctively opened her purse.

"What's the good of his paying me a shilling, if you give it back in sixpences?" demanded Henry Lambert reasonably.

Adelaide did not answer; if she had, she would have said that sixpence was a cheap price at which to buy back one's self-respect. It bought more; it bought something like friendship. She sometimes had quite long conversations with Old Bert, who in his prime had actually penetrated into drawing-rooms, entertaining children's parties. Only once or twice, he admitted; but he alone in the Mews (except of course Henry) had any idea of the sort of home Adelaide came from. He could describe carpets, window-curtains, which she almost recognized; for if an occasion is rare it leaves a deep impression, and an evening in Queen's Gate had left a deep impression on Old Bert. There was a piano in the room, he told Adelaide; there was a sofa covered in yellow silk; there was a wonderful great chandelier a-hanging from the ceiling. Adelaide would stand in the Mews and listen to the old man, the shabby booth tilted beside them; she felt a pang of sympathy as he stooped to its handles. It was too much for him; as Henry said, he needed an assistant.

"Can't you get anyone to push for you?" she asked one day.

The ancient man raised his head and looked slowly round, his rheumy eye travelling with cool judiciousness over the dwellings of his neighbours. Two of these neighbours were visible—male, able-bodied and unemployed, they leaned against the side-door of the Cock. Old Bert took them into his survey, and allowed his gaze to travel on till it had completed the circuit of the Mews. Then he spat.

With this judgment Adelaide thoroughly agreed. Habit had hardened her; her attitude towards her neighbours had changed from hatred to a profound contempt. The women in particular she

(105)

despised for their incurable slatternliness: they did not throw off altogether the burden of housewifery, but muddled and piddled at it all day long: they never finished one job before starting the next, their washing was never properly clean, their food never properly cooked, their persons never properly dressed. Adelaide found herself able to ignore them, almost as though they were so many animals—very dirty animals, whom one naturally avoided, but otherwise took no notice of. The one exception was Mrs. Mounsey, the Sow. Her Adelaide still feared, and this was the one feeling she had in common with the rest of the Mews.

Even the Blazer, even the bullies of the Cock, feared Mrs. Mounsey. As a rule she was not much seen, only once or twice a week she waddled by with her sack; but sometimes in the evening, when the Mews was at its liveliest, Mrs. Mounsey came out on her balcony. She stood there without speaking, merely watching; and these appearances always produced a curious tension. Voices quietened, eyes glanced furtively up, and glanced away; no one was quite easy until the Sow, her inspection over, heaved herself back within doors. Much later that evening a man or woman would be seen going quickly up her stair, the door opened a crack, something passed from hand to hand, the door closed again. "Why do they do it, Henry?" demanded Adelaide. "They give her money. Why do they do it?" "Because she knows too much about 'em," said Henry. "Didn't I tell you she was a witch?"

"If she's blackmailing them, they should go to the police."

Henry shrugged.

"The police know too much about 'em too. Once you're in the Sow's clutches, it's not so easy to get out."

Adelaide looked at him sharply.

"Have you ever paid her anything?"

"Not a penny."

"Then promise me, Henry, you never will. Promise me you'll never on any account give her any money. Never!"

He readily did so. Adelaide no longer put much faith in her husband's promises, but she felt that this one had a chance of being kept: partly because it might after all be superfluous. For Henry was the only person in the Mews who could look upon the Sow dispassionately; his draughtsman's eye took a detached pleasure in her enormous bulk, he more than once declared that he could make a damn fine drawing of her; and this attitude as it were insulated him from her malefic power. Adelaide had no such defence; and when Henry actually made such a drawing, from memory, super-stitiously burned it.

As for his other promises, she soon learned that Henry gave them simply to save trouble. He promised to go and see a headmaster, simply to get half a crown out of Adelaide for his fares. When she saw through this device he became more ingenious: he got two pounds from her by saying he had borrowed that sum off Miss Ocock. Adelaide in a fury of humiliation gave it him at once; then, preyed upon by doubt, posted a cheque to Miss Ocock direct, and it was not returned; as Miss Ocock's lessons then ceased, it seemed likely that the first part of his tale was true. This dishonesty in money matters, when she first discovered it, drove Adelaide again to tears; but she could, and did, take precautions; Henry got no more money from her. But he had acquired four pounds at one stroke, and four pounds, at the Cock, went a long way: night after night Henry came home the worse for drink. Sometimes, in this state, he was amorous, and when Adelaide shut him out from her room grew loud in anger and self-pity, asking what the devil she had married him for.

"I married you because I loved you," said Adelaide once. "I loved you and wanted to help you. Now I see you're past help."

"And you don' love me?"

"No."

He regarded her, for a moment, with a sort of surprised attention. "Love not stronger than death, and all that?"

"No," said Adelaide.

"Damn' shame," said Mr. Lambert sympathetically.

2

THERE were moments when her spirit almost broke. There was one very dreadful night when a knot of fighting men burst noisily through the door of the Cock and Adelaide, drawn in spite of herself to the balcony, saw a rough circle form round two grappled figures. One was much the more powerful, a brute notorious in the Mews as a bully; and the other man was Henry.

What followed was sheer nightmare. Adelaide heard her own voice raised in a shriek as she ran down the iron stairs, she heard her own voice screaming abuse as she pushed between filthy shoulders, thrust with her elbows, stooped over her husband and pulled him to his feet. The other man struck at her; Adelaide twisted back, still clinging to Henry's arm. No one helped her, but Henry was finding his feet, he was shouting too, cursing with a drink-thickened tongue; as his opponent lunged after him a woman interposed herself, giving them time to retreat. Adelaide pushed Henry against their own stair and stood at its foot while he stumbled up; but no one came any nearer. She waited perhaps half a minute, then turned her back and mounted after him, quite slowly, without once looking round till she turned to shut the door. The knot of men was still there, and the Blazer among them; and it seemed to Adelaide that the Blazer made her some sort of sign.

Henry was leaning against the table, dishevelled but apparently not much hurt. Adelaide attempted to walk past him to the bedroom, but he reached out and caught her wrist. She could feel the dirt of the Mews still on his hand.

"So you're blooded," said Henry Lambert thickly.

"Let me go!"

"You looked like a bloody what d'you call it—"

"Henry," said Adelaide curtly, "if you're able to talk—"

"A bloody Valkyrie—"

"I tell you now that we are going to leave the Mews."

"Didn't know you had it in you. Bloody Valkyrie!"

"If you will not, I shall," said Adelaide.

At that he dropped her wrist and tried to laugh.

"Do I oppose you? Wouldn't dare. Do whatever you damn well like. Go home to Mother. Go home, with your black eye . . ."

Adelaide looked at herself in the mirror. At some point, though she did not remember it, she must have received a blow. Her right eye was already discoloured, the flesh of her cheek felt bruised. For some moments she stared at her reflection unrecognizingly; then she perceived with great clearness the woman she had become.

She was no more fitted, now, for the life she had known than was Henry himself. She was no longer Adelaide Culver. She had been battered, toughened, into Henry Lambert's wife.

"Very well," said Adelaide to her reflection. "But when I am ready, I shall go."

CHAPTER V

IN A CURIOUS way, once Adelaide accepted the fact that her husband drank, life became easier. There was at least, in Britannia Mews, no need for concealment. Most of the men there drank, and a good number of the women; it was a perpetual wonder to Adelaide, as she heard their feet slip and stumble on the steep iron steps, that there were no fatalities from broken necks. Henry was cleverer than most: she quite often saw him, at the foot of their stair, stand eyeing the gradient, pulling himself together, before tackling the ascent: he came up hand over hand on the rail, keeping his gaze fixed on the door above. He was less noisy than most; he did not shout at Adelaide when he came in, or push the furniture over. Taking Henry in the setting of Britannia Mews, Adelaide had little cause for shame. Moreover, once all pretence at painting was given up, she had not to waste time posing as Pharaoh's daughter; she could devote herself to housekeeping, for which her budget of twenty-five shillings a week was perfectly adequate. She became a clever marketer at stalls and small shops; she became a clever cook. One part of her original programme, at least, was achieved: she provided regular and nourishing meals. If Henry were not there to eat them, Adelaide ate alone; with a certain grim determination she looked after herself. She ate well; she kept up an immaculate standard of personal cleanliness; she never went into the Mews without putting on hat and gloves. These were her defences, which she unconsciously feared to relax. Her character was hardening like a tree's bark.

Henry noticed the change in her almost before she did herself. Coming in one afternoon from the Cock, swaying a little in the doorway, he found her finishing a cup of coffee and reading *The Times*. (She had suddenly begun to take *The Times;* it was another of her defences.) He looked at the cleared table and frowned.

"You didn't wait for me?"

"No," said Adelaide. "Do you want anything?"

"Certainly I do. I want my lunch."

She silently went to the stove, and helped him from a casserole, and laid a place at the table.

"A wife," observed Henry sulkily, "usually waits for her husband."

"If I waited for you, I should miss half my meals."

He sat down and began to eat. Adelaide saw at once that he did not want the food, he had demanded it as a gesture. He said:—

"You've changed, Addie. You're getting damned hard. It doesn't become a woman . . ."

"Would you rather find me in tears?"

He did not answer. Adelaide refilled her coffee-cup. She could now consider him without emotion. It was a capacity which had grown very steadily, and which (like her acceptance of Henry's insobriety) brought a certain peace of mind. It gave her control of a situation which only a few months earlier would have reduced her to despair. It enabled her to talk to her husband, when he was in a state to be talked to, in an easy, almost social tone that put him at a disadvantage. She now said casually:—

"Shall you be in this afternoon, Henry? Because I'm having tea with Alice."

2

THE EMPLOYMENT of her niece as a decoy-duck had always been part of Mrs. Culver's design; as soon as Alice returned from Somerset she was admitted to a family council and instructed to write to her cousin inviting her to tea at Swan and Edgar's; Adelaide read the note a good deal more calmly than Alice had written it, and accepted because it would have been cowardly not to do so. When the two young women met that afternoon it was Adelaide whose calm carried them through the first moments of greeting, as it was Adelaide who ordered tea. Alice was decidedly flustered. Shocked as she was by Adelaide's dreadful conduct, hurt by the withholding of Adelaide's confidence, she could not help regarding her with a troubled admiration.

"I don't know how you *dared!*" breathed Alice.

Adelaide smiled. As Alice sat there staring, her two little front teeth more in evidence than usual—looking prettier than usual, too, with a diamond engagement ring on her finger, and all the force of public approval at her back—the adjective that rose in Adelaide's mind was "half-baked." Alice looked half-baked; she hadn't been through anything, she didn't know anything; she was still, in essence, the little girl of Kensington Gardens. Adelaide felt an extraordinary sense of intellectual, almost moral, superiority. The idea that Alice had come to lecture her, or in any way influence her, was so ludicrous that she felt it must be at once disposed of.

"Alice, I'm very glad to see you," said Adelaide deliberately. "I shall always be glad to see you. But if Mamma has sent you to persuade me to leave Henry, you had better know at once that it's a waste of time."

Alice looked very uncomfortable.

"I don't expect Mamma to understand," went on Adelaide, more kindly, "but how would you feel if as soon as you got married to Mr. Baker, your family decided you ought to leave him?"

"Freddy's different," said Alice quickly. "I know what you mean, dear; but you must admit Freddy's quite different."

"He's not nearly so clever as Henry." (Adelaide paused, in momentary surprise at the warmth, the naturalness of her tone. It seemed that the impulse to defend one's husband could co-exist with the most bitter knowledge of his deficiencies.) "He is not original. He's simply and exactly the sort of young man one's parents like.

I was wrong to compare them," said Adelaide loftily. "What I meant was, as you're going to be married yourself, you surely realize that a wife's place is with her husband."

"If he can support her," put in Alice rashly.

Adelaide withered her with a look. (This was how Alice afterwards described the incident to Freddy Baker; and indeed there had been something in Adelaide's expression that almost frightened her. "She looked at me as though she *hated* me," said poor Alice. "She really did, Freddy." "Nonsense," said Mr. Baker robustly. But he was not displeased. From all he had heard, Alice's cousin was a most undesirable connection; he thought the sooner Alice dropped her the better.)

"If any one has said that Henry can't support me," said Adelaide flatly, "it's a lie. Now tell me about Somerset."

Rather nervously at first, but with growing confidence, Alice did so. Somerset had been wonderful; all the Bakers were so kind, and there were so many of them, she and Freddy already had more invitations than they could manage; and if they waited to be married till the following August, two more Bakers, an Indian civil servant and his wife, would be there to swell the throng. "Of course you'll wait," said Adelaide blandly. "Oh, I expect so," said Alice, and chattered on. She was delighted to find Adelaide so sympathetic a listener; actually the latter was employing a technique learned in dealing with Mrs. Culver, that of encouraging the opposition to expend its energy on a side-issue. In describing her trousseau Alice quite forgot her original mission, and Adelaide, as she had enjoyed hearing about Platt's End, genuinely enjoyed hearing about her cousin's frocks. She still felt superior. What she didn't realize was that Alice had in fact influenced her—though not in the direction intended. The commiseration in Alice's first manner (which Adelaide had so quickly removed) was a foretaste of the commiseration which lay in wait at Platt's End and Kensington; and sitting there in the beautifully clean tea-room, out of sight and smell of Britannia Mews, Adelaide felt she could more easily bear life with Henry than life in the family bosom. This feeling was real. There was also the fact that in imposing on Alice a totally false picture of her marriage, Adelaide had also, for all practical purposes, imposed it on herself. Every word she now spoke would have to be eaten before she could make a first move towards Farnham; she was pushing a door shut which one part of her longed to leave open; and before the meeting ended, she had slammed it.

"When are you coming to see us, dear?" asked Alice.

And Adelaide answered deliberately:—

"After you have been to see me."

The risk she took was enormous. She passionately did not wish Alice to come to Britannia Mews. At Britannia Mews pretence was no longer possible, Henry's sobriety could not be relied on even for an afternoon. But the proposition followed too logically on what had gone before for Adelaide to shirk it. It was the touchstone of the whole false position on which she had taken her stand.

Alice flushed. For a moment she looked as though she were going to cry.

"Addie, dear, do be reasonable! You know how nervous Mamma is, she's always afraid I'll catch something . . ."

Adelaide saw at once that she was safe. She said coldly:—

"Does that mean you're forbidden to visit me in my home?"

"It's the *Mews,* dear—"

"My home," repeated Adelaide implacably. "Please tell Aunt I quite see her point, and no doubt she'll see mine. I hope you haven't caught anything to-day, dear."

Alice lifted her head with a look of sudden anger. She had been doing her best, chiefly for the sake of a family feeling which she was quite sure her cousin did not appreciate, and she did not mean to be sneered at.

"Addie, if you take up that attitude, we shan't see each other at *all.* I hate to say it, but I must, Mamma and Papa and Freddy are all absolutely agreed. You must behave sensibly. We all want to see you—"

"With my husband?"

Alice's silence was a sufficient answer, and watching her cousin's

(113)

unhappy face Adelaide suddenly thought of the twins. They got about so much. . . . They had seen Henry once, outside the Café Royal: had they seen him more often, and told what they had seen? It would explain much. Adelaide felt a great desire to bring the interview to an end. She stood up.

"Then this is good-bye for some time," she said harshly.

"I'm sorry, Addie."

"So am I, but there it is. When you see Mamma, as I've no doubt you will, give her my love and say Henry and I wish to be left alone for at least a year. And don't be afraid to ask me to your wedding: I promise I won't come."

3

As ADELAIDE walked back from Regent Street she went over this conversation very carefully in her mind. She had in the first place to prepare a version for Henry; for while she had long ceased to attribute to him any of her own pride, that pride could be buttressed by imposing on another person her chosen point of view. To present Alice as a silly little noodle—to protest that one simply couldn't take on all those Bakers—was to establish face-saving reasons for a breach whose true grounds were humiliating. So far it was easy; but when Adelaide took up Alice's point of view, she could not help wondering how far her cousin had been deceived. What sort of appearance had she, Adelaide, created? Not one of radiant happiness, that was impossible; but she looked well (Alice had said so), she had defined a not ungallant position; above all, hers had been throughout the dominating spirit. She could not have appeared ill-used. (Here Adelaide came very close to reading her cousin's mind, for Alice in fact told both Mrs. Culver and Mrs. Hambro, who were waiting for her in Kensington, that Addie hadn't changed a bit.) As for her defence of Henry, the success of that depended upon whether Alice had any other source of information. On whether, in short, the twins had talked. Adelaide had never treated them with more than a rather impatient kindness, she had no claim on their loyalty; but she thought she could trust their discretion. They got about so much, they had learned to hold their tongues. . . .

In sum, then, there was ground for satisfaction. A difficult passage had been carried through. But at the back of her mind something troubled her, and as she turned into Oxford Street, on the pavement opposite Jay's window, her own final words suddenly came back with peculiar force.

She thought, "Why did I say a year?"

For what could happen, in a year, to change her position? Was it possible that she still had hopes of Henry's reform? Adelaide smiled bitterly; that hope was dead. Certainly it was better not to see her mother, when at every meeting pride impelled her to build up the wall of separation with lies, and lies, and more lies again—each lie a brick that must be laboriously displaced before communication could be re-achieved. The less she saw her mother, the better chance of her return to a daughter's place. That was a good reason, but it was not the true one; and in a flash of lucidity Adelaide suddenly perceived that she had said "a year" because a year was the longest period of her present life that she could endure to contemplate.

But her father and mother had been married for a quarter of a century.

Adelaide stood still on the pavement, splitting the stream of shopping women, and felt panic touch her. She had said a year; there was in truth no period to her bondage. She was caught for life, held fast by a marriage ceremony and her own stubborn pride. Only Henry's death could absolutely free her—and the wickedness of this thought struck her like a blow. For there was nothing more wicked in the world—so all her training, all her beliefs had taught her—than for a wife to desire her husband's death.

She began to walk on again at extreme speed, as though to leave the thought behind her. She pushed it from her mind. But pictures formed there nevertheless—pictures of herself, widowed, unquestioningly received back into a life she should never have left. There was no shame in a widowed daughter's going home, it was natural, it was praiseworthy; and after a year of mourning life began again. How eager they would be, the Culvers and the Hambros, to help her forget! How eagerly would she herself forget, letting her bitter pride die with the memory! "For I haven't changed so much," thought Adelaide piteously. "I could go back and be a girl again. . . ."

There was a moisture on her cheeks; she put up her hand and found tears; she was crying, in Oxford Street. Women were beginning to look at her curiously. Adelaide wiped her eyes without pausing and hurried on. Every step she took was bringing her nearer Britannia Mews, but still she hurried. Her wickedness appalled her, she had to expiate it: she was hurrying back to Henry because only by long years of unremitting care for his welfare, by a lifetime of devotion, could she wipe out that one moment's mortal sin.

CHAPTER VI

THE EIGHTEEN months which elapsed before Henry Lambert's death saw a great change in the distribution of Adelaide's natural connections. The Culvers had moved out of town already; Alice and Freddy Baker settled in the new suburb of Surbiton, and shortly after the wedding, the Hambros followed. There were several reasons for this move: the social advantages of Kensington, successfully exploited by Alice, were as yet unimportant to her little sisters; the twins, who went to St. Paul's, were eager to make the daily journey by train; above all, Mrs. Hambro wished to be near her daughter, and Alice no less desired to have her family close at hand so that they could all run in and out. All Hambros adored running in and out, and Freddy Baker, a Hambro by nature if not by birth, was perfectly agreeable. They migrated therefore—carrying the Redan with them for totem—like a migrating tribe; they colonized Surbiton as they might have colonized Australia, and Alice at once invited two sisters-in-law from Somerset to come and reinforce the operation.

Adelaide was thankful. Isolation was a relief to her; it was a relief to know that her family no longer had an observation post, so to speak, just on the other side of the Park. When Alice wrote giving the new addresses—for she could not bear to think that any member of the tribe, however depraved, should not know where the other members were—Adelaide did not answer. She had not answered the invitation to the wedding, nor sent any gift. She did not answer the rare letters from her mother. In the last of these Mrs. Culver wrote angrily: if Adelaide wished to cut herself off she might; perhaps in a year's time she would show more sense. Adelaide tore the letter across and threw it out with the day's rubbish. From Treff she never heard at all; without resentment she realized that it would be very awkward for him to take her part, and that he indeed had probably no inclination to do so. They were fundamentally indifferent to each other, and indifference was something Adelaide could well bear.

So isolated, both voluntarily and by force of circumstances, Adelaide continued to keep her house and cherish her husband. She took, as she had not taken for some time, pains to be pleasant with him; and if Henry showed an increasing indifference, that was a relief too. He was drinking steadily, and Adelaide would have given much to know where he got the money; no longer from her, for on that issue she never faltered. When questioned he replied vaguely that he had a new pupil. "Where?" asked Adelaide. "Hampstead," said Henry—and Adelaide felt he spoke at random. But he did go out every afternoon, and on the one occasion when Adelaide followed him, he did go to Hampstead. But fearing to be seen, she lost him in the High Street, and after an hour's pointless wandering returned home unconvinced.

He did not go out in the mornings, because he did not get up till noon. This habit, in so small an establishment, considerably inconvenienced Adelaide in her domestic duties, but she was quick to see an advantage. She bought and set up for him a bed in the coach-house below; there he could lie as long as he liked, she explained, undisturbed by her housewifery. For once Henry looked at her intelligently, his indifference pierced by something she had said. He asked sardonically:—

"Are you turning me out of your bed?"

"No, of course not," said Adelaide.

But her body moved with anxiety, with the reverse of desire, as she spoke. The physical contact of her husband was now odious to her: she hated and dreaded the nights when he was sober enough to undress and go to bed. Then she lay close against the wall, rigid, listening to his raucous breathing: if he woke she herself feigned sleep; sometimes she crept out and passed the night in the living-room. But she said calmly:—

"If you don't want to, don't. I simply thought it might be convenient. And you often come in so late—"

Henry looked round with his usual grin. They were standing in the coach-house, the studio, under the Turkish lamp Adelaide had bought at Liberty's.

"It's very nice down here. It's a very good plan, my dear, to give your husband a bachelor's liberty. Some people might call it unconventional . . ."

Adelaide pretended not to understand. Part of what he implied she did not understand; but from her old life rose a disturbing echo. *They occupy separate rooms* . . . It was the most damning thing that could be said about any married couple. She thought quickly, But who will know? Not the Culvers, not the Hambros, no one who subscribed to her own creed of appearances. What the Mews said of her she did not care. With a brisk, matter-of-fact air she set about making up the bed.

Yet this relief in turn brought its dangers. Now, in the quiet of the room she could call her own, in the period before she slept, her thoughts turned uncontrollably to her home. So she thought of Platt's End, the house she had only twice entered; but she remembered perfectly the drawing-room with the bow-window, she knew by heart all the objects with which it was now furnished; she could walk in spirit from room to room and recognize all she found there. ("*You can have the corner room,*" said Mrs. Culver. "*Or the one at the back, with the pretty view.*") Nostalgia tortured her. Again and again she thought, If only I were there! It was not for her mother, for her father or Treff, that she so longed; it was for a life of order and uprightness. The afternoon calls she had once despised now appeared in their true light, as knots in the fabric of respectable society; she saw that it was well to move constantly among one's equals, for it proclaimed one's fearlessness of their judgment. To have nothing to conceal! There were hours when Adelaide envied her cousin Alice, blameless under the eyes of Surbiton; and presently she began to indulge herself in a dangerous fantasy. She lay with closed eyes and imagined she was at Platt's End in body as well as spirit, in the room with the pretty view: she pretended that when she woke it would be to go down to the sunny breakfast-room and find a letter from Alice on her plate. It was an invitation; but she could not accept it, for she was going to a garden-party; and at the garden-party everyone knew who she was, Miss Culver from Platt's End. . . .

Once or twice, breaking in on this dream, she thought she heard voices from the studio below. She shut her ears to them; or if they sounded through her sleep, the woman's voice was Alice's.

It was from these dreams that the climax and disaster of her life with Henry arose.

2

As TIME passed they invaded her waking as well as her sleeping hours; they drove her to make hopeless plans. Since pride forbade her to return alone, she must find a means of taking Henry with her. Her standards fell; she fancied that as the wife of an art-master—of a professional man—she could re-establish herself; and since it was out of the question that he could be employed by any reputable art-school, Adelaide hit on the idea that he might set up for himself. The coach-house had room for half a dozen pupils; easels were cheap, plaster casts not prohibitive; moreover the whole enterprise would carry on under Adelaide's direct supervision. Not only could she keep an eye on Henry, but young ladies would find a chaperone on the premises. To the two fundamental weaknesses of this scheme—the character of Britannia Mews and the character of Henry Lambert—Adelaide shut her eyes; her mind was working in a fever. She set to. Without consulting her husband she drew up an advertisement and copied it a hundred times on good quality, gilt-edged cards, which she meant to drop herself, after dark, through the letter-boxes of Chester and Bedford Streets.

Mr. and Mrs. Henry Lambert

have pleasure in announcing that their drawing-classes will reopen on October 1st at Studio No. 2, Britannia Mews, Albion Place. Hours, 2 to 6 P.M., or by arrangement. Terms, two guineas the course of six lessons. Individual tuition, drawing from the antique, water-colour and freehand a speciality. All information from Mrs. Henry Lambert, Studio 2, Britannia Mews.

At this disingenuous and able production Adelaide worked in secret until the hundred cards were finished, and then she showed them to Henry.

He had come up from the coach-house about noon, dressed but unshaven, with a bilious look that should have warned her. But Adelaide was too fevered to notice: she at once took a card from the neat stack on the table and put it into his hand. He glanced at it, turned it over, glanced with equal attention, or indifference, at the blank reverse, and threw it down.

"Read it, Henry!" cried Adelaide impatiently. "See what it says!"

"I can't, without a magnifying glass."

"I had to write small, to get it on the card. Do you think it's too small?" Adelaide picked up a card herself and scrutinized it anxiously. "Henry, I'm sure you can read it perfectly well!"

She gave him more of them, a handful, and this time he brought his vague attention to bear. But he did not seem to understand, he said stupidly:—

"What's it all about?"

"It's a—a prospectus. I thought you could take pupils again—here, in the studio. I'd look after them. All you'd have to do would be to walk round and criticize. You wouldn't have to go out to give lessons, they'd come to you. It would be so easy, Henry—"

"You're out of your mind. No one would come here."

"But they might," pleaded Adelaide. "We could try. I might lower the prices—"

"No one would come here. If they did, I couldn't teach 'em. I've had enough of it. If I ever see another fool with a drawing-board I won't be responsible for my actions."

With a gesture at once weak and violent he struck at the stack of cards and sent them scattering over the floor; he trod them underfoot as he turned and walked towards the door. Adelaide ran after him and caught him by the arm.

"Please listen, Henry. We must do something. We can't go on like this for ever—"

He thrust past her, knocking away her hand; but on the tiny balcony they were still close together, almost breast to breast. Adelaide hurried on:—

"You say I've grown hard, Henry, but I've had to, or I couldn't endure this life. If only you'll try again I'll be different. I'll believe in you. And why shouldn't you try? You're young, we're both young, there are so many years before us! Are we never to hold up our heads again? Why, when my mother writes to me I can't even answer—"

"The more fool you," said Henry Lambert. "If you weren't a proud bloody fool you'd get money out of her."

Without the least consciousness of what she did, in a purely physical reaction, Adelaide pushed him away from her. His balance was none too good, he was standing with his back to the top-most stair; he fell headlong on the cobbles a dozen feet below.

3

BRITANNIA MEWS was never over-anxious to call in the police; but when a man had his neck broken it recognized the necessity. Who ran for the constable Adelaide never knew; he seemed to appear within a few seconds, while she was still kneeling beside her husband's body. And as rapidly, the Mews filled. All around her faces like the faces in a nightmare pressed and muttered, none approaching too closely, but hemming her in. She felt their hungry excitement breathe upon her like the fumes of an evil spirit; their eyes watched her every movement, sucking at her, avid to miss no least detail. Violence, a violent death, stirred them like beauty. Adelaide shut her eyes; there were no tears under the lids, and in her numbed brain rose the first coherent thought: It would look better if I were crying . . .

A hand, heavy but not rough, fell on her shoulder; the constable was helping her to her feet. Adelaide saw that he looked at her with surprise: he had not expected to find her so respectable. She thought, I am not crying, but I am a respectable woman. I am a lady. And again her clever brain warned her: *If you are a lady, what are you doing here? You are just a respectable woman. . . .*

"Now then," said the constable. "This your husband?"

"Yes," said Adelaide.

"Name?"

"Mrs. Lambert. Mrs. Henry Lambert."

The constable stooped over Henry Lambert's body, while the spectators pressed closer. Now that Adelaide had given her name, had accepted so to speak responsibility, they grew more bold. They could even afford to show compassion, someone carried out a chair for Adelaide to sit on, and she accepted it, though she would have preferred to stand, because she feared to antagonize the oaf or slattern who had brought it. Already she was wondering who had been in the Mews below when Henry fell, and how much they had seen; she could not trust in the common front they usually presented to the Law, because she wasn't one of them. . . .

The constable straightened his back and looked at her uneasily.

"He's dead."

"Yes," said Adelaide.

"Can you make a statement as to how it happened?"

Adelaide moistened her lips.

(122)

"We were standing at the top of our stairs. Number 2. He went past me to go down and missed his footing on the top step."

She was aware that she spoke too calmly, too lucidly; she should have wailed and lamented, thrown herself down on her husband's dead body. From the back of the crowd rose a small impersonal whisper: "Did 'e fall or was 'e pushed?" The constable glared in the direction of the voice, saying, "Silence, there!" But he looked at Adelaide more uneasily still.

"Is there anyone who saw it happen?"

"I don't know."

He turned, not very hopefully, to the spectators. Again there was a drawing-back. But at the same time the hindmost rank parted, someone was pushing through; slowly, purposefully, there emerged the huge and obscene figure of the Sow. She said:—

"*I* seen it. I seen it all."

The constable stared at her, weighing her credit as a witness; she met his look and returned it without flinching.

"Name?"

"Mrs. Mounsey. Number 9, rags and old clo'."

"You say you saw the occurrence happen?"

"On me oath. I was in me winder opposite, which is on the same level, and I see Mr. Lambert and Mrs. Lambert a-standing like she said. 'E pushed past 'er and missed 'is footing. I'd 'a bin down sooner, but I move 'eavy."

Laboriously copying this statement into his book, the constable nodded.

"Accidental death," added Mrs. Mounsey. "Pore soul!"

She waddled up to Adelaide and enveloped her in a dreadful embrace. Adelaide dared not reject it; when her head was forced down upon a filthy bosom, she submitted.

"Stunned," explained Mrs. Mounsey, in a proprietary manner. "Stunned, that's what she is. If you knew your duty, young man, you'd be fetching the ambulance to take 'im away. 'Oo's the Crowner?"

The professionalism of this question cleared the air. On the outskirts of the crowd a brisk discussion arose as to whether the coroner would be Mr. Bickford or Mr. Mayhew; the police surgeon they all knew. The constable closed his note-book and raised an authoritative voice.

"I want someone to go to the station and tell them to send an ambulance and the surgeon. Those who have no business here will clear off. Mrs. Lambert, Ma'am, if you wish to go indoors—"

"I'll stay with my husband," said Adelaide.

She raised a face appropriately white, though less with sorrow than with nausea; already her clothes, her hair, her whole person, reeked with the horrible odour of the Sow's unwashed flesh. But the dead weight of an immensely ponderous arm still held her as the Sow said tenderly:—

"She didn't ought to be left. I'll stay 'ere too."

Adelaide looked quickly at the policeman's face and read there assent to a law older than that he served: *The bereaved must not be left alone.*

"You better have someone," agreed the constable gravely. "Can you send for any relation?"

"I have no relations," said Adelaide.

Even as she spoke she remembered that the whole Mews knew of Mrs. Culver's visit. The Sow knew of it, as she knew everything: Adelaide saw pass over her face a peculiar expression of complicity and approval. She said unctuously:—

"But she 'as friends. I'm 'er friend, ain't I, dearie?"

Adelaide nodded. She could do nothing else, her strength was leaving her, she felt tired and stupid. But she did not quite submit: with a last effort she raised her head and searched through the crowd for where Old Bert, too abject to approach nearer, hung on its fringe.

"Old Bert!" called Adelaide.

He came shambling up to her, gentle, oddly innocent, and stood obediently by her chair: humble as his own dog, he brought something of a dog's comfort. Under Mrs. Mounsey's malevolent stare he blinked and turned away his head, but did not budge. The constable took up his stand at the foot of the steps and withdrew into official stolidity. Of them all the dead man appeared most at ease: he lay in a relaxed and strangely natural attitude, his face hidden by his arm, as though he had flung himself down to sleep.

So they waited; and not unobserved. There were watchers at every window, the Blazer never left her door, women moved on constant vague errands from one end of the Mews to the other. Adelaide endured their looks as she had endured everything; she sat white and rigid, a stony figure of grief. But within her bosom her heart beat with a new life: her shocked brain held only one thought. She thought: Now I can go home.

CHAPTER VII

THE CORONER'S COURT had olive-green walls, panelled halfway up with newly varnished pine. The odour of varnish still hung on the air, mingling in Adelaide's mouth with a sickening after-taste of gin. Mrs. Mounsey had been waiting for her by the Cock, glass in hand; Adelaide dared not offend the conventions of the Mews by refusing it. Someone gave Old Bert a gin as well; Mrs. Mounsey took her third. As befitted her position as chief witness and friend of the bereaved she had drawn upon all the resources of the second-hand clothes trade to appear in deep mourning: her ancient skirt, rust-coloured rather than sable, had crape about the hem; her upper part was swathed in a black opera cloak ornamented with jet, worn over a black bodice and shawl; her bonnet elaborated the sombre theme with more crape, more jet, and a broken feather. Old Bert had a bit of black round his arm. Sitting between them in the Coroner's Court Adelaide felt her own hastily bought black dress to be insufficiently funereal. It had never occurred to her not to go into mourning, but the intricate detail by which a widow published her single-minded grief was conspicuously absent.

Adelaide looked round the room. At the far end was a raised desk for the Coroner, below it a desk for his clerk. Between the jurors' benches on the left and the witness-box in the centre ran a long table round which sat half a dozen men in attitudes at once alert and casual. They showed neither the uneasy importance of the jurors nor the furtive eagerness Adelaide could feel stirring the curiosity-mongers behind her. They looked—at home.

"Newspaper chaps," breathed Mrs. Mounsey.

Adelaide flinched. This was a danger she had not foreseen, and instinctively she shrank back. The Sow's evil-smelling bonnet nodded against her ear.

"They ain't 'ere for us, the next's murder. But don't you be'ave too ladylike . . ."

Adelaide nodded back. The gin had gone to her head a little, with excellent results. She felt detached yet extremely lucid: for once indifferent to the Sow's physical odiousness, and able to appreciate the sense of her advice. A lady, in that place, would attract attention even to an accident, even when the next was murder. . . . The *next*, thought Adelaide, with sudden resentment; remembering the sense of uniqueness and importance that surrounded a death in the Culver circles, her detachment was momentarily pierced: she felt resentful that Henry was treated so unceremoniously, given no more than a place in a series, a place on a list. But she could not pursue this thought, she had to think about herself. *I am not a lady, I am a respectable woman* . . . not too respectable even, if she were to merge into the protective background of Mrs. Mounsey and Old Bert. As though of its own accord Adelaide's hand went up to her throat, unhooking her collar; up to her brow, loosening a strand of hair; she let her shoulders sag, her stiff back slacken. The Sow's small eyes watched approvingly.

Adelaide sat with bowed head, seeing nothing. She stood, as they all stood, when the Coroner entered, but she did not look at him.

She did not see the jurors, their oath taken, file out of the Court and return with paler looks from viewing the body. Until her own name was called she sat blind and deaf, with only one thought in her mind to keep at bay a sensation which she feared to identify, lest it should be fear itself. The thought was a philosophical one, which had come to her before, in the church where she and Henry for the first and last time attended service together: she concentrated upon the importance of appearances.

Then she heard her name called; Mrs. Mounsey and a police officer were helping her to her feet. She was in the witness-box, a Testament in her hand: a voice rolled out certain sonorous periods: "The evidence which you shall give at this inquest on behalf of our Sovereign Lord the King . . ." Another voice prompted, "Kiss the Book," and Adelaide touched her lips to greasy leather.

"You are Adelaide Lambert, and you identify the body of the man now lying in the Mortuary as that of your late husband Henry Lambert?"

"Yes," said Adelaide. Instinctively she straightened her back; on a second impulse let her shoulders droop again, and added, "Yes, sir."

"On Monday last, at 12:30 P.M., Henry Lambert fell from the steps outside your dwelling at 2, Britannia Mews, and was fatally injured. Can you tell the Court how it happened?"

"My husband was standing beside me at the top of the steps. He was going out. He turned and missed his footing. When I got down to him he—he was dead."

The Coroner expressed perfunctory sympathy. With intense relief Adelaide realized that he was not in the least interested in her, but was favourably disposed because she made a good witness who would not waste his time. (The next was murder.) He turned and asked a question of the police officer beside her: How high were the steps from the ground, and were they steep enough to be dangerous? Nine foot, replied the officer, and not to say dangerous, but very steep. They would need care. The landlord wished to say

(127)

that they had been passed by the proper authorities; but in his, the officer's, opinion, they could be called very steep. The Coroner nodded, and turned back to Adelaide.

"Was your husband a temperate man?"

"Oh, yes, sir."

"No sort of quarrel or disagreement? You weren't arguing about anything?"

"Oh, no, sir. He was just going out . . . I said good-bye to him."

There was another touch on her lips, this time of clean linen. Again instinctively, Adelaide had covered her face with her handkerchief. It was the right, the sympathy-arousing move; before she had time to realize that no more questions would be asked, that her personal ordeal was over, someone had taken her by the arm and led her from the box.

When she looked up again, Mrs. Mounsey was in her place.

"You are Mrs. Sarah Mounsey, of 9, Britannia Mews?"

"Yes, sir."

"Will you tell the Court what you saw on the morning of Monday last?"

The Sow nodded gravely. In spite of her grotesque appearance she managed to give an impression of great judiciousness.

"I was standin' in me winder, which is opposite Number 2 and on the same level. I see Mr. and Mrs. Lambert a-standin' there as 'e was goin' out. 'Good-bye,' she says to 'im; 'e turns, misses 'is footing and falls like a stone. I see 'er rush down after 'im, and then I comes down meself; only bein' 'eavy I moves slow. An' seein' 'er too distracted to think fer 'erself, I says, 'Fetch the perlice.' So 'elp me God."

There was a brief silence. Adelaide looked not at Mrs. Mounsey but at the Coroner: he had the appearance of a clever man; the Sow's unctuousness was evidently unpleasant to him. He turned to another policeman, whose face Adelaide recognized, and asked sharply:—

"You were sent for as this witness says? Who fetched you?"

"A young lad, sir. He made off. But I found the body as stated, and not cold. There was no obstruction."

"Is there any other witness?"

"A party known as Old Bert, also living in the Mews, was about at the time."

"He must have another name than Old Bert," said the Coroner impatiently. "Is he here?"

Adelaide clutched her handkerchief tightly as the Old 'Un wavered to his feet. In a high, thin voice, like the voice he used for the Hangman, he cried shrilly:—

"Albert Daneslaw, your honour, Albert Arthur Daneslaw!"

"In the box," said the Coroner.

The Sow waddled out, angry, and, as Adelaide could see, disturbed. She sank down in Old Bert's place, muttering under her breath as he took the oath, thrusting her bulk against Adelaide's shoulder. Adelaide drew away.

"You wish to give evidence?" asked the Coroner.

Old Bert looked across at Adelaide and lifted his aged voice.

"I want to give evidence as I've known Mrs. Lambert ever since she come to the Mews . . . and 'er 'usband before that . . ."

"Yes?" prompted the Coroner. "If you have no direct knowledge of what occurred—"

"If you mean did I see it, I didn't. What I want to say is this: 'e treated 'er something shocking."

A stir of interest passed over the Court. One of the reporters turned and began to look for Adelaide among the witnesses. The Coroner frowned.

"Unless what you have to say is relevant—"

" 'E treated 'er something shocking," repeated Old Bert stubbornly. "She was too good for 'im. They're covering it up now, but 'e drank like a fish. What she 'ad to put up wiv, oh dear, oh dear."

The Coroner looked at him irritably. Old Bert wasn't a good witness, indeed his blinking and rheumy eyes, his high senile voice, made him seem almost half-witted: whatever he said would not weigh with the jurors, but it might confuse them. It was only, the Coroner admitted to himself, out of sheer dislike for the witness before that he had called the old man at all. The woman's evidence, and the widow's, was perfectly clear and largely corroborated by the police. Catching the foreman's eye, the Coroner read there sentiments exactly matching his own: they were wasting time, and the next was murder.

"Did you or did you not witness the deceased's fall?"

"Nay," admitted Old Bert. "Wot I want to say—"

"Then stand down," said the Coroner.

His summing-up took less than a minute, and the jury's consultation no longer. They returned without the least hesitation a verdict of accidental death.

2

THERE WAS still half an hour to wait, for the burial order. When Adelaide learned this she gave Mrs. Mounsey five shillings and Old Bert half a crown, and told them to go and get a drink. That the action was at all dubious, that it might be interpreted as a payment to witnesses, did not strike her; she only longed to be alone. Mrs. Mounsey accepted the bounty expressionlessly, Old Bert with a certain mild pride. "I done me best for you," he asserted complacently. "I wor the one as stood up for you, worn't I now?" "You were indeed," said Adelaide. The Sow looked at them both with contempt, but did not speak. Outside, she took the old man's money away from him.

Adelaide sat down in the sombre waiting-room and pushed the hair back from her forehead, and hooked her collar. She felt weak, as though after hard physical exercise; not her own minutes in the witness-box, but Old Bert's, had drained her strength. Yet things had been made easy for her, unbelievably so: she had simply had to tell the truth . . . leaving a little out. Leaving out, naturally, the worse side of Henry's character, for by convention one did not speak ill of the dead, and leaving out one slight action of her own. Indeed, Adelaide could so easily reconstruct the whole scene without it that it had begun to lose reality: might not Henry have fallen, was he not bound to fall, even without that thrust of her arm against his breast? In her distress and confusion, might she not have exaggerated its force? No more than the lightest contact would have sufficed to leave that mere physical memory of rough tweed under her wrist: in distress and confusion, one's senses played tricks . . .

So Adelaide's mind set about preparing itself for the return to Platt's End; for there were certain memories, certain doubts and self-accusations, which would be out of place there, which therefore had to be eliminated; yet strangely enough, as she worked step by step towards an acceptable position, the one obvious, all-exonerating circumstance for a time escaped her; when she realized it she was astonished by its simple logic. She thought: If I had really pushed Henry down those steps, Mrs. Mounsey would have seen. She did not see, so I did not push him.

This was the first time it occurred to Adelaide that Mrs. Mounsey, in the witness-box, on oath, might have been speaking the truth.

The idea was as surprising as welcome. Yet why should it be? Why, after all, had she assumed that the Sow was lying? Why should the Sow lie? It was not to her interest. She was no well-wisher to perjure herself on Adelaide's behalf. If she had thrust herself forward, taken control, it was because of a certain professionalism in regard to disaster and sudden death: an inquest was meat and drink to her. But there was no reason why she should have lied, and Adelaide, turning these new ideas over in her mind, almost laughed with relief. Not yet, not even in her reaction from fear, could she admit how afraid she had been: the bald summary of the facts, *I thrust Henry to his death, I killed him, I was seen,* was still too terrifying to face. But now it need never be faced. In her own eyes, as in the eyes of her Sovereign Lord the King, she stood acquitted. I have been distracted, thought Adelaide. I must forget all about it. I shall forget easily, when I am at home.

The door opened and a man came in: a clergyman with a kind and troubled face. He said:—

"Mrs. Lambert? I thought I would bring you this myself. I am Mr. James, the Court Missionary."

She took the paper and looked at it: it was the Coroner's order for burial.

"Thank you," said Adelaide.

Mr. James was regarding her with interest, almost with curiosity, but holding that paper in her hand Adelaide felt safe. If he recognized her for a lady it no longer mattered; it might even be an advantage.

"If there is anything I can do to help—if there are relatives to be informed—"

"My husband had no relatives."

"But your own, Mrs. Lambert? Surely your own people will not allow you to bear this burden alone?" He moved a step nearer, evidently disturbed by her extreme tranquillity. "Forgive me if I seem to pry, but if there has been any—estrangement, an outsider like myself, and in my position, can often be of help. I need not assure you of my willingness."

Adelaide straightened her back. It was a relief to do so, and a relief also to speak to someone of her own class, in her own language.

"I don't think you are prying, I think you are very kind." She hesitated a moment, and added deliberately, "I should like to be frank. My family did not approve of my marriage; it led, as you say, to an estrangement. Now that it is ended, I shall of course go home."

"May I say how glad I am to hear it?"

"Thank you. But I wish them to be spared as much as possible. They do not yet know of my husband's death, and I hope they never will know the—the circumstances. Papa is an invalid. Do you think it will be reported in the papers?"

Mr. James, who at the mention of an invalid parent had prepared a fresh expression of sympathy, altered it to one of reassurance.

"I doubt it. I trust not. The next, you see—"

"Was murder," said Adelaide. "And none of my people live in London. They take *The Times*."

"It's extremely unlikely that any report should be in *The Times*. I think you may set your mind at rest on that account."

"Then I shall say my husband died suddenly, of the influenza. There's a lot of it about. If I sound heartless, it is because I have so much to think of. The arrangements for the funeral—"

"That I can take off your hands."

"I should like it to be as soon as possible. I can't go home, you see, until it is all over; I've caused too much grief already. I know I sound heartless."

"If I may say so, you sound as though you are bearing up most bravely under a great strain. I only hope it may not prove too much for you."

She looked at him searchingly; but Mr. James returned her gaze with genuine admiration. He was a man of wide experience; he could reconstruct very easily the story of her married life; he guessed at once that her late husband had drunk like a fish, had probably been drunk when he died. A dreadful end . . . Mr. James had seen it before, he would doubtless see it again; the whole squalid story was thoroughly commonplace—save for the personality of the young woman before him. A fine character, thought Mr. James; been through too much for her years and never given in; desperately eager—and how naturally!—to put the whole tragedy behind her; eager like a child to go home. He only hoped she would find there the sympathy and understanding she deserved.

"Must you tell that untruth?" he asked abruptly.

"I think so. If Papa knows it is any sort of accident, he will know there has been an inquest. He'll make enquiries. He will learn what sort of people gave evidence. I don't want him to know what my life has been like."

Mr. James sighed. There was reason in what she said, and the risk of discovery was very slight; it simply grieved him that she should be forced to take on the additional burden of a lie. He said very kindly:—

"Then give me back the order and I will make all arrangements. I will call and tell you of them. Quite simple, I suppose . . . ?"

"But good," said Adelaide.

With that, suddenly, her tears flowed. They were tears as much of fatigue as of grief, but they made a profound impression on Mr. James, who led her out, and put her into a cab, promising that so far as in him lay she should have no more trouble.

He was as good as his word; Adelaide did not even have to see the undertaker. Two days later Mr. James called for her in a closed carriage, and alone they followed the hearse to the Paddington cemetery. They stood side by side at the lip of the grave, in a downpour of rain that spared them the attentions of any bystander. No one followed from the Mews; and thankful as she was Adelaide subconsciously noted the fact as strange, almost disturbing. It was not like Britannia Mews to boycott death.

Before returning she left with Mr. James the inscription for her husband's tombstone: HENRY LAMBERT, BELOVED HUSBAND OF ADELAIDE LAMBERT, the date, and REST IN PEACE. And because she was not heartless, she directed that the mason should carve as well an artist's palette, crossed by a spray of laurel, at the head.

3

THE INTERVENING days had been spent by Adelaide cleaning and clearing the flat in Britannia Mews. The work was valuable to her, occupying her thoughts and tiring her body; it was also part of her plan for immediate flight. She had little to take away, only her own personal belongings, and little to destroy, since Henry seemed to have kept neither papers nor letters; his clothes, his books, his painting materials, she simply stacked in the coach-house below. They would not stay there long, the Mews would scavenge them up in a morning; Adelaide contemplated this dispersal of her husband's property not only with detachment, but with a sense that it was somehow fitting. *Ashes to ashes, dust to dust* . . . Nor did she care what became of the furniture; if she left the rooms clean it was because the landlord would see them; but she did not bother to give him notice. The rent was paid to the end of the month. All her other dealings had been for cash. It was, in fact, extraordinarily easy to be rid of Britannia Mews.

(134)

To defray the unusual expenses of the funeral and her own mourning she sold a heavy gold necklet of her grandmother's, and found herself with a sufficient balance to return to Farnham first-class.

The morning after the funeral, therefore, Adelaide had no more to do than pack her own clothes in the trunk she had brought from Kensington. It did not take long; by eleven o'clock she was standing in the clean bare room, drawing on her gloves, ready to go out and find a cab; first, as she now decided, to send a telegram. She had originally planned to arrive at Farnham unannounced; so obsessed with the idea of going home, so nearly romantic in her longing, she imagined herself walking into Platt's End as simply and naturally as she might have walked into the house at Albion Place after a morning in Kensington Gardens. But as her mind returned to its old habits she perceived that from her mother's point of view even a few hours' notice would be valuable. There must inevitably be some little talk about the sudden appearance of a daughter; there would be less if Mrs. Culver had dropped a word in advance. "We are so happy, my daughter comes home this afternoon"; and then with a melancholy look, a lowering of the voice, "She has lost her husband. . . ." For Adelaide now saw that it would be wise to give this information too, and with a certain fullness. She took off her gloves and looked round for a scrap of paper on which to compose the message; there was none, she had cleaned too thoroughly; only by a blackened mass in the hearth lay a clean white rectangle, a single card of the hundred on which Mr. and Mrs. Henry Lambert had announced their intention of opening a school.

Adelaide picked it up, drew her pencil through the neat copper-plate, and turned it to the other side:—

Dearest mother and father, she wrote. *I am coming home this afternoon. Henry passed away a week ago after a short illness, influenza. I long for you with all my heart. Your loving Addie.*

Never since earliest girlhood had she so signed herself; never before with such sincerity. She felt the springs of youth begin to flow again, warm with a new affection. I have been hard and ungrateful, thought Adelaide; I have been too selfish. Please God, I'll be a good daughter.

There was a sound behind her as someone pushed at the outer door. It moved slowly, clumsily; halfway it stuck, then grated on; for it had to open to its widest extent to admit the huge swaddled bulk of Mrs. Mounsey, the Sow.

She looked round the room, taking in the strapped trunk, the charred hearth; then she looked at Adelaide.

"You bin cleanin' up."

"Yes," said Adelaide cheerfully. "I'm going home."

The Sow waddled across the room and sat down in Henry's chair.

CHAPTER VIII

FOR PERHAPS HALF a minute the two women looked at each other without speaking. The narrow room was perfectly still: a brief silence had fallen even on the Mews without. Mrs. Mounsey sat like an image: her smooth, dirty-greyish face might have been carved from soapstone, her eyes were mere opaque slits between the creases of fat above and below. She was a dirty and probably a diseased old woman: with loose discoloured teeth, bits of wool stuck in her ears, every squalid sign of decay; and she also looked immensely enduring, able to carry disease as a powerful creature carries lice, in sum formidable.

Adelaide moistened her lips and said pleasantly:—

"I wanted to see you, Mrs. Mounsey. You will find some things in the coach-house which may be of use; I should like you to have them."

The Sow said nothing.

"Clothes, and books," persisted Adelaide. Her voice sounded unnatural in her own ears: too high, too sweet, too fluent. "And if

(136)

there is anything up here—china, or bedding—please take what you like. There's a kettle and teapot, besides cups—"

The wicker of the chair creaked as the Sow settled herself more easily. In her dull eyes flickered a gleam of pleasure; why should she not be pleased? She had just been given the substance of a month's trading. But still she did not speak, and her silence was disconcerting. Adelaide moved towards the door.

"Indeed, I'll leave you in possession," she said, "while I go for a cab. All I'm taking is that one trunk, and the handbag. Everything else—"

"Come 'ere," said the Sow.

She did not even turn her head. She gave the order; Adelaide, however, thought it best not to show offence.

"I'm sorry, Mrs. Mounsey, I've very little time if I'm to catch my train, and as I've got to go at once—"

"You ain't goin' nowhere," said the Sow. "You're stayin' 'ere."

2

AGAIN they faced each other in silence, Adelaide with her hand on the door, the Sow at ease in Henry Lambert's chair. She had been in the room five minutes, and looked as though she had been there always.

Adelaide gave a high, artificial laugh.

"Stay here? I don't know what you mean!"

"I've took a fancy to yer," said the Sow.

"Indeed that's very kind of you—"

"A real fancy." The Sow paused, with the air of one examining and condoning an amiable weakness. She said, "Not but what you knows already . . . fer if I 'adn't took such a fancy to yer, would I 'a said what I done in the box?"

Adelaide closed the door and came slowly back into the room. She was not entirely unprepared; from the moment of the Sow's entry she had feared, if not foreseen, mischance. She had made propitiatory gifts. Now it was time to fight. Without any pretence at misunderstanding she said coldly:—

(137)

"If you mean what I think you do, you're accusing yourself of perjury. Do you know the penalty for that?"

"Term o' imprisonment," said the Sow, unblinking. "Better'n bein' 'anged by the neck till yer dead. You let perjury alone, an' take it I done you a good turn."

"You simply told the truth."

The Sow moved her head ponderously on her thick neck.

"If I'd told the truth, dearie, you wouldn't be 'ere now. You'd be in the Tench awaitin' trial. If I'd told 'ow I seen you push yer pore 'usband to 'is death—"

"My husband fell. Everyone knows it."

"Because I told 'em," agreed the Sow. "Though if they'd took the Old 'Un first, the Crowner mightn't 'a bin so believin'." She swayed her head again, this time in a gesture of impatience. "But what's the use talkin'? You knows, and I knows, you killed yer 'usband. You knows, and I knows, you 'ad good cause. Motive, they calls it: you 'ad good motive. Every night almost 'e went with that red-'eaded slut. . . . But so long as you be'ave sensible, you don't 'ave to fear. *I'll* look arter yer."

Adelaide steadied herself against the table. Her knees were suddenly shaking, but she would not sit; she felt she could fight better on her feet. But now she was on the defensive, her weapon of attack had failed, she was in deadly peril . . . and all at once, as the soft threatening voice ceased, Adelaide heard another voice, her own, speaking out of the past: *"Promise me, Henry, you'll never give her any money!"* She remembered feeling contempt for the blackmailed wretches who crept to the Sow's door. . . . Well, now she was one of them. She knew, as they had known, that there was no alternative. She said:—

"How much?"

"Ten bob a week."

The smallness of the sum brought so great a relief that for a moment Adelaide could not speak. Ten shillings a week—twenty-five pounds a year—was easily within her means; as the price of what it bought it was ludicrous. "Why, the woman's a fool!"

thought Adelaide sharply; and as sharply checked herself. Mrs. Mounsey was no fool: but she bought a man's coat for eightpence, and sold it for one and three: ten shillings a week was wealth to her. Adelaide said cunningly:—

"Eight."

"Ten," said the Sow.

With returning confidence, a sense of power almost, Adelaide allowed herself to hesitate.

"Very well," she said at last. "But not because I believe you. Because I'm grateful for your—your kindness, I'll send you ten shillings a week."

"Not send, give it. 'Ere."

Adelaide looked patient. It might have been a pension they were discussing, a pension to an ex-housemaid.

"My dear Mrs. Mounsey, I can't possibly come to London every week to pay you ten shillings—"

"You'll 'ave no call to. I told you, you ain't leavin'!"

A slow smile creased the folds of Mrs. Mounsey's cheeks, her bosom heaved with enjoyment as from the depths of her shawls she fumbled out a dirty scrap. It was the upper half of a sheet of note-paper: Adelaide recognized at once the Platt's End address, and below a line of her mother's writing: *My dear daughter* . . . She remembered how she had torn that letter across and thrown it with other rubbish for the dust-cart; throwing her life into the Sow's hands.

"I never was a one fer travellin'," said the Sow, "but I can find me way. 'Oo knows, if yer set on the place, I might set up a little business there; you recommending me ter yer nice friends. But 'ere or there, we'll not be parted; jus' you say, dearie, which it's to be."

3

ADELAIDE's thoughts were under control no longer: they raced desperately—as she had once seen a dog race, long ago in Kensington Gardens, running desperately and hopelessly from inescapable terror. The dog whimpered as it ran; and she knew that if she spoke her voice would break on a whimper like a dog's. Twist and turn, plead and whimper as she might, there was no escape. To go back to Farnham with the Sow as her familiar would defeat the whole purpose of her return; would undermine not her own prosperity alone, but that of all the Culvers together. Them at least she could protect—only at the thought of the price, the true price, Adelaide's mind swung away sickened, as her body swayed and sickened, so that she clung with both hands to the table's edge. To stay there, in the Mews, all her life, with no hope of release but by the Sow's death . . .

Her thoughts steadied again. She turned away her head, so that the Sow should not see her eyes. But there was no evil thought of hers the Sow could not anticipate.

"Not twice you couldn't," said the Sow, almost kindly. "Not with the same Crowner. . . . Made up yer mind yet?"

"I'll stay," said Adelaide.

PART THREE

CHAPTER I

IT WAS SUNDAY afternoon: Alice and her mother, surrounded by their families, sat under the big cedar on the Hambros'
lawn.

By 1890, two years after Henry Lambert's death, of which they
did not know, the Hambros at the Cedars and the Bakers in Oakley
Road had been domiciled in Surbiton almost three years: they had
made many friends, and indeed become popular in the neighbourhood, but no new ties affected their family attachment. Alice saw
her mother almost daily: Mr. Hambro and Freddy Baker travelled
up to London on the same train, and frequently travelled back with
the twins. To make quite sure they shouldn't miss each other, however, there was a standing engagement for tea on Sunday at the
Hambros'; every Sunday afternoon the Bakers walked round—at
first Alice and Freddy, then Alice and Freddy with Archy in the
pram, then Alice and Freddy with Raymond in the pram and
Archy alongside in the go-cart—all in their best clothes, all beaming
with expectation. In summer tea was on the lawn: the infants
sprawled on rugs, in charge of their juvenile and enthusiastic aunts,
the twins were allowed to bring out books (of travel only, in deference to the Sabbath) and while the men smoked Alice and her
mother peacefully reviewed the events of the week. If Alice had any
sister-in-law staying with her, as frequently happened, they came
too. After tea they all played croquet. Strangers glimpsing the party
through the hedge often received the impression that some sort of
reunion was going on—possibly a Silver Wedding; and it was a
reunion, only it happened every week.

"Really, Mamma," said Alice, "whatever did we do without a
garden?"

(143)

It was a remark she made regularly, because it regularly occurred to her, and no Hambro ever refrained from saying anything merely because he had said it before. Mrs. Hambro made her usual reply.

"I'm sure I don't know, dear. Of course, there weren't the babies."

"But it's so nice to sit outside without one's hat." Alice leaned back luxuriously against the cushions of her basket-chair. "And it's such good exercise for Freddy and Papa to cut the grass."

"Your father hasn't cut the grass once."

Alice laughed.

"Freddy doesn't often either. . . . He did last month, though."

They relapsed into silence. The twins, lying on their stomachs, were reading the same book: they reached the bottom of the page at precisely the same moment, and Johnny turned it as unthinkingly as if he were alone. Raymond slept in a sort of nest made for him by the bodies of his two young aunts: Archy had wandered as far as the herbaceous border, where he stood lost in contemplation of a lupine. It was the moment of peace and repletion, when tea was over, and before they started to play croquet.

"We ought to cut the lavender," said Mrs. Hambro drowsily.

"There isn't much, Mamma. That's the one thing I envy at Platt's End . . . that gorgeous hedge."

"It's an older garden . . ."

Alice's eyes, which had been closing, suddenly opened.

"Mamma."

"Yes, dear?"

"Do you know if they ever hear from Adelaide?"

For a moment Mrs. Hambro, sunk in a delicious coma, pretended not to hear. But Alice repeated her question more vigorously and forced an answer.

"No, dear. They only know she's left the Mews."

"*How* do they know, if they don't hear from her?"

"Your aunt went to see her."

"I *thought* so!" Alice sat up, letting her cushions slip to the ground. "I *thought* that was what you were talking about, last time we were over there! You might have told me."

"There wasn't anything to tell. Your Aunt Bertha went up to town last month, meaning to see Adelaide, but Adelaide wasn't there. A neighbour told her they'd gone a year ago, without leaving any address. It's not surprising."

Alice reflected.

"If they've left Britannia Mews, it must mean Mr. Lambert's doing better."

"I'm sure I hope he is."

"He *was* rather fascinating, you know. You know, Mamma," said Alice, in a lower tone, "I could have forgiven Addie anything, if only she'd confided in me. But I remember one afternoon, when I was telling her about Freddy, before we were engaged, she had such a queer superior manner; and I suppose now it was going on all the time."

"You may be thankful she didn't confide in you," said Mrs. Hambro practically. "You'd have been in a most unpleasant position."

"She wasn't even at my wedding, and I wasn't at hers. Oh, dear, the boys want to play croquet."

Alice jumped up. At the same moment the infant Raymond woke, stretching soft pink fists and toes into the delighted faces of his aunts; and with all her kind heart Alice regretted that Adelaide was not there to share the delicious spectacle. She didn't often think of her cousin; her life was too full of immediate, absorbing detail, her mind too preoccupied with intimate family concerns; she was also honest enough to admit that if Adelaide should suddenly reappear she might prove rather an awkward customer. Would she fit in? To "fit in" was one of Alice's pet phrases, and covered a good deal of moral ground: it implied the complete acceptance of her own view of life, the practice of all her own cheerful virtues, the absence of anything disturbing, unkind, or even out of the way. Adelaide was hardly unkind, but she was certainly disturbing, and she didn't seem to accept anything. . . . Selecting her own particular mallet, the one with the blue band, Alice unconsciously shook her head. Despite these moments of regret, and sharp as they were, she no longer felt any impulse to seek Adelaide out.

2

IN DESCRIBING her abortive visit to Britannia Mews, Mrs. Culver had given her sister only the barest outline, and the latter would have been surprised to know that neither Mr. Culver nor Treff had been told any more. "Adelaide has been gone a year," said Mrs. Culver, on her return to Platt's End. "There's no address. I did what I could, Will, I enquired of a neighbour; that's all they know"—and then she went upstairs and lay down. Later that evening Mr. Culver said abruptly, "I suppose we don't want to go to the police?" and his wife shook her head. She had in fact had a very unpleasant experience: though there were several people about when she entered the Mews, no one came forward to answer her question but one grossly fat old woman, who indeed replied civilly enough; but when Mrs. Culver turned to go this creature followed, jostling her in the archway to Albion Alley, demanding money. Mrs. Culver opened her bag. She did not give to beggars as a rule, but the Alley was deserted and the Mews behind ominously quiet. Mrs. Culver opened her bag—and suddenly a heavy, foul-smelling arm thrust against her breast, she was pushed back against the wall, and a filthy hand closed over her sovereign-purse. For almost the first time in her life Mrs. Culver felt physical fear; it lent her strength to jerk herself free; and she actually ran as far as the corner of Chester Street. Her lungs cramped by her corset, her feet cramped in her pointed shoes, her heavy petticoats twisted between her knees, Mrs. Culver ran. A horrid, an undignified, experience! She did not tell a policeman, she did not tell her husband; she wished neither to think nor to speak of Britannia Mews.

The move to Farnham had been an unqualified success. Platt's End received them kindly: Mrs. Culver had known at once that she would like the house, and she grew to like it more and more. Her drawing-room in particular was a pleasure to her: all through the summer she kept the bow-window full of flowers, arranged on tiers of bamboo stands—"My flower show," she called it—and it had become quite a feature of her At Home Days. These Days were well attended, for she had managed to bring with her a certain urban consequence; upon the quiet ladies of the neighbourhood Mrs. Culver's London talk made an impression; they were also flattered by her preference for Farnham. "Never again," exclaimed Mrs. Culver, "would I live in town!"—and Mrs. Hume and Mrs. Blake and Mrs. Howard, whose experience of London was confined to a day's shopping, all agreed that the bustle and rush there had become quite unendurable. Their daughters sometimes looked blank; for they all had daughters, among whom Treff moved with rather the air of a *jeune premier*.

Treff, a detached young man, was extremely popular, and improved his tennis on every court in the neighbourhood; he had just come down from Cambridge. Mothers fished a little now and again, trying to find out what his profession was to be, and, particularly, if it was a profession which would soon support a wife; on this subject Mrs. Culver was very discreet, for the good reason that she did not know, herself. Charming, good-tempered, without vices, Treff was still, from a professional point of view, an unknown quantity. He had read History, and his father thought he might become a schoolmaster. Treff promised to think it over, and continued to play tennis.

Platt's End, however, and the houses like it, did not form all of Farnham's society. There was an upper crust, with which the Culvers mingled more rarely, though still on equal terms; a retired admiral, a retired judge, a dowager viscountess, added lustre to the neighbourhood. Mr. Vaneck, at Bishop's Lodge, untitled but wealthy, played almost the part of a squire in his patronage of cricket clubs, flower shows, and the Cottage Hospital. Without a wife to entertain for him, he still entertained more than anyone else, and always on a large, almost impersonal scale. No one dropped in on him. The Vicar's wife, calling on a charitable errand, and with no fear of being refused, sent round a note in advance. There was a ceremoniousness in all his dealings which made him undoubtedly impressive, and Mrs. Culver was more flattered than she liked to admit when he called at Platt's End. He came at the proper time, though not on her Day, accepted tea, inspected the garden, gave advice on the management of the green-house, and paid his next call exactly a year later. No one expected more from Mr. Vaneck.

In these pleasant surroundings the years passed swiftly. Mr. Culver's heart gave no trouble, though Dr. Howard very properly warned him against over-exertion; he took to gardening, and achieved a mild local reputation with his phloxes. He never spoke of Adelaide, nor did Treff. Mrs. Culver occasionally mentioned her in public, being too wise a woman to suppress altogether a married daughter; but she gave the impression that Adelaide lived abroad—so successfully that a new-comer introduced by Mrs. Blake made conversation by observing that she knew a gentleman in the Consular Service, like Mrs. Culver's son-in-law. Mrs. Culver replied that it was a most interesting career, only it took one out of England. But apart from such politenesses no one showed any interest in Adelaide; no one ever was interested, as Mrs. Culver well knew, in other people's absent female relations.

CHAPTER II

IN THE SUMMER heat Britannia Mews sweltered and smelt: Adelaide Lambert propped her door open all day long, and sent Mrs. Mounsey for beer instead of gin.

So, after two years, had their relationship established itself, and not without a great moral danger to Adelaide. For she had not long accepted her fate passively, and the ensuing struggle drove her more and more to use the Sow's weapons: as their wills met and locked Adelaide found she could draw strength only from the worse part of her nature, from pride, bitterness, and hate; finding these qualities serviceable, she cultivated them. Anger, too: since it was her first movement of anger that gave her the clue to the Sow's one weak point. This happened on the fourth day after Henry Lambert's funeral: the first three Adelaide had passed cowering in her room like a wounded animal, lying fully dressed on her bed, moving only to fetch bread and water—for there was a loaf thrust within the door each morning, placed there indeed by Mrs. Mounsey, who had no intention of letting her victim starve. But on the fourth day stupor gave place to restlessness, and Adelaide got up, and bathed her face, and went slowly down to the coach-house below.

She found it stripped. The Turkish lamp was gone, Henry's stool and easel, his bed, all the bedding; his clothes were still there, but tied up in bundles, obviously ready for removal. These signs of the Sow's activity roused Adelaide to sudden fury; and anger overcoming weakness, she walked straight out of the Mews to a locksmith's and brought the man back with her to affix padlocks to both upper and lower doors. It was done in an hour. The Sow, re-entering the Mews, passed the man leaving; she waddled up to the coach-house doors, looked at them, looked at Adelaide and silently thrust out her hand.

"What d'you want?" snapped Adelaide.

"The key, o' course, 'and it over."

"I shan't," said Adelaide. "I'll have no more thieving here!"

For some reason Mrs. Mounsey appeared to resent the term.

"I've took nothing but what you give me—"

Adelaide laughed loudly.

"When I thought I was leaving. Now I've changed my mind. You've had all you're going to get."

The Sow blinked her small eyes.

"And suppose I change me mind and go to the perlice?" she insinuated.

"You'll lose ten shillings a week," said Adelaide.

Almost to her surprise, the threat took effect. Mrs. Mounsey's hand dropped, her eyes blinked again over Adelaide's haggard, venomous face; and she turned and shuffled away.

Adelaide's knees gave beneath her, she sat down on the iron steps and bowed her head in her lap. Her first thought was simply of food, she had to get some food; her second, that she had found her weapon of defence, and it was the ten shillings a week.

So it turned out. On this sum the Sow's miserly spirit fastened and fed; to retain it she would give up all other perquisites. It was sweeter to her even than revenge. So long as Adelaide could produce ten shillings every Monday, Mrs. Mounsey would not go to the police; and because she could produce it, Adelaide was condemned to imprisonment. So, in some Eastern country, debtor and creditor are chained together with an iron chain; but at least Adelaide was imprisoned on her own terms.

This was the first phase. Not until a few months later did Adelaide give Mrs. Mounsey her first order. A clammy fog had settled over the Mews; only the children were driven out to steal from coal-carts, their elders creeping no further than the Cock, and Adelaide no more than any one else wished to venture forth. But she had no book. She had now become a voracious reader, drugging her brain with the works of Miss Braddon, Rhoda Broughton, Ouida, Edna Lyall—anything and everything procurable from either the public library or a private establishment in String Street where volumes were hired out at a halfpenny a time; but now, owing to the fog (and many subscribers to Mudie's were suffering for the same reason) she had no book. She put on her coat and stepped out on to the balcony; fog billowed up in a yellow acrid wave and made her cough; she could just discern the houses opposite, but no more. Against their smoky façade, however, someone was moving: the Sow, her bulk swollen to even more monstrous dimensions by the murky atmosphere, was coming slowly down her steps. She carried a jug; she was going to the Cock.

"Mrs. Mounsey!" shouted Adelaide.

The Sow paused, peering out from the folds of the shawl over her head. So muffled there was nothing human about her outline; only bulk.

"Go to the shop in String Street where I get my books and fetch me two more," directed Adelaide. "Ask the woman to choose them —and be quick."

The shawl slipped back as the Sow raised her head; her face made a lighter but still shapeless patch in the fog.

"You fetch yer own bloody books. I ain't yer servant."

"Don't I pay you?" asked Adelaide.

And in spite of the icy damp, the blood burned in her cheeks. She was deliberately pitting, as she had not done for months, her will against the Sow's; she was re-testing the strength of her own hold, exploring the limit of the other's cupidity. She had a foretaste of the pleasures of bullying. . . . And throwing into her voice all the menace and harshness of which she was capable, she cried, "Do as you like, you old fool! It'll be long before you find such another fool as I am to pay you ten shillings a week!"

She made as if to go in; and out of the corner of her eye saw Mrs. Mounsey move a pace nearer.

"I'll do it this once . . ." said the Sow.

"You'll do it as often as I tell you," said Adelaide. "Take these back." She tossed the two books she was holding over the rail; it gave her great pleasure to see the Sow stoop laboriously to pick them up. She added, "And as you come back by the Cock, I'll have fourpennyworth of gin."

For Adelaide had now begun to drink a little; not much, but a little; and not at the Cock, where she would have had to encounter the eyes of her neighbours, but in the Ladies' Bar of a rather superior house in Paddington. But this was ten minutes' walk away, and Adelaide at once saw the advantage of being able to procure spirits from the Cock without entering it. Sitting by the fire, waiting for the Sow to return (as she punctually did) Adelaide smiled grimly. She thought, I've a dog to fetch and carry. Only her lips moved, her eyes remained hard and cold; and in expression at least she bore, at that moment, a strange, fleeting resemblance to Mrs. Mounsey.

Thus the Sow became Adelaide's servant, as Adelaide was the Sow's victim; there arose between them the evil relationship, not unknown among women, of the maid who blackmails and the mistress who bullies: they were complementary to each other. To gloss over her subservience Mrs. Mounsey sometimes put on an air of unctuous geniality; sometimes, to show that all she did was of her own free will, she brought up a pennyworth of gin unasked; and Adelaide, so long as she tolerated, and even demanded, these attentions, with however open a contempt, could not deny the familiarity that springs from habit. In the eyes of Britannia Mews they appeared almost cronies; presently Adelaide became aware that as the Mews had once avoided her from a mixture of dislike and resentment, she was now avoided from something like fear. She partook of the Sow's ominousness. Old Bert no longer looked out for her to come and talk to him, but slunk away, or shuffled behind his booth, not wishing for her notice; after one or two attempts to win back his confidence Adelaide let the Old 'Un go.

She let so many things go: the habit of pleasant courtesy, scruples of speech and thought; the habit of consideration for others. In Britannia Mews these were not qualities but weaknesses; Adelaide discarded them without a pang. She still took care of her person, for this was instinctive, and her instinct of order still ruled in the flat. She ate wholesomely, refraining from the papers of cooked foods on which her neighbours appeared to subsist; what with housewifery, shopping, visits to the library, Adelaide's time was sufficiently occupied. When she had nothing else to do, she read. She never went into the Gardens, for fear of meeting anyone she used to know. It was in many ways the life of a hermit; and hermits, it is said, find the days pass swiftly enough.

2

ADELAIDE did not hear of her mother's visit until some days after the event. She heard of it from the Blazer, who vaguely hoped to do Mrs. Mounsey an ill-service by "splitting," and one morning waylaid Adelaide under the archway to tell her. Adelaide had many reasons for disliking this young woman, and would have passed on; but the Blazer planted herself firmly in the path.

"Pity you was out t'other day; you missed yer ma."

Adelaide halted. She would not answer, but she listened. The Blazer set her fine arms akimbo and laughed raucously.

"Good as a play, it was: yer poor ma banging at the door, askin' does anyone know if Mrs. Lambert is 'ome, till up steps the Sow, lookin' like butter wouldn't melt in 'er mouth, and tells 'er you bin gone a twelvemonth. . . ."

Still Adelaide did not speak; and the Blazer, piqued, threw more drama into the recital.

"'Ain't she left no address?' asks yer ma. 'Ain't my cruel daughter left no word?' 'Nary a word,' says the Sow. 'She's gone, leavin' no address.' And with that yer ma goes away, the Sow seein' 'er off; and I shouldn't be surprised if she got some tin out of 'er."

At last Adelaide spoke. She said stiffly:—

"You're in my way. Get out."

For a moment the Blazer tried to outstare her; she met the cold and snakelike look which even Mrs. Mounsey feared. For Adelaide had not given the tale more than a moment's attention; she accepted it as true, realized the spring of the Sow's action, and indeed approved it; her mind was on what had gone before, on what had once passed between her husband and this creature; and hatred showed so nakedly in her eyes that the Blazer's eyes fell. With a shrug of her magnificent shoulders, half-defiant, half-defensive, she swung away; and Adelaide walked on without a backward look.

She did not mention the matter to the Sow. But Mrs. Mounsey by some witchcraft learned what had happened, and made an oblique reference to it.

"If anyone was to come arter you," she said cautiously, "I take it you don't want no interferin' with. . . ."

"No," said Adelaide. It amused her to watch the Sow's tortuous approach.

"If anyone was to come askin' where you was, I'd tell 'em you was gone . . . ?"

"Leaving no address," supplied Adelaide. "I dare say you'd get a shilling for your trouble."

Mrs. Mounsey gave her a sly look. She knew a lot, this young Tartar, but she didn't know all; she didn't know what had happened outside the Mews. In the long game of bluff and counter-bluff, blackmail and chicanery, it was a point to the Sow.

CHAPTER III

ON THE LAST Sunday in August the weather broke in a thunderstorm, and though the temperature scarcely dropped, by nightfall there was a perceptible lightening of the atmosphere. The rain ceased, leaving a freshness on the air: the wet leaves of the lime-tree gave off a faint country scent. At such an hour, when a failing light blurred its more squalid details, Britannia Mews showed at its best: a stranger glancing through the archway from outside might have called it picturesque, and envied its tranquillity. Adelaide, standing on her balcony within, took no such exaggerated view; but she was grateful for the absence of her neighbours, whom the rain had driven indoors, or into the Cock. The quiet soothed her nerves, as the cool air her face; she stood on, scarcely thinking, giving herself up to a temporary respite from noise and heat. The years had not altered her carriage: she still stood easily erect, her hands lightly clasped before her—as she used to stand at Mrs. Orton's parties; seen thus in silhouette, she was unchanged, for the dusk was as kind to her as to the Mews, and hid the stony set of her features.

A quarter of an hour passed, and still the silence was untroubled. The air was so still that the lime-tree's foliage stirred only when a leaf shook free from its weight of rain-drops; then the tiny sound was perfectly audible. Adelaide could see the tree distinctly, for the lamp on the angle of the Cock cast its light through the branches, throwing up each twig with theatrical precision. This light seemed to increase as the sky darkened, but at the other end of the Mews the archway loomed darker than the sky. Through that archway Adelaide had entered the Mews four years ago—fifteen years ago; but if she suddenly moved and sighed it was not because of any such memories; she had learned not to give memory rein. She sighed because she knew that if she stayed there much longer the character of Britannia Mews would inevitably reassert itself, and with some grotesque or sordid incident mar her interlude of peace.

As it was, she had lingered over-long. At that moment the side-door of the Cock clashed open, and a man was thrown out.

2

THE IMPULSE of a powerful hand, perhaps a powerful knee, flung him halfway down the Mews, still on his feet, but staggering; as the door clashed to again he lost his balance; his final collapse took place almost directly under Adelaide's balcony, where he pitched forward and lay motionless, his head in a puddle, his limbs cast north, south, east, and west to the four points of the compass. The suddenness and violence of his appearance—a man cast up so to speak at her feet—made Adelaide start back; she put her hand to the door. But there was no one else in the Mews, and the man's stillness frightened her. Leaning over the rail she called sharply down to him, asking if he were hurt.

To her immense relief, he stirred; reassembled his sprawled limbs, propped himself on an elbow, and with only a little difficulty focussed his gaze on herself. He spoke:—

"But, soft! what light through yonder window breaks?
It is the east, and Juliet is the sun.
Arise, fair sun . . ."

Far more than by his words, unexpected as they were, Adelaide was struck by his voice. It was unmistakably the voice of a gentleman. This was a point on which she could not err, for her life with Henry Lambert had perfectly familiarized her with the accents of the gentleman-drunk, and so slightly softened her tone.

"If you're not hurt," called Adelaide, "please get up."

And now her own voice, heard the second time, appeared to make a similar impression upon the stranger. He stared; scrambled up; and moved his hand to his head with a gesture she had no trouble in interpreting: he was raising a non-existent hat.

"I beg your pardon," he said, quite clearly. "No idea ladies present. Lemme call you a cab."

Adelaide was extraordinarily touched. His swiftness in recognizing her for a lady, his immediate appreciation of her incongruousness with her surroundings—and at a moment, too, of great physical distress—showed, she thought, a most remarkable understanding. And he not only realized and sympathized with her position, he was prepared to take steps to relieve it. How many gentlemen, wondered Adelaide, thrown out of a public-house, would immediately rise up to fetch a lady a cab?

"Thank you," she said gratefully. "I don't want a cab; but thank you."

He looked at her with increasing bewilderment: every word she spoke, all he could see of her, confirmed his first impression. She must want a cab. He became persuasive.

"Would you object to a hansom? They are more easily found, at this time of night, than the growler. The growler, as its name suggests, belongs to the dog-and-daylight order of vehicles; the hansom to the cat—nocturnal and amorous. However, in an emergency—"

"I don't want either," said Adelaide. "But I do wish you'd tell me whether you are hurt."

"Not in the least. Not physically. Morally, yes, because I perceive you do not trust me even in the capacity of cab-hailer. Will you tell me, please, how you propose to get home?"

Adelaide laughed. It was not a very pleasant sound.

"This is my home. This is where I live. I live here, in Britannia Mews."

The stranger sat down again, this time on the bottommost of the steps, and stared up. He did not express incredulity: did not exclaim or commiserate. Instead, he made another extraordinarily perceptive remark.

"I had an aunt who lived in Kensington. Beauchamp Place."

Adelaide leaned impulsively towards him.

"What was her name?"

"Ferrier. Perhaps you knew her?"

"No, we didn't, but I believe *my* aunt did; they had a much wider circle . . ." Adelaide's expression changed, and she looked at him resentfully. "But you're quite right, of course; I did live in Kensington. It's so long since I've talked to any one, you'll find it easy to trick things out of me."

In a swift movement—all his movements were remarkably rapid —he was up, and up the remaining steps, and standing beside her.

"Please forgive me. I'm unforgivable, but forgive me. You can't imagine how extraordinarily interesting and fascinating you are—a woman, a lady like yourself, here in this place. You say it's long since you've talked to any one: when I heard your voice just now I thought it was a delusion. It's so long—"

He broke off, turning away from her. The lamplight reached towards his face, exaggerating its bony structure, deepening the hollows round his eyes, making him look older, Adelaide thought, than he probably was; for in spite of the brindled hair over his ears she did not take him for more than thirty. His appearance appealed to her strongly. To find out his name, she told him hers; and saw nothing odd in using the conventional phrase.

"Let me introduce myself," said Adelaide. "I am Mrs. Lambert."

He bowed.

"My name is Lauderdale. Gilbert Lauderdale."

"I feel more and more convinced that I once met Mrs. Ferrier. Do you keep in touch with her?"

"As a matter of fact, I haven't seen her for years; it's odd how one's relations are always bores. I've a brother in the Church who is the greatest bore alive. You know, from this level, and in this light, the Mews is really quite picturesque."

"So my husband used to say."

"Used . . . ?"

"He passed away two years ago."

There was a short silence. Already, and despite the politeness of these exchanges, they had crossed the border into familiarity. Naturally, thought Adelaide; for if, while making a gentleman's acquaintance, one was at the same time remarking how quickly he sobered up, one already knew a good deal about him. His mind was probably working along the same lines; when he spoke again it was with complete frankness.

"You know, you oughtn't to be living here alone," said Mr. Lauderdale.

With equal frankness Adelaide answered him.

"I have no choice."

He nodded understandingly.

"One has, as you say, no choice. One takes a first step, and the rest follows. I'm the man you see, because I have no choice."

"You're not drunk now," said Adelaide baldly.

"I have a remarkable faculty of sobering up. When I was on the stage I could start a scene stewed, and finish in full command of my faculties. However, the managers didn't think it good enough. Before that, of course, I was reading for the Bar. At the moment I address envelopes, at two and six per thou'; my feet may betray me, but my hand remains faithful." He paused, and looked at Adelaide shrewdly. "Now you, I take it, have a private income?"

She nodded in turn.

"I knew it. There's nothing gives a woman so much dignity as the possession of a private income. And you don't drink—much."

"How did you know *that*?"

"That you drank a little, by your humane attitude when I was thrown out of the pub. The other's obvious. You're a most remarkable woman."

"I am what my life's made me," said Adelaide.

It was almost a repetition of his own phrase. Mr. Lauderdale, who was now leaning comfortably on the railing, glanced over his shoulder with a smile.

"Frankly—certain obvious disadvantages apart—isn't this life more interesting than the one you led in Kensington?"

"No," said Adelaide.

"Then that's because you haven't realized its opportunities. I wish I had a cigar," added Mr. Lauderdale irrelevantly. "With a cigar I could imagine myself on the balcony overlooking Lake Como: it's really a remarkably warm night."

"You must have a remarkable imagination," observed Adelaide. But she too rested her arms on the rail, and leaned beside him. "What opportunities do you mean?"

"In the sphere of human relationships. One's so completely free from all but purely personal considerations. In this life a man and woman meet, and within half an hour may be on terms of completest intimacy. They may be attacking each other with bottles, or deciding to set up house together. And if they do decide to set up house together, no one minds; it's entirely their own affair. On the other hand, if they feel no mutual interest, they needn't pretend to it. They just ignore each other. My dear Mrs. Lambert, if you and I had met for the first time at your father's table, how long would it have been before I could talk to you like this?"

"You would never have talked to me like this."

"No, we should have conversed for years about the Savoy operas. Or rather, owing to my unconventional career, we should never have been allowed to converse at all. As it is—"

"Hush!" said Adelaide sharply.

His hand, which just then touched hers, drew back; but Adelaide had not noticed the contact. She was looking across the Mews, at the balcony opposite; upon which, framed in the open door, stood the monstrous, watchful figure of Mrs. Mounsey.

3

THE Sow remained there only a few moments, turning her squat head this way and that, as though tasting the night air; then deliberately began to descend, lowering her great carcase painfully from step to step.

"What a horrible creature," said Mr. Lauderdale.

"Hush! She may be coming here."

"Here? Why should she?"

But the Sow did not pause—or only long enough, in passing, to give Adelaide a familiar nod; then she waddled on towards the Cock. That was all. Adelaide drew a long sigh of relief, and turned to find Mr. Lauderdale looking at her with astonishment.

"She's hateful," explained Adelaide weakly. "Isn't she hateful?"

"Yes, but why are you afraid of her?"

"Because . . . because she's so hateful."

"She has certainly spoiled the picturesque illusion," agreed Mr. Lauderdale. "May I come in a moment?"

Without waiting for an answer he opened the door and stood aside to let her pass. Adelaide hesitated; the appearance of Mrs. Mounsey had jarred their curious and pleasant intimacy; on the other hand—by such minute considerations is a life swayed—it was the first time in four years that any one had opened a door for her. She passed through.

4

THE ROOM was as usual neat and well-ordered; Adelaide observed with pleasure her companion's appreciative look. She observed also that his face and hands were extremely muddy, and with a hostesslike gesture—as her mother drew attention to the flower-stands—indicated the water-bucket by the sink.

"If you would care to wash . . . ?"

Mr. Lauderdale gratefully removed his coat. His shirt was cleaner than might have been expected, his waistcoat much too large and pleated with safety-pins behind. Adelaide saw at once how it could be made to fit. When he had finished washing she offered him a clothes-brush, and within ten minutes Mr. Lauderdale's appearance was greatly improved.

"If you would like some tea, I can easily light the fire."

"Won't that be a great trouble to you?"

"Not in the least. But if this were Kensington"—Adelaide smiled—"I should simply ring for the maid."

(160)

"No, you wouldn't," said Mr. Lauderdale. "
scandalizing her."

They both laughed. Adelaide set a match to the
fires burned well—and filled the kettle; and as they sat
for it to boil it struck her that Mr. Lauderdale was the fi
she had ever entertained in Britannia Mews. No one before
ever come to sit sociably by her fire. The sensation was extrad
dinarily agreeable. They discussed the weather: to both the most
trifling civilized chat was a novel pleasure. But Adelaide had,
gradually forming in her mind, a matter of greater importance:
she had glimpsed what might be a great opportunity; and when
about half an hour had passed, and the teapot was empty, she
came to a decision.

"I think you said you'd been a barrister. Could you give me
some legal advice?" And in the moment before he answered—for
her change of tone surprised him—she added hastily, "I should
tell you it's not for myself, but for a friend . . ."

Mr. Lauderdale smiled.

"I'll give you any advice I can. I don't guarantee it will be sound.
What is your friend's difficulty?"

"She is being what I suppose one would call . . . blackmailed."
Adelaide paused; it both relieved and disconcerted her that he
took the word with complete calm. "That might happen to any
one, mightn't it?"

"Especially to an inexperienced young woman—as I take your
friend to be."

"She was young, and inexperienced, and a complete fool," said
Adelaide deliberately. "She married like a fool, through her own
fault. Her husband drank; like a fool she thought she could alter
him. Well, she couldn't, of course. They became on bad terms. In
the course of an argument she—she pushed him away from her.
That was all. Only they were standing at the top of some steps. He
fell, and was killed. And someone saw."

Still cool as a cucumber, Mr. Lauderdale reflected a moment.
"When did this happen?"

"Some time ago."

e been an inquest. What was the verdict?"

ath."

friend has nothing to worry about."

t finished. The chief witness, at the inquest, was this
who saw. She perjured herself. She said he had simply
ed. Otherwise—I don't know what the verdict would have
en. Everyone knew they were on bad terms. Afterwards this
person, this witness, asked for money, and my friend gave it her.
She's been giving it ever since. That's all."

Adelaide was sitting with her elbows on the table, her chin
resting in her palm; now she moved her hand slightly to cover
her eyes. The memory of Henry Lambert's end aroused in her no
feelings of guilt, or even of remorse; she could tell the tale without emotion; what she felt was a weary despair, an immense
fatigue in the face of her own future: a deepening and embitter-
ing of the mood which in her girlhood she had called "the Hollows." Even as she finished speaking she asked herself what good
she had done, what help she could possibly expect from this repu-
tationless stranger. She wished she had kept silence, and that he
would go.

Mr. Lauderdale, on the contrary, showed no misgivings whatever. His advice was prompt, brief, and to the point. He said:—

"Tell the old bitch to go to hell."

Adelaide gasped. Her hand fell, she stared across the table with
incredulous eyes.

"I beg your pardon," added Mr. Lauderdale. "But it's really the
only sensible thing to do. Why not?"

"Because . . . because she would go to the police."

"Let her. They'd never take her word against yours."

Adelaide gasped again.

"I told you it was a friend!"

"Of course," agreed Mr. Lauderdale. "When a woman asks advice for a friend who's being blackmailed, she is invariably speaking for herself; I let you go on because I thought it made it easier
for you. I presume the blackmailer is that peculiarly horrible old

party we saw in the Mews?" Adelaide nodded dumbly. "What you don't realize is that blackmail is a criminal offence. She'd never dare go to the police. She's simply foxed you. And moreover, whatever she'd said at the inquest, I believe the verdict would have been the same, because it was the true one."

Adelaide leaned back in her chair, weak with relief. She believed him implicitly: not only his words, but his whole tone—the tone of a man laying down the law—commanded her trust. He knew what he was talking about. Because she had not quite recovered herself, she began to laugh.

"To think that all these years—two years!—I've been paying her hush-money!"

"How much?"

"Ten shillings a week."

"All that!" (It surprised her, and she laughed again, to see that he took the same view of this sum as the Sow.) "You must never pay her another farthing. If she comes here, turn her out. Simply have nothing whatever to say to her."

Adelaide stopped laughing. At the realization that she was not yet free, but had still to free herself, her courage ebbed. However strong her legal position, it was not so strong as the habit of fear. She said weakly:—

"I—I don't know if I can . . ."

"Nonsense. It shouldn't take five minutes."

"You don't know her. She's evil. And it wasn't only what she could tell: she said that if I went home she'd follow me. That was the real hold . . ." Adelaide shuddered. "She's like a—a nightmare. Always there, even if you don't see her. Every one in the Mews is afraid of her. I've never given way, I've even ordered her about; but I'm still afraid. I'm afraid of her, and that's the truth."

Mr. Lauderdale glanced at Adelaide's face, and glanced away again. A moment passed before he said abruptly:—

"Would it help if I were here when you saw this woman?"

"Yes," said Adelaide at once. The offer did not even surprise her; from the beginning of their consultation—for that was what

(163)

it was—she had been unconsciously demanding his masculine support. "You're so very kind, I don't know how to thank you. Could you come to-morrow?"

"I'll be round in the morning."

With an easy and businesslike air he rose to take his leave. It was now nearly midnight, and as they moved towards the door Adelaide was struck by a sudden thought.

"Mr. Lauderdale, where are you going?"

He had to think.

"I'm a bit late for the doss-houses, but there's a very sheltered seat by Blackfriars Bridge to which I have practically a squatter's right."

"Do you mean you have nowhere . . . permanent . . . to sleep?"

"Not at the moment. I find landladies so narrow-minded about money. Very few rate a Shakespearian soliloquy at a bob a night."

Adelaide reflected a moment, and then said calmly:—

"If you like, you can sleep here."

5

HE SLEPT in the living-room. Through the thin wall Adelaide heard him moving quietly about, using the sink again, shifting a chair. He wasn't nearly so noisy as Henry, but the sounds had a certain naturalness, and Adelaide noted them with complete coolness. The enormity (by Kensington standards) of the situation did not trouble her in the least; her thoughts were all fixed on the prospect before her—the blessed prospect of release at last. Indeed, she had offered Mr. Lauderdale hospitality not so much out of gratitude or liking, as because she wanted to make sure of him. Once out of sight, what hazard might not befall the man? Hazard evidently ruled his life: a chance had brought him to her door, another chance—accident, drunkenness, or even jail—might well prevent his return; Adelaide heard with great satisfaction Mr. Lauderdale take off his boots.

She liked him too, of course; and strangely enough, having regard to all the circumstances of their acquaintance, trusted him. She felt she could trust Gilbert Lauderdale to behave like a gentleman; and did not even wedge a chair against the door of her room.

CHAPTER IV

THE SCENE PRODUCED by the dismissal of Mrs. Mounsey was more horrible than Adelaide ever contemplated.

It began quietly enough. The Sow panted up the steps, punctual as usual, on Monday morning; knocked as Adelaide had taught her to do, and confidently entered. At the sight of Mr. Lauderdale she paused, her small eyes moving quickly from him to Adelaide; if she were surprised she did not show it; but Adelaide, who by this time was able to follow the processes of the Sow's mind with great accuracy, saw her examining the possibilities of this new development. She could have sworn that the idea of fresh blackmail for a moment entered Mrs. Mounsey's mind; she saw the idea dismissed and give place to a neutral wariness.

The Sow wasn't looking for trouble.

" 'Mornin', dearie," she said affably. "If you got company, I won't keep you."

"You'll stay a moment, because I have something to say to you," stated Adelaide. "You've come for ten shillings—"

The Sow shot a warning glance in the direction of Mr. Lauderdale.

"Want 'im to 'ear?" she murmured.

"Certainly."

"Then I don't. 'E's a stranger to me, and I don't do business afore strangers." Mrs. Mounsey's tone hardened; she had evidently decided to change her tactics. "What's 'e doin' 'ere, anyway? 'Oo is 'e?"

"He's a witness," said Adelaide deliberately, "to the fact that I am no longer going to pay you ten shillings a week."

"I am also," cut in Mr. Lauderdale, "a lawyer. I've just been telling Mrs. Lambert that if she likes she can prosecute you."

Under this combined attack the Sow blinked a moment—but only for a moment. Draping her shawl more closely about her, folding her huge arms over her huge bosom, she faced them both with amused contempt.

"A lawyer!" she repeated sardonically—and indeed Mr. Lauderdale's appearance gave ground for the irony. "'E looks like a lawyer, don't 'e? I wonder you've bin so took in."

"Did you understand what I said?" asked Adelaide sharply.

"A narsty little sponger, that's what 'e is. Tryin' to prey on yer innocence. I only 'ope you 'aven't told 'im nothing you didn't ought."

"I've told him everything," said Adelaide.

"Then it's lucky you got me to look arter you," said the Sow, with a return to blandness.

There was an impudence, a speed of manoeuvre about this, for which Adelaide was unprepared. She saw that it was a mistake to admit any sort of discussion whatever, that she should simply have stated her position and ordered the creature out. And Mr. Lauderdale evidently agreed; for he now stood up and, interposing himself between the two women, said roughly:—

"You hear what Mrs. Lambert says. She'll pay you no more money. You don't dare go to the police, and she knows it. There's to be no more talk of following her about. You're being let off lightly: now get out."

The Sow did not budge. She stood there, huge, ponderous, unshiftable, her eyes on Adelaide.

"Very well," said Lauderdale. "Then Mrs. Lambert will prosecute you for the theft of household goods."

Adelaide sometimes wondered why Mrs. Mounsey so objected to

being called a thief. She was a thief, everyone knew it; in Britannia Mews stealing was hardly a misdemeanour; but now as always the word released a flood of angry denial.

"Thievin', indeed! When she give me the stuff 'erself! Everything there was she give me, out o' gratitude for me kindness in 'er trouble! Not a stick I laid 'and to but what she give me 'erself! An' two years gone at that! Two bloody years—"

"If she says you took stuff last week, the police will believe her and not you."

"And if necessary, I shall say so," said Adelaide.

The remnants of Mrs. Mounsey's self-control left her. Her voice rose in a husky shriek, she began to shout abuse, all the grudges of two years' servitude found voice as she called Adelaide by every filthy name she could lay tongue to. It was like the bursting of a sewer: Adelaide instinctively put her hands to her ears, but the horrible voice rose louder, the language grew more and more obscene, hardly recognizable except as foulness. For perhaps a minute the evil flood rose inexhaustibly; then Mr. Lauderdale advanced and with his open hand, but with great force, struck the Sow across the mouth.

She rocked back, spat blood, and launched herself clumsily upon him. Lauderdale stepped easily aside and let her impetus carry her past him. She blundered against the table and stood there panting, her face congested, as though she could not draw enough breath into her vast bosom. She turned and faced him; a curious, rudimentary weaving motion of the head showed that she had once been a practised fighter; now it was the only movement she was capable of. Her enormous weight was no longer a weapon, but a handicap, for that one blind rush had exhausted her. When Lauderdale approached again she did not even turn away.

"Oh, don't!" cried Adelaide instinctively.

"I must," said Lauderdale, white-faced as herself—"it's the only thing she understands"; and he struck again, again with his open hand. The Sow snapped with her toothless gums, and that was all; only the table prevented her from falling. "If you ever speak to Mrs. Lambert again," said Lauderdale, "I'll break every bone in your body. Now get out."

Very slowly, the Sow moved. Helping herself by the table, by a chair, she crossed the short space to the door; pulled it open and dragged herself through; and there on the threshold paused and gave Adelaide a last backward look.

It was, strangely enough, a look of reproach; and in the strangest manner Adelaide felt that somehow she had deserved it. The misery and squalor of all her relations with the Sow infected them to the very end.

Lauderdale shut the door and went to the sink and washed his hands. It was an action Adelaide understood; it did away with the repugnance she had momentarily felt for him. Over his shoulder he said:—

"Go and lie down a little. I'll make you a cup of tea."

2

It was much later in the day, when Adelaide had sufficiently recovered to prepare a meal which they ate together, and when they were drinking coffee afterwards, that Mr. Lauderdale broached the question of the future.

"And now," he said casually, "I suppose you'll go home."

Adelaide did not immediately answer. Like so many people to whom a long-desired wish has been granted, she did not know quite what to do with it. She was free; she could go home; and two years before would have gone home, at once, without considering an alternative. Now she hesitated. Lying on her bed, thinking steadily, she had perceived that for two years, within one great limitation, she had enjoyed the completest independence, filling each hour of the day exactly as she pleased. To return to Farnham meant readapting herself to a daughter's docility, putting her time at other people's disposal, conforming to other people's tastes and opinions instead of following her own. Adelaide had no illusions about this, she saw the Culver point of view too clearly: a daughter come to grief through self-will could return to the bosom of her family only on the condition of surrendering all self-will for the future; having flung one's cap over the windmill, one went bareheaded all one's life. Two years ago, battered and shocked by disaster, such a condition would have been acceptable; but now . . .

"I don't know that I can," said Adelaide slowly.

Mr. Lauderdale, who had been watching her with great attention, nodded.

"Would it mean such a deal of humble-pie?" he asked sympathetically.

"Not exactly. But I've got out of the way of . . . listening to Mamma." Adelaide smiled. "Perhaps I was never very good at it. I shall have to consider."

"You know what that means."

"That I don't really want to go? And yet I have wanted to so badly! I used to picture myself doing the flowers, going calling with Mamma, simply waking up in a pretty room. . . . Now I wonder what we should talk about."

Mr. Lauderdale rose and began in an absent-minded way to examine the objects on the mantelpiece. He picked up the Indian shell and turned it in his hand, running a finger over the blunt spines.

"You would certainly find conversation more restricted."

"It could hardly be that, for here I've talked to no one. But I've a suspicion I should be bored."

"When I was a boy," said Mr. Lauderdale reflectively, "I travelled abroad a great deal with my parents. Then they sent me home to school. I found all the boys there great fools. But it was undoubtedly a healthier life."

Adelaide sighed.

"You'll think me sentimental; but I had planned to go home . . . rejoicing. I don't want to go because I have no alternative."

"Is there no alternative?"

"On an income of two pounds a week? I might get work, I suppose, but I doubt it. I don't imagine anyone would employ me as a governess."

"No, you don't look like a governess. You look like a gentle-woman, of course, but insufficiently distressed. Any really nice family would be afraid of you."

"In fact the only place where I can live, on my income, is Britannia Mews."

At once he said, as he had said the night before:—

"You can't live here alone."

Adelaide reflected.

"I think I could. It's not exactly a pleasant way of life; but I'm used to it. Perhaps that's what I've brought on myself: that I'm no longer fit for ordinary pleasant living."

"There is nothing ordinary about you." Mr. Lauderdale replaced the shell and stood frowning down on her; he added abruptly, "The curse of it is, I'm married already."

Adelaide did not pretend to misunderstand him. Their common history of the last few hours had begun to seem the inevitable con-clusion to their separate but oddly similar histories in the past; the end, for both, of one period, the beginning, for both, of another.

"I'm sorry," said Adelaide, simply. She didn't ask whether he were living with his wife; she knew that he was not.

"That would have been one solution," said Lauderdale seriously. "However, owing to the peculiar circumstances in which we have both somehow landed ourselves, there's another. We can simply join forces. I've the greatest respect and admiration for you. I can't ask you to marry me, but I do ask you to let me live with you, in every sense of the term except the technical one."

There was a considerable silence. Adelaide sat perfectly still, looking not at her suitor but at her hands folded in her lap. The proposition was one which appealed to her strongly, it seemed to offer exactly what she needed—a man's company and protection, without any emotional demand. She liked Mr. Lauderdale, his un-spoken desire to protect her from annoyance was matched by her own impulse to mend his clothes for him; each had benefits to confer on the other, the greatest being simply understanding; but for all that, if there had been anything lover-like in his attitude, if she had glimpsed any of the amorousness of which Henry had so thoroughly sickened her, she would have refused. But there was nothing to alarm. Even his suggestion of marriage—and Adelaide really believed that Lauderdale would have married her if he could—sprang, she felt sure, from a wish to regularize their position. For they had one rather curious trait in common: neither, though forced to inhabit Bohemia, and indeed appreciating certain of its advantages, was a natural Bohemian.

"Why not?" said Adelaide.

Mr. Lauderdale smiled.

"You're more than remarkable, you're unique."

"There's nothing unique, in this neighbourhood," said Adelaide rather dampingly, "about taking a lodger. You can sleep in the coach-house. It's a nuisance that Mrs. Mounsey took the bed, but I'll get another. At any rate, we can try the experiment."

Mr. Lauderdale reflected.

"Speaking as a lodger—I believe I told you that my source of income was addressing envelopes. If I make ten shillings a week I do well."

"Then you can give me five, and I shan't be out of pocket for your food."

"Or I might even find more remunerative employment. Especially if I stop drinking."

Adelaide surveyed him with a perfectly friendly cynicism.

"That I shan't expect. If you drink . . . badly, I shall of course turn you out; but I don't expect you to stop. I've seen too much of it."

"You aren't going to try and reform me?"

"Indeed I'm not. I do think, as I believe you do, that we may get on very well, and be—and be—"

"A comfort to each other."

"A comfort to each other, if you like; but I don't expect miracles."

Adelaide rose and began clearing the table. Lauderdale watched her a moment (standing out of the way, for he was already at home in the small room) with an expression of great thoughtfulness. He said slowly:—

"At the same time, there is something slightly miraculous about it. If I hadn't been thrown out of the Cock—"

Adelaide turned and looked back at him and made a completely incomprehensible remark.

"If Alice hadn't had a cold!" she said bitterly. "How I hate that word 'if'!"

With the tact that was always to be so valuable to them both, Mr. Lauderdale replied that he would be back about six, if that suited her, and went out.

He was so deep in thought that he passed not only the Cock, but five other public-houses as well, without even observing them; and arrived at his place of employment, for the first time that quarter, in a state of complete sobriety.

3

Mr. Lauderdale's place of employment was situated in a large basement, the area of which had been roofed in to form a private office for the proprietor, an elderly and lizard-like Welshman who had seen better days. He thus resembled his helots: they had all seen better days, for all had to be literate; and indeed a mouldering flavour of gentility characterized the whole establishment. On the damp and peeling walls ceremoniously worded notices requested gentlemen not to smoke; gentlemen were also requested not to spit, lay bets, or bring in spirits. No one paid any attention to these injunctions, but if one fell off Mr. Evans punctiliously replaced it. The temperature, even in summer, was cellar-like; gas burned all day, one naked jet above each long table, and gave a special quality to the atmosphere. The tables themselves were rather interesting: each habitué knew his place by a familiar pattern of ink-stains, and some of these stains had been minutely elaborated into likenesses of women, domestic animals, and maps; over all lay the rich patina produced by years of contact between greasy cloth and greasy wood. At one end of the apartment gaped a doorless cupboard containing on its upper shelves a supply of envelopes and wrappers, and in its lower half great jorums of ink—or rather of the inky fluid which Mr. Evans prepared himself every Monday morning: it was compounded of a black powder and water, in very unequal proportions. Directories, reference-books, and special lists were housed in the office and dealt out as occasion required. Gentlemen supplied their own nibs.

Such was Evans's, familiarly known as "the Club"; and in spite of its melancholy appearance, it was a going concern. There was always work on hand for the big shops, whose circular wrappers provided the backbone of the trade; charitable organizations did not disdain Evans's, nor political candidates. Sometimes the lists came complete with addresses, sometimes a blanket order was given to cover a whole district, and the addresses had to be looked up. A tricky but profitable customer was a large firm of second-hand booksellers, who required envelopes of superior quality, and no abbreviations; it was the general opinion that they supplied erotica to the gentry.

Lauderdale ran down the area steps, nodded to Mr. Evans through the office door, and passed into the workroom. Monday was always, from the employees' point of view, a slack day, for they had the upper-class habit of taking a long week end, and to-day only two tables had occupants. Lauderdale nodded again, to Mr. Bly and Mr. Samson, and sat down opposite the inky likeness of a flying pig. He sat some moments, regarding it attentively, until Mr. Bly turned round and thrust over a tattered portion of a directory. At this sign that they were on a Belgravia "blanket" Lauderdale pulled himself together, fetched a stack of wrappers, fitted his nib into the holder, and sat down again. As a rule he was quick and accurate; not to-day. He wrote four addresses, blotted the fifth, laid down his pen, took it up again to add a twist to the pig's tail; he could not re-immerse himself in the familiar atmosphere. Something important had happened to him. Adelaide Lambert had happened to him. It was enough to disturb any man. And strangely enough, what disturbed Mr. Lauderdale most, as he sat there reflecting on their whole encounter, was not the fact that Mrs. Lambert had (though inadvertently) killed her husband, but the fact that she could still flash such bitterness at the thought of an unknown female named Alice, who had once had a cold. . . .

For it was a cardinal point of Mr. Lauderdale's philosophy never to cry over spilt milk; that they inevitably did so, one of the things he most disliked in women; and he had seen, or thought he had seen, in Adelaide such a capacity for cutting her losses as set her apart from her whole sex. Only . . . who the deuce was Alice? Part of that other life, no doubt, which Adelaide had seemed so admirably ready to jettison; Mr. Lauderdale had felt confident that she would jettison it; but if she continued to yearn after it, and particularly if yearning embittered her tongue, he foresaw that the new arrangement wouldn't last long.

Mr. Lauderdale seriously considered not returning to Britannia Mews at all.

It also occurred to him that if he did return, he might not find any one there. That phrase might have marked the beginning of a reaction: the recollection of Alice, bringing no doubt a flood of other memories, might set Adelaide Lambert's thoughts so strongly towards her home that neither the desire for independence, nor the fear of humiliation—nor the prospect of his own companionship —could turn them. Perhaps she was already packing; perhaps already gone. "And yet I'll swear she'd have married me," thought Lauderdale, "as I'd have married her. We both felt the . . . fatality. But she may be subject to other fatalities as well—and then where the deuce am I?"

At this point Mr. Bly, sensing his colleague's idleness, turned again. He was a man about fifty, but so shrivelled as to look much older: nature had provisioned him with a bit of skin and bone, just enough, a dab of hair on top of his head, and two more dabs growing out of his ears. With a monkey-nut and a little wool it was possible to make not so much a caricature of **Mr. Bly**, as a miniature likeness.

"What's your opinion of women?" asked Lauderdale suddenly.

"Pah!" said Mr. Bly.

This however was more an immediate reaction than a considered answer; he thrust his chair back, crossed one leg over the other, and mused. Mr. Samson too turned; there was a Mondayish mood about the place which inclined them all to conversation. One sometimes heard very good talk at the Club, each member having a wide experience, mostly unfortunate, to draw upon.

"In general, or in particular?" enquired Mr. Bly, who was fond of chopping logic.

"Either."

"In general, a soft and charming sex, designed for the pleasure of mankind and consequently the propagation of the race. In particular, hellcats."

"I take issue," said Mr. Samson formally.

"What has chiefly struck me," said Lauderdale, "is their persistence in following their own ends. It's a very remarkable woman who can suddenly, so to speak, change direction."

"If you've met a remarkable woman," said Mr. Samson shrewdly, "steer clear of her. But all women are remarkable in some way, and that is where I take issue with the Chairman. To say 'charmers' or 'hellcats' is over-simplification."

"Then I'll say hellcats," offered Mr. Bly.

"You miss the point. I fear we are not giving our young friend much assistance."

Lauderdale tilted back his chair and considered them. They were both fairly intelligent; both (if their general conversation were any guide) frequenters of women; he himself was fairly intelligent, and a married man; and there they all three sat, discussing women as though women were some unknown fauna of the Antipodes.

"It's their damned conventionality," he said abruptly. "How deep does it go? Can they ever really get rid of it?"

"No," said Mr. Bly.

"Yes," said Mr. Samson, at the same moment. "Conventionality has been bred into 'em, by man, for man's protection; but they can get rid of it, with a man's help—and then God help man."

Mr. Bly spat neatly into the empty grate.

"If I may illustrate from my own experience—I was once a puppet-master. I am probably still the best manipulator of puppets in the three kingdoms. In the summer I travelled with fairs, in the Christmas-party season entertained the coroneted brats of the nobility. I was equally at home in the caravan and the servants' hall. There I observed the two extremes of the basic female character: the pampered female servant, untouched by education, engaged in purely feminine activities; the toil-worn gipsy, equally uneducated, equally restricted to female avocations, a great breeder, but exposed to all the hazards of an inimical world. And what had they in common? A rooted, an intense conventionality. The conventions differed, of course, but that was all. Mrs. Lee as conventionally poisoned a pig as Mary Ann went to church. In dealing with any women whatsoever the mind, as such, may be written off." Having delivered which judgment Mr. Bly added tolerantly, "Just go for a dark 'un with a small waist and a big bust."

Mr. Samson, for once in agreement, nodded.

"And don't be put off by a mole or two on the face, a blemish of that kind, in the big-built sort. It's a good sign." He looked at Lauderdale inquisitively. "Dark or light?" he prompted. "You being so black yourself, I'll wager she's light. . . ."

But Lauderdale let his chair drop forward with a clatter. The conversation had not exactly cleared his mind, but it had produced a sensation which he recognized as important. He felt, in fact, that he shouldn't be discussing Adelaide, even anonymously, with Mr. Samson and Mr. Bly. It was such a feeling as a husband might have about his wife; and Lauderdale knew that whatever the upshot, he would at least go back to Britannia Mews.

"Light as a fairy," he said flippantly, reaching again to his wrappers.

Mr. Samson and Mr. Bly, however, continued the conversation

behind his back; and became so engrossed by it that Mr. Evans, emerging from the office in one of his Welsh humours, cursed them as roundly as if they were being paid by time. Mr. Samson cursed back; Mr. Bly quietly extracted from his tail-pocket a pair of bloaters, and set about grilling them at a gas-jet; the Club was itself again.

About six o'clock Mr. Lauderdale returned to Britannia Mews. Adelaide was still there, she had bought a truckle-bed for him, and prepared him a meal.

CHAPTER V

AND NOW, as Lauderdale had foretold, the Mews showed its more amiable side. In no other society could his domestication with Adelaide have caused so little stir: a state of affairs that in Kensington, in Surbiton, in Farnham, would have led to complete ostracizing raised not an eyebrow in Britannia Mews. There was a certain amount of comment; a certain amount of ribaldry, Adelaide suspected, at the Cock; women looked more curiously at her as she passed; but in general her new situation put her on slightly better terms with her neighbours. It was felt that she had come down off her high horse. As for Lauderdale, the fact that he had given Mrs. Mounsey a beating (which was known almost immediately after the event, since the Blazer had been listening on the steps) won him universal respect.

Between him and Adelaide, relations became increasingly delightful.

They were so peculiarly well suited to each other; as though each, starting out from the same point, had described half the perimeter of a circle to meet at the point opposite, their common upper-middle-class tradition suppled and broadened by experiences the same in kind if differing in detail. Both knew what was implied by "church parade," "tea on the terrace," a "drawing-room" or a "small-and-early"; both knew also the remedy for a black eye, and the price of gin. Nor did Lauderdale, as Henry Lambert had done, despise what he had lost; he shared Adelaide's nostalgia for it. With her, he would have returned if he could. But in the meantime they found considerable satisfaction in applying to the very different life in Britannia Mews the surface conventions of life in Kensington. Gilbert went off to address envelopes as he might have gone off to the City, with *The Times* under his arm; lunched off pease-pudding at a cook-shop (as though at Simpson's), and returned to afternoon tea. They dined at seven—"We don't pretend to be fashionable!" said Adelaide, with only the least touch of mockery.

Inevitably, they returned to the question of marriage, because to get married would have been so natural. They felt so like a husband and wife it was hard to realize that Lauderdale had a wife already.

"At least, I suppose I have," he said one day, with a flash of hope. "Adelaide, can it be possible that I am a widower?"

"It's possible," said Adelaide practically, "but I should think extremely unlikely. Surely some one would have let you know?"

"They wouldn't know where to get hold of me. They'd put a notice in *The Times,* but I haven't been reading *The Times* for years. However, Milly had an excellent constitution; and she can't be much over thirty."

"I think you were very careless not to come to some arrangement," said Adelaide disapprovingly. "There's her point of view as well. *She* may be wondering if she's a widow."

"She may be hoping she's a widow," agreed Gilbert, without resentment. "Still, I don't see what's to be done. There might be some point in letting her know I was dead, but there's none in letting her know I'm alive. I don't think she'd divorce me."

"I'm quite sure she wouldn't," said Adelaide. "No nice woman would."

"Unless of course she wants to marry someone else, too. Even so—

I tell you frankly, Adelaide, I've a possibly fatuous conviction that once Milly got hold of me again, she'd want to hang on. And when I think of all the business of tracking her down—she went to India, good God!—and then getting the lawyers on to it, or perhaps having her refuse to see a lawyer, and then the whole thing beginning all over again—it doesn't seem worth it."

"Which brings us back to where we started," said Adelaide. "Dear me, Gilbert, there seems nothing to be done."

"Of course, if I die you can put a notice in the *Times of India*. Milly'd be certain to see that."

"Assuming that she's still in India."

"Well, she's not in the London directory. My dear, does our situation trouble you very much?"

Adelaide shook her head. Strangely enough, it troubled her hardly at all: her life with Gilbert was so perfectly satisfying she felt married to him, even if she were not. What, after all, made a marriage? Community of interest, complete mutual trust, the accepting of both as permanent; by these high standards she and Gilbert were as thoroughly married as any couple in England. In her relation to him, for the first time in her life, she had pierced below appearances to reality. She said thoughtfully:—

"No, Gilbert, it doesn't trouble me. That is, I'm not in the least unhappy about it. I don't feel guilty. Do you?"

"Not in the least. However, at the end of seven years, Milly and I could presume each other dead. I wonder if she knows?"

Adelaide smiled.

"You may be quite certain of this, my dear—if she needs to know, some one will tell her."

So the question of their marriage was shelved, with, on Adelaide's part at least, a rather remarkable large-mindedness. In a peculiar way she felt it less important to be married to Gilbert, because she had been married already, to Henry; she was a married woman. The ring on her finger, legitimately placed there, gave her a feeling of respectability. Adelaide was quite struck by the fact that the initials engraved inside, A. L., corresponded so neatly, so providentially, with her new status; it looked almost as though Providence shared her point of view.

2

IN TIME, Adelaide came to know quite a lot about Milly, and even to feel that she understood her rather better than did Lauderdale.

"I married so young," he once said, "I didn't know what I was doing. It sounds absurd when a man says that, but it can quite well happen. Milly was pretty and well-bred, and had a good deal of money, and when she said she'd marry me I couldn't believe my luck."

"I'm surprised that her family let her," said Adelaide.

"She was twenty-five, and her own mistress. Her people were Army, mine were Church; they couldn't make me out an adventurer. And if a girl makes up her mind to marry any one, she'll do it."

Who should know this better than Adelaide? Out of her own memories she said, almost anxiously:—

"But you were in love with her, Gilbert?"

"Of course I was. My dear, what a generous nature you have!"

"Then why weren't you happy?"

"I found I didn't like her," said Gilbert simply. "She had a mean and petty mind. She disliked everything she didn't understand, and she understood practically nothing. We got along for two years, and then she did something I couldn't stomach. Do you want to know what it was?"

"If you want to tell me."

"I want to justify myself to you. Milly was a great snob; we used to give pretentious dinner-parties. At one of them, as a great feather, she got a Dowager Countess of Thingmajig. The old girl started talking about burglaries, said she'd had a diamond star stolen only the previous week. Milly, not to be outdone, said *she'd* lost a diamond ring. So she had; but she'd found it again exactly where she'd put it down, in the bedroom. The Dowager was extremely interested, in fact this was the only topic she did show any interest in, and wanted particulars. Milly, not to look a fool, said she suspected one of the maids. By this time the whole table was listening. Another woman there, who came to the house a lot, asked was it Blandford. That was a maid Milly'd just dismissed, she was always dismissing maids; Milly said, 'I'm afraid so.' She had the ring on her hand all the time. If any one asked me why I left my wife, that's what I'd have to tell them. Does it seem to you an adequate reason?"

Adelaide considered. To some women the ugly little incident would have seemed trivial enough; women did such things, she was aware, more often than men, and thought less of them; she knew, too, to what straits a hostess might be reduced to keep the conversation alive. But her judgment was not deflected.

"It was adequate, because it shows so much else."

"It shows she had an odious nature."

"And that you didn't love her. If you'd loved her, you'd have . . . glossed it over. Why do you look at me like that?"

"Because first you wanted me to be in love with the woman, and now you're pleased that I wasn't."

Adelaide smiled, as though admitting her own lack of logic.

"Did you leave at once?"

"Next day. We hadn't any quarrel. I simply said I had to grind for an examination, and went to dig with a man I knew in the Temple. I said I could work better there. As a matter of fact I'd stopped working. I knew I should never make a success at the Bar, I'd neither the brains nor the industry; I'd a house and a wife already, the things a man works for; there was something fictitious about it all. I began to hang round with the theatrical crowd; I ran into a man I knew who'd gone on the stage and made a success of it, and I didn't see why I shouldn't do the same. I fancied myself in Arthur Cecil parts. One day a fellow offered me a job with a touring company, and I took it. I went and told Milly I was going on the stage." Gilbert looked at Adelaide and laughed. "Then there was a row. At first Milly didn't believe me. When she saw I meant it she said she'd give me six months to come to my senses, and she'd tell everyone I'd gone to Edinburgh. She thought Edinburgh sounded somehow legal and convincing. Oddly enough I did go to Edinburgh; that was where we were stranded. I got a job as scene-shifter. I got a job as conjurer's assistant. I got back on the stage in *Scenes from Shakespeare*. I liked it. I liked the rag-tag and bob-tail I mixed with. They all drank more or less, and so did I. The idea of going back to Milly became simply fantastic. But I went, because I thought she'd better have a look at me. However, she was so glad to recover her property that she received me with open arms. She said very sweetly that she and her father had decided I wasn't cut out for the Law, and I'd better chuck it. They were Army people, as I've said, but there was an uncle in the House, who agreed to take me on as unpaid private secretary. That meant Milly could tell her friends I was going in for politics. My penny-gaff experience came in useful, I used to touch up his speeches for him; I also used to make out his wife's invitation cards. I'd rather address wrappers for Evans. At the end of two months I was back on tour in more *Scenes from Shakespeare*. That was three years ago, and I'll spare you the rest; but I did get a letter from my father-in-law, when a manager had me up for assault and battery and the papers printed my address. He said Milly had gone to her sister-in-law in India, and I was to consider myself dead to her. Like a short-sighted ass I left it at that. And I wouldn't give a tinker's curse, if only it didn't involve you."

As Adelaide listened to all this she sometimes had the extraordinary sense that she was hearing Henry Lambert's side of his and her story. She hadn't behaved as badly as Milly—or rather, she hoped her character was less unamiable; but she could perceive a similarity of outlook. *"That meant Milly could tell her friends I was going in for politics"*—had not she herself desired to force Henry into any occupation that would sound well to the Culvers? Had not she too been governed by the desire to keep up appearances, regardless of what lay beneath them? It seemed to Adelaide that she and Milly had committed the same great fault, of approaching marriage from the outside, accepting the outsider's point of view, preferring, in short, appearance to reality. She would never like the woman, but she could understand her.

3

As a matter of fact Gilbert Lauderdale made Milly a much better husband in India than he had done in England. All Simla knew her sad and interesting story: how she had been married out of the nursery, how her husband, immersed in scientific research, had reverted immediately after the honeymoon to his bachelor habits; how she had gradually perceived herself to be no more than a burden to him and a drag upon his genius; how after long searchings of the soul she had one day met him at luncheon with the words, "Dearest, I am going to India. When you need me, send for me; I shall be waiting." The source of this fable was necessarily Milly herself, but she had not deliberately invented it; it had simply grown, out of a word here, a hint dropped there, an after-the-ball confidence to her sister-in-law, Mrs. Macintyre. Milly's character, which prevented her from telling the flat lie that her husband was dead, also prevented her from holding her tongue; her self-importance demanded a husband of standing; since successful Queen's Counsel had a knack of making their names known even in India, and since the name of Lauderdale was not so known, she retrieved the situation by switching Gilbert from law to science, whose practitioners, however able, as a rule achieve fame only after death. The luncheon-table episode owed a good deal to Mrs. Macintyre, a devotee of amateur theatricals and a very sympathetic nature. This lady was undoubtedly widowed, the late Colonel Macintyre was dead as mutton under a tombstone in Umballa cemetery; and the two sisters-in-law kept house together in a very pleasant aura of mingled irreproachability and broad-mindedness. They were on the Government House list, and their many callers were chiefly male.

It was in connection with one of these, however, a Major Philpot, that Milly Lauderdale had lately begun to reconsider her hitherto entirely agreeable situation; for rumour had it that Mrs. Philpot—

poor Mrs. Philpot, whose health kept her at home—had recently passed away. No one knew where this rumour came from. The Major continued to dance, dine, ride, and picnic with no sign of mourning; but there the rumour was, and it made Milly thoughtful; and at last, at a certain dinner-party, at which Major Philpot had been put next to the Rowland girl, her thoughts took a direction which would have interested Adelaide and Gilbert very much indeed.

Through five courses Mrs. Lauderdale's pale pretty face continued to turn this way and that as she shared her light, expert small-talk between the Woods-and-Forests boy on her left and the Bengal civilian on her right. (All the women were pale—except the Rowland girl, just out from Home; all the men's faces were tanned; the contrast round the table made the Rowland girl think of almonds and raisins. She was only eighteen.) After three years in India, however, Mrs. Lauderdale knew exactly what to say to any dinner partner, from policeman to commissioner; her thoughts were quite free, and already they had leapt ahead, past the tedium of female conversation in the drawing-room, to the moment when the gentlemen joined the ladies and Tom Philpot would find himself close to her chair, which should be close to the long windows, so that a step would take them unobtrusively to the verandah. . . . They were to ride together next morning, but Milly made a poor and preoccupied horsewoman (the Rowland girl could flirt at a canter) and the conversation she had in mind was one which might require to be interrupted; a roomful of people in the background was a positive advantage.

The whole manoeuvre carried through smoothly, and as Mrs. Macintyre sat down to the piano, Milly and Major Philpot slipped out.

Mrs. Macintyre began to sing "Juanita." The enormous Indian stars blazed like lamps. The Major's hand under Milly's elbow tightened. But she sighed.

"Out of sorts, little woman?" asked the Major tenderly.

She shook her head; then smiled whimsically.

"I've food for thought, Tom—and it doesn't agree with me."

"I'll send you some chocolates from Peliti's instead."

"They always agree with me. Tom. . . ."

"Yes, dear?"

"I'm wondering what I should do if Gilbert asks me for a divorce."

Was it imagination, or did his hand under her arm not so much tighten as stiffen? Milly saw his other hand go up and tug at his big moustache. When he spoke again all playfulness had left his voice as he said:—

"What makes you think he may?"

"Just—just the tone of his last letters." (Milly had carefully built up the fiction that she heard from her husband. She often had mail from home.) "I believe as we've been separated so long—if we pretended he'd deserted me—"

"Rubbish!" said the Major firmly. "I can't believe, Milly, that any man you married would be such a cad."

"Perhaps not, dear."

"You must have mistaken him," declared Major Philpot. "Besides—dash it all!—what the deuce does he want a divorce for?"

These last words told Milly all she needed to know. Nor did her adroitness, or indeed her courage, fail her. She drew only one deep breath—and used it for her soft pretty laugh.

"And what should I want a divorce for?" she asked lightly.

"What indeed?" The Major, simple soul, smiled down at her in open relief. "You've all the hearts in Simla to break—and your own safe at home. If you weren't the dearest little woman in the world, I'd say you didn't deserve such luck."

"And if you weren't—the biggest flatterer in India, I shouldn't like you half so much!"

At that moment, pat, came the needed interruption: a burst of clapping as Mrs. Macintyre finished her song. Milly joined in, with a humorous glance at her companion: it was an old joke that she and dear Dora always applauded each other with reciprocal enthusiasm. "Clap hard!" whispered Milly. "Come in and clap!"—and so in the neatest, smoothest way possible made the transition back to their normal relationship.

The rumour of Major Philpot's widowerhood was eventually confirmed by a back number of *The Times*. His new situation did not affect his conduct. If anything he became even more devoted to Mrs. Lauderdale. The Rowland girl married an Assistant.

4

So THE DAYS passed, the months passed, the year ended; for the first time Adelaide received no Christmas card from Alice. But in the following May an encounter took place which threw the latter into a great state of excitement. Alice had been in town to shop, and in particular to buy material for the children's Sunday smocks, and on her return to Surbiton hurried straight to the Cedars without even going home first.

"Mamma! Who on earth do you think I saw in Regent Street? Adelaide!"

"Dear me," observed Mrs. Hambro, more moderately. "Did you speak to her?"

"No," said Alice. "I would have, Mamma, because whatever Addie's done she is my cousin, and I *don't* agree with the way Aunt Bertha's behaved, but she didn't give me a chance. It was so odd! I was going into Liberty's, and Addie was coming out, we met absolutely face to face! Of course I simply stared; and then before I had time to say anything she just *bowed* to me—actually bowed to me, Mamma, as though I were a casual acquaintance, and walked on. I was so astonished I went straight on in and bought three yards of tussore instead of three and a half, and now I believe it's the wrong shade."

"One can always use three yards of tussore, dear. Let me see."

Alice whipped open her parcel, shook out a length of green silk, and draped it expertly over her own bust.

"Too yellowish," she lamented. "Poor Archy will look positively seasick. But Mamma, wasn't it extraordinary, meeting Adelaide like that? She must be living somewhere in London, even if they've left the Mews."

"How did she look?"

"Very well. She was wearing that brown cloth coat with the black braid she had when I had my blue with the blue braid, it must be at least seven years old; but she looked very well. And, Mamma— she looked so happy!"

Mrs. Hambro removed the silk from her daughter's shoulder and examined it carefully. She had never really loved Adelaide, even while allowing her the greatest intimacy with Alice: two cousins, girls, living in the same neighbourhood, were intimate as a matter of course. Now she thoroughly agreed with her son-in-law that the less they saw of each other the better. It was unpleasant to drop such a close relation, but at least Adelaide had made it easy. She had made it inevitable. Alice, sitting there bursting with family affection, showed considerably less wisdom than her cousin.

"My dear," said Mrs. Hambro, rather impatiently, "I hope Adelaide is happy. At least she has had her own way. But she has shown very clearly that she means to have nothing to do with us."

"All the same, I wish I knew her address. . . ."

"If she wants you to know it, she has only to write. But she doesn't even write to her mother."

"Because she feels she's still in disgrace. Mamma, have you ever thought that perhaps they never left Britannia Mews at all?"

"No," said Mrs. Hambro repressively.

"Because she didn't want to see Aunt Bertha, so she pretended she had?"

"Alice, if you don't go, Freddy will be home before you."

"I shall ask him what he thinks."

"He'll think exactly as I do," said Mrs. Hambro.

Perhaps because she knew this to be so probable, Alice on second thoughts did not mention the incident to her husband. But she felt vaguely defrauded; she had to tell someone; and in the end she told Treff.

5

THE GREAT EVENT of the Farnham summer was always Mr. Vaneck's garden-party. The first year the Culvers were invited Alice chanced to be staying with them; the invitation was extended to include her also, and subsequently, owing to Alice's genius for family reunions, became an annual engagement. Mr. Vaneck blandly co-operated by inviting Hambros and Bakers to any number, and if Alice had commanded a motor-car she would have undoubtedly packed all her family in and driven triumphantly to Farnham; as it was, making the journey by train, she regularly produced her mother and father and Freddy. (The twins despised parties, Sybil and Ellen spent a rapturous day with the babies, and even Alice hardly regretted them.) They went first to Platt's End, where the ladies refreshed their toilets, and then walked all together to the scene of the festivities. Alice organized the whole thing.

This year, for the first time, she was struck by a change in Mr. Culver's appearance. It was only momentary, but as she waited with Treff to speak to Mr. Vaneck, she happened to see her uncle step back from the crowd and stand a moment alone. His face had a greyish tinge; he held his left shoulder hunched forward as though to ease a pain in his chest. Alice exclaimed in sympathy.

"Treff! Isn't Uncle Will well?"

Treff however followed her glance without any sign of apprehension.

"It's just the walk up the hill," he said casually. "We came a bit fast for him."

Alice took a step forward, and paused. Even as she watched, Mr. Culver's distress passed; she saw him turn and speak to Mrs. Howard with his normal slow politeness; but she was still uneasy. In the time it took her to raise her parasol a whole train of anxious thought flashed through her mind; and she came to a rapid decision.

"Treff . . . I've seen Adelaide. In London."

He at once looked blank.

"Have you?"

"I mean your only sister," said Alice sharply.

"How was she?"

"She looked very well. I didn't speak to her. And I'm not trying to interfere in your affairs, and I haven't told Aunt Bertha. I'm simply mentioning it because if ever Adelaide has to be sent for, I should try Britannia Mews."

Treff nodded and walked away, leaving Alice to many sad reflections. What a state that family had got into! But Alice could not be sad for long at a garden-party, especially at Mr. Vaneck's garden-party, where there were so many people to talk to, and so many dresses to notice, and so many strawberries to be eaten; and conscious of looking very pretty herself, and of having the prettiest parasol, she whisked into the crowd and gave herself up to enjoyment.

It was one of the best parties Alice remembered. By this time she knew all the Farnham ladies, and year by year gave them the latest news of her children, to which the Farnham ladies listened very amiably, considering such a topic natural and proper to a young matron. Farnham gentlemen appreciated her prettiness, and voluntarily admired her parasol. (It was of white lace, with an enormous white moire bow on top.) Nor were the rest of Alice's party discontented with their fare of strawberries, strolling, and mild conversation; in a beautiful garden, on a fine afternoon, nothing could have been more agreeable; they were sorry to leave, but glad to find a first-class carriage to themselves on their way back.

"What a lovely party it was!" cried Alice, throwing herself into the corner seat. Coming, she had sat bolt upright on one of Freddy's handkerchiefs, to save her muslin; now she could relax. "Didn't you enjoy it, Papa?"

"I did indeed," said Mr. Hambro. "For once I had a talk with my host. He's a nice fellow. I said, 'Look here, sir, for several years I've enjoyed your hospitality, I don't quite know why—'"

"Papa! You didn't!"

"I did, my dear— 'And if ever you're in Surbiton on a Sunday, you'll find a minor affair going on at the Cedars in Elm Road. I've four other children,' I said, 'and two grandchildren, and if you care for that sort of thing we'll be delighted to see you.' I gave him fair warning, you observe, and at the same time delicately pointed out that there might have been six more of us."

"I call that a very honest statement," said Freddy. "How did he take it?"

"With a gentlemanly bow and three words. He looked me in the eye and replied simply . . ."

Mr. Hambro paused, while his daughter bounced with impatience.

"Papa! What did he reply?"

"He said, 'I like Alice.'"

Alice turned quite crimson with pleasure. Freddy Baker looked gratified. Mr. Hambro turned to his wife and smiled indulgently; but he too was sensible of the compliment. There was a prestige about Mr. Vaneck which none of them attempted to deny.

CHAPTER VI

As ALICE HAD guessed, Adelaide and Gilbert were by now permanently settled in Britannia Mews. If from time to time they talked of moving to a more respectable neighbourhood, nothing ever came of it; they had got used to the Mews; and they had also, as Adelaide pointed out, got used to being well off.

"And where else could we be well off, Gilbert, on two pounds ten a week? I've got used to having money to spare; if we moved only a step up, I should have to pinch and scrape. And we live very comfortably here?"

"Very. You're such an admirable cook."

"It is such a pleasure to me to see you enjoy your meals. No, dear, if I can't have three maids, I'll have none."

"I wish I could give you three maids."

"You give me everything I need," said Adelaide.

It was true. His constant thoughtfulness for her had never flagged; he was never ill-humoured, or even casual in his manners; as for his drinking, it was automatically cut down by the fact that he gave Adelaide five shillings a week. Unlike Henry, he refused to become indebted to her; he even brought her small presents—a bunch of flowers, a piece of china from a street stall; his raffish side was catered to at the Club, and outside it he genuinely preferred Adelaide's society to that of the public-house. Never had one man more literally stepped into another's shoes, for Henry Lambert's wardrobe, so fortunately saved from the rapacity of the Sow, was now Gilbert Lauderdale's; but with what a difference he wore it! Adelaide sometimes smiled to think how she had promised not to try to reform him: it was he who had reformed her. Under his influence her character gradually shed its acquired harshness, its acquired brutality: gratitude at being treated like a lady made her once more ladylike, she recovered her old delicacy of thought and speech. They were devoted to each other; and because their relation was not passionate, it was serene. At night and morning they kissed, but their most familiar gesture of affection was a quiet caress, Gilbert's arm about Adelaide's shoulder, or Adelaide's hand slipped through the crook of his elbow, a dozen times a day.

When Adelaide saw Mrs. Mounsey in the Mews, she smiled and nodded to her. The Sow was no longer an object of fear. Indeed she had lost, Adelaide fancied, much of her local power, for Gilbert's unprecedented and successful revolt undermined her prestige. Moreover, many of her victims had disappeared, flitting, shooting the moon, drifting east to the rookeries of Clerkenwell and Bethnal Green; a new class of tenant took their place. In 1892 rents were raised; Adelaide, faced with a demand for two shillings a week more, tartly informed the collector that unless certain amenities were forthcoming as a *quid pro quo,* she was prepared to lead a tenants' strike. Something inspired her to mention the name of Miss Octavia Hill, and there was that in her appearance and manner which did most forcibly remind the collector of certain other young women—ladies sticking their noses in where they had no business to be—whom Miss Hill had apparently trained up with the sole idea of giving trouble to landlords. Apart from this, Britannia Mews was of comparatively modern construction: the fabric was sound, it was worth improving. Workmen came in; plumbing, and even paint, appeared where neither had been before. In a spirit of emulation, the brewers improved the Cock. Britannia Mews was on the up-grade.

These changes did not take place all at once; many of the old inhabitants hung on—and among them, the Blazer and her child. The Blazer, after Mrs. Mounsey, had been Adelaide's chief object of aversion; now Adelaide began to shrug off this enmity, as she shrugged off her taste for gin—as part of the old unhappiness she wished to forget. "We were all unhappy," thought Adelaide, "I, and Henry, and perhaps the Blazer too . . ." For a time this new tolerance lay dormant, but in August an incident occurred which precipitated them both into something like friendship. It also had unexpectedly far-reaching effects upon the status of Gilbert Lauderdale.

2

A VERY FINE MORNING led Gilbert to take the day off: Adelaide went out early to do her shopping (they proposed an excursion to Hampton Court), and as she returned met the Blazer and Iris in the Mews. It was so rarely that one saw the Blazer and her child together that Adelaide instinctively paused: there they stood, the magnificent brazen-headed woman, running now to fat, but still with something monumental, Caryatid-like about her—and the scrap of a child like a frightened white mouse. (What was it Gilbert had said about them? *"Parturiunt montes, nascetur ridiculus mus . . ."*) Moreover, Iris had been smartened up; instead of her usual ragged shawl she wore a woman's jacket—it came almost to her knees—and on her feet a pair of old dancing-shoes not many sizes too large. Adelaide, struck by this phenomenon, and in a very good humour, spoke without thinking and asked where they were bound.

The Blazer looked at her suspiciously. No more than any one else in the Mews was she quite accustomed to Adelaide's new manner. But she was also very full of the importance of the occasion, and replied civilly enough.

"If yer wants to know—she's goin' for a fairy."

"A fairy!" repeated Adelaide in astonishment.

"In Panto'. A bloke come into the Cock—an actor-bloke—told me there's an agent wantin' fairies. Kids as can dance. So I'm takin' Iris."

Adelaide could not fail to be interested by this evidence of maternal care. In the Mews, in the Blazer, it was really remarkable; and seeing Gilbert appear at that moment on their balcony, she impulsively called up to him.

"Gilbert, do listen! Mrs. O'Keefe is taking Iris to be a fairy!"

These words produced an unexpected effect. Adelaide had not only remembered the Blazer's proper name, but as an instinctive tribute to the occasion had given her her courtesy title; the Blazer's whole person surged forward to receive it. She expanded, she beamed—and she returned the compliment.

"Mr. Lambert's bin a pro 'imself, I believe?"

This was the first time that anyone in the Mews had given Gilbert a name; till then he had simply been "the New Bloke." Adelaide met his eye and saw that he was as amused as herself by this regularizing of their position. She said good-humouredly:—

"Yes, Gilbert, perhaps you can help. See which agent they're going to."

With great willingness the Blazer passed over a dirty piece of paper, and Adelaide ran up the steps with it. It appeared that Gilbert knew the name, and could vouch for the man's comparative honesty; but while he gave the Blazer more precise directions Adelaide, re-examining the grotesque figure of the child, began to be concerned. She said softly:—

"Gilbert, is it any use? The child's a perfect fright!"

"Old Fitz won't mind. He's used to rags and tatters."

But now Gilbert too looked at Iris more closely, and his expression became dubious. The child was not merely lost in her hideous and unsuitable attire, she was not, so to speak, visible. There was nothing to notice in her pale face and light eyes; her almost colourless hair—though she had plenty of it, like her mother—fell lankly over her shoulders; she was worse than insignificant, she was positively depressing. Both Adelaide and the Blazer waited anxiously; though the latter had not heard the brief question and answer, she was aware that her child was being judged. She said encouragingly:—

"Go on, Iris, do yer splits or I'll knock yer block off."

At once the child collapsed, one skinny leg extended before, one behind; they stuck out like chicken-bones from a bundle of old clothes; Adelaide caught her breath in pity. With a powerful hand the Blazer hauled her offspring up again, and again waited for Gilbert's judgement.

Like a Solomon he delivered it.

"Mrs. O'Keefe: you must wash her hair."

The Blazer looked injured.

"I 'ave. Leastways, I've combed it. I've combed it meself, till there's not a nit to be seen."

"But you must wash it. She's got a lot of hair; it's her best point. I don't say it will ever equal yours, but it's something."

"Wash it with carbolic soap," put in Adelaide, "and then brush it."

"Wash it several times, and then brush it for an hour," added Gilbert.

The Blazer looked uncertainly from one to the other.

"But we're just goin' off . . ."

"I know these auditions, they last all week," said Gilbert firmly. "And I tell you frankly that if you take the child as she is it's a waste of time. Hair's what they look out for. You wash it—and Mrs. Lambert will give you a pretty ribbon."

The washing of Iris's hair turned out to be a major enterprise. Her mother supplied the soap, but it was Adelaide who, abandoning Hampton Court, went out and bought a new brush and comb, and the operation took place in Number 2's coach-house. Apparently incapable of resistance, Iris was plunged headfirst into a bucket, lathered, scrubbed, rinsed, then lathered, scrubbed, and rinsed all over again. They used four bucketfuls before the water ran clear, and in the last Adelaide put a spoonful of vinegar. Iris was then set in the sun to dry, and to everyone's surprise dried wavy: a strong natural ripple ran from a point level with her ears to the extreme tips of the hair. She also dried tangled. Adelaide produced a second comb, and for an hour she and the Blazer sat on either side of the child patiently combing. (Halfway through the Blazer went for a drink. She brought Adelaide back twopennyworth of gin, which Adelaide gracefully accepted.) Then they brushed, ruthless of Iris's whimpers, till their wrists ached. At the end of two hours Iris had to be helped to her feet; but she staggered up a new child.

The change was amazing. Her hair was still colourless, but it was colourless like moonshine. It stood away from her head in an enormous bush, at once light and sleek, rippled as regularly as watered silk. "Now do your splits!" said Gilbert; as the child collapsed and bowed, her hair flew up in a silver spray, and the Blazer shouted with enthusiasm.

There was some discussion as to how this phenomenal hair should be arranged. The Blazer wanted to cut a fashionable fringe, but at last Adelaide persuaded her to comb it all straight back, with a cherry-coloured ribbon drawn up behind the ears and tied in a bow on top. At this point Adelaide thought to give the child a mirror; and as Iris stared at her image expression flickered for the first time in her pale eyes. It was an expression merely of vanity, but it was at least better than her habitual blankness; and Adelaide, quite worn out, felt she had done a good day's work.

Iris slept that night with her hair in paper bags. The next day her mother led her in triumph to the agency, and in greater triumph returned with the news that Iris had been picked first go off. Her remarkable career, though none of them yet suspected it, had begun.

3

THUS LAUDERDALE became known throughout the Mews as "Mr. Lambert." Newcomers naturally accepted this title without question; Mr. and Mrs. Lambert, leaders of the respectable element, were looked up to by all.

"Do you mind, dear?" asked Adelaide, rather anxiously.

"Not in the least," Lauderdale assured her. "It gives me a certain feeling of security."

"Do you mean—from Milly?"

"From my whole past. I always wanted to make a fresh start with you, my dear."

"It may lead to complications."

"I don't see why. I haven't a bank account, and no one is likely to leave me any money. In fact, it will avoid complications. If we were in America, I could even more accurately call myself Henry Lambert II."

"Not Henry, Gilbert. I won't have that."

"Just as you like. Dear me," said Gilbert, "I'm getting rather deeply into Henry's debt."

He showed no embarrassment about referring to his predecessor, and though Adelaide did not guess it, this was a definite policy on his part; he did not wish the ghost of Henry Lambert to lurk hidden and unmentionable in the depths of her mind. Adelaide was nothing if not plainspoken about him, unlike most women she could not sentimentalize the dead; on the other hand, she did not nag his memory.

"We were both to blame," she said, "and we were both unhappy. I used to think I could never forgive him, but I have; and it's a great relief."

One day she showed Gilbert the collection of puppets. The wicker basket was still there, still under the table, still an inconvenience; Adelaide longed to get rid of it. But Gilbert, as the puppets were lifted out, astonished her by his enthusiasm.

"My dear Adelaide, they're superb!"

"Really?" Adelaide surveyed the creatures with a mixed expression; she had never got over her dislike of them, but if Gilbert considered they had merit, she was perfectly prepared to agree. "I know Henry said they were the best work he ever did: he made them when he was in France. Are they really worth anything?"

"In cash, I don't know how you'd set a price. They must be unique. But they ought to be shown."

Gilbert lifted the Marquise by her slender waist; she dropped amorously against his arm—just as she had done against Henry's. Adelaide sniffed.

"They're supposed to be characters from Molière—but we did Molière at school, and it wasn't anything like *that*."

Gilbert laughed absently.

"It wouldn't be, my dear. But—good Lord!—in a proper puppet theatre, they'd make a sensation. They've got to be shown, and I've got to learn how to handle 'em."

"Gilbert!" Adelaide stared at him in alarm: there was a look in his eye, a look of rapt preoccupation, which she instinctively mistrusted. "Gilbert, for heaven's sake don't *you* begin wasting your time on them!"

"It wouldn't be waste. We'd make money out of it."

"But they're just for children!"

"Not these."

"And there aren't any puppet theatres!"

"Then we'll start one. We could fix one up in the coach-house."

"You're mad," said Adelaide patiently. "If they *were* for children, you might get some engagements at parties, as Old Bert used to, but you say yourself they're not."

"Can Old Bert handle puppets?"

"He has a Punch and Judy."

"That's not the same thing. . . . Who *was* it told me he was a puppet-master?"

"Oh, dear, I don't suppose any one did," cried Adelaide. "They've just started you imagining things. . . ."

"Mr. Bly!" exclaimed Gilbert. "I'll bring him round to-morrow night."

4

ADELAIDE simply could not understand it. The sight of the puppets threw Mr. Bly too into a state of high excitement. He pronounced them priceless, unique, superlative: he and Gilbert squatted by the basket exchanging an antiphon of praise. "If you don't clear them away I can't get dinner," said Adelaide sharply; whereupon the two men carried them all down to the coach-house and stayed there till she had to go and call them up. Mr. Bly returned almost solemnized; a vista, he told Adelaide, was opening before him: at last he had found material worthy of his own surpassing skill (there was no false modesty about Mr. Bly), he had found in Gilbert a worthy heir to his art, he would not go down to the grave (as he had sometimes feared) leaving the world his creditor.

"We're going to start stringing them at once," added Gilbert. "How long will it take, Bly?"

"Weeks," replied Mr. Bly gravely. "Possibly months. And before you are competent to manipulate them—I dare say several years."

Adelaide was glad to hear it. She thought that as a hobby, and kept within bounds, Gilbert's interest in the puppets might even be tolerable. A hobby was a domesticating influence on a man, and though Gilbert had so far shown himself domesticated by nature, one could not have too many safeguards. She said more amiably:—

"I suppose they are very nice. My husband always thought a great deal of them."

"I don't wonder," said Mr. Bly—naturally glancing at Gilbert, and then, as a thought struck him, glancing away again. "What's their provenance?"

"French," said Gilbert. "They were made in Paris."

"One sees the Gallic touch. The wit, the workmanship. And we'll advertise them as French, of course; it'll attract the snobs. *Le Petit Guignol* perhaps; or *Le Guignol de Molière*." Mr. Bly leaned back, replete with steak-and-kidney pudding, and sketched a proscenium-arch in the air. "For the opening, it would be nice to give a little performance at the French Embassy."

Adelaide laughed.

"It's surely too soon to approach the Ambassador yet, Mr. Bly? If you won't be ready for several years?"

"When we are, we'll send you to plead for us," said Mr. Bly courteously, "for such distinction could not fail."

From that moment Adelaide began to like him rather better; and if she sometimes referred to him, to Gilbert, as a "blarneying old rogue," his elaborate compliments continued to amuse and please her. For they were sincere; Mr. Bly on his side developed a deep admiration for Adelaide, setting her in a class by herself as neither charmer nor hellcat, but an experienced woman who could cook. He also admired her appearance, which reminded him, he said, of the Duchess of Connaught's.

Regarding the relation between her and Gilbert, Mr. Bly proved himself a model of tact, simply assuming that they were married to each other, and taking the latter's new nomenclature in his stride. "It's done again and again," he assured Gilbert, "in the best families, when there's no male heir, it's a matter of course. I simply mention it, my dear fellow, in case you mean to retain your professional name at the Club." Gilbert said he might as well, but Mr. Bly did not always remember; however, since several other habitués used more than one name, his lapses drew no comment.

Mr. Bly, in fact, gradually became a good deal confused as to who Gilbert really was. Adelaide's references to her husband, meaning Henry, were often applied by him to Gilbert, producing the hazy impression that they had been married for many years. A separation, perhaps, thought Mr. Bly, also common in the best families, followed by a reuniting . . . happy pair to have discovered their error before it was too late! His shrivelled face lit with benevolence whenever he regarded them; he warmed himself at their domestic glow.

In the first flow of enthusiasm Mr. Bly appeared nearly every night, discreetly bringing his own supper (pease-pudding wrapped in newsprint) and the two men spent hours together in the coach-house, sometimes under Adelaide's eye, sometimes alone; but both she and Gilbert missed their quiet evenings, and soon, on a hint from the latter, Mr. Bly appeared only once a week. Gilbert's progress in his new art was steady rather than rapid; Adelaide, no longer fearing any violent upheaval in the smooth tenor of their life, grew to tolerate the puppets as she had grown to tolerate Mrs. Mounsey and the Blazer. They were a nice hobby for Gilbert; and Mr. Bly slipped into the position of family friend.

Another friend, an older one, reappeared. Old Bert got wind of the new activities, and came sidling back to the coach-house to offer professional advice. Adelaide found Mr. Bly and Gilbert inclined to snub him, and laid herself out to be pleasant to the old man; she was touched by the alacrity with which he met her advances. But he at least had no doubts as to Gilbert's identity; this obviously wasn't the man he'd helped the Crowner sit on; and Adelaide sometimes caught his rheumy eye fixed on her in a very withdrawn and considerate look. She found herself attaching an absurd importance to his judgement, and grew impatient waiting for it; but at last the Old 'Un made up his mind. In the midst of a heated discussion as to whether the Camargo should or should not rise upon her points, Old Bert shuffled deliberately across the floor and applied his lips to Adelaide's ear. "Second time lucky!" snorted Old Bert; and the pronouncement (which threw Mr. Bly into renewed mental confusion) pleased both Adelaide and Gilbert equally.

It was an odd enough circle of which Adelaide was now the centre. Neither Old Bert nor Mr. Bly could by any stretch be called presentable, but they behaved to her with as much courtesy as she had ever received in a Kensington drawing-room; and no woman is displeased to be the sole feminine influence in the lives of three men. It was at this time that Adelaide acquired the habit of imperiousness which later generations were to consider so typically Victorian. She owed it chiefly to those typical Victorians, the Old 'Un and Mr. Bly.

In 1893, a few days after Adelaide's twenty-ninth birthday, Mr. Culver died.

CHAPTER VII

T HE TELEGRAM, signed by Treff, arrived before Gilbert had
left for the Club. Adelaide passed it over to him without speaking.
She was surprised and shocked to find that she felt almost no
emotion: to find that her thoughts at once turned from the fact
of her father's death to the fact that at last her return to Farnham
had been made inevitable.

"I must go at once," she said, after a while.

"Of course, my dear. I wish I could come with you."

"I wish you could. You're always such a strength to me, it seems
hard—" Adelaide broke off, and sighed. "But of course it's impossible."

Gilbert reflected a moment, then came and put his arm gently
round her shoulders.

"Adelaide, why don't you tell your people that Henry is dead,
and that you have married again?"

"Because I haven't married again." Adelaide smiled. "I don't
think you realize, dear, the appetite women have for marriages.
They're like detectives. My mother, my aunt, my cousin Alice—
for of course they'll be there—would want to know every detail
of where and when. I should have to tell more lies than I could
think of. And then about poor Henry . . . Gilbert, you'll think me
a coward: but all that time—I mean at the very end, at the inquest
—is still so dreadful to me, I couldn't bear to be questioned."

"You'll be questioned anyway, my dear."

"But so very little! My mother will ask, 'Is your husband quite
well?' and I shall say, 'Yes, Mamma,' and she'll be only too glad
to let the matter drop. They'll consider he's shown a sense of
decency in not coming. If—if I do get an opportunity, perhaps I'll

tell everything; but I don't think so. They wouldn't understand."
Adelaide considered. "You know, Gilbert, it's very odd: when I
think about the whole thing, and how it's arisen, I believe the only
person who would understand is—Henry."

It was in the black dress she had bought for Henry that Adelaide
went down to Farnham. With his usual care for her comfort Gilbert
took her to Waterloo, and put her into a ladies' first-class compart-
ment, and waited by the door till the train moved out. He had
nothing to say, nor had Adelaide; their silence was even painful,
for each knew how the other suffered at parting—the first time
they had been parted in three years. But Gilbert could not tear
himself away, and Adelaide did not wish him to; only the movement of the train separated their hands.

The other lady in the carriage, observing Adelaide's mourning,
sympathetically enquired whether she would like the window up.
"No, thank you," said Adelaide; and closed her eyes on the thought
that a first-class carriage was a great equalizer: little did the lady
guess that Gilbert had paused en route to pawn his overcoat because
he wished to send Adelaide first-class out of his own pocket. Adelaide looked at her ticket, and hoped the weather would continue
warm.

2

TREFF was waiting for her at Farnham; but even as she
hurried towards him Adelaide's heart dropped. His whole bearing,
the way he stood, was eloquent of nervousness and constraint; his
voice when he spoke to her was without warmth. She saw that he
had come to meet her because he had to, because it was the proper
thing; he occupied the first moments of their reunion by hurrying
her into a cab. Even there he sat speechless, while Adelaide cautiously examined him: at twenty-four he still looked younger than
his years; he had grown rather handsome, in a delicate and fine-
drawn way; and his straight dark hair still fell untidily over his
forehead. . . .

"Well, Treff?"

He turned his head and gave her a formidably reserved look. Adelaide thought, He hasn't forgiven me. He resents even this occasion of our being brought together again. But it's because there was never any affection between us; and why there was no affection, I don't know. It was too late now to bridge that gap; but she felt regret. She said gently:—

"All this must have been very dreadful for you, dear. But if you can tell me just what happened, it will spare Mamma."

Treff averted his head again and looked straight before him.

"He'd been digging in the garden . . . you know about his heart. He wasn't to take any strenuous exercise. Only he'd got awfully keen on gardening. Mother went out to call him, and he said he'd just finish the last strip. When he came up to the house he looked queer, but nothing much. He sat down, and—and just in a moment—before anyone realized—he'd popped off."

Adelaide was silent. The incongruous slanginess of that last phrase did not deceive her: Treff was badly shaken. But she didn't know what to say to him, they were so far apart, like two strangers. They were separated even in their grief, for Adelaide, who had not seen her father for over seven years, and who indeed had never really known him, was painfully aware of not grieving enough. She felt sad and solemnized; but in truth the death of Mr. Culver was hardly a personal loss at all.

After a few moments Treff said formally:—

"And how are you, Adelaide? Getting on all right?"

"Quite, thank you."

"Is—is your husband coming to the funeral?"

"No, dear."

Treff nodded, as though this were what he had expected to hear, and made no further reference to his brother-in-law.

3

THE SIGHT of Platt's End with the blinds down gave Adelaide another shock. She had forgotten about the blinds; in all her dreams of this house, which at one time had been so real to her, she had pictured it cheerful and welcoming, and the blank windows were like a rebuff. A strange maid, red-eyed, opened the door; no one else was in the hall. Adelaide stood like a visitor, waiting to be told what to do. "Show Mrs. Lambert to her room, please," said Treff; and then to Adelaide, "I'll let Mother know you're here." Adelaide followed the maid upstairs into the room at the back, the room with the pretty view—and at once found herself standing before her own dressing-table. She looked round: her wardrobe was there, her bureau; she recognized the new casement-cloth curtains she had machined herself during the last days in Kensington; only they weren't new now, they were slightly faded. Every object, even the arrangement of them, was familiar; only her own face in the glass had changed.

Adelaide took off her hat and scrutinized herself carefully. She was pale, of course, but not haggard; did not, to her own eye at least, look so very much older than the girl reflected in that mirror over seven years before; but the change was there. "I look unsuitably experienced," thought Adelaide dispassionately. She smoothed her brow, but still could not achieve a blank girlishness. "But was I ever girlish?" she wondered. "I don't believe so. I look more like myself to-day than I did then . . . and Gilbert calls me 'distinguished' . . ."

She was still staring at herself when the door opened, and in flew Alice.

"Addie! How glad I am to see you again!"

There was no lack of warmth about Alice. She embraced her cousin and kissed her with the greatest enthusiasm—indeed Adelaide could almost see Alice damp herself down, as she remembered the mournfulness of the occasion and drew away with a graver look. Alice too was in black, and she had been crying, but her vitality was unimpaired.

"I'm very glad you're here," said Adelaide sincerely. "Treff didn't tell me."

"Of course I'm here. So is Mamma. She's with Aunt Bertha. Oh, Adelaide, isn't it dreadful! I do so feel for you!"

"How is Mamma?"

"Well, she's bearing up wonderfully. Just imagine the shock, Addie! Without any warning! Though of course we'd all known for years that Uncle Will wasn't strong. Treff went at once and fetched the doctor and the Vicar, and Mrs. Howard stayed with Aunt Bertha all night, she didn't leave until Mamma and I got here this morning, though of course the doctor gave Aunt Bertha a sleeping-draught. Everything was done, Addie—"

"Even though I wasn't here."

"How could you be?" cried Alice warmly. "It's not as though Uncle had been ill first. Whatever you do, you mustn't reproach yourself."

Adelaide looked at her cousin with affection. How really good Alice was! How quickly she seized on what was most painful in Adelaide's position, and tried to put it right! Now she fell tactfully silent, but she wasn't idle. She did Adelaide's unpacking for her. She went and fetched her a cup of tea—and only then asked her first question.

"Mr. Lambert hasn't come with you, then?"

"No," said Adelaide.

Alice nodded vigorously.

"I must say, dear, I think that's very wise. Freddy hasn't come either." (Adelaide appreciated her cousin's generosity afresh.) "I must say," elaborated Alice, "I think it's so much nicer—I don't mean *nicer*, I mean more suitable—if it's just ourselves."

"Much more suitable."

"It's the first death we've ever had in our family," pursued Alice seriously. "Not counting grandparents, of course. Now if you've finished your tea you shall see Aunt Bertha, unless . . . unless you want to see Uncle Will first."

Adelaide straightened her back.

"Where is he?"

"In the corner bedroom, dear. Shall I come with you?"

"No," said Adelaide.

But with unusual demonstrativeness she kissed Alice's cheek;

and with the warmth of that contact on her lips, walked slowly across the landing.

4

THE ROOM was full of flowers—no wreaths as yet, but bouquets of white phlox and carnations, their scent strong on the air; more garden scents came in through the open windows, round the edges of the blinds; and since these too were white, the room wasn't dark, but only pleasantly shady, a cool place in which to lie.

Adelaide braced herself a moment, then walked steadily to the bed and drew down the sheet. Her father's pale, composed face was in no way terrifying or unfamiliar: as Adelaide gazed on it what struck her most of all was its expression of profound indifference. And even that, she presently realized—for she stood there some time—was an illusion, at most a carelessly-left mark of the soul's passing; for the conviction grew upon her that wherever else her father was, he was not there. He had gone.

Adelaide drew up the sheet again and knelt down at the bedside. The action was purely formal, but she felt it could not be incorrect: Mr. Culver had always been a stickler for the conventions, and though Adelaide could hardly believe, after seeing that face, that he cared for them now, still one never knew. At least her prayer was sincere.

"O Lord, Who knowest the secrets of all our hearts, my father is in Thy safe hands. If I have been hard and undutiful, pardon and soften me. If I am acting a deceitful part"—here Adelaide paused, and after a moment's thought found she could do no better than repeat herself—"Thou knowest the secrets of our hearts. Amen. Amen."

She rose almost cheerfully; for the thought that the Lord knew all about Gilbert and herself, without its having to be explained to Him, was a sudden and a great comfort.

5

THE THREE DAYS which elapsed before the funeral were varied by many visits of condolence. The duty of receiving them fell chiefly upon Adelaide and her aunt: for Mrs. Culver remained in her room, with Treff in constant attendance, and Alice went back to her babies. Adelaide found the exchange of platitudes easy enough, though wearisome; whatever curiosity the ladies of Farnham might feel about her, convention forbade its unleashing; convention also very usefully defined her own rôle as the daughter of a bereaved house. Perhaps she should have spent more time with Mrs. Culver, but the latter showed little desire for her daughter's company: the calls on her self-control were so many that where Adelaide was concerned it broke down, allowing all the old grievances to find outlet. After the first moments of natural emotion they had drawn apart.

"Mamma," said Adelaide gently, on the second morning, "what is Treff going to do?"

"To do?" repeated Mrs. Culver. "What do you mean?"

"What profession is he going to adopt? For I suppose he's down from Cambridge?"

"Of course."

"Did he take a degree?"

"Of course. You've never done Treff justice," said Mrs. Culver, in an irritated voice. "He's an extremely clever boy. And what is more exceptional, he's thoroughly unselfish. With Treff, his mother has always come first."

Ignoring the hit at herself, Adelaide reverted to her original question.

"But what is he going to do, Mamma? What did Papa expect for him?"

"Your poor father had no time to expect anything. If he'd lived, of course," added Mrs. Culver illogically, "Treff would have gone into the family business. That I do know. But now as things are so altered, and I must say Mr. Blore hasn't at all come forward in the way one would expect, Treff has decided against it. And I thoroughly agree with him."

Adelaide saw no reason to oppose this opinion, and waited with all the more impatience for the arrival of Mr. Hambro. He was, she knew, her father's executor; neither Mrs. Culver nor Treff had said anything to her about their financial position; Adelaide had no expectations for herself, but did not see why she should be kept in ignorance. Soon after her uncle arrived she tackled him alone, and he gave her a very plain statement of the situation.

"Everything goes to your mother, and if she buys an annuity she'll get about three hundred a year. This house is freehold, and she could of course sell it, but I hope she won't. In Farnham, on three hundred, she'll do very well."

Adelaide nodded. Then she said baldly:—

"Uncle Ham, what's going to happen to Treff?"

At once his expression changed. It became extraordinarily bored.

"My dear girl, I don't know. He's very thoroughly educated, so all careers are open to him. He appears to have no inclination towards any."

Adelaide sighed.

"I wish I knew what Papa thought."

"I believe your father was considering the Church."

"Uncle Ham!"

"Why not? He'd make a very good pale young curate," said Mr. Hambro cheerfully. "In any case, there's no need for you to feel responsible for him." He considered her pleasantly. "And how are you, my dear? You look to me like a contented woman."

"I am," said Adelaide. She hesitated; her uncle's kind, quizzical face inspired confidence; for the moment she was on the verge of opening her heart to him; but just then another caller arrived, and she had to go.

It was Mr. Vaneck. Adelaide could not have been twenty-four hours in Farnham without hearing his name, and had even felt a slight curiosity about him; but just then he was an interruption, and she received him almost with brusqueness. Mrs. Hambro immediately left them to go to her husband, and for a moment Adelaide could really think of nothing to say. Mr. Vaneck sat opposite her, large, ponderous, very well-groomed, apparently in the same case. Their silence became noticeable. Adelaide racked her brains to remember what she had last said, and unconsciously repeated herself.

"I'm afraid Mamma is not able to see anybody; but she is so grateful for everyone's kindness."

"Your father will be a great loss to the neighbourhood."

Adelaide gave him a quick glance. He too had repeated himself, and this time she realized it. She said frankly:—

"Did I say that before?"

"As a matter of fact, you did. It's very natural."

"I have said it a great many times," admitted Adelaide.

"One does. What else is there to say?"

"Oh, nothing." She reflected. "Yet I think it helps, to let conventions . . . float one over the bad patches."

"We've learned to handle death very competently," agreed Mr. Vaneck. "Dogs, for example, have been known to starve to death on their master's graves."

It took Adelaide a few minutes to recollect why her mother's seclusion in a comfortable bedroom was really the more admirable behaviour.

"Dogs don't know about the immortality of the soul."

"Ah," said Mr. Vaneck, "but you weren't speaking of religion, you were speaking of the conventions. The distinction was as clear in your mind as it is in mine. Now convention tells me that I've stayed long enough, and that's a very good thing, for you might otherwise find it difficult to dismiss me."

He stood up, easily, like a man used to the control of all occasions. Adelaide walked out with him to the hall and opened the door; as the sunlight fell full on her face he added:—

"You don't get enough fresh air."

"I go in the garden."

"You should walk, or ride. Good day," said Mr. Vaneck.

6

ON THE MORNING of the funeral Alice and Freddy arrived early from Surbiton, bringing the Baker flowers with them. The hall was already full of such tributes, which Alice immediately set about reviewing.

"Seventeen," she counted approvingly. "If you don't mind, Addie,

(209)

I think we should make sure all the cards are quite firm, because they do so tend to come off."

Adelaide plunged her fingers into a great circle of arums, and felt for the pasteboard.

"This one's all right."

"It would be," said Alice, "it's Mr. Vaneck's. Mrs. Blake's is hanging by a thread."

They went methodically from wreath to wreath, tightening and re-knotting; Adelaide observed that the Hambros had sent roses, the Bakers lilies, the little Bakers—Alice always did this sort of thing beautifully—a simple bunch of garden flowers. Her own card, on a sheaf of iris, bore her own name alone, for on this minor point her conscience had suddenly pricked her.

"I like the Howards'," remarked Alice.

It was like working in a hot-house: the strong scents gave Adelaide a headache. And she was haunted by a memory she could not quite recapture—something that had happened a long time ago, her cousin there too, sharing the same sort of task. . . . She said suddenly:—

"Alice, do you remember once, in Kensington, sorting out Treff's toys? And tying cards on them?"

"Oh, Addie!"

For the first time since her home-coming, Adelaide burst into tears. She wept and wept, with Alice's arms around her; she wept uncontrollably, and not for her father; but because time passed, and young girls grew older, and because days gone by would come no more.

CHAPTER VIII

ALTHOUGH, AS SHE told Gilbert, Adelaide had not expected her family to show much curiosity about her, the indifference she actually met was so complete as to be startling. The change from London to Farnham had no doubt much to do with it, and the mere passage of time; in seven years Mrs. Culver had gathered a new set of interests, a new series of memories, in which her daughter played no part, and Adelaide was a stranger at Platt's End as she could never have been a stranger in Kensington or Bayswater. She saw, moreover, that in a way her return had been a relief, as showing that she was still presentable, and not in want; nothing need be done about her; but neither her mother nor Treff wished to probe this appearance, in case what lay beneath it should be less reassuring. All their future plans excluded her; it was only by chance she learned what those plans were.

Walking in the garden, the day after the funeral, Adelaide saw Treff at the bow-window of the drawing-room, and to make conversation, as she might have done with an acquaintance, began to praise Platt's End.

"What a pretty house this is, Treff! So beautifully sunny!"

Treff looked pleased.

"That's what everyone says. And it's a convenient size. It ought to be quite easy to sell."

"To sell?" Adelaide looked at him in astonishment. "Does Mamma mean to sell it?"

"If we go abroad."

"I didn't know you thought of going abroad!" Adelaide hesitated. "Have you talked to Uncle Ham about it? I dare say Mamma needs a change—"

"I'm taking her to Brighton for a week the day after to-morrow. But we shall probably decide to live in Florence. Italy's cheaper than England, and more agreeable."

Treff said all this rather rapidly, as though admitting Adelaide's right to the information, but no more. He was obviously not admitting any discussion. As he saw Adelaide about to speak again he added pointedly:—

"I'm perfectly capable of looking after Mamma's affairs, and as a matter of fact, Florence was her own idea."

Adelaide very much doubted it. Mrs. Culver's liking for Platt's End was incontestable, she had thoroughly settled herself there, and she was fifty-two. Her devotion to Treff, also incontestable, might well persuade her to Italy—or to the North Pole—but how would she bear the transplanting to alien soil? Though Florence was known to be full of English tea-shops, one could not spend one's life drinking tea. . . .

With a disturbed face Adelaide went into the house and up to her mother's room. She did not for a moment imagine that her advice would be welcome, but the Hambros had gone, and there was no one else except herself qualified to speak on the matter. Adelaide wondered whether the Hambros knew any more than she did, and decided they did not; the mere rumour of such an upheaval (the first members of the family to settle abroad) would have found Alice on the spot.

Adelaide tapped, and went in. Mrs. Culver was seated before her bureau, going through the drawers; she often did this, it was a favourite occupation with her, but for a moment Adelaide saw it as the first step in the dismantling of Platt's End. She said impulsively, "Mamma, Treff tells me you're thinking of selling this house and going to live in Italy!"

Mrs. Culver turned, her face at once setting in obstinate, almost angry lines.

"Have you any objection?"

"No, of course not." Adelaide moved a step or two nearer, and tried her best to make her voice affectionate. "Only it would be such a very great change, and I thought you liked Farnham so much— Mamma, all I want to say is, don't agree to anything . . . final just now, while you're still upset. Don't sell the house. I know it's Treff's idea—"

"And a very good one," said Mrs. Culver.

"But you haven't had time to consider it—for I'm sure Papa never thought of living abroad. It's only come up in these last few days. Why, what would you do in Florence?"

"I should make a home for my son."

"And what would Treff do? Really, Mamma, I'm sure it would be the worst thing possible for him, to live there with no occupation, no career—"

"That's just where you're mistaken," interrupted Mrs. Culver. "It's on account of Treff's career that we're going." She paused impressively. "He has decided to become an art-expert."

For a moment Adelaide could not speak. She was too astonished, too indignant, and finally, too much amused. At least he hadn't the effrontery to tell *me* that! she thought. Nor Papa . . . I wonder if he'll tell Uncle Ham? . . . But how clever of Treff to light on so shadowy, so aloof a career! How beautifully it would cover his do-nothing habits! And how well it would sound on his mother's lips! Adelaide had heard enough of art-experts from Henry to form a very low opinion of them.

It also occurred to her, as she stood there reflecting, that the Culver line was taking an unexpected turn. Grandfather Culver had been a prosperous publisher, Grandfather Trefusis a prosperous land-agent; behind them busy generations of the same ilk had carried on the country's trade, filled the country's minor professions, for as long as their records existed. Now she, Adelaide, had married an artist, and Treff was to make art his precarious career. Adelaide contemplated this decadence of a sound commercial line with genuine misgiving. Where had it begun? Not, surely, in the Trefusis strain: look at Aunt Ham and Alice and the twins, all sound as bells, their feet firmly planted on solid middle-class ground, with never an æsthetic idea in their heads; but on the Culver side there was—well, there was Belle Burnett; and in Mr. Culver himself a failure of practical energy, Adelaide suspected, as well as a weak heart, had been responsible for his early retirement. Adelaide began to feel the whole problem too much for her. She said rather wearily, "Very well, Mamma, I hope whatever you decide will turn out satisfactorily. Treff also said you were going to Brighton on Thursday; so I shall leave to-morrow."

To her extreme surprise, Mrs. Culver turned on her.

"No doubt you'll do exactly as you please, as you always have done—without consideration for me or anyone else. It's fortunate I have a good son. Treff doesn't go off and leave his mother in her grief!"

Adelaide was taken aback afresh. The Brighton plan had been made without any reference to her, and quite naturally, but no hint had been thrown out that her company would be acceptable; indeed, she was quite sure it would not. However, she made haste to offer it.

"I'll certainly come to Brighton if you wish it, Mamma."

"If I wish it!" repeated Mrs. Culver resentfully. "It's no good saying that now, my dear. When have *you* ever paid any attention to your mother's wishes?"

Adelaide considered. She wanted to answer fairly, as much for her own satisfaction as her mother's.

"For about twenty years I paid every attention to them."

"Because you had to! But you were always—oh, I don't know—critical of me. You were never a proper daughter to me as Alice was to her mother. The whole house was run for you—"

"No," said Adelaide quietly. "The house was run for you and Papa. I dare say that was quite right. And there was a daughter's place in it which I was to fill, whether I fitted it or not."

"I don't understand a word you're saying."

"I mean that I was often extremely unhappy, and you never even noticed it. But there's no use talking, Mamma. Shall I come to Brighton?"

"When Treff has made all the arrangements? Why should you?"

"Because I thought you wanted me."

"I want nothing but the love and respect to which I'm entitled," said Mrs. Culver.

She pulled out a box of gloves and began sorting them with quick, angry movements. Adelaide went away.

2

LOOKING BACK afterwards on this period, this interlude, Adelaide saw it marked by a series of dialogues. There had been no family discussion, very little general conversation; she had talked to one person after the other, alone, the impulse coming always from her side—with one exception. Her last conversation was with Mr. Vaneck, and initiated by him.

When she left her mother Adelaide put on her hat and went out for a walk. Except for the short drive to the church, it was the first time she had been outside the garden; she did not know Farnham at all. The high ground beside the castle, however, was a natural objective; Adelaide climbed a slanting path and was walking on without any sense of direction when a broad shadow overtook her own and Mr. Vaneck came up beside her.

"May I join you?"

"Do," said Adelaide.

"I see you are taking my advice."

"Am I? Oh, of course. It's very pretty up here."

"There's a fair view. This avenue"—they were approaching a double row of trees—"is said to have been planted by one of the old bishops."

They entered it. The evening was very fine and still. Below, on the easier slopes, quite a number of strollers were taking the air, but Adelaide and Mr. Vaneck had the summit to themselves. He said abruptly:—

"You know, you're very unexpected."

Adelaide smiled.

"It was kind of you to have a preconceived idea of me."

"Why do you say that?"

"Because you're so obviously the great man of the neighbourhood."

"Am I so insufferably pompous?"

"Oh, no. But you live in the great house, you do all the right things, you're very important. Everybody in Farnham is pleased by your notice. I assure you that *we* were very pleased that you came to the funeral. . . ."

"Do you wonder I call you unexpected?"

"But I mean it!" protested Adelaide. "Isn't it natural, in a place like this, that one should be pleased by the attention of an important neighbour?"

Mr. Vaneck considered her thoughtfully.

"You say 'a place like this' as though it were strange to you."

"So it is. I've never lived in the country."

"In fact, you give me the impression of a visiting anthropologist. You observe. And you're not, as you suggest, observing the beauties of nature."

Adelaide felt a slight alarm. Unlike her mother, unlike Treff, Mr. Vaneck evidently had a taste for probing beneath appearances. Raising her eyes in a glance as girlish as she could make it, she said ingenuously:—

"Mamma always used to scold me for absent-mindedness; she said it made me seem critical and conceited. I'm afraid I've never grown out of it."

He looked at her again, more thoughtfully still. They reached the end of the avenue, where a fallen trunk lay slantwise across the path; to go farther was not impossible, but just difficult enough to halt so desultory a promenade. Both paused, Adelaide gazing at the view (which here was rather inferior) and waiting for Mr. Vaneck to take up the conversation. His interest in her was flattering; though she mocked a little, she could not help being impressed. He was, in his appearance, his manners, his possessions, an impressive man.

(216)

A thought entered her mind, distinct and dispassionate: If I had come here to live, I should probably have married him.

"How long are you staying in Farnham?" asked Mr. Vaneck.

"I go to-morrow."

"So soon! But of course you have other ties."

"Treff will take Mamma to Brighton. We think she needs the change."

"You yourself, I believe, have come from town?"

Adelaide smiled again. The vision of Mr. Vaneck paying a call in Britannia Mews was diverting.

"I am just going away, too . . ."

Mr. Vaneck bowed. They turned and began to retrace their steps. The air was so pleasant, the evening light so golden, that Adelaide felt reluctant to reach the avenue's end. She wondered what her companion's reaction would be if she were to tell him the plain truth about Henry, about Gilbert; she thought he would take it calmly enough; she thought that his own past might hold just as incongruous matter. And considering herself through Mr. Vaneck's eyes, Adelaide suddenly perceived a circumstance which she usually overlooked: she was not, in fact, married.

In the eyes of the world and the law, she was perfectly free to marry again.

At this moment chance brought them to a gap in one side of the avenue, through which could be seen the roofs and gardens of Bishop's Lodge. It lay not far below them, halfway up the hill: a gentleman's residence, almost a gentleman's seat, complete and handsome in all its parts, from that viewpoint most advantageously displayed. Adelaide could not withhold her admiration; nor could she fail to realize all that the ownership of such a property implied. With Bishop's Lodge went wealth, position, the gratification of taste, the exercise of power—and not the mere appearance of these desirables, but the reality.

"It's a pleasant place," said Mr. Vaneck, nodding towards his house as to a friend. "I'm always glad to get back to it."

"You travel a great deal?"

"No, but I have a fondness for Persia."

Of course, thought Adelaide; there would be that too; and he is probably an authority on some Persian poet. What an interesting man! And then she smiled, for none of this really concerned her. She had lost herself for a minute like a girl day-dreaming over a romantic novel. But it was only a tale, nothing to do with real life. Her real life was with Gilbert, in Britannia Mews; and suddenly wanting him with all her heart, she wanted nothing more.

She began to walk faster; and Mr. Vaneck, falling into step, did not speak again till he bade her good-bye.

3

ADELAIDE left the next day. The parting was decently affectionate, but on both sides felt to be final. Treff promised to let her know the Culver plans, Adelaide approved them in advance; her mother vaguely enquired whether there were any pieces of furniture she wanted from Platt's End, and Adelaide politely refused the offer. In the last few minutes, however, while they waited for the cab, Mrs. Culver said unexpectedly:—

"Adelaide, there's something I want you to do for me." She drew a deep breath. "Your father had a sister, Mrs. Burnett. You never knew her—"

"Yes, I did," said Adelaide. "You took me to call."

Mrs. Culver frowned.

"Did I? Well, I've neither seen nor heard of her since, and I can't say I wish to. But she is Papa's sister, and she should be told." Mrs. Culver paused again. "I didn't write to her, I had too much to think of; there was the notice in *The Times,* I thought if she were in England she'd see it. But now it's on my mind. I want you to go to Chesterfield Street, and if she's still there just tell her, simply and quietly, and explain I'm too ill to see anyone."

Adelaide readily promised, for she was glad to be of use at last; but at the same time, and though Belle Burnett was one of the most fascinating memories of her childhood, the errand now appeared to her as an extension of her duty at Platt's End, something she wished to clear up and be finished with before returning to Gilbert; and for this reason she went straight from Waterloo to Chesterfield Street, on her way home.

CHAPTER IX

MRS. CULVER had thought the number was 5 or 7; Adelaide found herself remembering quite clearly that the windows were to the left of the door, and went unhesitatingly to Number 6. No page, but a parlour-maid, opened to her; Mrs. Burnett still lived there, and to the name "Adelaide Culver" was At Home. Adelaide was shown into the remembered drawing-room; it looked just the same, except that there were more ornaments—more vases, more figurines, more snuff-boxes, more fans: the trophies of a successful and acquisitive career covered every available inch of space, the forget-me-not monkeys on the mantelpiece rose like rocks from a precious shingle of porcelain and ivory and jade and silver. Adelaide instinctively looked round for the cigar-box; and there it was! In the same place, with the same picture glowing from the lid. . . .

On a wave of perfume, with a rustle of silk, Belle Burnett swam into the room; for the first time Adelaide realized that over eighteen years had passed since their last meeting. Mrs. Burnett's hair was still auburn—more than auburn; her cheeks were still bright, but with the brightness of painted china. Only beneath the eyes lay shadows like the bruise on a magnolia petal, the white throat was withered, the pretty hands grown bony. She must be, thought Adelaide, about fifty-five—but her dress was so youthful that she had succeeded in making herself look much older.

"My niece!" exclaimed Mrs. Burnett dramatically. "Great heavens! Have you brought your husband?"

"No," said Adelaide. "I've just come from Farnham—from Mamma's."

Mrs. Burnett brushed Farnham and Mamma aside in a gesture Adelaide remembered.

"But you are married, are you not? And to a penniless artist? My dear, I felt such a sympathy for you! But I never interfere with Culvers, they're too formidable. Who told me? A very fast young woman called Ocock, or Ozanne, who became engaged to a man I'd done a great deal for, and who insisted on being brought to call on me—what the modern girl is coming to," threw in Mrs. Burnett parenthetically, "I really don't know. *No* sense of decorum! And she actually told me your tale, my dear, apparently as evidence that the wickedness of Mayfair was as nothing to the wickedness of Kensington! 'Take her away, George,' I cried, 'and never let me see her again—and if you're imbecile enough to marry her, you shall never see *me* again!' He broke the engagement at once."

So Providence, thought Adelaide, is just after all. She would have liked to dwell on this remarkable circumstance more thoroughly, but her errand weighed on her. She said gently:—

"The reason I have come, Aunt Belle, is to bring bad news. Papa died just a week ago. Mamma wasn't capable of writing, she isn't able to see anyone; so I came to tell you."

There was a long silence—rather like the silence, Adelaide thought, when a canary stops singing. Mrs. Burnett's painted face showed neither grief nor shock; it simply became immobile, so that each pencil-stroke about the eyebrows, each graduation of colour in the cheeks, showed with rather dreadful distinctness; and with sudden insight Adelaide guessed that over a long period of time that had been Mrs. Burnett's automatic defence against the ravages of emotion: tears would have washed her face away. She now put up a tiny lace handkerchief and held it in readiness under her eye-lids; but it remained dry.

"*Mon dieu,*" she said at last. "I won't pretend to be heart-broken. But one doesn't like to hear of people dying. Was it sudden?"

"Very sudden, without any pain. It was his heart."

Belle Burnett shivered.

"But he was older than I am—much older, wasn't he? He must have been quite an old man. And it is all over—the funeral, and so on?"

"All," said Adelaide gently.

"Then we will not talk about it. Thank you for coming, but we will not talk about it." Mrs. Burnett shook her shoulders delicately, as though against the rain of sorrow. "And now let me look at you, my dear, for you've turned out better than I expected. In fact," said Mrs. Burnett frankly, "you're quite distinguished. Heaven knows where you get it from, unless from me. Do you really live in a slum?"

"Oh, yes," said Adelaide. "I like it."

Belle Burnett threw up her hands again, seizing volatility out of the air.

"*C'est incroyable!* Of all my dreadful relations the only one with an appearance tells me she lives in a slum. I suppose that's at least better than living in a suburb."

"Mamma and Treff are going to live in Florence."

"Which is precisely what I mean. Treff is your brother? What does he do?"

"He's going to be an art-expert."

"How ridiculous," said Mrs. Burnett cheerfully. "However, perhaps he'll marry one of those rich American girls who are always hanging round the Pitti. And I, my dear, am leaving England myself. I'm going to Vienna."

To Adelaide's astonishment, Mrs. Burnett actually blushed. The colour swept up from her withered throat to the dyed hair at her temples, making her look almost girlish; confusion rejuvenated her. She laughed and said quickly:—

"Oh, I know I'm a fool, but someone's ill there and wants me. I'm in the middle of packing now, and my maid is such an imbecile —you must really see for yourself!"

In the full flow of spirits again she swept Adelaide across the landing, into a bedroom strewn with luxurious gear. Adelaide

(221)

marvelled at the enormous quantity of hand-made underwear—embroidered chemises, petticoats three frills deep in lace—which Mrs. Burnett apparently considered the necessary equipment for visiting a sick friend. ("I'm still waiting for the *négligées*," she explained, "but it's no use hurrying an artist like Hortense.") On the dressing-table lay a pile of jewel-cases, glove-boxes, sachets of all sorts; parasols, one open, added to the confusion. It seemed plain that the stay in Vienna was to be of some length.

"How long shall you be away?" asked Adelaide.

"My dear, how can I tell? Perhaps for years, perhaps for ever. I've let this house furnished, the lease is up next year, I shall very likely tell my man of business to arrange a sale while I'm not here to be heart-broken by it. Money's very important to me," said Belle Burnett, without rancour. "Is your husband still penniless?"

"Oh, no. We could be described," said Adelaide truthfully, "as very comfortably off."

"I'm glad to hear it." Mrs. Burnett looked at her shrewdly. "You know, in spite of your very distinguished and decorous appearance, I've a feeling that you live, as I do, outside the rules. I wish you'd come to see me sooner. I'd like to give you something to remember me by. You must take a little souvenir!"

At that Adelaide laughed.

"I have one already. Don't you remember giving me an Indian shell? A pink Indian shell, with spikes on it?"

Up flew Mrs. Burnett's hands again.

"*Tiens!* That horrible object! Have you really got it still?"

"It's on my mantelpiece."

"That is absolutely touching. That shows sentiment. Here, take my pearls!"

She swooped upon the dressing-table, seized a red morocco case, opened it, hastily closed it again, opened a slightly smaller box, and thrust a gleaming handful under her niece's nose. The reckless good-nature of the action struck Adelaide with wonder: it was unlike anything she had ever known, it gave her a glimpse into a world where the easy-come, easy-go of Britannia Mews was translated into terms of unimaginable extravagance—a world still nearer to Britannia Mews, however, than to Kensington or Platt's End. But she instinctively protested.

"My dear aunt, I can't possibly take them!"

"Why not?" argued Mrs. Burnett energetically. "You'd take them if I left them to you—and I quite possibly shan't have anything to leave at all. Put the box in your pocket, my dear, sell them if you like, and give my love to your wicked husband!"

As many people had found in the past, there was no withstanding Belle Burnett. When Adelaide left the house, she took the pearls with her.

2

THIS WAS THE LAST Adelaide saw of her blood-relations for many years. She had seen them all—her mother, Treff, the Hambros, Alice, Mrs. Burnett; and with none of them had she discovered any real tie. They had no use for her, nor she for them; and the tacit admission of this fact marked the end of a long period in her life. Henceforward the centre of her life was to be Gilbert alone, without doubts, without backward glances; when four years later Alice broke silence to write announcing the birth of a daughter, Adelaide did not reply. She did not even write to Italy. Such extreme concentration upon one subject might have become dangerous, for Adelaide's devotion and energy were both unlimited; but both presently found full scope, as she herself found a modicum of fame, in the new enterprise with which she was to be associated for the rest of her life. In 1905 a long dream of Gilbert's was at last realized, and the Puppet Theatre was born.

CHAPTER X

BRILLIANT in maturity, the Puppet Theatre was of slow growth. As Mr. Bly had foretold, it took Gilbert many years to become an expert manipulator, and for long periods the puppets were laid aside. But he always returned to them, they exercised a fascination over him: at last he rigged up a booth in the coach-house, and one Christmas-tide the Lamberts entertained their neighbours with a performance. This was in 1901. The French dolls were quite overshadowed by a comic singer and an acrobat constructed by Gilbert and Mr. Bly, which the neighbours found much more to their taste. But the show was altogether a success, and led to several professional engagements among Friendly Societies and at Smoking Concerts. Gilbert and Mr. Bly set to work and completed a whole music-hall troupe; they put their names down at an agency, and presently were able to give up addressing envelopes and devote themselves to this new career. The advent of the gramophone was a great help to them, and in a modest way they flourished. But Gilbert still hankered after a theatre, and when the coach-house next door fell empty, boldly proposed to Adelaide that they should take it and build a permanent stage. Adelaide considered the whole project extremely rash, but Belle Burnett's pearls had been valued at six hundred pounds; she sold them, put four hundred in the bank, and gave Gilbert the rest. (At the same time his bed was moved up to her room; it was the sensible thing to do.)

So the Puppet Theatre was born, in 1905; it might have died soon after, but for the intervention of Iris O'Keefe.

The career of Miss O'Keefe, now at Daly's, had been immensely successful. A genuine talent for dancing, a mediocre voice, a spectacular appearance, and a cold heart carried her to the top of her own particular tree; and unlike many of her rivals, she stayed there. Stage-door Johnnies dogged her footsteps, more serious admirers invested her earnings for her; she lived in St. John's Wood, and the Blazer—but how altered, how chastened a Blazer!—lived with her. Iris was far too wise to discard her parent, she rather went in for being respectable, and an icy will-power cramped the Blazer into corsets, clothed her in subfusc hues, limited her to half a bottle of gin a day, and propped her up as a symbol of decorum in the front window of St. John's Wood. "You must meet my mamma," Iris would say, at the beginning of each new friendship; and each new friend, gazing into Mamma's cowlike, slightly bewildered, but stubborn eye—noting perhaps Mamma's still powerful physique—realized at once that the O'Keefes were not folk to be trifled with. Iris had never married, and did not wish to; but she soon enjoyed, quite apart from her professional earnings, a considerable and steady income.

In one corner of this stony heart, however, there lodged a small plant of gratitude. She never forgot how Mrs. Lambert had washed her hair. From that moment, and rightly, she judged her success to have been born: to Mrs. Lambert's labours with the rinsing-water she owed her first engagement, half a dozen rôles as First Fairy, an adolescent success as Queen of the Moonbeams, and then the steady glories of Daly's. On every picture postcard—and she was photographed by Downey's, twice a month—her extraordinary, abundant ash-blonde tresses flowed in undulant, incredible waves. They were what she was famous for. At some point in the third act of each of her musical comedies, her hair came down. If it hadn't, patrons would have asked for their money back. So she felt she owed Mrs. Lambert much; and every now and then came to pay a visit in the Mews, her brougham waiting outside, her lace petticoats held delicately from contact with the cobbles, indubitably with a sense of going slumming, but nevertheless, as has been said, from a feeling of genuine gratitude. One of these visits occurred just as the workmen were out of the Puppet Theatre, leaving Gilbert slightly at a loss how to proceed next; Miss O'Keefe took the situation in at a glance, promised her patronage, and personally saw to procuring the licence. She was at that moment rehearsing only; her evenings were free; on the opening night the minute auditorium was so packed with her personal friends that patrons from the Mews had to stand at the back.

That first night was undoubtedly Iris OKeefe's. She had a new dress by Worth, and looked partly like a sheaf of white roses and partly like a moonbeam; but the brain behind the roses and moonbeams invented the idea of selling tickets by the set of six; invented, in fact, the idea of the Theatre Club. Moreover one of her followers, an unsuccessful poet, stayed behind to offer ideas for a modern pastoral, and an attaché from the French Embassy asked for a closer view of the figures from Molière. These had been shown only in tableaux; but some time later the attaché returned with an elderly, witty Frenchwoman, a *diseuse,* who had a little idea for a little *divertissement* at the Embassy itself. This took place, again with success, and led to an odd incident.

Adelaide, accompanying Gilbert and the radiant Mr. Bly (his wild, early prophecy come true), was presented with them, after the performance, to His Excellency. She had a new evening gown, the midnight-blue velvet of her dreams; if she had no diamond star, she wore tuberoses at her breast; and the Ambassador, after one split second of surprise, bowed over her hand in the most complimentary way. He praised the puppets, praised the performance, but in a manner which put them, so to speak, outside their personal relation; it was obvious that he couldn't place Mrs. Lambert in the *milieu* of paid entertainers. He asked her if she knew Paris; she replied composedly that she did not—though her aunt, Mrs. Burnett, had lived there for many years.

At once His Excellency's face expressed the most lively interest. He regretted extremely that Mrs. Burnett had left London. Did Mrs. Lambert ever hear from Vienna? No, said Adelaide, her aunt did not write; and then she added sincerely—thinking not of their last meeting but of their first:—

"But I always remember her as the loveliest and kindest person I ever knew."

The old man smiled at her so brightly and fixedly that, if he had been a woman, Adelaide would have thought he was trying to keep back tears. He said nothing more; but several times after, that winter, *Le Guignol de Molière* was seen at the French Embassy; and fashion carried the Puppet Theatre along through two highly successful seasons.

Fashion dropped it again. For the next few years Gilbert was back at the agency, though with enhanced prestige. He found a new opening: the witty Frenchwoman, condescending to a finishing school in Wigmore Street, introduced the French puppets to a whole series of such establishments. Molière was undoubtedly educational —if properly presented; and it was edifying to see how Madame Dulac threw away, before a schoolgirl audience, points so wickedly made at the Embassy. She became a sort of partner, and it was she who introduced Yvette Guilbert, who with the greatest amusement and good humour offered not only her own songs, but her own person, to the puppet world.

The unsuccessful poet also joined them, developing a talent for burlesque and also spending more time than the Lamberts could spare talking about Iris O'Keefe. Adelaide sometimes thought it fortunate that that beauty had so little use for him: her image remained garlanded and intact. This young man, whose name was Amos Jackson, but who wrote under the pseudonym and wished to be known as "Plantagenet Desmond," occupied rather the position that had belonged to Old Bert. (The Old 'Un was long dead; the Lamberts went to his funeral. It was paid for out of the three pounds fifteen found under the current Dog Toby's bed. The Dog Toby had to be destroyed.) Neither Mr. Bly nor Gilbert paid much attention to Plantagenet, but Adelaide had a liking for him. He was simple, trusting, and worked for a firm of insurance agents. Unlike Madame Dulac, he never made disconcerting or improper remarks. "You and your 'usband do not sleep together," Madame had once observed. "Why?" This was in English. The other remarks were in French, and Adelaide could only suspect their impropriety; but her suspicions were very strong.

So the Puppet Theatre, now flourishing in fashion, now modestly paying its way, took root and grew. Between 1914 and 1918 it closed altogether, while Gilbert worked in the Ministry of Pensions and Adelaide sewed at the Red Cross. Plantagenet Desmond went to France, behaved with unexpected heroism, and came back with a row of ribbons to write a rather different kind of poetry under his own name. Madame Dulac died at Verdun—in spirit, if not in flesh. And then, in the 'twenties, a new spirit of gaiety flared over London as the rockets had flared over the trenches, and the Puppet Theatre, along with bottle-parties, night clubs, short hair, short skirts, and the saxophone, again caught the mode.

So did the Mews. By 1922, for the first time in its history, Britannia Mews was a fashionable address.

PART FOUR

CHAPTER I

THERE HAD always been this quality about Britannia Mews, that to step into it from Albion Alley was like stepping into a self-contained and separate small world. Its character might change, its Dark Ages alternate, so to speak, with its Christian Eras, but always it retained this strong individuality. No one who passed under the archway ever had any doubt as to what sort of place he was entering—in 1865, model stables; in 1880, a slum; in 1900, a respectable working-class court. Thus, when an address in a mews came to imply a high degree of fashion, Britannia Mews was unmistakably smart.

To step under the archway, in 1922, was like stepping into a toy village—a very expensive toy from Hamley's or Harrods: with a touch of the Russian Ballet about it, as though at any moment a door might fly open upon Petroushka or the Doll, for the colours of the doors, like the colours of the window-curtains, were unusually bright and varied: green, yellow, orange. Outside them stood tubs of begonias, or little clipped bushes. The five dwarf houses facing west were two-storey, with large downstairs rooms converted from old coach-houses: opposite four stables had been thrown into one to make the Puppet Theatre. The Theatre thus dominated the scene, but with a certain sobriety: its paintwork was a dark olive, the sign above the entrance a straightforward piece of lettering, programmes were displayed in plain oak frames which somehow suggested church notice-boards: it was the village church, completing the toy village, as the Cock, with its new bright signboard, was the village inn.

People often said that the Theatre had made the Mews. This was only partly true: the post-war passion for living in cramped quarters, the Back-to-a-Cottage-in-Mayfair movement, would certainly have found out Britannia Mews sooner or later; the Theatre simply made it more quickly known. No time was lost; the new settlers hurried in, and the cocktail bar in Number 8 (where once the Blazer's Iris shivered on the step) was the first cocktail bar in all London to be installed in an ex-stable. The bottle-parties at Number 6 (once the humble lair of Old Bert) were almost historic. Indeed, the new denizens drank almost as heavily as the old, and had the same taste for gin. (Another minor but curious parallel was that at Number 9 a lady of title unwittingly followed in the footsteps of her predecessor Mrs. Mounsey by selling her own and her friends' cast-off clothes.) Their standard of sexual and financial morality was about the same, but their standard of cleanliness far higher. They put in bathrooms recklessly. They were also better-educated, and generally artistic; no more industrious, but better-tempered, owing to their easier circumstances—for several were wealthy, and the rest ran up bills.

The most damaging criticism of these new-comers was voiced by Iris O'Keefe. In her forties Miss O'Keefe was still a popular favourite: with her customary good sense she had ceased to let down her hair and usually played Queens, Empresses, Czarinas—rôles undemanding but spectacular—in which she wore her own diamonds. Miss O'Keefe surveyed the new inhabitants of Britannia Mews and said that they lacked style.

"It may be the war," said Miss O'Keefe to an old friend of hers, "or it may be this free love, but whatever the cause I cannot admire the result. For what is the result? That men nowadays can hardly distinguish between one woman and another, and I dare say the reverse applies as well. *I* have been called hard, and cold," said Miss O'Keefe reflectively, "and it's true I never lost my head about a man; but I always had style, dear, which was far more to the point. I don't think you ever saw my bedroom?"

The friend said she had not.

"Pale blue brocade. The bed-curtains, all the upholstery; and the sheets and pillows pale blue silk. To show up my hair, you know.

I'm told," said Miss O'Keefe impersonally, "that the effect was quite breath-taking. Let's be frank, dear: I know it was. Poor Charlie used to fall on his knees. But what I mean to say is, in those days there was a glamour and romance about it all; one didn't just push the overcoats off the divan."

2

NUMBER 7 was occupied by Miss Sonia Trent, a young lady of independent means. She had many friends, but only one who lived in Surbiton. This was Dodo, or Dorothy, Baker; and after a party at Sonia's Dodo usually contrived to spend the night in Britannia Mews.

In Miss Trent's sitting-room, at about nine o'clock of an October morning in the year 1922, Dodo awoke.

As she yawned and stretched her right hand encountered parquet, her left sheepskin; for her bed was on the floor. Through the orange curtains enough light filtered to show looming over her head the end of a glass-topped table; and staring up through the glass she saw gin bottles, glasses, ash trays, some one's evening bag, all vaguely distorted like objects seen through water. The air was still heavy with cigarette smoke, and the fainter smell of unfinished drinks.

This, thought Dodo joyfully, is life.

She was twenty-five, but in many ways young for her age, and she lived at Surbiton. Propping herself on her elbow, gazing appreciatively about, she next perceived that she was not alone. Beyond the table, under an overcoat on the divan, slumbered a perfectly strange young man.

This, thought Dodo, is heaven!

She exaggerated a little, however, in her thoughts. The young man was not an absolute stranger, she remembered seeing him come in the night before—very late, and rather intoxicated. But she didn't know his name. She had to all intents and purposes spent the night in the same room with a perfectly strange man.

At this moment the telephone rang. Dodo knelt up and grabbed the receiver, for she knew how Sonia hated to be disturbed, and heard—how incongruous, how unwelcome!—her mother's voice.

"Hello?" said Alice Baker sharply. She was always rather sharp on the telephone, hoping thus to disguise an ineradicable mistrust of the instrument. "Hello, hello, who's that?"

"Hello, darling."

"Is that you, Dodo?"

"Yes, darling."

"I've been expecting you to ring up," complained Alice.

Dodo remembered that she had promised to do so; had promised anything, the night before, when explaining that she was going to stay in town. She said softly:—

"It's only just nine, darling . . ."

"I can't hear you!" shouted Alice.

"I said, it's only just nine."

The young man stirred. Dodo, kneeling up in her cami-knickers, could not repress a giggle. The contrast between the scene at one end of the line—her father had probably just issued, bowler-hatted, from the front door—and the scene at the other was really priceless.

"When are you coming back?" demanded Alice. "It's Saturday, your father will be home to lunch. You can catch the 10:15. . . . What did you say?"

"I said, Don't fuss."

"I'm not fussing." Alice's voice rose a little. "I don't even know where you *are*, Dodo. Where *is* Bayswater 0716?"

"It's in Britannia Mews, darling."

There was so long a silence that Dodo, believing her mother to have rung off, thankfully did so too.

3

At the other end of the line Alice Baker sat in her pleasant, well-dusted morning-room, and for ten minutes never stirred: the name *Britannia Mews,* dropped so insouciantly by her daughter—chucked as a child chucks a pebble into a pool—set such memory-ripples widening that she could only sit and think, and think and sit, with the receiver still in her hand. . . .

She hadn't seen Adelaide for nearly thirty years; not in fact since the day of Mr. Culver's funeral; and though the sadness of that occasion had momentarily drawn them together, Alice never took any step toward a further meeting. A whole complex of emotions prevented her: the break after all had been so complete, and Freddy so stubbornly disapproving, and Adelaide so uncommonly stiff-necked —and moreover, why didn't Adelaide take any further step herself? "She knows where I live," Alice used to argue; "if she wants to, she can come and see me!"—and once or twice, at the sight of a tall woman walking briskly in Oakley Road, had hurried forward, imagining it to be Adelaide. It never was Adelaide; it was generally the new headmistress at the High School, who indeed had so much of Adelaide's imperious bearing that even after she ceased to be new, Alice was sometimes deceived. But it never was Adelaide; nor did a letter ever arrive, or the telephone ring. "She knows where I live," thought Alice stubbornly.

Poor soul! She could ill spare a first cousin. The war, robbing her of both sons, also robbed her, indirectly, of two brothers, for in 1914 the twins insinuated themselves into the A.S.C. as privates, rose to the rank of quartermaster-sergeants, and at the conclusion of hostilities departed to British Columbia. "But I should have thought you'd be so glad to get home!" wailed Alice. The twins looked at each other, said nothing, and went to British Columbia. Milly and Sybil, the two little girls who had sat up in bed to admire Alice's party frocks, both married Yorkshire parsons. (This was not a coincidence, but a natural sequence of events: Milly married first, and had Sybil to stay with her.) Alice saw so little of them that she sometimes complained she might as well have no sisters at all— momentarily forgetting her youngest sister, Ellen, still unmarried, still inhabiting the Cedars, all alone there since the elder Hambros' deaths. As for the Bakers in Somerset, they had formed the habit of staying in Somerset, and not asking one to visit them.

Poor Alice! It was indeed hard on one so devoted to family life that all the rich potentialities of Hambros, Culvers, and Bakers had thus dwindled off; no wonder she sometimes thought longingly of Adelaide. But as Dodo grew up—and grew up virtually an only child—another element entered into the one-sided argument. Alice's love for her pretty daughter became so possessive as to raise bogies where none could be. She saw Adelaide, the flouter of family ties, as a potentially bad influence; and in time, by following this line of thought with resentful persistence, arrived at the conclusion that it was entirely for Dodo's sake that she had given up Adelaide.

"I give up everything for my daughter!" said Alice aloud—and suddenly wondered whether Adelaide had any children. She thought not: and she thought that Adelaide's husband was probably dead, and that Adelaide lived somewhere in a boarding-house, and had grown very bitter and disagreeable. Alice did not exactly hope that this was her cousin's fate; she just felt it was the fate appropriate to all undutiful daughters.

4

Dodo meanwhile had slipped into the rest of her clothes as quietly and swiftly as possible. Her body had its own modesty, partly innate, partly the result of a training too thorough to be quickly cast off: it still disliked the casual bold caresses which in Sonia Trent's circle the sexes almost automatically exchanged; it did not now wish to be observed half in and half out of a suspender-belt. The strange young man, however, never stirred. Above, too, all was quiet; and presently Dodo hesitated at the foot of the tiny stair wondering whether Sonia were yet awake. Probably not. And if she was, she probably wasn't alone, since her lover Robin had been at the party. Dodo savoured this situation to the full. She thought it would be frightfully amusing to make some tea and take it up to them. But in the end she didn't. (She often had these second thoughts, and they often led to arguments with young men in taxis.) Moreover, she was hungry: Sonia's lavish hospitality was largely alcoholic—never taking breakfast herself, she didn't expect anyone else to. After a moment's thought Dodo ran up the narrow stairs and tapped discreetly at the narrow door.

"Sonia!"

Nothing happened. Dodo glanced over her shoulder at the young man below; he was sleeping so soundly, she didn't want to disturb him; on the other hand—and here, oddly enough, it was her mother's careful training that again came into play—one simply couldn't run off without a word to one's hostess. . . . Dodo slightly opened the door and applied her lips to the crack.

"Sonia! Are you awake?"

This produced results. A bed-spring twanged, and Sonia's husky, sleepy voice replied.

"Who the hell's that?"

"It's me, Dodo."

"Good God, are you still here?"

"Well, you said I could stay," Dodo pointed out; and giggled. "As a matter of fact, some one else has stayed too. . . . I don't know who he is."

"Good God!" said Sonia again. "Am I never to have the place to myself?"

Dodo did not consider this rude, but merely frightfully amusing. She said tactfully:—

"As a matter of fact, I'm just going out to get breakfast. Shall I come back?"

"Do whatever you damn well like," said Miss Trent.

Dodo closed the door. She had been conscious throughout of someone besides Sonia on the other side of it; of vague muffled stirrings, not caused by Sonia. Some people no doubt would have been shocked—and in the early days of their friendship Dodo herself had looked askance at Robin's pyjamas in the laundry-basket. "Are you going to marry him?" she asked naïvely. "Hell, no!" yawned Sonia. "But I don't mean to be sexually repressed." Since then, of course, Dodo had learned to fear sexual repression as her mother feared scarlet fever; and to conceal the fact of her own virginity as though it were some sort of preliminary rash.

(237)

She picked up her bag and stepped out. The fresh air tasted delicious; a leaf or two from the lime-tree crunched underfoot, and from the chimney of the Cock a thread of smoke rose against the clear October sky like the smoke from a bonfire. Dodo sniffed appreciatively, just as she had sniffed up the smell of stale gin—and at the same moment observed someone else also taking the morning air. At the door of the Puppet Theatre stood a very tall, very upright old woman with a face like ivory under a crown of white hair.

Dodo instinctively paused. She knew who this person was; everyone who frequented the Mews knew Mrs. Lambert; she was the object at once of their derision and their awe. "Darling," they said, "she's too Victorian and stuffy for words—but the Puppet Theatre *is* an artistic achievement, you can't get away from it, Diaghilev has been there himself!" So they put up with Mrs. Lambert—having really no alternative, for when she complained about noise the landlord always took her side, she'd had poor Drogo actually turned out of Number 10 for giving the tiniest cocaine-party—and told themselves they didn't want to upset the old girl because after all the Theatre *was* an artistic achievement. All this flashed through Dodo's mind as she stood staring across the Mews, and she hastily assumed an expression of supercilious amusement.

Mrs. Lambert glanced back at her. Dodo's expression changed. Mrs. Lambert raised her hand. Dodo at once advanced and stood waiting to be spoken to.

"I wish," said Mrs. Lambert, "to see Miss Trent."

"Well, I'm afraid you can't," said Dodo, speaking as airily as possible.

"Thank you," said Mrs. Lambert.

Dodo at once felt a lout. She added hurriedly:—

"I mean, she isn't up. We were all rather late last night. As a matter of fact, I've only just got up myself."

Mrs. Lambert merely withdrew into the foyer and sat down at the desk before a large account-book. Seen in profile, she was beautiful: the delicate strong lines of brow and nose and chin had the precision of a fine drawing. Her perfectly white hair was pinned with tortoise shell; a net collar, boned to the ears, covered her throat; and these touches of handsomeness looked neither out of date (as they were) nor ridiculous (as Dodo would have expected) but simply appropriate.

Dodo took another step forward. She belonged, and consciously, to a generation that plumed itself on its assurance—a generation unabashed before its elders, because its elders had made such a mess of things. It was a point of dogma that in any encounter with the old, the young always came off best. But there had to *be* an encounter. . . . She said hopefully:—

"I suppose you think we're awful!"

"No, only ill-bred," said Mrs. Lambert.

Her pen moved swiftly down a column of figures, paused, and filled in the total. She turned the page. Dodo hung about a few moments longer, and turned away. She was still within the Mews, however, when a door opened on the Theatre balcony and there stepped forth Gilbert Lambert himself—insubstantial as a puppet, thin as paper in his shepherd's plaid suit, a flower in his buttonhole and a monocle in his eye. At the same moment—she must have had very sharp hearing—Mrs. Lambert called quietly:—

"Yes, dear, what is it?"

"I want you, dear. Will you come up or shall I come down?"

"I'll come up, dear."

Mrs. Lambert emerged from the foyer and mounted the outside stair, her husband waiting above. Dodo saw him hold the door open for her, saw them pass in with some indistinguishable exchange of words—some joke apparently, for they both smiled; then the door closed on them, and Dodo went on through the archway. The incident left her thoughtful, and slightly puzzled, because everyone knew that the Victorians were sexually repressed; and everyone knew what *that* did to you; and it was inconceivable that these established propositions could be shaken by a momentary glimpse of two old people on a balcony. . . .

They must have sublimated it, thought Dodo uneasily—and of course the Theatre *is* an artistic achievement—Diaghilev went there himself. . . .

CHAPTER 11

WALKING SLOWLY from Surbiton station—for she was never anxious to return to her comfortable home—Dodo was overtaken by a young man named Tommy Hitchcock who had been on the same train. He was always on that train, as he was always on the 8:15 in the morning. All his habits were regular, and all good.

"Dodo!" he called. "Have you just come from town? Why didn't I see you?"

Dodo said she hadn't the faintest.

"But didn't you see me?"

"Obviously not," said Dodo.

In spite of her brusqueness they fell into step and walked on with the ease, the indifference, almost, of complete intimacy. They were in fact engaged to each other; and sometimes, particularly when she had just left the company of Sonia Trent, Dodo wondered how on earth this had come about. Tommy on his side was perfectly clear: he had fallen in love with the prettiest girl in Surbiton, and a long wooing confirmed him in the habit. They were to marry in the spring, and he thought it only natural that meanwhile Dodo should want to run up to town and see her friends as much as possible—the implicit corollary being that after marriage, she should stay put.

"Been shopping?" he asked amiably.

"No," said Dodo. "At least, I looked in windows. I'm sorry I didn't see you, old thing, I must have been thinking of something else."

"Darling, I don't expect to occupy every moment of your thoughts," said Tommy cheerfully.

Dodo looked at him.

"And of course I don't occupy every moment of yours . . ."

"Well, hardly, old thing. I should soon be in a nice mess at the office if you did."

"I wonder where Mr. Vaneck is?" said Dodo.

The remark was by no means irrelevant, and they both smiled. For two years earlier the Bakers had been going to Mr. Vaneck's garden-party; even after the Culvers left Farnham, a *carte blanche* invitation continued to arrive every year, and Alice, not unaware of Tommy's interest in her daughter, had suggested that he should accompany them. The day was a Thursday; he regretfully refused. He was then a newly fledged chartered accountant, his firm had a big audit on hand, and to take Thursday off would be the equivalent, he told Dodo, of cutting his professional throat. Dodo looked even prettier than usual, and said she quite understood. But when on Thursday the Bakers reached Surbiton station, there stood Tommy, immaculately attired, a first-class ticket to Farnham in one hand and a spray of orchids in the other. He looked desperate but exalted. All through the afternoon he stuck close to Dodo's side, and Dodo, wearing his orchids, could not help feeling fond of him. They wandered through Mr. Vaneck's beautiful gardens, played to by a string quartet; nothing was lacking to make the occasion romantic—not even peril, for at one terrific moment Tommy actually perceived, strolling towards them, the head of his own firm: Mr. Humphreys too had taken the day off. Tommy seized Dodo by the hand and drew her rapidly away, through a box hedge, past a tennis-court, into a kitchen-garden; and there they hid, eating raspberries off the bushes, till the danger was past. And when he got home, Tommy deliberately threw himself down a flight of stairs, in order to turn up at the office with a convincing bruise. . . .

That was two years ago; Mr. Vaneck had given no more parties, he was said to be abroad; and Tommy committed no more such follies. His calm nature, it seemed, had boiled over once for all; he had succeeded in fixing Dodo's attention; a course of earnest, unremitting devotion did the rest. . . . But how sad it is, thought Dodo (walking beside him, two years later, along the station road), that all that's in the past! Sonia would adore the bit about the raspberries, it was all very sweet and pastoral—but is that all I'm to have, ever, in the way of love and peril and despair?

"I don't know how I had the nerve!" said Tommy, in genuine astonishment.

At the end of the road their ways parted, they separated without difficulty, and Dodo went on home. Her mother was waiting for her in a state of great mental agitation; and no wonder.

"There you are!" cried Alice. "Darling, who ever do you think is coming to stay with us? Your Uncle Treff!"

2

ALICE BAKER was a great believer in coincidences, and a great discoverer of them; but they never failed to excite her. Scarcely had she got over the shock of finding that her daughter was in Britannia Mews (a remarkable coincidence in itself) when a letter arrived from Italy. She was thinking about Adelaide, when she heard from Treff. It was as though one cousin reached out of the past, the other across a continent, to pluck her by the sleeve; a movement of dismay was countered by a movement of pleasure; for Treff confidently announced his intention of coming to pay her a visit.

Alice was delighted. She had never liked the Italian scheme, which defrauded her of two close relations; when Mrs. Culver died Alice didn't know a thing about it till long after the funeral; and Treff was a very bad correspondent, writing solely to draw attention to occasional articles, signed TREFUSIS CULVER, in the *Connoisseur* or the *World of Art*. They were usually about painters Alice had never heard of, but she cut them all out and kept them in her bureau drawer, and referred to her cousin, "the writer." "You don't mean to say he *lives* by writing?" Freddy Baker once asked; and even Alice's loyalty had to admit that it seemed unlikely. How then did Treff live, after Mrs. Culver had departed, and her annuity with her? The truth was that Treff had solved all economic problems by a simple extension of his original plan; he had become a *resident* art-expert, attached to a wealthy American widow whose æsthetic and maternal instincts he equally gratified.

It was hardly to be expected, however, that Dodo, who hated all relations on principle, should share her mother's enthusiasm at the prospect of this visit. She merely said, "Oh," and "When?" and "Won't that be nice for you, darling?" and prepared to mount the stairs.

"Just imagine," cried Alice—almost imploringly—"we haven't seen him for almost thirty years!"

"I've never seen him at all," observed Dodo.

"Then I should have thought you'd be all the more interested. He's one of your closest relations!"

Dodo shrugged indifferently, and went on upstairs.

The relations between mother and daughter were often thus unsatisfactory, and it was hard to tell which of them was to blame. Dodo, arriving belatedly in 1897, when Alice was thirty-four, sometimes felt that her mother might be her grandmother; and Alice, hopelessly trying to share her daughter's life, sometimes felt as though she were imposing herself upon a stranger. Her hungry heart, still mourning for her son Archy and her son Raymond, both killed in the war, longed to receive as well as to give affection; whereas Dodo's grief for her brothers too often merged into what could only be called resentment. They had left her to bear the burden of too much love. Dodo could remember a family circle in which Raymond and Archy, Uncle James and John, Grandpa and Grandma Hambro, all played parts far more important than her own; she ran about amongst them all, petted and spoiled, but as often ignored, unconsciously happy, unconsciously content to take a third share in her mother's affection. Then, suddenly, all was changed; Dodo could not well recollect the sequence of events; but she did remember that on her mother's fifty-fifth birthday there sat down to dinner only her father and herself and her Aunt Ellen.

Alice was rather emotional, at that birthday dinner; and Dodo went to bed with a great feeling of responsibility. She had all a twenty-one-year-old's appetite for self-sacrifice; she was prepared to devote her entire life to her mother. It was her father who suggested her going up to Oxford; Dodo scouted the idea indignantly. A year later she was clamouring to go to an art school. She went to the Slade. There, having no talent, she naturally drifted into the company of the idlers; met Sonia Trent; acquired a taste for cocktail parties, an interest in free love, and a contempt for Surbiton. At twenty-five she was in some ways still childish, in others sophisticated; without direction (in spite of her engagement); and unhappy.

3

ALICE naturally had to carry her news round to the Cedars, and she went that same afternoon, taking Dodo with her. "You know how Aunt Ellen loves to see you!" she said reproachfully, when Dodo hung back; and presently they were following the familiar route along Oakley Road. "We used to come along here every Sunday, with the babies," said Alice reminiscently. "You don't remember, darling . . ." "I wasn't born," said Dodo. But she had a dim recollection of being pushed herself in a go-cart, with her big brothers walking alongside; and then there was Grandma, and Grandpa, and aunts and uncles, and a mug of milk on the grass, and overhead a confusion of grown-up noise. . . .

There was no noise, now, at the Cedars: Aunt Ellen lived there alone. The house was far too big for her, but she refused to move; it was her own property, left to her as the only unmarried daughter, and she was fond of referring to it as "the old home." Alice and Dodo as a matter of course ignored the front-door and walked round to the back, where on any fine day the long drawing-room windows always stood open. Cedars are tidy trees: the stretch of lawn was not melancholy with fallen leaves; Michaelmas daisies filled the borders; but it was very quiet. It was all quiet: when Alice walked through the untenanted drawing-room and called up the stairway, her voice echoed as though in an empty house.

"Are you there, Ellen? Are you coming down?"

"You come up!" called Aunt Ellen.

"What are you doing?"

"Things for the Jumble Sale!"

"Then we'll wait!" shouted Dodo. She was half a Hambro; it was natural for her to call up and down stairs.

"No, come up and help!" shrilled Aunt Ellen.

"Come down!" cried Alice.

For a moment the hall, the house, came to life; then in the pause that followed the grandfather clock struck three, and the big booming strokes when they died away left a deeper silence behind. "I believe that stag's head has moth," said Alice.

Somewhere above a drawer was slammed shut, and Miss Hambro appeared on the landing. She had never been pretty like her sisters, and in middle age was rather ugly, with a tight, sallow skin, a little blotched about the forehead, yellow-grey hair, and pale lashes. She was devoted to Dodo, who did not return her affection.

"We've only popped in for a moment," said Alice, "to tell you we're going to have a visitor. I'll give you three guesses."

"One of the Somerset lot."

"Wrong."

"Then it's Milly."

"Wrong again."

Dodo, fidgeting against the banisters, marvelled at her elders' foolishness. At that age, she thought, at *that* age! They were behaving like a couple of children. She said impatiently:—

"It's Uncle Treff, Aunt. He's coming—"

"Next week," put in Alice quickly. "Just think, my dear, after almost thirty years! You can't have been more than ten—"

"I was eleven and a half—"

"Of course in Kensington we were always in and out—"

"I also remember at Farnham . . ."

Dodo, bored by this highly allusive exchange, strolled back into the drawing-room. She was already impatient to be gone; though the house had none but festive memories for her—of summer teas and Christmas parties—now that she was grown-up she always felt oppressed in it. It was too full of furniture: Miss Hambro, with a single maid, was known to spend three hours each morning dusting. The furniture, in fact, kept *two* maids. . . .

Dodo giggled at the thought and automatically glanced about for a gramophone, remembered that there wasn't one, and began to wander round the room examining the innumerable family photographs which Aunt Ellen persistently collected. They were all, thought Dodo, quite sickening, but she mastered her nausea until she found what she was looking for—the fading likeness of a slim young man with a high collar and a lock of hair a-droop over his forehead. When had she been told that this was her Uncle Treff? Dodo couldn't remember; she knew indeed very little about him beyond the fact that he was her mother's cousin—and so not really an uncle at all. But he lived in Italy. He had left Farnham and gone to live in Florence; which for a Culver was surely very enterprising. Dodo knew little about the Culvers either, but all she heard left a general impression of Victorian stuffiness, from which Uncle Treff had somehow broken loose. He had been a rebel, and a successful one. Dodo began to feel quite an interest in him. Experience had taught her that her mother could be influenced only by members of her own elder generation; however benevolently disposed towards the young—and no one could be kinder than Alice over picnics or amateur dramatics—she never allowed them the possession of common sense. It would not have done the slightest good, for example, to bring Sonia Trent to Surbiton to plead for the London flat on which Dodo's hopes were just then pinned—indeed a sound instinct had led Dodo to keep Sonia away from Surbiton altogether; but if Uncle Treff could be induced to take her part, there might be a chance of success. "Just for six months!" thought Dodo—already rehearsing her arguments. "Just till I get married!" But in her heart of hearts she believed that once she got away she would never come back to Surbiton and never marry Tommy Hitchcock, because someone else, far wealthier and more interesting, would ask her to marry him instead, unless someone else, wealthier still, wanted to make her into a film star. . . .

Most young people have an exaggerated idea of their own importance, it is very useful to them and helps them to push them-selves out a little breathing-space in the world; the curious part about Dodo's conviction that she was too rare for Surbiton was that Surbi-ton had given it to her. Daughters at home were less numerous than they used to be; many of Dodo's contemporaries, and many of the most intelligent among them, went to work, or had been to the university and adopted a profession; as a daughter at home Dodo had the approval of all elders; and as a very pretty girl, with ample leisure to improve her tennis and learn long dramatic parts, she naturally took the lead among the young. She couldn't help but think herself something out of the ordinary. (At the Slade, where her talents had met genuine competition, her looks had not; it was Dodo who posed as Lady Hamilton in the tableau for the Arts Ball.) She was not however particularly vain; but she believed she had personality. She had an idea she could make some sort of mark on the world. Born a generation earlier, she would have been a suffragette; Octavia Hill could have turned her into a rent col-lector; a fervent evangelist might have sent her to missionize among zenanas. But in the ears of Dodo's generation no such calls to faith and work sounded; so they believed in free love and the Ballet Russe.

That Dodo, wishing to share a flat with her raffish and unprin-cipled friend Sonia Trent, was really seeking after faith was some-thing no one—not even Dodo—could guess.

"Hello, Uncle Treff!" said Dodo softly; and with childish super-stition moved his photograph into a better place. Then she grew restless again; in the hall outside her mother and aunt talked on; presently, to her extreme annoyance, she heard them both go up-stairs. "She can't be showing mother the *house!*" thought Dodo in-dignantly; and presently went out into the hall again, and again called out.

"Mother! I'll have to go! I'm playing badminton at the Club!"

There was a whispered conversation on the top landing—"So they *are* going over the house!" thought Dodo. "The old really are incredible!"—and then Alice called back.

"Very well, dear. Don't be late for dinner."

Dodo let herself out of the front door. Walking swiftly down the drive—and here, under the chestnuts, the leaves lay thick—she wondered how any one could bear to live in so melancholy a place.

4

LOOKING back afterwards on the events of that remarkable Saturday, Dodo thought that the surprise sprung on them by Miss Hambro was due partly to the surprise which had been sprung on her by Alice; for she always tried to cap anything her sister said or did. (When the Bakers had vanilla ice at their garden-party, Miss Hambro had pistachio. When Alice had a musquash coat, Ellen had a sealskin.) In this instance she produced a counter-interest so effective that for some days Treff's impending visit was completely forgotten.

Dodo got back rather late for dinner, and slipping into her place was at once aware of something unusual in the wind. Her mother looked almost solemn, though at the same time pleased; there was an odour of cigar smoke about her father; and as they both looked up Dodo perceived that the event, or surprise, or whatever it was, had something to do with herself.

"Did you have a nice game, dear?" asked Alice.

"Yes, thanks."

But the question, like the answer, had been purely automatic, as Alice's next words showed.

"You shouldn't have run off like that, Dodo; it was very rude."

"Good heavens, I don't suppose Aunt Ellen minded!"

Alice glanced at her husband, received a confirmatory nod, and said impressively:—

"As a matter of fact, she has something very important to say to you. You must go round again after dinner."

Dodo gaped.

"Go *round*? Why can't I ring her up?"

"You're to go round," said Freddy Baker sharply.

(248)

Dodo put down her fish-fork and looked stubborn.

"I've just played three sets of badminton, it's the Tennis Club dance, and Tommy's calling for me at nine."

"Tommy had better go with you."

"Then we'll be late. Anyway," persisted Dodo, "it's perfectly obvious that you both know what she wants to see me for, so why can't you tell me? If she's just decided to give us some ghastly piece of silver for a wedding present—"

"Oh, Dodo!" cried Alice reproachfully. "She's going to give you the house!"

Dodo sat back, her mouth and eyes wide open, and stared incredulously. Indeed, at that dreadful moment, she felt incredulity to be her only hope.

"There, darling!" said her mother sympathetically. "Isn't that marvellous? I don't wonder you're surprised—but she really does feel it's too big for her—"

"It's too big for Tommy and me," gasped Dodo.

"It won't always be too big, darling."

"Mother, we can't possibly live at the Cedars. It's out of the question. Tommy couldn't afford it."

"Rubbish. Anyone can afford to live rent free," said Freddy. "It's a freehold house, and a valuable property."

"Well, where would Aunt Ellen live?"

"She'll take a nice little flat," said Alice reassuringly.

Dodo almost laughed aloud at the irony of it. Though astonished and perturbed, she was not yet seriously alarmed. It seemed too impossible that one could be saddled, against one's will, with a thing like a freehold house; and she relied on Tommy to share her point of view. But Tommy, when he arrived and was told of this stupendous wedding present, was extremely pleased. He agreed that the house was large, but he had always looked forward to having a large house in due course, and the Cedars—so substantial, with such a good garden—most adequately filled the bill. "But how in hell's name are we to run it?" wailed Dodo. "That's your job," pointed out Tommy reasonably. "There are dozens of houses that size in Surbiton, and some one runs 'em. I do hate to hear you swear, darling." "If we ever live at the Cedars, you'll hear me swearing all day long," snapped Dodo.

This conversation, so nearly a quarrel, took place at the Club dance, after they had paid a visit to Miss Hambro on the way— Tommy had absolutely insisted on doing so, and quite charmed Dodo's generous aunt by the warmth of his expressions. For once he had definitely taken the lead, forcing Dodo into the distasteful rôle of a child overcome by a Christmas-tree. They were now sitting out, like the engaged couple they were, in a corner of the lounge. Through the archway from the dance-room floated the strains of piano, saxophone, and drums, playing "K-K-K-Katie"; but though it was one of Dodo's favourite tunes, she had refused to dance.

"Tommy," she said suddenly, "why do we *assume* we're going to live in Surbiton? Why shouldn't we live in town? It's where you work—"

But Tommy was looking at her in the blankest amazement.

"*Not live in Surbiton?* My dear girl, it's where every one we know lives—"

"Not everyone I know," put in Dodo.

"And where all our people live, and now your aunt's given us a house we could never afford anywhere else! I never heard such an idiotic suggestion."

"That house," said Dodo distinctly, "is an octopus."

"And I suppose Surbiton's an octopus, and I'm an octopus," said Tommy, with justified annoyance. "You talk the most utter bosh, darling, and even if you don't mean it—"

"I do mean it. At any rate about the house," added Dodo; for she had not the heart to call Tommy an octopus. He looked so puzzled and distressed, like a good dog in unmerited disgrace. With genuine curiosity she said, "I wonder why you want to go on being engaged to me?"

"I suppose because I'm used to it," said Tommy, with a brighter look; and dropping into the current idiom he added cheerfully, "I'm used to you, old thing; I can't think of any other reason, can you? So come and shake a leg . . ."

This time Dodo rose, and they joined the dancers. She was by now very tired: it had been a long and full day, and looking back to its beginning, Dodo was struck with astonishment. Here every face was familiar—every name, even the women's dresses; Dodo knew exactly where they all lived, she could have made a good guess at what they had all had for dinner; and that morning she had woken up in the company of a perfectly strange young man. . . .

Dodo hid a smile against Tommy's shoulder. She hadn't told him, of course; he would have been shocked to the core. She was leading, in fact, a double life. And who would have thought it? Who, judging by her present appearance and circumstances, would take her for anything but a thoroughly nice girl who never slept anywhere but in her own virginal bed? Appearances are the thing, thought Dodo vaguely. So long as you keep up appearances, I believe you can get away with murder. . . .

She was so tired that she stumbled. Tommy looked down at her anxiously.

"Like to stop, old thing?"

"Yes, please," said Dodo meekly. "I think I'd like to go home."

"You've had too much excitement," pronounced Tommy, not displeased. "In London all morning, and then playing badminton—besides having a house given you."

His tone was slightly interrogative; Dodo knew he wanted her to admit having been foolish about the Cedars, so that they could drive home in the affectionate amity proper to an engaged couple. They had come to a halt in the centre of the floor; every one was looking at them; and though all the glances were friendly, Dodo (perhaps fatigue heightened her imagination) thought she could perceive under the friendliness a movement of curiosity. She knew from experience that the evening, in all its least particulars, would be discussed and re-discussed for days afterwards; could guess at the very phrase even then forming, perhaps, behind the smooth, friendly brows—"*And there they stood glaring at each other, darling, in the middle of the floor!*"

Dodo tucked her hand closer against her fiancé's side and smiled up at him.

"I'm an idiot, Tommy . . ."

He responded with touching eagerness, pressing her hand more closely still. Dodo turned towards him, so that they could dance down the length of the room, and let her soft hair touch his chin. Tommy responded again; as the kiss brushed her temple Dodo indeed felt a slight pang of self-reproach. But at least she had killed that obnoxious, imagined phrase—let them repeat as often as they liked, "*And he actually kissed her, darling, in the middle of the floor!*"

CHAPTER III

"YOU'VE JUST come from Florence, sir?" observed Tommy Hitchcock, politely. "Very picturesque, isn't it?"

"Very," said Mr. Culver.

It was a week later; Treff Culver had arrived. Unswathed from the ulster, scarves, comforters, and additional waistcoats in which he had faced the journey, he emerged slight, stooping and dandified. Even his stoop was dandified, suggestive not so much of age—and indeed Treff was only fifty-four, though he appeared much older— as of a life-time spent bowing over ladies' hands; he wore ghosts of side-whiskers, a lock of silvery hair drooped over his forehead. Both Alice and Dodo also received the impression that, though he moved so spryly, he was extremely brittle. Spry, delicate, dandified: Italianate, expatriate—trailing an aura of Pater, Ruskin, and the

Brownings, Treff Culver returned to his native shores; and Alice was giving a little family dinner-party to welcome him.

"The way Italians treat their animals is abominable," observed Aunt Ellen.

"Though I doubt," continued Mr. Culver precisely, and ignoring the interruption, "whether 'picturesque' is an accurate description. To me 'picturesque' suggests a ruined mill and a duck-pond—a page, in fact, from a young lady's sketch-book; Florence is a beautiful and an historic city."

His head as he spoke revolved slowly from left to right, so that he began by addressing Alice and finished up at Dodo, taking in Tommy, Miss Hambro and Mr. Baker on the way. He was evidently used to a small, attentive audience. There was now a slight pause. Tommy, perhaps feeling he had got more than he asked for, fell silent; Freddy Baker was carving a partridge; Dodo, though she kept her eyes fixed on her uncle, appeared to be lost in thought.

"Mrs. Ambrose was in Florence two years ago," said Alice. "She stayed in such a nice guest-house, run entirely by English people—"

Dodo emerged from her dream to interrupt.

"You don't live in a guest-house, do you, Uncle Treff?"

"The Gods forbid, my dear." Mr. Culver turned to Alice. "The architecture of the Palazzo Venezia, which I am sure your friend would detest, is as far removed from the cosiness of a guest-house" —here his eye caught Tommy's—"as the crypt of Saint Paul's from the domestic cupboard-under-the-stairs."

"Platt's End was a nice house," remarked Freddy Baker suddenly. "Alice and I always liked it."

"I loved it," agreed Alice warmly. "And I remember how pleased Aunt Bertha was . . ." She broke off, fearful lest she had introduced an inappropriately mournful note. She looked at her cousin anxiously. But Treff went on eating partridge without a tear. "I remember how proud Aunt Bertha was of her garden," finished Alice.

"She grew bulbs and stuff in Florence."

"Poor soul!" ejaculated Miss Hambro ambiguously.

(253)

"And I remember your lavender hedge." Alice always enjoyed these excursions into the past. "It was a lovely garden altogether; I'm sure I don't know how you could bear to leave it."

"I do," said Dodo, under her breath. No one heard her but Tommy, who glanced at her sharply. He had several times tried to catch her eye, he wanted to share his amusement in this extraordinary old party who had suddenly been sprung on them as a long-lost uncle. Tommy prided himself on being tolerant—"Live and let live" was his oft-declared motto: though he could not help scenting something fishy about an Englishman who chose to live abroad, he was perfectly prepared to treat Mr. Culver with benevolence. But when Dodo did meet his eye she frowned repressively, as though—as though, damn it, he'd been laughing in church. . . . Tommy turned to Miss Hambro, to whom he was in these days extremely attentive, and began to talk eagerly of lawn-mowers.

About an hour later, in the hall, he asked Dodo how long Mr. Culver was expected to stay.

"I don't know," said Dodo vaguely. "As long as he wants to."

"He isn't going to make life any jollier."

"I think he's interesting."

"He's like one of those old music-boxes where you shift a little pointer and out comes a little tune."

Dodo smiled mysteriously—she didn't in the least mind being the only one to understand her uncle—and bade Tommy an affectionate good night. They still enjoyed kissing, though there was no longer any excitement in it; but he walked out of the front door and out of her mind at the same instant.

2

THE PRESENCE of any guest, however welcome, in any family, however loosely united, cannot fail to produce certain minor alterations in that family's habits. Shortly after Treff's arrival Alice surprised her husband by reverting to her long-discarded practice of walking down to the gate with him each morning, and waving to him as he turned the corner. "It's so nice to see you go off," observed

Alice guilelessly. Freddy, rightly referring this remark to the presence of her cousin, merely nodded, and that night brought back a piece of fish. Alice did not quite know what to do with it, she happened to have a rather large salmon in the larder already, but she appreciated his motive. They were always sure of each other's sympathy, however obliquely expressed.

The problem of a man perpetually about the house was not one which Alice had previously encountered. When Treff told her he had come home on business, to renew acquaintance with London art circles, to see editors and arrange for the publication of more articles, Alice of course believed him, and in her innocence expected him to be very fully occupied. But after one or two calls on the editors, Treff's business was apparently accomplished; one or two visits to art exhibitions sent him home quite depressed; and he soon stopped going up to town at all. It was difficult to know what to do with him. The gaieties of Surbiton (And it *is* gay, thought Alice patriotically; there's the Tennis Club and the Golf and the Amateur Dramatic, I'm sure Dodo has a wonderful time) were all run by a younger generation. (And quite right too, thought Alice.) One could invite older people to dinner; one did; they asked one back. One had people to tea, went out to tea in return; but even so great stretches of each day remained untouched.

"He's used to artistic conversations," Alice told her husband uneasily.

"They go in for that sort of thing in Florence," agreed Freddy.

"I mean all day. In cafés. I take him to the Copper Kettle every morning, and it holds up my shopping dreadfully, but I'm sure I don't know whether he enjoys it."

There was room for doubt. When Treff Culver, hunched in his overcoat, endeavoured to draw preoccupied housewives into a leisurely discussion of the merits of Perugino, frustration was inevitable. "How very interesting, Mr. Culver!" they said. "I could listen for hours—couldn't you, Alice? I suppose you didn't notice whether Davies had any prawns? I'm going to try an aspic." It was unsatisfactory. And when he tried London again, making his way to the Café Royal, to the purlieus of Bloomsbury, it was no better. A violent young generation, spouting incomprehensible shibboleths, elbowed him aside. Not literally, to be sure; they grinned tolerantly when he asked if he might sit at their tables; but when he spoke of Florence, referred to an article of his in the *Connoisseur,* they showed their boredom. Their own conversation was marked by iconoclasm based on ignorance. In the course of a single evening Treff heard Swinburne called a "tripe-merchant," and Lord Leighton a "photographer manqué." He also learned that the adjective "Victorian" was purely abusive (if frequently misapplied), and that any one over thirty was a "back number."

Mr. Culver returned to Surbiton almost as to a refuge.

He trusted it was not to be his sole refuge.

For the motive of Treff's repatriation was in fact twofold, and beneath the official motive, the motive he gave Alice, lay another and a far more important. Treff had no objection to picking up a commission or two in London, but what he chiefly desired was to be missed in Florence. A sudden coolness, for the first time in ten years, marred the relations between himself and his patroness; he had carelessly bought a Tiepolo for her which was not only not the work of Tiepolo, but which could be proved to be the work of someone else. Treff hadn't lived thirty years in Florence without making enemies; rival art-experts rose on all sides to deride him. He looked a fool, and so did Mrs. Van Thal. She reproached him with incompetence, dishonesty, and a too warm admiration of her serving-maid Bianca—this last thrown in at first as a mere make-weight, but later developing into a major charge. Life in the Palazzo Venezia became very uncomfortable. Bianca was dismissed, and no one else could manage Mrs. Van Thal's hair; on the evening of the Principessa's ball, Treff strolled into Mrs. Van's dressing-room (such was his naïf habit) and saw Fury mirrored in the glass. "Look at me!" cried Mrs. Van Thal: she was indeed a heart-rending spectacle. One side of her hair was up, the other down; before her on the dressing-table lay a number of the wire frames known as "rats," a dozen combs, hundreds of hairpins; the new maid was weeping into her apron. "An hour's work!" cried Mrs. Van Thal, "and look at me!"

Treff, however, glanced first at the maid, who thankfully fled. Then he advanced towards the dressing-table, smiling at Mrs. Van Thal through the glass. In the early days of their acquaintance her beauty had been opulent—already verging on the over-blown, but still able to command admiration. Italian cooking and Italian siestas had made her gross. Her big cheeks ballooned, she had three chins; as she now sat—her dressing-jacket flung open in the heat of despair, her stays still unlaced—betrayed by nature, abandoned by art—she had all the dreadful pathos, without the dignity, of a stranded whale.

"You always look beautiful to me," said Treff.

Mrs. Van Thal turned and faced him. Above her fat mottled cheeks her eyes were suddenly shrewd.

"You'll have to do better than that, Treff Culver!" said she.

Treff at once recognized a crisis. A little roughness, a little high-handedness, he was used to; never before had his patroness addressed him in precisely that voice. He said lightly:—

"I don't call you a pretty young girl, Madonna, but as something of an expert—"

"Expert, indeed! What about my Tiepolo?"

Treff Culver's was not a courageous character—he did not reply, "Oh, damn your Tiepolo!"—but he did make a swift and in the circumstances an almost heroic decision. He said:—

"I'm going to London. It's time I looked up some of my editors; and there's family business I ought to settle on the spot. You won't mind if I leave early next week?"

"You can leave to-morrow!" snapped Mrs. Van Thal.

Treff in fact did so. He was luckily in funds, for he had made fifty pounds commission on the Tiepolo deal, and managed to hang on to it. Mrs. Van Thal relented so far as to come and see him off—her countenance already the ample battleground of conflicting emotions. In another couple of days, thought Treff, regretfully, she would have relented altogether; as it was, he had to pin his hopes on her knowledge of his Surbiton address.

The saddest part of the whole affair was that Treff, when he paid that fatal compliment, had been speaking the truth. He possessed the rare quality of gratitude. Gratitude and affection blurred, or rather reduced, Mrs. Van Thal's current shape, and fixed her appearance as it had been when he first saw her. (When he told her she was like a magnolia: her full smooth curves and white skin made the simile not inapt.) How foolish of Mrs. Van Thal to quarrel with such true, nay blind devotion! How damnably unfortunate for Treff, to have his truth taken for the grossest flattery! Now Treff was alone in Surbiton, and Mrs. Van Thal alone, or so he hoped, in the Palazzo Venezia. He hoped this very much. He hoped she wasn't making a fool of herself. Above all he hoped that she would soon write to him and tell him to come back.

3

It was inevitable that, between her brother and her cousin, Adelaide's name should be mentioned.

It was mentioned, indeed, within half an hour of Treff's arrival, while he was taking his first cup of English tea. Freddy Baker had not come home, and Dodo was out of the room, when Alice rather hurriedly enquired whether he ever heard from his sister.

"From Adelaide? Never a line," said Treff. "I don't even know whether she's still alive."

"Nor do I," confessed Alice. "It does seem dreadful, but it's her own doing. She knows where we live, and she's never made the slightest move . . ."

"Do you want her to?" asked Treff shrewdly.

"I naturally dislike losing sight of a first cousin."

"I dare say it would be natural in me to dislike losing sight of a sister. In fact, I feel nothing but relief. When we were children, Adelaide used to bully me; even at the time of my father's funeral I could see her working up to bully me again; she would certainly attempt to bully me if we met to-day. I'm very glad you don't see her."

Alice looked up, hearing her daughter's step in the hall; but Dodo went into the dining-room. The movement was not lost on Treff. His stay abroad seemed to have developed in him a quite feminine power of intuition.

"Does Dodo . . . ?"

"No," said Alice. "It simply hasn't arisen." She paused. Should she mention that odd little incident, Dodo's night in Britannia Mews? She had never questioned her daughter on the subject; first Treff's letter, then Miss Hambro's munificence, drove it from her mind; afterwards she told herself that if the Mews had become a smart address Adelaide certainly wouldn't be living there, and that in any case questions would only point Dodo's interest in an undesirable direction. . . .

"It simply hasn't arisen," repeated Alice, "and I don't imagine it will."

CHAPTER IV

THE DAYS PASSED, and no letter came with an Italian stamp. Treff wrote once, a chatty casual note—containing nevertheless the names of two editors—and then pride forbade him to write again, and every day his anxiety grew. Surbiton, for all its creature comforts, did not suit him; he caught cold out shopping with Alice; he had nothing to say to Freddy; and there was something about young Dodo which positively worried him. Pretty as she was, and quite surprisingly attentive, he had the uneasy feeling that she was about to call his bluff. Treff was a Culver as well as an art-expert: there were moments, usually very early in the morning, when the Culver hard-headedness in him blew away his slender achievements in print, and blew cold on Mrs. Van Thal's loyalty, and left him naked —friendless, incomeless—in a world of Philistines.

In point of fact, he misread Dodo's attitude. Her eager eye was beseeching, not critical; it was a growing anxiety to her that none of the tunes her uncle played—and Tommy had really hit on quite a clever simile—was the one she wanted. In variations on the twin themes of art and Florence he was inexhaustible, one had only to pronounce the name Botticelli, or Perugino, or the Brownings, and out came a perfectly polished (perhaps perfectly practised) little disquisition, lasting several minutes and in its way admirable; but other key-words, such as "family," "marriage," "stagnation," and "suburbia," found him mute. Dodo was baffled. Could one who had himself escaped from the Philistines really look so indifferently upon a kindred spirit still struggling to be free? Could it be possible that he did not *recognize* a kindred spirit? Dodo, by being extremely short with her mother, unkind to Tommy, and curt with Aunt Ellen, did all in her power to prove herself one. But the object of these manoeuvres remained obtuse, and at last Dodo determined on a frontal attack.

The occasion was propitious: it was the night of the Police Concert. Alice and Freddy, like all prudent householders, took tickets; their originality lay in attending the concert. (Alice believed that the Force would be gratified, and come more quickly in case of burglars. Freddy honestly enjoyed the comic songs.) Treff and Dodo stayed at home, and after dinner took their coffee tête-à-tête.

"Uncle Treff," began Dodo at once, "have you had a happy life?"

Treff did not much care for her use of the past tense; but it was a question he could answer.

"Yes, my dear. It's been spent in beautiful surroundings, studying beautiful things. No one could ask more."

"Oh," said Dodo. "Yes, I see that. But I'm not particularly artistic. I mean, I went to the Slade, but it's not my whole life. Uncle Treff, if you were me, would you marry Tommy?"

"Yes," said Treff promptly. "He seems a very nice young fellow."

Dodo jumped up and stamped her foot.

"Of course he's nice! But is that enough?"

"Well, what else would you do?"

"Exactly." Dodo took a quick turn round the room—she had her mother's habit of walking about when under any emotional stress—and Treff prudently drew in his feet. "I'm to marry Tommy because otherwise there's nothing for me to do but stay messing about at home. It isn't good enough. The trouble with me," said Dodo violently, "is that I'm too old and too young. I'm too old to marry Tommy blindly, as I might have done two years ago, only we had to wait till he got more money, and I'm too young to settle down for life. I feel my life's just beginning. I want to take a flat in town with Sonia Trent. You don't know her, but she's wonderful. I want to make a fresh start. I've *exhausted* Surbiton, Uncle Treff! I don't want to live here all my life! I want something big and real and tremendous!"

Treff sighed. He found the company of his niece very tiring. If she hadn't been so pretty—if she hadn't turned to him now with such a sparkle of admiration—he would really have had to go upstairs.

"That's why I admire *you*, Uncle Treff," went on Dodo rapidly. "Because you didn't just drift. You had enough of Farnham—do you know we used to go to Mr. Vaneck's garden-party every year? —and so you cleared out to Italy. I can just imagine the struggle it meant."

Treff could not but remember his mother's eager acquiescence in his slightest wish; but after fifty the admiration of the young is very precious. He said sententiously:—

"Most things worth having must be struggled for. I was fortunate in that I had a definite vocation."

"All the same, I can't think how you did it. I couldn't even make Mother and Dad move into town. And as for letting me take a flat . . . ! But I suppose you had your own money?"

"I was soon earning some."

"Of course, your generation doesn't like to talk about money. Or sex." Dodo flashed him a quick, considering glance. Repressed?

Was Uncle Treff repressed? Could one put the straight question? One could try. . . . "You can talk to me just as though I were a man," said Dodo. "Have one of Dad's cigars. Uncle Treff, don't you think sex is terribly important?"

Mr. Culver stiffened. His hand, reaching towards the cigar box, halted in mid-air. But it was not because of his niece's straight question: it was because he had just heard, crunching up the path, the tread of the postman bringing the last delivery. The next moment a loud double-knock resounded through the house; before it died away Treff was on his feet and making for the hall.

There was no letter for him, only a postcard, but it had an Italian stamp. Treff read it in one burning glance:—

Amico mio, will you get Bumpus or Hatchards to send me *A Sabine Farm* by T. Fowler Cox, Oxford University Press, also anything else he has written. Best love, M. VAN THAL.

Impatient of the interruption, Dodo appeared behind him in the drawing-room door.

"Uncle Treff—"

"Oh, hold your tongue!" cried Treff violently.

"Uncle *Treff!*"

Under her astonished gaze he pulled himself together, thrust the card into his pocket, and turned back to her with a pallid smile.

"I'm sorry, my dear; I've just found that all my correspondence has been sent to the wrong address. What were you saying?"

Dodo hesitated a moment, wishing that he would come back and sit down. But he looked as though he might be going upstairs. . . . She said uncertainly:—

"Well, I'd just asked you what you thought about sex. . . ."

"Sex!" Treff smiled again. "No sane man wastes much time on it." Inside his pocket his fingers were busy at the pasteboard, crumpling and twisting it into a bit of rubbish. "Women and flowers are both very charming things, my dear; neither men nor bees could do without them; personally I've always considered the bee a very sensible fellow."

Dodo looked at him sombrely. A tune on a music-box! Without another word she turned her back on him and walked into the drawing-room; and Treff Culver crept upstairs.

2

AT BREAKFAST next morning Alice was very cheerful, and full of the concert; Dodo and her uncle were both rather silent, and ready to be disagreeable. It rained hard. Freddy Baker armed himself with umbrella and mackintosh and splashed gamely down the path, every inch a bread-winner. No sooner had he disappeared, and Alice returned to her description of Constable Bright singing "Old Black Joe," than Treff announced that he was going up to town himself.

"In this weather! Nonsense, Treff," cried Alice. "You'll catch cold."

Treff pointed out that he had a cold already.

"Then you'll make it worse."

Treff got up with a defiant sneeze and asked if he might borrow an umbrella.

"Have mine," said Dodo gloomily. "It's got a hole in it."

"If you *must* go," cried Alice, now really annoyed, "why couldn't you have gone with Freddy? And anyway, can't you telephone?"

"I happen to have an appointment with an editor."

"Have my mackintosh," added Dodo. "It's green silk."

In the end Treff went off wearing his own overcoat and two scarves, under an umbrella which had belonged to Mr. Hambro. It was a handsome silk one with a gold band.

"I expect he'll lose it," said Dodo.

She herself spent an hour or two pottering about, rang up Sonia, got no answer, and finally drifted into the morning-room. Alice was sitting at the bureau, doing her accounts, and when Dodo asked to look at Uncle Treff's articles, very willingly produced the big Manila envelope in which she piously preserved them. Dodo sat down on the floor with it and began to examine the contents with great attention.

The result was surprising. Treff Culver had reached Florence in 1893. His first article—"A Stroll round the Pitti"—appeared in the *World of Art* in May, 1894. In September of the same year appeared "Some Notes on Perugino." Between 1894 and 1900 he apparently published some half-dozen articles a year; in 1901 the high water mark was reached with eight. After that his output—or at any rate his printed output—declined, until in 1914 only one article saw the light. Then came a gap, no doubt due to the war. In 1919 the *Connoisseur* printed "A Stroll through the Pitti." In 1921 appeared "A Note on Botticelli"; and that was the last. Dodo sat back on her heels and gathered all the cuttings together; they made a noticeably slender sheaf.

"Mother, is this *all?*"

"I believe so, dear," said Alice absently.

"But he can't have lived on this!"

"People asked his advice as well, and I dare say paid him for it. Treff always managed to get along. . . ."

"Do you mean he sponged on people?"

"Dodo, I will not have you speak of your uncle in that way!"

"I'm simply curious," said Dodo reasonably. "I just want to know how he got enough to eat."

Now, this was something Alice had wondered about, herself; and putting down her pen she said thoughtfully:—

"I did hear—from Mrs. Ambrose, you know—that that Palazzo place Treff wrote from wasn't a guest-house at all. It belonged to a rich American lady. Perhaps Treff was staying with her. . . ."

"I bet he was staying with her!"

"Dodo!"

"Well, how long has he been using that address?"

"Oh, for years and years," admitted Alice vaguely.

"Then I bet he was her lover."

"*Dodo!*"

"I *hope* he was her lover!" cried Dodo furiously. "It would be the only excuse! And he's quite capable of *not*—I can just see him living there like a cat on a cushion and lapping up the cream and being too terribly æsthetic and sneering about sex! And now he's simply deserted the poor old thing just because he thinks he'd like to come back to England! I call it disgusting!"

There were moments when Alice Baker surprised everyone by her clear-headedness. No one could have run a house as well as she did without mental ability, as a rule the house absorbed it—her small-talk was woolly, and any serious conversation with her daughter fogged by emotion; but now, looking straight from her account-books to her daughter, she said deliberately:—

"You're being extremely illogical. You young people always talk about being 'hard-boiled.' If your Uncle Treff *has* been . . . accepting a woman's hospitality all these years, and giving her no affection in return, he's beaten you on your own ground, and you ought to admire him. But if you call his ideas disgusting, so are your own. You must make your choice."

Dodo was silent. Put like that, the argument seemed valid: only she knew it couldn't be, because—because she was young, and her mother and uncle were old. . . . After a moment's thought she said:—

"*We're* all hard-boiled together, Mother; that makes it fair. Uncle Treff's sucker is probably some helpless little female who can't take care of herself."

But Alice for once had the sense not to argue, and presently Dodo put the envelope back in the bureau and silently departed—a good deal more disturbed than she wished to admit.

3

MR. CULVER meanwhile was standing with splashed trousers in Hatchards ordering *A Sabine Farm* to be sent to Mrs. Van Thal. The price, two guineas, struck him as ridiculous. He wasn't paying it himself, Mrs. Van Thal had an account; he simply objected to it on principle.

"Very small edition, no doubt?" he suggested hopefully.

"About average for its class, sir. *Conversations in the Campagna* went very nicely."

(265)

"Ah! Send that as well," said Treff, remembering the rest of his commission. "Anything else of his in print?"

"Only the *Latin Grammar for Middle Forms*—with T. E. Parker."

"Send it," said Treff. "Let Parker have his cut. That the lot?"

"That's all, sir."

But Treff paused, as though struck by a sudden thought.

"By the way, I want to get in touch with Mr. Cox myself. Have you any idea where he is?"

The assistant took in Treff's rather peculiar but rather academic appearance, and smiled.

"I can easily find out, sir, for he's one of our regular customers; we're always sending parcels to him. Will you wait a moment?"

Treff waited, his gaze fixed furiously but unseeingly on a pile of sensational novels published by Blore and Masterman. In five minutes the assistant returned with a slip of paper.

"He's in Italy, sir; an address in Florence. Mr. Cox won't be back till March."

4

TREFF returned to Oakley Road sneezing violently and went straight to bed. *Trays!* thought Alice crossly. There was nothing that put a house out so as the perpetual carrying up and down of trays; and she was all the more annoyed because Treff's heavy cold was the direct result of not taking advice. Old people and children! thought Alice—managing to put her cousin into both categories at once. They were in fact almost contemporaries, Alice some years the elder; but the mornings in Kensington Gardens— she and Adelaide strolling like grown-ups while Treff played at soldiers—had established him for ever as belonging to a younger generation. At the same time, finding him now so finicking and old-fashioned in all his ways, she tended to lump him with the old. The combination of these two attitudes led her to indulge all his physical requirements, and pay slight notice to his conversation.

Treff, laid up in the best spare room, was thus treated kindly but firmly; he was kept in bed for three days, and Dodo wasn't to go near him for fear of catching his cold. Dodo was to take plenty of exercise, and gargle every morning—and go and see Aunt Ellen, and take an interest in the house. "Good gracious!" cried Alice. "One would never think you were going to live there!" "Perhaps I'm not," said Dodo sulkily—and went to see Sonia Trent.

CHAPTER V

"HELLO, OLD THING," said Miss Trent. "Have a drink. You might pour me one. You might get a clean glass. . . ."

Dodo did all these things, and sank down on the orange cushions with a sigh of pleasure. The untidy room, the slight smell of gin—the bottles on the gramophone and the gramophone records on the floor—how delightful, how welcoming it all was! How wonderful of Sonia to greet her like that, as though only an hour, instead of three weeks, had elapsed since their last meeting! Dodo gazed at her friend adoringly. She said:—

"I couldn't get up before, because my uncle's staying with us."

Sonia raised her eyebrows—hair-thin, with a narrow line of goose-flesh above and below. She had been plucking her eyebrows for years.

"How ghastly for you!"

"Ghastly! He's lived all his life in Florence and is too repressed for words. If any one mentions sex he simply goes upstairs."

"I didn't know any one did mention sex, in Surbiton."

"Well, I do," said Dodo. "In fact, at first I thought he might know something about it. But you know what that generation is."

"Ghastly," agreed Sonia.

"Utterly ghastly. You can't imagine what a relief it is to get some civilized conversation."

Sonia said idly, "You can always come here if you want to. . . ."

That afternoon was marked for Dodo by two very important events. This was the first of them. Never before, however much she fished, had Sonia made so definite an offer; and Dodo was on it in a flash.

"Can I really? Can I come and *stay* here? Of course I'd share expenses—"

Sonia lowered her eyelashes—very black, slightly sticky with mascara—over the long grey-green eyes that always made Dodo think of a mermaid's, and said thoughtfully:—

"I'd better warn you, old thing, it would come to about five pounds a week. Or you could come for a month for twenty quid in advance."

"I've got that much in the bank," said Dodo promptly.

"Lucky infant."

Something in her friend's voice made Dodo sit up.

"Sonia, you don't mean you *want* twenty pounds? Why on earth didn't you tell me? I could easily lend it you!"

The eyelashes flickered.

"Could you, old thing? I'd be frightfully obliged . . ."

"Of course I can. I haven't got it on me—"

"Use one of my cheques," suggested Sonia. "Just cross out the name of my bank and put yours. It's perfectly legal."

Considering the confusion of the desk, she found her cheque-book with remarkable speed. Dodo used the big green quill pen and signed her name with a flourish. So honest was Sonia that she wouldn't accept the money as a loan, but insisted on calling it a month's prepayment; and Dodo could arrive whenever she chose!

"I shall come straight away!" cried Dodo joyfully.

"To-morrow, if you like."

Dodo giggled.

"What about Robin?"

"My dear, you won't mind poor Robin just for the odd night? You'll be sleeping down here on the divan, and he's the quietest soul alive. Did I ever tell you he was devoted to you?"

Dodo was both pleased and surprised to hear it, for Sonia's lover, a highbrow film critic, had never appeared to take the least notice of her. He was tall, very good-looking, and exasperated in his manner; Dodo was rather afraid of him. It just showed, she supposed, how little experience she had of really interesting men; and she was naturally eager to pursue the subject. But Sonia—just as Dodo tucked up her feet and reached for a cigarette—suddenly looked at her watch, exclaiming that if she didn't fly she'd be late for a lunch date. It was very disappointing. "I'd hoped you could lunch with me," said Dodo, in the ingenuous hope that her friend might ask her to come too; after all, the date was probably with Robin. . . . "I can't, what a damned shame!" cried Sonia, not ceasing to apply powder. "There's some cold ham in the kitchen, why don't you picnic here? God knows when I'll be back"—she stuffed the compact into her bag; out fluttered Dodo's cheque; she thrust it back—"but I tell you what you can do, darling, you can go to the Puppet Theatre. I've a member's ticket for this afternoon, matinées are ghastly, but they're doing Music Hall. Want it?"

She flipped the ticket across; and Dodo, all disappointment forgotten, seized on it with joyful hands. She had never been to the Puppet Theatre, she longed to do so; and she thought it was just like Sonia—darling Sonia, with her wonderful flippant manner, and all that wonderful kindness underneath—to give her the very thing she most wanted, and not even wait to be thanked.

2

THE COLD HAM was not very nice; but Dodo found plenty of bread and butter, and also made herself tea, and this simple repast left her time to wash six pairs of Sonia's stockings. Then she waited until she had seen three people go into the Theatre, and entered the foyer on the heels of the fourth.

This was the second important thing.

From the moment she stepped inside Dodo experienced a most definite feeling of satisfaction. The tiny lobby was painted a pale green, and hung with small brightly coloured sketches, designs for costumes or settings, some in narrow white frames, others simply pinned to the wall; and these last gave the place an air of informality.

The booking-office was simply a nice old desk; the person seated behind it, Mrs. Lambert herself in her usual dark gown. She looked like a hostess who has sat down for a moment; she was indeed chatting pleasantly with an elderly gentleman, and Dodo, as she hung back a moment, caught their last words—"My dear lady, I always come to matinées now: I prefer the audience." "I entirely agree with you," replied Mrs. Lambert, in a clear voice. "In the evenings we get the riff-raff." The preferrer of matinées passed on: Dodo presented her ticket almost with trepidation. But Mrs. Lambert barely glanced at her, being now busy with a seating-chart; and Dodo hung back another moment to admire at close quarters the magnificent white hair, the extraordinarily fine texture of an unpowdered skin. If Mrs. Lambert were aware of this scrutiny, she did not show it: her complete unselfconsciousness was evidently part of a supreme self-assurance, and in result highly impressive. I suppose the Victorians *were* self-assured, thought Dodo—poor saps! But she added the last phrase mechanically; for poise, in the degree attained by Mrs. Lambert, was something even Sonia had a good word for.

The auditorium, made out of four coach-houses, seated about three hundred. Its walls were green like the foyer, but undecorated. The seats showed great variety, for some had been picked up secondhand when a theatre or cinema was being remodelled (these had tip-up seats) some were plain wood, fastened in rows by a plank beneath; at the back were even some benches—and, astonishingly, a rocking-chair (unnumbered, and in fact permanently reserved for the Lamberts). The seating thus had no homogeneous colouring, but the curtain was a deep plum, emblazoned with the heads of Punch and Judy, father and mother of all puppets, on crossed staves.

Dodo found her place and settled down to watch the people come in. There were a good many children, who all sat in the front rows. Dodo saw one of them approached by an adult, apparently holding a ticket for the same seat: the child merely handed over its own stub, and the adult found a place further back: it was evidently a recognized procedure. But adults formed the great majority, and were certainly not riff-raff. Somewhere behind the curtain a person of catholic taste began to play the gramophone: Chopin's "Tristesse" followed the "Robbers' March" and "Life on the Ocean Wave"—someone playing to amuse himself. Dodo found that the odd mixture of tunes, the rather tinny tone of the machine, produced almost exactly the same effect on her as an orchestra's tuning-up. Then silence; lights down, a bright ribbon widening on a plum-coloured hem; and curtains apart upon enchantment.

What Dodo loved was the brightness and smallness of it. The technical skill was beyond her; after the first few moments she forgot she was watching puppets at all, or rather forgot that any one was manipulating them. They seemed to move of their own volition, only more precisely, more exquisitely than was usual. Looking back afterwards, she was not sure whether they had all talked, or only some of them. Certainly all the members of the concert-party sang, and certainly the acrobat, like a silver flying-fish, was mute; but the speaking glances of the female impersonator were so eloquent as to be confusing. Music Hall was followed by a short ballet starring the Camargo, and this made the transition (as the programme curtly remarked, *No Intervals at Matinées*) to scenes from *Les Précieuses Ridicules*. A peculiar stillness fell on the audience as the curtains again parted: not this time on fantasy, but on magnificence. Now the puppets moved stately in spreading brocades: each gesture began, made its point, and finished with classic assurance: they spoke in clear, ringing tones, giving each vowel its value, biting off the last syllables, slurring no stress or accent of the great lines. One Frenchwoman was speaking for all of them; yet the illusion was complete —and the more so because only the puppets took their curtain-call. The second call, indeed, caught them unawares: Madelon was yawning, Du Croisy had removed his wig, and the rest were already strolling off the stage. . . .

The lights went up. Dodo came out of her trance blinking. Her neighbours to right and left looked unnaturally large, and how clumsily they moved! People pushed between the rows and stamped down the aisle like a herd of elephants, bumping against the end seats, bumping each other, as though they hadn't proper control of their limbs. Dodo hung back till the line thinned; in front of her two men had also paused, and she heard one say to the other:—

"What is it that's so satisfying?"

His companion shrugged.

"The perfection, old man. The sheer damned classic virtuosity. And of course artistic integrity and all that—"

"I should like to hear you talk to Mrs. Lambert about artistic integrity—"

"It's her husband who is the artist, of course. He made the Molière lot. He was manipulating this afternoon, I can always spot his style. There's nothing slipshod, nothing left to chance—"

"And it's all so small and bright," added Dodo.

They turned and looked at her in surprise. Then the taller said:—

"Exactly. Perfection in miniature. The only perfection we're now capable of. Sonnets and string quartets. Have you seen the Yvette Guilbert?"

Dodo shook her head. The man at once turned away again, and both moved on. Dodo followed reluctantly, hating to leave.

CHAPTER VI

S HE RETURNED to Surbiton, with a head full of dreams and a flat in Britannia Mews, to find her mother wrapping Christmas parcels for the twins in British Columbia.

Simple as it seemed, when actually with Sonia, in the Mews, to transfer herself thither from Surbiton, once she was in Surbiton it became extraordinarily difficult.

Christmas, for example. Already, at the beginning of December, plans had been made in detail: Tommy Hitchcock invited to eat his midday dinner at the Bakers', and Dodo invited to eat a second dinner with the Hitchcocks at night. On Boxing Day Dodo and Tommy were invited together to Aunt Ellen's, and in the evening there was a Tennis Club dance. For these two days each hour al-most was consecrated to food or relations. Then on New Year's Eve there was a dance at the Town Hall, and on New Year's Day dinner at Aunt Ellen's (because she came to the Bakers' at Christmas). Working backwards, there was carol-singing on Christmas Eve, the Dramatic Society show on the twenty-second, review of puddings, mincemeat and lemon curd on the twentieth, and Christmas shop-ping for a good two weeks before that. Alice Baker adored Christ-mas (often referring to it as "the family festival") and she spread it out as long as she could. Dodo thought it all bosh; but lacked the courage to throw a spanner into such complicated works.

If I were like Sonia, she thought, groaning over her diary (*Bazaar on the twenty-first*), I'd cut the lot! But Sonia was an ideal, an exemplar, towards which she was still only striving; and the morn-ing of Christmas Eve found Dodo as usual on top of a step ladder, putting holly over the lights.

2

SHE WAS in the hall when the postman arrived; Alice hurried from the morning-room, and Treff downstairs, to see what he had brought. It was Alice who found the letter with the Italian stamp, addressed to Treff, and he was thus forced to open it in public.

It was from Mrs. Van Thal.

Amico mio,

I have a little commission I am sure you will be glad to execute for me, or rather for my friend Mr. Cox. It is a special kind of eye-lotion, none of the chemists here stock it, but Burroughs and Wel-come (Wigmore Street) will surely send it out if you just say who it is for. Mr. Cox would write them himself only he has forgotten the name—he is just too impractical to live!—but it is something be-ginning with an O. I know you will be happy to oblige your old friend

M. VAN THAL

To this address.
Either the largest size bottle, or two small ones.

Alice looked up from her own mail.

"Dodo, dear, don't grind your teeth so!"

"I'm not," said Dodo, from her ladder. She looked at her uncle, and Treff immediately went upstairs again. Dodo said:—

"He's had a pathetic letter from her."

"From whom, dear?"

"From the Principessa."

This was the name Dodo had given her uncle's unknown victim, because she lived in a *palazzo*. In point of fact, the Principessa was Mrs. Van Thal's dearest enemy. The whole situation was one of complicated misunderstanding.

"Well, he can't go and sulk just when it's lunch-time," said Alice. "There's the soup now; if he's not down in five minutes I shall fetch him myself."

She did fetch him; her manner throughout the meal remained severe, and Dodo unkindly persisted in talking about Florence. "How on earth could you bear to come home for the winter, Uncle Treff?" she asked. "Away from all the balmy breezes?" "The balmy breeze on the Prado can be a damned east wind," said Treff crossly. After lunch, taking coffee in the drawing-room (Alice had started this elegant habit on Treff's arrival, but now thought it a waste of a fire) Dodo sat down at the piano and strummed what she believed to be Italian airs—"Funiculi, Funicula," and the "Soldiers' Chorus" from Faust. "Do you mind?—I've a headache," said Treff pointedly. Dodo at once stopped, and complete silence reigned until Alice, remembering that she had six spare Christmas cards, asked Treff if he wanted any for his editors.

"No," said Treff shortly; and a moment later, with the malice of wretchedness and bad temper, added that of course he could always send one to Adelaide.

3

ALICE closed her lips as firmly as possible. With age her front teeth had become more prominent, giving her a rather rabbity look. Treff continued to annoy.

"I dare say she'd find a robin or two very gratifying. On the other hand, being Adelaide, she might not."

"I'm quite sure she wouldn't."

Dodo, bored as usual by her elders' conversation, swung round on the piano-stool and asked idly:—

"Who's Adelaide?"

Alice at once dropped her defences and shot Treff an imploring look, which unfortunately irritated him. He said happily:—

"Adelaide is my sister, dear child. Your mother's cousin, and the family skeleton."

"I didn't know we had one," said Dodo. "How perfectly priceless!"

"It wasn't priceless at all," said Alice angrily, "and I don't wish it talked about. I shall send one of these cards to the curate."

"But I must know what she did! Uncle Treff, what did she do?"

Treff put on a melodramatic air.

"Horrible as it is to relate, poor Adelaide eloped with a drawing-master—"

"How *priceless!*"

"Whereupon Culvers and Hambros alike cast her off—"

"They did nothing of the sort!" snapped Alice.

"And never mentioned her name again. It was quite barbarous."

"I hope you remember how relieved *you* were," cried Alice, "when Mr. Lambert didn't come to Uncle's funeral!"

"Naturally. In those days I was a barbarian, a prig, myself."

"Well, what happened to her?" asked Dodo, beginning to lose interest.

"Nothing, my dear. They simply lived in squalor. I hope they're not living in squalor still, Alice?"

"How should I know?"

"It seems unnatural that you do not. I can't believe that you've never taken a basket of goodies to Britannia Mews."

Dodo, her hands on the piano keys, struck a violent chord and swung round to stare.

"Britannia Mews! They live in Britannia Mews?"

"Or some such slum. Poor Adelaide—"

"Britannia Mews isn't a slum! It's one of the smartest places in town! It's where the Puppet Theatre is! Mother, *what* did you say was her married name?"

"Lambert," supplied Treff maliciously.

"Mrs. Lambert! It's their theatre! Mother, why on earth didn't you tell me?"

"My dear, I didn't know it would interest you," protested poor Alice. "I didn't even know they still lived there—or that they had a theatre. I must say it sounds most unlikely."

"Not interest me!" Dodo pounced across the room and stood over her parent accusingly. "The one relation who *is* interesting—Mrs. Lambert! I've seen her! She's the most wonderful-looking person—"

"Dodo, when did you see her?"

"At the Theatre. And last month, after I stayed the night with Sonia. If only I'd known she was my aunt—"

"She is not your aunt. She's a second cousin."

"If Uncle Treff is Uncle Treff his sister must be Aunt Adelaide. My aunt." Dodo turned on Treff and stood over him in turn. "Tell me everything about her!" she ordered. "When did they elope? What was he like then?"

"Dear child, I never even saw him. I was away at school."

"At school!" Dodo stared, making an obvious effort to grasp so great a passage of time. "Good God, it must have been crinolines!"

"Nonsense," said Alice sharply. "It was in 1886."

"Then they've been married over thirty-five—nearly forty years. I think that's wonderful."

Alice put down the Christmas cards and with a certain dignity rose from her seat.

"Your father and I have also been married nearly forty years: I have never thought of myself as wonderful. Adelaide persisted in the course she had chosen, though she was given every opportunity to return to her proper life—"

"You mean her family wanted her to leave him?"

"And I cannot see that the mere passage of time makes her into a heroine. If they have become the successful proprietors of a Punch and Judy show, I'm glad to hear it; but you're throwing yourself into a great state of excitement over nothing."

The door closed behind her. In the silence that followed Dodo stood for a moment so completely lost in thought that her uncle's voice made her start.

"What are you thinking about, child?"

"I'm thinking," said Dodo slowly, "about something that's lasted nearly forty years."

"A good many things have lasted forty years. I myself have lasted over fifty."

"Oh, you," said Dodo absently.

"And as your mother pointed out, such duration of a marriage isn't uncommon."

"But against opposition!" flashed Dodo. "Her family wanted her to leave him. And you said yourself, they lived in squalor. And out of all that they've built up the marvellous Puppet Theatre and—and she heard him come out on the balcony . . . I saw her. I think it's wonderful."

Mr. Culver hunched himself in his chair and closed his eyes. His spurt of malicious energy was dead; its only result had been to kill in him all desire to meet his sister Adelaide, who was evidently still the vigorous and overbearing character he remembered, and to make his situation with the Bakers extremely uncomfortable.

4

"Dodo, my dear," said Mr. Hitchcock, "I'm drinking your health!"

Dodo smiled automatically. He was a nice old duck, and very fond of her. At the other end of the Christmas dinner-table Mrs. Hitchcock looked a little sour; she thought Dodo had had too much sherry before dinner. (And so Dodo had; there weren't any cock-tails.) Tommy beamed, and Aunt Ellen—for Aunt Ellen was there too, the Hitchcocks were making a great fuss of her—observed, without false modesty, that Dodo was a very lucky girl. "They're coming to-morrow," she told Mrs. Hitchcock, "to go over the whole house from top to bottom; it's the first time Tommy's really seen it." Tommy turned his beaming eye on her in a grateful look. ("He's had too much sherry too," thought Dodo unkindly.) It became obvious that everyone was waiting for her to say something, but Dodo successfully pretended to be overcome by shyness. She was pretending so much, these days, that it made her quite tired.

At the Cedars, on Boxing Day, she had to pretend for three solid hours.

Tommy called for her immediately after lunch, and to every one's surprise Mr. Culver volunteered to join the expedition. "Now, Treff, you know they won't want you," said Alice briskly; but Dodo, still vaguely hopeful of her uncle's support, said that they did. "The more the merrier," said Dodo glumly. Tommy, on the other hand, obviously if silently agreed with Alice, and in the end it was decided that the young people should set out first, and Mr. Culver follow them in an hour's time. "I dare say we shan't have got farther than the basement," said Dodo.

If she was being thoroughly perverse, it was because she was thoroughly troubled; and all through the afternoon her trouble grew. For Tommy, going eagerly round the big house, was really rather sweet, and the sweeter and more enthusiastic he became, the more Dodo's heart sank. What stairs, what corridors, pantries, cupboards! Tommy leapt up, along, into them with indefatigable energy, as though he were a house-agent. How *can* he, wondered Dodo, when he knows I hate it? When he knows I don't want to live here? . . . As for Aunt Ellen, she was simply unprincipled. She didn't want the Cedars, she wanted a flat; she was *unloading* the Cedars—on to Dodo. Dodo was to wrestle with eleven grates and a boiler, while Aunt Ellen luxuriated in electric heat. . . .

Aunt Ellen was being brave about it.

"You mustn't feel you're turning me out," she explained. "You can think of me quite cosy and snug in my two rooms and a kitchenette!"

"And a bath-room," put in Dodo, who had seen the apartment contemplated.

"Well, of course, dear."

"And isn't there a maid's room?"

"There's a cubby-hole which my old Martha says she can make do." Miss Hambro laughed. "Martha and I are really too old to be separated."

"I suppose this had got rather beyond her."

Tommy said quickly:—

"Dodo's unnaturally modest about her housekeeping. Aren't you, old thing?"

Dodo gave him a long look, and for the first time read in his face something obtuse, almost relentless: the bland assurance of the male. In a gust of panic she thought, We've both changed! Tommy's changed too! He—he's dug himself in! She thought, I must talk to him at once, we must talk things out! And then a third thought struck her, so simple and obvious that only an hour or two earlier it would have made her hoot with laughter. She thought, I must talk to Mother. . . .

When Treff arrived they were all, even Tommy, glad to see him, for he ignored altogether the immediate purpose of the visit and plunged into a vein of reminiscence which Miss Hambro at least found very agreeable. Treff had a good memory for bric-à-brac, and easily identified, for example, the Chinese vase cracked by Jimmy on a Guy Fawkes Day in the previous century. "That's Rex," he announced confidently, before an aged rocking-horse. (For the work of inspection continued; they reached the box-rooms.) "The one before was called Roy. And that—great heavens, that's the Redan! My dear Ellen, do you remember Redanning?" "We all used to slide on it," explained Aunt Ellen to Dodo, "when we were all children together"; and she looked at her cousin kindly. Hitherto Miss Hambro had shown rather a dislike for Treff, considering him selfish and affected, but the charm of these shared memories was irresistible. "The twins went down head-first," mused Treff. "I wouldn't. I remember I much preferred playing with you girls." "You used to cut out paper dolls for us," said Miss Hambro, "before we were allowed to use the scissors." "My dear Ellen, when were you Hambros not allowed to do anything?" "That was Alice," said Miss Hambro. "Alice all over," agreed Treff.

The young people listened to this conversation with natural indifference. Dodo was very tired—too tired even to recollect that one of the children sliding on the Redan had been, in all probability, her Aunt Adelaide; and genuinely too tired, that night, to go to the Tennis Club dance. She persuaded Tommy to take a sister instead, which regained her the ground lost with Mrs. Hitchcock, and herself went to bed at nine. She was still awake, however, when Alice came up an hour later—and called softly to her mother to come in.

5

ALICE did so very willingly; there was nothing she liked better than to sit on her daughter's bed and have a nice chat, and only regretted that Dodo offered her so few opportunities. She switched on the fire, to be cosier, and settled herself plumply by Dodo's feet. "Now, isn't this nice?" said Alice. "You were so sensible not to go out, my darling, and by to-morrow you'll be quite rested!"

Dodo said:—

"Mother, I don't want to marry Tommy!"

To her utter amazement, Alice received this announcement with complete calm.

"Don't you, dear? That's nothing to worry about."

"Nothing to worry about!" repeated Dodo indignantly. "When I'm engaged to him! When we're supposed to get married in April—"

"I mean," explained Alice comfortably, "all girls have moments when they want to cry off. I had myself. It's the idea of leaving home."

"It's nothing of the sort. I *want* to leave home. I want to go and stay with Sonia in the Mews. I *don't* want to go and live at the Cedars—and marry Tommy."

"That's nonsense, dear. I know it's a big place, but you'll always have me to run to. And I must say, Ellen really surprised me: I'd no idea she could be so generous."

"Why is it generous to give me something she doesn't want when I don't want it either?"

At last Alice began to look disturbed.

"Dodo, don't be so unreasonable. Of course you want it, really—just as you really want to get married. Every girl wants a house and a husband and a home of her own—"

"I don't," said Dodo.

"You make me wish I'd let you get married two years ago!"

"Well, it would have been better, in a way. I mean, we were still in love then. Now Tommy just takes me for granted."

Alice brightened. For here was something she *could* understand —and with the greatest kindness and sympathy she reassured her daughter. No young man, explained Alice, could be expected to keep up for more than a month or two the first ardours of courtship. She drew examples from her own experience: Freddy, who began by being really wonderful with the twins, lost interest in boat-sailing almost as soon as Alice accepted him; quite often, in Somerset, he went fishing for the whole day without her. Girls just had to learn, said Alice wisely, not to think too much of themselves; there had to be give-and-take on both sides . . .

Dodo listened for five minutes, her cheeks scarlet, her eyes very bright; then threw her pillow across the room, buried her face in the bolster, and burst into tears. Alice's reassurance was complete; she knew what this was too, it was a plain attack of nerves, such as she had had herself—only much later, actually the night before her wedding. With soothing little words and gestures she put Dodo's bed straight, and brought her a glass of water, and Eau-de-Cologne on a clean handkerchief. "There, my darling!" murmured Alice tenderly. "Mother understands!" Dodo's lips moved against the pillow. "Good night, mother's precious," said Alice—and turned off the light.

CHAPTER VII

HOW DECEITFUL appearances could be! What pains, as well as pleasures, a double life can produce! What a lucky girl Dodo was, and how unhappy! She had kept up appearances so successfully that now she was the victim of them. Her mother couldn't believe she didn't really want to marry Tommy, just as Tommy couldn't believe she didn't really want the house: Dodo was honest enough to admit that both had reason. With one foot in Sonia's camp she had kept the other firmly planted in Surbiton—consciously enjoying, for example, the contrast between the gin-parties in Britannia Mews and the dances at the Town Hall, encouraging Tommy in Surbiton, because there it was the thing to be engaged, and suppressing him in the Mews, because there it wasn't. Now life had so to speak caught up with her, offering a definite and final alternative; but when Dodo made her choice, and the honest one— life wouldn't accept it. . . .

After meditating earnestly for several days, she perceived, however, a ray of hope. Her mother couldn't understand, nor her uncle —but what of Tommy himself? Was it possible that he too had been victimized? That he didn't really want the house either? (The obvious corollary, that he didn't really want to marry herself, Dodo simply put out of court.) But was it possible, even, that he didn't really want to be a chartered accountant? Suppose that he too had secret ambitions, longed to be a writer, or a painter, instead? This idea put a totally different complexion on him: Dodo quite jumped at the notion of sharing penury, cooking meals, darning his socks. Had not Mrs. Lambert done the same for her husband? And now look at the Puppet Theatre! The bright confusion of these ideas made Dodo happier than she had been for some months, and naturally impatient to put her unsuspecting fiancé to the test.

About a week later, when Tommy was dining in Oakley Road, Alice and Freddy went out afterwards to play bridge with the Ambroses. Treff was at the Cedars. Dodo waited to be sure her mother wasn't coming back for anything—Alice often forgot her handkerchief, or her money, or a last message—and let Tommy kiss her once or twice, and then thrust him resolutely down at one end of the sofa while she faced him from the other.

"Tommy, let's talk," said Dodo. "I don't know why it is, but we never seem to talk to each other."

Tommy grinned affectionately.

"My dear old thing, considering we see each other nearly every day—"

"I know we do, but we don't *talk*. We just chatter. I sometimes feel you've no idea what I'm really like. Perhaps I don't know what you're like." Dodo looked at her fiancé with great earnestness. "Tommy, if you told me for instance you really hated being a chartered accountant, and wanted to chuck it and start something else—even if it meant being poor and having to struggle—I shouldn't mind a bit. Truly I shouldn't! I'd understand. I don't *need* a big house or a car—"

"Darling, you must have gone bats. I like being a chartered accountant."

"Oh, God!"

"I do wish you wouldn't swear. And even if I weren't particularly keen, after all the money it's cost my people, I certainly wouldn't be such a cad as to chuck it. I don't see what the deuce you're driving at."

"We've got such frightfully different outlooks."

"Well, you don't seem to have much sense of obligation."

"I think one's obligation is to oneself, you think it's to other people."

"And I should be a pretty poor specimen if I didn't." Tommy

(283)

frowned. "Look here, Dodo, you know I never interfere, but I think some of your clever unconventional friends in town are having a pretty rotten influence on you. Incidentally, I notice you never ask me to meet them."

"You'd hate them . . ."

"Very probably."

"At least they're not smug. In fact, they drink a lot," said Dodo recklessly, "and sleep together, but they aren't stuffy and Victorian, and I like them very much."

There was a short, an ominous silence. Tommy had gone perfectly white. Without looking at her, he said:—

"Then I suppose because I haven't asked you to sleep with me before we're married, I'm Victorian and stuffy. Is that it?"

For a moment Dodo felt almost frightened, but she answered steadily:—

"No, because you'd think it was wrong."

"And you wouldn't?"

"No," said Dodo.

Again there was a silence. Making an obvious effort, Tommy took out and lit a cigarette before he went on. He said:—

"Tell me the truth, Dodo."

"I've told it."

"Tell me the rest. You wouldn't have gone this far unless there were something more."

"I haven't a lover, if that's what you mean."

The match burned his fingers, he dropped it and let it flare out on Alice's rug. He said:—

"That night you spent in town last month, when we met coming from the station. I thought there was something queer about you. Where had you been?"

"With Sonia."

"Only Sonia?"

"Yes. At least—"

"For God's sake tell the truth!"

"At least, Sonia had her lover upstairs, and there was another

(284)

man where I was, in the sitting-room. I didn't know till morning, and I'd gone before he woke up."

"I don't believe you," said Tommy harshly.

Dodo shrugged.

"I swear there's nothing to go off the deep end about."

"Isn't there? A slut and her lover upstairs—"

"Sonia isn't a slut!" Dodo's cheeks flamed till she was as scarlet as he was white. "They've been devoted to each other for years, it's exactly the same as being married, only they stick together of their own free wills. *They* don't need any legal ceremonies to make them faithful. And as for the other man, I don't suppose he knows of my existence. The whole thing is so utterly unimportant—"

"Not to me."

"Very well." Dodo tried to smile. "I told you, didn't I, it was time we talked to each other? For years and years, ever since we stopped being in love, we've just made conversation. Now we can be honest."

"Honest." Tommy walked to the window and pulled aside the curtain and stood looking out at the bitter weather. "I apologize for calling you a liar. I believe you've told the truth. But all the time this was going on—while you were getting all these ideas, going about with these people—you were engaged to me. That's what I can't get over. You behaved as though you cared for me."

"I did, Tommy. I still do."

"I'm not a fool, though you evidently think me one. Perhaps you cared for me at the beginning. But if you'd gone on caring, you'd have been—have been on my side. The decent side. All the time you were really on the other. Whether you ever really intended to marry me I don't know."

"I felt I was being pushed into it. I didn't want to hurt your feelings."

"That's quite humorous. You didn't want to hurt my feelings, so you went on letting me be engaged to you, and making plans for my whole life, and all the time you thought me dull and stuffy and Victorian and a bore."

"I did try—over the house," said Dodo, in a small voice.

"So you did. That was another push, of course." With a peculiar unconsciousness Tommy rubbed the palms of his hands over his eyes. "Well, it's over now and you needn't pretend any more. I'll tell my people to-night, and you can tell yours."

Dodo began to cry. She cried as noiselessly as possible; she did not wish him to hear her, and suspect an appeal to his pity. Nor were her tears for her broken engagement. She was crying because even her own generation had let her down, because Tommy hadn't for one moment understood what she was trying to say, because he had somehow turned a confession of faith into a confession of shabby misbehaviour. . . . She steadied her voice to say proudly:—

"You're thinking worse of me than I deserve. But I'm very sorry to have made you unhappy."

Tommy jerked round and for a moment looked at her. He was still very pale, but his features were under control. Without another word he walked past and out of the room, and Dodo heard the front door close behind him.

2

TEN MINUTES later the maid, going into Dodo's room to turn down the bed, found her young mistress feverishly throwing clothes into a suitcase. She glanced enquiringly at the clock, and withdrew. Dodo also kept glancing at the clock: it was ten to nine, there was a train to London at twenty past, she could just do it. What she could not do, that evening, was embark on long explanations, listen to her mother's remonstrances, argue with her father. She couldn't, in fact, face the music. She had to get out. She wanted above all to get to Sonia Trent, that fount and origin of the modern ideal—who wouldn't ask questions or expostulate, but simply take her in and let her sleep among the gin-bottles and wake up next morning in a world where no one was conventional or stuffy or old. . . . Bliss! thought Dodo. What heavenly, heavenly bliss!

She ran downstairs, her case in one hand, her bag and hat in the other; flew into the morning-room, dropped case and hat, seized paper and pencil from the bureau. *Dear mother,* scrawled Dodo, *I've gone to stay with Sonia. My engagement to Tommy is off. Don't worry, Dodo.* She pulled off her engagement-ring, thrust it into an envelope with the note; on her way out dropped it on the hall table. Then she ran, ran as fast as she could, her suitcase bumping against her legs, all the way along Oakley Road. The London train was in. Dodo hurled herself past the barrier and into a carriage. She had no ticket, but she could pay at the other end.

CHAPTER VIII

D ODO REACHED Britannia Mews shortly after eleven; not late, by the Mews' standards, but it was Monday, when the Puppet Theatre did not open, and week-enders hadn't returned, so that there was no one about, and very few lights showing. Dodo thought quickly that she had never seen the place so quiet, and hurried on to Number 7.

She knocked at the door; but there was no answer. She listened intently; nothing made a sound but her own taxi turning in Bedford Street, and the bare branches of the lime-tree creaking against each other in the small wind. It was as quiet as—as a churchyard! Dodo knocked again, more loudly. Could Sonia be away? She pushed up the letter-flap and peered through. A light burned within —not that that meant anything, for Sonia would leave a light on for days together. Dodo rattled the flap and knocked again. She couldn't bear Sonia to be away! Suddenly a door opened, the door of Number 10, and a woman's voice asked what the row was. Dodo spun round and enquired in turn whether Miss Trent were known to be in or out. "Oh, definitely out," replied the voice; and Dodo stared at a small, intelligent face behind horn-rimmed glasses. A new-comer to the Mews—staring back at her rather curiously. "I'm terribly sorry if I disturbed you," said Dodo, "but I've simply got to find Miss Trent. Have you any idea when she'll be back?" "Not the faintest," said the woman; "I shouldn't wait." But she waited a moment herself, apparently to see whether her advice were taken; and at that moment Dodo thought she heard a sound in Sonia's room. She pounced back to the door and beat again; and sure enough, Sonia opened it.

She did not look at all welcoming. She was wearing a grey brocade housecoat, her feet, thrust into slippers, were bare, and her hair was tumbled—which of course made her first words less of a shock.

"Damn you," said Sonia, "I was asleep . . ."

Dodo almost pushed past her into the room, dropped her bag and dropped into a chair.

"Darling, I'm terribly sorry if I woke you, but I had to. I've come!"

"What the hell do you mean?"

"I've come to stay. You know it was all arranged! What's the matter, darling? Is Robin here?"

"No, he isn't," snapped Sonia.

"Well, then." Dodo pulled off her hat. It was unlucky, she told herself (fighting down a doubt too dreadful to contemplate) that she had found Sonia in such a peculiarly foul temper; but then Sonia's temper was notorious. It didn't mean anything. It didn't mean, for example, that Sonia wasn't really and truly very glad to see her. It couldn't. . . .

"I've had an awful day," said Dodo simply. "It was all so utterly ghastly I simply couldn't stay at home. I hadn't time to phone. And you did say I could come any time I liked. . . . You're not angry, are you?"

"Of course not. You simply made such a hellish row on the one night I'd gone to bed early." Sonia moved across to a mirror and began smoothing her hair, sleeking it back behind her ears; her long grey-green eyes smiled at Dodo through the glass. At once Dodo sank back in her chair, relaxed and happy again. Of course it was all right, of course Sonia wanted her. She said solemnly:—

(288)

"Darling, if you hadn't been pleased to see me I'd have jumped into the river. I'm *dead*."

"You'll have to sleep on the divan."

"All I care is that I'm here. You're the only person in the world, Sonia, who hasn't let me down."

Sonia yawned.

"My poor infant, you shall tell me all about it in the morning; I've just taken two sleeping tablets, and I'm going straight back to bed."

Dodo now regarded her friend more closely. She did look—not exactly sleepy, but lethargic, relaxed. All her movements were peculiarly slow. . . . Sleeping tablets, of course. Sonia took them recklessly, they were her only remedy against all ills. A wave of grateful tenderness warmed Dodo's heart as she said:—

"Of course, old thing. And I'm going to tuck you up and give you a hot-water bottle."

Sonia smiled.

"I've got a hot-water bottle—"

"I bet it's cold. I bet you've been lying on your bed for hours and got it all in a mess. Darling, you need a nurse."

Dodo jumped up. At once Sonia whipped round, but she wasn't quick enough, Dodo was up the stairs and at the bedroom-door before she could be stopped. At its threshold, however, she stopped of her own accord, for on the edge of the bed (tumbled just as she had expected) a man sat hurriedly lacing his shoes.

He wasn't Robin.

Dodo automatically backed away and stumbled downstairs, all her Hambro and Baker blood burning in her cheeks. So few moments had elapsed that Sonia was still moving across the room; they nearly collided. Sonia flung out her long, scarlet-nailed hand in a gesture of warning; and instinctively, shamefully, Dodo spoke in a lowered voice.

"It—it isn't Robin!" she stammered.

"My good idiot, I never said it was."

"But—" Dodo broke off, summoning all her sophistication to

(289)

meet this new development. It proved inadequate. She couldn't keep the reproach out of her voice as she said childishly, "If it had been Robin, I shouldn't mind. . . ."

"Why the hell should you mind anyway?"

"I don't," said Dodo stoutly. But she did. She minded so much that to her horror she felt her eyes brim with tears. In the little mirror, so lately filled with Sonia's drowsy elegance, she saw her own face scarlet and blubbered like a schoolgirl's. She said wretchedly, "It's only because you and Robin have been a—a sort of ideal to me. But if you're in love with any one else—"

Sonia began to laugh. Her laughter was curiously explicit: it told Dodo more about her friend than she had learned in two years. There was a brutality about it, a pleasure in deriding; above all, there was contempt. Dodo turned and stared; Sonia had collapsed on the divan, her head thrown back, the beautiful line of her throat quivering with mirth. She raised herself on an elbow and tried to speak; but at the sight of her friend's face laughter took her again.

"Darling," she gasped. "Darling . . . !"

The word of endearment stung most of all. In a moment of blind misery Dodo rushed to the door, and pulled it open, and fled out into Britannia Mews.

2

THE BRANCHES of the lime-tree creaked a little as they touched; there was no other sound. Dodo ran a few paces towards the archway, then her knees gave and she stopped, leaning against the brick wall. Her physical fatigue was greater than she had realized; that brief moment of relaxation had unbent her will; as for her controlling mind, it was still shaken beyond bearing by the collapse of an ideal. Nothing held. Free love, the gay and casual intercourse of the sexes—but the man on the bed hadn't looked gay or casual; he had looked a gross, guilty, undignified fool. The room itself, Sonia's gay modern room, had been made squalid by his presence; Sonia herself, angry at being disturbed, heavy like a cat with cream . . .

(290)

"Of course she didn't want me!" thought Dodo bitterly.

Because the man wasn't Robin.

Dodo shut her eyes, trying to blot out his heavy, startled face. "If I'd telephoned first," she thought, "Sonia would have bundled him out, and I shouldn't have known. Perhaps she often has to bundle men out. When Robin's coming. Or doesn't Robin mind either?"

The small wind blew colder; Dodo turned up the collar of her coat. Her hat, her bag, her suitcase, were all still inside Number 7. Well, she couldn't go back for them. Not to-night. Perhaps even now Sonia was upstairs again, making her peace, making jokes about a country cousin. . . . Sliding between the sheets like a long white mermaid with her grey-green eyes . . . Dodo, back to the wall, pressed hard with her hands against the grimy brick on either side. "I've made a fool of myself," she thought. "An utter, complete fool. I don't suppose any one's ever made such a fool of themselves before." And then another thought occurred to her; that if the man came out, he would see her standing there and recognize her, and perhaps, if Sonia had sufficiently soothed him, think it funny.

At that she moved, and took another step towards the archway. But her knees were still weak; she had no money, no luggage; where was she to go? She couldn't walk all night, she couldn't walk a hundred yards; only within the narrow compass of Britannia Mews could she reach sanctuary.

Dodo turned round and without any conscious effort of thought, by blind instinct, made her way to the Puppet Theatre.

This time her knock was light as the scratch of a stray dog at a door; she stood on the balcony and waited, shivering. The stars seemed much nearer, which was ridiculous, for what difference could nine feet make to a distance counted in millions of miles? But they blinked and flickered, they were almost dazzling; Dodo blinked back and found that the light in her eyes came from an open door.

Mrs. Lambert stood before her, tall, erect, fully dressed, speaking in a low cool voice.

"Who is it? What is the matter? Please don't make a noise."

And Dodo said, very quietly:—

"I'm Dodo Baker. My mother's your cousin. We've got Uncle Treff staying with us now. You're my Aunt Adelaide. I want to come in."

3

THE SMALL ROOM was extraordinarily clean and orderly. A bright fire woke flickering lights in well-polished surfaces of wood and brass, there was old-fashioned china on the mantelpiece, and a curious shell; the chairs had antimacassars. A room unimaginable in Britannia Mews! Victorian! Dodo stared about, wondering why it should all seem so agreeable; why she should suddenly feel at home, and safe; and while she looked at the room, Mrs. Lambert looked at her.

"So you're Alice's daughter," said Mrs. Lambert. "I can see the likeness. . . . How's your mother?"

"Very well, thank you," said Dodo politely.

"She is probably in hysterics. You had better telephone at once." Dodo shook her head.

"That's all right, I'm supposed to be at Sonia's. That part's all right. But now I've nowhere, unless you let me stay here. I'm afraid I'm a nuisance."

"Not so long as you're quiet; I'm sitting up because my husband isn't very well." Mrs. Lambert continued to regard her visitor thoughtfully, but without much sign of excitement. She remained indeed most beautifully calm, as though nothing in the situation were in the least out of the way. "We have a spare room, over the Theatre; sit down a moment, while I see to things."

Dodo sat down by the fire, in a Windsor chair with a patchwork cushion tied to the seat, while Mrs. Lambert moved quietly in and out. There were two more doors besides the one on to the balcony, one leading to a room behind, the other pierced through the wall on the side over the theatre—all neatly edged with rubber tubing, to keep out draughts. The small cold wind couldn't get in.

"I've put you between blankets," observed Mrs. Lambert. "They're warmer."

"Thank you very much," said Dodo; and added painfully, "I suppose the whole trouble is that I'm not logical. If I were logical, I suppose I wouldn't have minded."

"Drink this," said Mrs. Lambert.

It was a cup of very hot milk, laced with something stronger. Dodo drank it in long steady gulps and felt much better. She looked round the room again and said intelligently:—

"I know now why people go into convents."

"That *would* upset your mother. Why?"

"Because they're so clean."

"One can be just as clean—or cleaner—outside one. The Carmelites I believe don't wash."

"Oh?" said Dodo, momentarily interested. "Why don't they wash?"

"They are too holy. Haven't you even a toothbrush?"

Dodo shook her head.

"You haven't by any chance run away from home?"

"Not exactly. But I can't go back."

A curious expression passed over Mrs. Lambert's face.

"I gather you are not eloping with any one, or you wouldn't be here alone."

Dodo put her elbows on her knees and her chin on her fists.

"Aunt Adelaide, you've read all those books where the hero sees two yokels making love in the cowshed and hates sex ever after?"

"I have not," said Mrs. Lambert. "But I can well believe that they exist."

"Well, nothing like that's happened to me. I'd broken off my engagement anyway. If it had been Robin, I shouldn't have minded in the least. It was just—finding the whole thing out. There *may* be people who believe in it and act up to it, I don't say there aren't; but I couldn't go back even to get my suitcase."

"Child," said Mrs. Lambert, "go to bed."

"I'm not tired now, thank you. I was tired, terribly, I was dead.

Therefore," said Dodo, very logically, "I haven't any one. Tommy's no use, nor Uncle Treff, and now—nor is Sonia. I feel worst about Tommy, because I once did such a beastly thing to him. I made him kiss me, in public, to keep up appearances. It was like—like—"

"Like taking away a maid's character, to provide light conversation."

"Yes, it was rather. Aunt Adelaide, can't I do something for you? Won't you go to bed, and let me sit up?"

Mrs. Lambert smiled.

"Thank you, no. You seem to be a kind child."

"Oh, no, I'm just a mess," said Dodo, very earnestly. "I don't know exactly where it started, but things have been collapsing so. Even Tommy, though he was almost too solid—"

A firm hand descended on her shoulder; still talking, Dodo found herself on her feet, propelled through a door into a queer room full of boxes and miniature scenery, where a truckle-bed had been set up, with blankets and a white pillow, and a flannel nightdress folded round a stone hot-water bottle. Still talking, she found herself undressed; the clean flannel, smelling like nursery bed-time, descended over her head; the blankets tickled round her chin; still in the middle of a sentence, Dodo slept.

Adelaide Lambert went quietly out of the flat and let herself into the foyer. She remembered Alice's address perfectly, and had no difficulty in finding the phone number; nor, though it was by now long past midnight, had she to wait for an answer.

"Good evening, Alice. This is Adelaide."

The startled silence lasted only a moment. Alice's voice said "Freddy! It's *Adelaide!*"—and then, very quickly:—

"Yes, what is it?"

"I rang up to say I had Dodo here."

This time the pause was longer; when Alice spoke again her voice had risen a note, sharpened to suspiciousness.

"Dodo? What's Dodo doing with you? She said she was going to a friend—"

(294)

"There has been a change of plan. I'm speaking from Britannia Mews. Dodo's in my spare room."

"Then please fetch her at once!"

"My dear Alice, the child's asleep."

"Adelaide, I will not have you shielding her. Tell Dodo to come and speak to her mother immediately! Both her father and I wish to speak to her! Adelaide, will you tell Dodo—"

Mrs. Lambert laid down the receiver for a moment or two, until she judged Alice would have exhausted herself. Then she took it up again and said firmly:—

"Dodo will telephone first thing in the morning. She is perfectly safe here—"

"She's to come *home* first thing in the morning!" cried Alice.

"That you must settle between you. *I* don't want your daughter, my dear; but I'm not going to bully her. Alice, control yourself."

"I am controlling myself! No, Freddy, let me speak! Adelaide: Dodo is not to stay with you. She's to come home at once. You're not to keep her there, or encourage her to be disobedient—"

"Alice."

"Yes, what is it?"

"I'm going to ring off. If you ring up again I shall not answer. Dodo appears to be over twenty-one, and I do not consider myself a disreputable influence. Good night."

CHAPTER IX

DODO RANG UP Surbiton next morning, but she didn't go back, because there was too much to do. Gilbert still required his wife's constant attention— "He's better," said Adelaide; "but he likes me to be there." She smiled as she spoke; but her face, after the night's vigil, was so white and fine-drawn, and at the same time so clear, that it made Dodo think of a shell worn thin to transparency by sea and sand. "You ought to lie down yourself," said Dodo anxiously. She was standing just inside the bedroom door; Adelaide sat by Gilbert's bed, and from his pillow the invalid regarded them both with an expression of great complacency. "I am being coddled," he announced, in a rather cracked voice. "Tomorrow I shall get up; in the meantime my wife, regardless of her own fatigue, will continue to coddle me. What have you to say to that?" "I think Aunt Adelaide ought to rest," said Dodo stoutly. "So do I," said Mr. Lambert. "You make her; I can't." "I am resting at this moment," said his wife, leaning back in her chair and pointedly closing her eyes. Dodo slipped away to clear up the breakfast, leaving each, for the sake of the other's peace of mind, feigning deep sleep. . . .

This was about nine. By ten Dodo had gone out to do the shopping, come back, and made Bovril all round. By eleven she was established in the box-office, answering the telephone, running up between calls to report, making marks in blue pencil on a seating-plan, and generally having the time of her life. She had all the natural resilience of her age; but nothing could have been more beneficial to her than this burst of enthralling and necessary activity. When about eleven-thirty Sonia came out of Number 7, Dodo called across to her with scarcely a moment's hesitation. "Sonia! You might bring over my suitcase. And my hat and bag." Miss Trent was the startled one. "What the hell are you doing there?" she demanded, dumping those objects in the foyer. "Mrs. Lambert's my aunt. Didn't you know?" said Dodo casually; and this did her as much good as anything. With a slight effort she looked her friend in the eye: Sonia's green glance was as mocking as ever, but in the cold morning light she had a raddled look. "Darling, you *are* such a little fool!" she said amiably. "Does this mean I'm to be cut off with a shilling?" Dodo nearly said, "No, with twenty pounds," but a certain schoolboy sense of honour restrained her; and Sonia shrugged and went away laughing.

By comparison, the three-cornered interview with her mother and Mrs. Lambert was positively agonizing.

Alice arrived, inevitably, about noon, and no sooner did Dodo see the familiar figure appear under the archway than she instinctively pressed the buzzer communicating with the flat above. Mrs. Lambert came out; paused a moment on the balcony; and slowly descended to meet her cousin.

"Well, Alice?" she said pleasantly. "It's nice to see you again."

The two women looked at each other; and each saw that the other had grown old. Half a lifetime, indeed, had passed since their last meeting; the gradual work of unshared years confronted them with its sum. Alice brought her little rabbit-teeth down on her lower lip to stop its trembling; if Adelaide had shown the least sign of emotion, she would have thrown herself on her cousin's neck and wept. But Adelaide stood impassive, erect, her hands clasped lightly before her—just as she used to stand at the Kensington parties, looking superior; and in Alice's breast an old resentment stirred. She said bluntly:—

"I've come to take Dodo home."

"So I see. Well, she has only to put her hat on."

Dodo threw her aunt an agonized look, which Alice fortunately failed to notice. She said more graciously:—

"It was good of you to put her up, Adelaide. I'm afraid Dodo's been very silly."

"Girls are silly things," agreed Mrs. Lambert pleasantly. "Don't you remember?"

Alice did not care for this remark at all. She could remember that her cousin had been silly, in fact quite wickedly so; she herself had not.

"Though I do think," continued Mrs. Lambert, still in an agreeable, speculative tone, "that this generation takes longer to grow out of it than we did. They are younger for their age. Dodo is . . . ?"

"Twenty-five," snapped Alice. Though she secretly agreed with every word of the implied criticism, she resented it as coming from Adelaide.

"All the same, she's been very useful to me this morning. My husband, whom you haven't asked after, is not very well. How's Freddy?"

"Freddy is always well, thank you."

"So you see, my dear, I won't ask you to come up."

And as though, after almost thirty years, that was all she had to say to her first cousin, to the companion of her youth, Mrs. Lambert turned to the stair. At once Dodo jumped up with a confused and desperate cry.

"Aunt Adelaide, wait! Mother, I'm not coming back with you. I'm not a child! And anyway, who's to answer the telephone?"

2

MRS. LAMBERT halted. Alice said angrily, "Dodo, don't talk nonsense!" Dodo sat down again and grasped the desk with both hands, as though prepared to resist physical force, and addressed her aunt.

"You said I'd been useful, didn't you? Aunt Adelaide: may I stay here and help with the Theatre in return for my keep?"

"No, you may not!" cried Alice.

"I'm asking Aunt Adelaide."

Mrs. Lambert looked from one to the other with a faint smile.

"It depends on your mother," she said. "Don't argue, Alice, I'm too tired. I don't particularly want the child, we employ all the assistance we need; Dodo has been busy this morning simply because I have been busy upstairs. I am not asking for her. Still, she may stay and make herself useful—but not if it's to involve periodical scenes. Is that quite clear?"

Immediately mother and daughter turned to confront each other; and Mrs. Lambert went quietly up the steps. Her demeanour gave no clue to her thoughts: she was in fact reflecting that at least Alice and Dodo were not about to attack one another with bottles. The

Blazer and Iris, before Iris finally gained the upper hand, had once had a great set-to on that very spot.

3

LIKE the Blazer, Alice was defeated: Dodo stayed. And another pattern oddly repeated itself: Alice, scanning the narrow confines of the Mews, assured herself that her daughter would soon be glad to return to a comfortable home. So had Mrs. Culver thought, thirty-six years earlier. (Perhaps with more justice; but then Adelaide had a stronger stomach than her niece.) Like the Blazer, like Mrs. Culver, like all mothers faced with a stubborn daughter, Dodo's mother was forced to yield; even to promise discreet behaviour; and went back to Surbiton alone.

Alice always had a great instinct for platitudes. When Freddy returned that evening he found her crying in Dodo's empty room.

"I've lost my daughter," said Alice, at the end of her sad tale. "I keep telling myself she'll come back, but in my heart I know she won't."

Freddy sat down beside her, on Dodo's bed, and kindly took her hand.

"Why should you say that, my dear? Dodo's always been interested in the theatre, it must seem a great opportunity to her to dabble in it a little, until—"

"Until what?" asked poor Alice. "She won't marry Tommy, she'll probably never marry any one; my only daughter will be an old maid. It's as though—as though Adelaide had cast a spell over her! After all these years! You always disliked her, and you were quite right!"

Freddy Baker, sitting there holding his wife's hand, tried to think back down the years and remember why. Why had he disliked Adelaide? She'd gone off with the drawing-master; caused a great family rumpus; hurt Alice's feelings. But all that was very long ago. . . .

"What's she like?" he asked suddenly.

"Old," said Alice. "She's gone quite white—much whiter than I am. I didn't see Mr. Lambert, he wasn't well. Dodo said Adelaide had been up all night. She said it was bronchitis." Alice wiped her eyes. "One thing I must say, Freddy; that marriage *has* lasted."

"I remember you were all very down on it at the time."

"Well, he drank, dear. I wasn't supposed to know, but Miss Ocock told me he once came absolutely intoxicated to a drawing-lesson." ("I haven't thought of *her* for years!" exclaimed Alice, quite pleased by the recollection.) "I suppose he must have given it up, or he wouldn't be alive to-day; and Adelaide *did* reform him." Alice sighed. "Oh, dear, what a long time it is!"

"We're all getting on," agreed Freddy comfortably.

"And how *unjust* it is! There's Adelaide, who's always done exactly as she pleased, with no thought for any one else, and—and now she's got Dodo too! It makes me feel I haven't been a good mother to the child, and yet I'm sure I don't see how I could have done better!"

Freddy put his arm round his wife's plump shoulder and gave her a gentle, clumsy hug.

"You have always been an excellent mother, and an excellent wife. Only Dodo's young, and we're rather elderly—"

"So is Adelaide elderly!"

"And Dodo's always wanted to live in London, and she sees her opportunity. Let's have a little peace and quiet, my dear, just the two of us; for what with Dodo and young Hitchcock, and your cousin Treff and your sister Ellen, I've found the last few months uncommonly wearing."

He could have said nothing more apt to distract and animate the current of his wife's thoughts. Alice sat bolt upright and stared at him.

"Freddy! Don't you feel *well?*"

As a matter of fact Freddy Baker's excellent health was a matter of great pride to him; for the last half-century he had never spent a single day in bed. But he was a very good fellow. Before the evening was out he had allowed Alice to persuade him about two things: that he ought to drink a glass of milk every night, and that he ought to retire at sixty.

4

AMONG the persons most put out by Dodo's flight was Aunt Ellen; she had no one to give her house to, and though there was no material reason why she should not have completed her design of moving into a flat, the idea of either letting or selling the Cedars was anathema to her. As she never tired of pointing out, it was the family home. "Good gracious," exclaimed Alice impatiently, "you'd think we'd lived there for generations!" And this from Alice, usually so loyal in all that concerned the clan, produced a coolness. (Alice couldn't get it out of her head that but for the house, Dodo might still have married Tommy.) Miss Hambro sought sympathy elsewhere, and found it in Treff, who for some time had been seriously concerned about his future. The friendly assistant at Hatchards informed him that T. Fowler Cox proposed to remain abroad indefinitely, on learning which Treff impulsively cabled asking for his summer underwear; when he opened the trunk and found not only his entire wardrobe, but his books, his few bibelots, and a sketch of a ruin he had actually presented to Mrs. Van Thal, he knew that he had cooked his goose. All was over; the breach complete. At the same time, Freddy and Alice showed a perverse tendency to talk about Florence. . . .

In these circumstances Treff did the best thing possible: he turned to the nearest unattached woman. Miss Hambro, who began by disliking him, now found him extraordinarily sympathetic. He alone seemed to appreciate her feelings; they were always going round the Cedars together, and as each room, each square yard of carpet almost, produced its appropriate reminiscence or anecdote, Treff's sympathy grew. He said he could enter into her feelings because he remembered his own on leaving Platt's End. He admired the Cedars extremely. ("In Florence, of course," he remarked, surveying the drawing-room, "this would have been called a *palazzo.*") The upshot was inevitable; shortly afterwards Miss Hambro informed her sister that she intended to stay on at the Cedars to make a home for Treff.

"But he's going back to Italy!" exclaimed Alice in surprise.

"No, dear, he isn't," said Ellen. "Perhaps he talks more freely to me, dear, than he does to you; but I know for a fact he means to stay in England. Surely you realized that when he sent for his things?"

"There was only one trunk."

Miss Hambro smiled. Treff had been living under the Baker roof for nearly five months, and Alice knew no more about him than that!

"All his life," explained Miss Hambro, "Treff has avoided possessions. He's like Epicurus—all he wants is a piece of bread, and on holidays a little bit of cheese."

Alice, who took this remark as a reflection on her housekeeping, said sharply that that was the first she had ever heard of Epicurus, and no doubt the first Ellen had either; but the arrangement was too agreeable to all parties to produce ill-feeling. Treff made the move a day or two later, and was installed in the large bedroom once occupied by the twins. Martha carried up his breakfast each morning without the least complaint, for she liked having a gentleman in the house again; and indeed Treff, by his mere masculine presence, seemed to bring the whole establishment to life, to give point to the eternal polishing of the furniture and the eternal cooking and serving of meals. As for Aunt Ellen, she blossomed. The constant small attentions with which Treff was so effortlessly lavish fell upon her like a gentle rain. She lost her tartness and learned to play bézique. (Martha learned to make ravioli.) Neither Alice nor anyone else knew whether Treff paid his share of expenses, and in fact he did not; but he certainly earned his keep.

Now and again, alone, at night, the image of Mrs. Van Thal still rose to torment him, the image of T. Fowler Cox leered; Treff bore his pangs in silence. He could recognize luck when it came his way. He wasn't a conceited man; he knew that he had only one real talent, and that was for making women feel comfortable. He was genuinely grateful to Miss Hambro, as he had been genuinely grateful to Mrs. Van Thal—and this time he meant to be more careful. Fortunately Ellen had no desire to buy pictures, and Martha, besides being over fifty, was quite uncommonly plain.

Freddy and Alice were thus left to keep each other company, and if their life was monotonous, it was remarkably comfortable. Monotony, indeed, was their deliberate choice; they could have travelled, abroad or at home, as much as they wished; their means were ample. But Freddy Baker did not like foreign food, and Alice was a bad sailor; even the best English "hydros," at guineas a day, could not quite supply the comforts of Surbiton; after Freddy took to gardening they never left home at all. His roses were a picture, and so was Alice's house. They entertained much less, for Alice unfortunately developed a tendency to self-pity which only her husband could cope with; but they were very comfortable.

Several years later, when the Puppet Theatre was putting on *The Brave Tin Soldier,* Dodo re-read all Hans Andersen. When she came to the story of the two snails who lived under a burdock-leaf, she smiled. They were so like Alice and Freddy! She took the book with her next time she went to Surbiton, but on second thoughts did not show it, and the joke was never shared; for amongst the many things her aunt taught her—such as simple arithmetic, method, and the habit of hard work—was respect for parents, and all persons older than herself.

CHAPTER X

THE HANS ANDERSEN series was a great success. Puppets were made for *The Little Mermaid, The Nightingale,* and *The Emperor's New Clothes,* all of which went into the permanent repertory. The big baskets in the store-room now held nearly a hundred puppets, not counting the characters from Molière. These were frequently on loan to museums or exhibitions, and an earnest young man from the Victoria and Albert acquired permanent possession of Tartuffe and the Marquise. Persons writing a week in advance could examine the rest of the set by appointment.

In 1928, the Theatre gained a brilliant recruit in the person of one Mark Bartholomew, a young student from the Slade whose satires on the Bright Young Things of the period gained piquancy from the fact that Bright Young Things filled the Theatre. (They filled the Mews. The goings-on of 'twenty-two were as nothing to the goings-on of 'twenty-eight.) The Bartholomew puppets marked a new epoch, and also found their way into exhibitions. A few years later new blood flowed in again, this time from the Continent: an Austrian Jew walked in with an entire *Danse Macabre* in a sack sewn out of his overcoat, asking fifty pounds, or ten pounds, or five pounds for the lot. Mrs. Lambert engaged him as a manipulator, for by this time Gilbert was too frail to do anything but sit at rehearsals with a rug over his knees. The business side of affairs fell more and more upon Dodo; acting first as her aunt's adjutant, she acquired both Adelaide's capability and her imperiousness. She worked hard, but it was a satisfying life, and full of human contacts: there was Bartholomew to be encouraged while he was working, and driven when he was not; the Jew Gerhardi to be encouraged all the time; odd assistants and cleaners about the Theatre to be kept up to the mark; and over all Mr. and Mrs. Lambert, the proprietors, the only begetters of the whole enterprise, to be cherished, shielded, deferred to—and made to rest in the afternoons.

In her thirties Dodo was as pretty as she had been as a girl; both Bartholomew and Gerhardi asked her to marry them. The one was so much too young, the other so much too Austrian, that Dodo refused almost without thinking; she would have missed their companionship; but that, the Theatre assured her. They lived for the Theatre, all three of them; when the war came, the Theatre was their first thought.

2

OF COURSE they would keep open. On this point they were all in complete agreement—congratulating themselves, moreover, on the possession of a company whose members would never be called up, never needed holidays, and whose limbs could be replaced in a matter of hours. And of course, added Dodo, the Lamberts would leave London.

"I think not, dear," said Adelaide gently.

Dodo drew a deep breath. She meant to speak casually, as though referring to an accepted plan, but in spite of herself her voice sounded thin with anxiety.

"I'm sorry, Aunt Adelaide, but you must."

"Well, we'll see, dear."

Nothing could have alarmed Dodo more than this unusual mildness: it meant that her aunt's will was so firmly set that she wouldn't even bother to argue. But Dodo also had a will, and a great fund of persistence; and continual dropping was said to wear away stone. . . .

"Very well," said Dodo grimly. "We'll see."

Once again a redistribution of the family was imminent. When war broke out Adelaide and Gilbert and Dodo were in Britannia Mews, the Bakers, Miss Hambro and Treff Culver at Surbiton; Dodo, confident of herself remaining fixed, waited impatiently for the shake of the kaleidoscope. But the characteristic of the kaleidoscope is unpredictability, and when the new pattern emerged, it was by no means the one she expected.

3

THE FIRST months of the war—the phony war—produced no violent changes but a great deal of extra work. Both Dodo and Gerhardi became air-raid wardens, and spent all spare moments hearing each other repeat the unpleasant symptoms produced by different gases: their A.R.P. Post was conveniently situated in Chester Street, and Dodo could get from her bed to her telephone in four minutes flat. For three days they worked almost continuously on the distribution and fitting of gas-masks; then a lull—the phony lull—succeeded, and the Post became a tea-drinking Cave of Adullam. At the Theatre they made blackout boards from old sets, and these, painted on the inside with masks and wands, rather added to the general effect. A selection of the Molière puppets was taken by cab to the Victoria and Albert Museum and deposited there for safe-keeping; Gerhardi slipped in one or two of his *Danse Macabre* figures as well, and insisted on seeing the same young man who had previously acquired the Tartuffe. "If I am killed," said Gerhardi impressively, "I wish the Museum to retain them. I have written a card, for when they are on show; and please do not let them be confused with the rest." Dodo, unpacking the hamper, glanced over his shoulder: *The work of Anatole Augustus Franz-Josef Gerhardi, 1890–19—.* ("You will please fill in the date," explained Gerhardi.) Dodo looked at the half-sheet of note-paper supplied by her aunt, and found it more optimistic. *Property of Mrs. Lambert,* wrote Adelaide curtly. But Gerhardi's precaution was not unreasonable, and under the serious young man's approving eye Dodo added the words, *Work of Gilbert Lambert.*

She did not, on her return, mention this addition to her aunt, but she did point out the paradox of sending puppets into safe-keeping while remaining in danger oneself. Adelaide at once retorted that if Dodo wished to leave town, the Theatre could perfectly well carry on without her. Neither took this remark seriously, but it roused Dodo to the point of swearing at her aunt.

"Damn it all, Aunt Adelaide, it's not just I who want you to go! The Government's asked every one who can to leave London—"

"I don't believe in all this gadding about the country."

"You can't call a Government evacuation scheme gadding about the country!"

"Nor do I see myself joining the queue of snotty-nosed school-children. Nor do I yet consider myself a superfluous person. If we do manage to keep open, I shall probably be back in the box-office."

"That's my job."

"You will probably be scrubbing the floor—I remember how difficult it was last time," said Adelaide, "to get a charwoman. When was Gerhardi naturalized?"

" 'Thirty-five," said Dodo. "Thank goodness." She frowned. Gerhardi was a tower of strength—an ingenious craftsman, an expert manipulator; but Dodo worried about young Bartholomew. He was twenty-eight, and much fitter than he looked; his puppets were in a class by themselves, finer than Gerhardi's, finer than anything the Theatre possessed except the original French set. He had just produced a Leda and Swan of extreme beauty—the Museum wanted these too, but Barty, with the prodigality of genius, refused them; he said they could take their chance, and if they got bombed he could make better—he had designs in hand for a whole Olympus. Dodo had been talking about him that afternoon, and now, shelving for the moment the major problem of the Lamberts, she said briskly:—

"That reminds me—will you write a letter to the War Office?"

"I cannot imagine," said Adelaide, "that even at this juncture they require my advice."

"And to the Council of Arts, or whatever it is?" went on Dodo, unheeding. "I've got the exact address. They're making out a short list of artists and writers and dancers and so on, who oughtn't to be called up, I believe they don't want more than a hundred names on it, so you ought to write at once and apply for Barty. He'd make a rotten soldier, and he *is* a genius."

Adelaide considered this proposal for a moment or two in silence. At seventy-five she was no longer so upright as she used to be; but she straightened her shoulders.

"Have you asked young Bartholomew's opinion?"

"No," admitted Dodo. "But you know he'll do whatever he's told. And he *oughtn't* to go, Aunt Adelaide; it would be such a waste."

Ever since her marriage Adelaide had had a low opinion of artists, which even the success of the Puppet Theatre had not altered. She said tartly:—

"There was none of this nonsense last time. Young Jackson volunteered immediately. We have enough puppets to carry on with for years. If young Bartholomew is called upon to die for his country instead of making more, I certainly shall raise no objection."

"One man," said Dodo, "can't make any difference."

"That is no reason why one man should be excused from his duty. It would be most unfair."

"Aunt Adelaide, you can't talk of fair and unfair when it's a question of artistic value! Why did we take the Molière lot to the V. and A.? Why are they sending all the pictures out of London? Because they're irreplaceable! And so is Barty irreplaceable! It's absurd!"

"I shall write no letter," said Adelaide.

As a matter of fact, it would have made no difference had she done so: the War Office took precisely her view. With great courtesy it admitted the artistic standpoint; and with equal firmness pointed out that such discrimination would be un-English, and therefore unfair.

4

AFTER the fall of France, after Dunkirk, with the first raids on London, the tempo of change quickened. Britannia Mews emptied—the simile was Adelaide's—like a sink. The gay amusing cottages stood empty; at the A.R.P. Post one or two glamour girls were missing—called to the side of friends in safe areas; other glamour girls remained, drove through the blitz, clung to their telephones under tables, and emerged to polish their scarlet finger-nails and complain about the shortage of cosmetics. Dodo clung to her telephone along with them, and every morning waited anxiously for Gerhardi to report. He was now attached to Light Rescue, and often sick when he came in. The Puppet Theatre opened for matinées only, and indeed they could hardly have managed more; but both were glad to escape, for an hour or two, into the small bright world of illusion.

Not Dodo and Gerhardi alone found comfort there. The Puppet, since so many theatres had closed, was extremely popular, and Adelaide never ceased to marvel at the number of Tommies in the audience. For Adelaide still called them "Tommies"—her vigorous mind was beginning to harden; any private soldier was a Tommy to her, and all Tommies by definition were rough, brave—and uneducated. Her niece pointed out in vain that many of those in the audience were actually old Members disguised by uniform. "Nonsense," said Adelaide. "They would have commissions." This attitude so exasperated Dodo that she began to look out for some identifiable individual, and in due course produced a young man named Warbeck who had occupied the end seat in Row F twice a month for three years; he was now a private in the London Scottish. Adelaide was forced to admit the fact, but interpreted it as pointing to something discreditable in Mr. Warbeck's past.

The point was important, because it was Adelaide who directed the Theatre's policy, and with sincere patriotism she wished to provide these brave Tommies with suitable entertainment. She proposed to cut out all items except Music Hall and a knockabout farce invented by Gerhardi to show off his technical skill, and ordered Bartholomew to lay aside a Europa for a Charlie Chaplin. "They must have what they want," said Adelaide firmly. "You can't tell *me* Tommies enjoy Molière." . . . "But they do," said Dodo. . . . "Or mythological *pastiche*." . . . "But they do!" cried Dodo— "We cater for the ones who don't want to go to the Windmill." In the end Dodo won by pinning up in the foyer a large sheet of paper with the name of every item on it and a notice beneath: SERVICE PATRONS ONLY: PLEASE TICK YOUR FAVOURITES. It remained up for a month, during which Dodo and Gerhardi went about with smugger and smugger looks. The Hans Andersen and Ballet tied for first place, with Molière second; Music Hall was third, and the farce at the foot.

While the serenity of Adelaide and Gilbert remained unshaken, Dodo found it unnerving. They refused to patronize the shelter under the Cock, they refused even to leave their beds, during the heaviest raids. "After threescore years and ten," observed Adelaide, "one doesn't go traipsing about in one's night-clothes"; and in the veiled allusion to the Biblical span Dodo divined a sort of gambler's theory: until the age of seventy, one should take reasonable care of oneself; but after that it was up to the Lord.

She was thankful that her own parents did not share this view: Alice and Freddy were in Somerset. The Somerset Bakers, in a recrudescence of family affection, had urgently summoned them, and Alice was to seek accommodation in the same village for Aunt Ellen and Treff. Her joy in this reunion was marred only by the thought of leaving Dodo behind: she came up to the Mews, tearfully imploring; Dodo, her tin hat still on the back of her head, grinned cheerfully and swore that the moment she felt nervous she would take the next train out. But it was her father's eye she caught as she spoke, and Freddy Baker grinned back. While Alice was talking to Adelaide he gave Dodo fifty pounds in notes, to buy, he said simply, drinks with. (He wasn't grinning as he added, "I'm about eighty, Dodo, and your mother would be wretched without me. I still feel a rat.") But Dodo thought their behaviour exemplary, and said so, and said so again to Adelaide as soon as they were gone.

"It's what I call being really sensible," she repeated pointedly, "and thoroughly considerate. Don't you, Aunt Adelaide?"

"Filial piety in reverse," agreed Adelaide briskly. "Dear Alice always was a bit of a mouse."

"And please don't sneer at her."

"Filial piety in the ascendant," said Adelaide, unabashed.

Dodo sat down on the edge of the desk—they were in the foyer—and marshalled her forces for argument. She didn't want to argue, she had had only three hours' sleep and was very tired, but she had learned something during the night which thoroughly upset her.

"Aunt Adelaide, have you or have you not been into the Post while I wasn't there and told them no one slept over the Theatre?"

"I have."

"And would you mind telling me why the hell?"

"I can see you've had a bad night, dear," said Adelaide sympathetically. "I told them no one slept here, of course, because you are always out on an Alert, and your uncle and I don't wish people to take risks rescuing us."

(310)

"That's exactly what I thought. It simply means that Gerhardi and I now have an added anxiety. Of course some one's got to rescue you!"

Adelaide sighed.

"I do think that at our age—"

"I know, threescore years and ten," interrupted Dodo rudely. "The whole trouble is you simply imagine you'll be killed outright. You never think of being trapped and injured."

"Yes, I do. But you know, dear, even a slight injury, even the shock, would be too much for Gilbert—"

"That's all the more reason why you should take him away. Every rational person is getting out as fast as they can—"

At that moment, as though to point her argument, in swooped a young woman in a mink coat, carrying a jewel-case and a small bag.

5

Both Adelaide and Dodo knew her, though only as Cyclamen—Number 1 having been redecorated from top to bottom in that tender hue for her reception. This had happened in the autumn of 'thirty-nine, when the first alarms were over, and before the war, as one said, had got rough: Cyclamen was fond of telling her friends how she had snapped up her darling little cot under the noses of the 'fraid-cats. Hers was the wide-eyed, kittenish, little-girl approach: *démodé,* but eternally bringing home the goods.

"You're not going, are you?" now cried Cyclamen breathlessly. "I mean, shall I leave my key here? There's a bucket of water upstairs, and a bucket of sand down, and if you'd got the key you wouldn't have to break in. Would you?"

On the other side of the desk aunt and niece presented a suddenly united front.

"I should be obliged if you would tell me," said Adelaide, "what exactly you have in mind?"

"She has incendiaries in mind," said Dodo grimly.

Adelaide's eyebrows shot up.

"Do I understand you wish to leave your key so that my niece may go and put them out for you?"

"Well, aren't you a warden?" asked Cyclamen, turning to Dodo in simple confidence. "I thought that was what wardens were for."

"You have undoubtedly," said Dodo, "the right idea."

Cyclamen rolled her big eyes from one to the other of them, sensing, it seemed, and incredulously, an implied criticism.

"But I'd stay myself if I could do any *good*," she explained. "I'd love to. It's just that my nerves let me down."

"You look as strong," observed Adelaide dispassionately, "as an ox."

Cyclamen brightened a little.

"That's what's so funny about me. I *look* strong, don't I?—but I'm not really. I'm not wiry, like Miss Baker. My doctor says that if I don't leave London at once I shall have a complete breakdown and just be a nuisance to every one . . ."

"He is probably right," said Adelaide.

Cyclamen brightened still more.

"I knew you'd understand," she said gratefully. "And I may leave my key, mayn't I? I mean, I've some quite nice things—I do wish I had time to show them you!—and of course I'll be back as soon as my nerves are right again, only I must go now because my friend's sending his car, and it's the *last* of his petrol so I mustn't keep him waiting. But I'll tell him how sweet you've both been, and one day we'll all have a party!"

On this generous note she skimmed away, moving really very gracefully, turned to wave under the arch, and was gone. Aunt and niece looked at each other.

"And the damnable thing," said Dodo, "is that if incendiaries do land in her beastly pink love-nest, I damn well shall have to go and put 'em out."

"However, all rational people are leaving London," said Adelaide.

Dodo, who did not feel the moment propitious for further argument, went rather wearily into the Theatre to prepare for the matinée.

The work grew harder. Bartholomew was still with them, but the electrician, having influence, got into the army; Gerhardi produced an elderly compatriot who was clever but unreliable, and a theatrical agency sent a Punch and Judy man whom they had to train. (He brought with him a mangy Dog Toby; Adelaide took a liking to the animal, washed it with disinfectant, and carried it up to show Gilbert.) Dodo and Adelaide managed the box-office between them, and the former, as her aunt had prophesied, also did a good deal of scrubbing: all front-of-the-house duties, and many domestic duties as well, fell upon her shoulders. Adelaide could tidy the flat, and cook, but she was a bad war-time shopper, for she couldn't bring herself to stand in a queue, and persisted in addressing tradesmen as though she were their social superior. "You don't realize," complained Dodo, "that the butcher has power." Adelaide sniffed, and said she supposed the fishmonger had aristocratic connections. "No, darling; the fishmonger has glamour," said Dodo, with a grin; and subsequently did the shopping as well.

But relief was on the way. Miss Hambro rang up one morning to say that a furnished house had been found for herself and Treff, near the Bakers in Somerset, and there was room for the Lamberts as well: would not Adelaide and her husband go down with them in two days' time? It was fortunately Dodo who took the call, and she knew better than to give the message directly; instead she suggested that Treff should come up in person and apply fraternal pressure. Brother and sister had met once or twice during the intervening years, if not with enthusiasm, at least with decent affability; and family affection seemed to be in the air. To herself Dodo admitted only an outside chance of success, but she was ready to take any chance at all.

Treff arrived. He hadn't changed much since his first appearance in Surbiton; after looking older than his age for years, he now looked younger. It was evident that Aunt Ellen had taken great care of him, for he had all the easy assurance of the cockered male.

"Of course Adelaide and Gilbert must come with us," he announced competently. "We'll pick them up to-morrow morning. . . ."

With a first gleam of hope Dodo led him upstairs and put him into the flat (rather as one popped a ferret into a rabbit-hole) and almost immediately withdrew; she had an idea that Adelaide would find it easier to climb down without a witness. But she was working in the store-room next door, and their first exchange was distinctly audible.

"My dear Adelaide, it's the common desire of all of us—"

"You're not addressing a meeting," said Adelaide.

Dodo groaned, and dived into a stack of old sets (they were feeling the three-ply shortage) and began to go through them methodically. "When on earth did we do Cinderella?" she wondered, as a pasteboard pumpkin collapsed in her hands. But she couldn't help cocking an ear, and presently Adelaide's voice rose high and peremptory.

"As you rightly point out, my dear Treff, we are not a service family; on the other hand, I never heard of the Culvers being notable for cowardice."

Dodo put her head round the door and said, "Treff isn't being a coward. He's simply being reasonable," and went downstairs. There was plenty to do in the box-office, and she realized that it would be less trying to wait out of earshot.

A whole hour passed; with every minute hope ebbed. When Treff at last reappeared Dodo felt it hardly worth while to put a question. But his manner was extremely agitated, and she felt bound (having summoned him on his bootless errand) at least to sympathize with its failure.

"I'm so sorry," said Dodo. "I'm afraid you haven't been able to persuade her?"

"No, I haven't," snapped Treff.

"I never really thought you would. She's so dreadfully stubborn—"

"Stubborn!" Treff dashed his hat down on the desk and glared. "She's a damned bully! She won't leave herself, and now she won't let me leave either! That's so *like* Adelaide—"

Dodo jumped to her feet.

"What on earth do you mean? Of course you're leaving!"

"No, I'm not. I'm coming to live up here." Treff glared crossly round the Mews. "Which is Number 1, Dodo? Adelaide says I'm to have Number 1."

"You wait here," ordered Dodo.

Almost beside herself with indignation she swung up the iron staircase and burst into the flat. Adelaide had retired to the inner room, where she was placidly engaged in amusing Gilbert, and educating Dog Toby, by teaching the latter to beg.

"Aunt Adelaide, what *is* all this nonsense?" demanded Dodo. "Treff comes up to take you to Somerset, and now he tells me *he's* going to stay in town!"

Adelaide looked complacent.

"I thought he'd be useful about the Theatre, dear. He can jelly the programmes. You know how short-handed we are, and Treff's a great deal more capable than he looks."

"But he doesn't *want* to stay in London! It—it's positively cruel!"

"Of course he doesn't," agreed Adelaide. "He'd much rather be a coward—and I will say this for Treff, he has no false shame about it. However, I don't choose to have a coward for a brother."

As Dodo had realized, family affection was in the air; but this particular manifestation of it disconcerted her.

"You're talking," added Adelaide blandly, "as though he weren't a free agent . . ."

Dodo at once flew downstairs again and turned her wrath on Treff.

"For heaven's sake stand up for yourself!" she adjured him. "All you've got to do is just *go*! Aunt Adelaide won't come after you! You're not locked up here! Haven't you any will of your own?"

"Not much," said Treff disarmingly; and regarding him with extreme repugnance (for she already saw him as some one else to be rescued), Dodo saw that this was only too true. Already he was becoming reconciled to his lot; already his flash of temper had subsided. "And you know," he went on, "to tell you the truth, Dodo, your Aunt Ellen can be a great bore. Your Aunt Ellen in the country might prove quite unendurable. I'm about ready for a change."

"But to come *here*! At this time!"

Treff said irrelevantly, "After all, it's where we used to live. I can remember as a small boy—"

The wail of the siren drowned his last words. Dodo seized her tin hat and bolted for the Post. Nothing fell, however, in their area, and the alert was a short one; when she ran back she found Treff and Adelaide in Number 1, making poor witticisms about the colour scheme.

6

THUS it was that Alice, meeting the train, saw her sister descend from the carriage alone.

"Where's Treff?" she cried at once.

Ellen dropped a rug and a suitcase on the platform and replied dramatically:—

"In Britannia Mews!"

"Ellen!" Regardless of interested bystanders, Alice seized and shook her sister's arm. "Ellen, what can you mean?"

"What I say. He's in Britannia Mews with Adelaide. He went to persuade her to come down here with us, and she persuaded him —or I should say browbeat and bullied him—into staying there. It's sheer madness."

"You shouldn't have allowed it!" cried Alice indignantly.

"My dear Alice, I don't remember that you exactly *allowed* Dodo to do exactly the same thing."

This was so dreadfully true that Alice could not answer. In silence she stooped and picked up Ellen's bag, and Ellen picked up the rug, and they joined the stream making for the barrier. It was a slow business; the train had been very full. When they had moved about a dozen yards Alice said suddenly:—

"What *is* it about Adelaide?"

"*I* don't know," said Ellen.

In the minds of both was the same thought: that life was grossly unjust to good women.

They moved on a few yards more. A small boy carrying a cat in a basket edged between them and rested his burden against Alice's

(316)

plump side. "Is that your pussy?" asked she—kind as ever even in distress. "No, it's my mum's," replied the urchin. Alice looked at him with approval: what a good, helpful child!

"Never mind, dear," said Ellen encouragingly. "At least *we're* all together here."

"And *they're* all together in the Mews!"

"I dare say even if Adelaide left, Dodo wouldn't."

"That's what Freddy says, but I don't believe it. And I know Adelaide won't leave. She gets her own way in everything, and always has done, simply by being as stubborn as a mule."

Ellen did not answer, and Alice knew why. There was at that time a conviction abroad that stubbornness had become a virtue. Was not the whole country drawing on its stubbornness, retreating into its old citadel of blind obstinacy? When to be clear-sighted was to admit defeat, thick-headedness offered an alternative. Moreover the country as a whole, making this choice, did not even see there was a choice at all, but felt itself to be following the only possible course; instinct took the place of reason; and as always when this happened with the British, they felt a deep, if unadmitted, sense of relief. Inside the thick heads certain racial memories stirred, all heartening; time was found to remark the peculiar beauty of that English summer. It was a wonderful year for buttercups. Each field was a cloth of gold, hedged by the upflung spray of hawthorn—as the island itself was moated by the sea. But if the sea, if its old ally the sea failed, the only defence was stubbornness. Already the great cities crouched under bombardment with no other shield. Stubbornness, in whatever manifestation, was not to be disparaged.

PART FIVE

CHAPTER I

FOUR YEARS LATER, in Britannia Mews, Adelaide lay awake listening to the barrage. She could identify three distinct sounds, like three instruments in an orchestra: a sharp *plan,* as of a finger flicked against taut parchment; an enormous fart; a rumble like a cartload of bricks being emptied—and then all three merging into great waves of noise, like the waves of the sea, as the barrage moved farther out. This pandemonium was very agreeable to her; like all other Londoners, she remembered nights when the only sound in the sky was the scoff-and-throb of Jerry engines.

"Well, we're still here," thought Adelaide.

She turned and glanced across the narrow space to Gilbert's bed. He slept peacefully on his back, his short white beard pointed defiantly at the ceiling. In an odd way it made him look more lively asleep than he did awake; he had become a very old man, rarely leaving the flat, except when he crept down once or twice a month to watch a performance in the Theatre, and taking all his airings on the balcony. Even by day he snoozed a good deal; he could snooze through a warning, a stick of bombs, and an All Clear; his increasing deafness had its compensations, and Adelaide's voice was always perfectly distinct to him. He took very little notice of any one else, and indeed very little notice of the war.

They had been very lucky. Bombs had dropped all around, in Paddington, in the Bayswater Road, by the Marble Arch; the Albion Place houses had all their front windows blown out; but nothing (except of course shrapnel, and tiles, and a few chimney-pots) fell upon the Mews. The Puppet Theatre still flourished (in 1942 they had resumed evening performances, at six o'clock) and shared with the Windmill the proud motto, WE NEVER CLOSED.

(321)

Adelaide became aware that the skies were quiet again; presently Dodo would come pounding back from the Post. At the thought of her niece Adelaide smiled in the darkness: good, brave, dependable child, how well she had turned out! Not that Dodo was a child any longer, she was in fact forty-seven, what some people might consider middle-aged; but she looked much younger, there was a sort of perennial girlishness about her—the girlishness of the woman who hasn't married and doesn't regret it.."Is Dodo happy?" Adelaide wondered for a moment . . . "Would she like to get married?" —and then shrugged the doubt aside as unimportant. "Dodo is stout-hearted," thought Adelaide. "That's all that matters . . ."

For this was one result of the war: it had reduced life to first principles. If you weren't stout-hearted, you didn't matter. You might be rich, or beautiful, or clever, or industrious, but your courage was what you were finally judged by. There was no longer any need to keep up appearances, except the appearance of being brave.

The All Clear sounded; Adelaide slept.

2

DAY was breaking as Dodo re-entered the Mews. In the cold February dawn the little houses looked bleak and shabby: without their bright paint, without their tubs and window-boxes, they had reverted to type. But Cyclamen's pink shutters still made a patch of pale colour, and on a sudden impulse Dodo went in to see if her uncle were awake. Treff always left the door on the latch, in case he needed rescuing: he had turned out quite as brave as could be expected, but he took precautions. Dodo at once looked under the stairs, and there he was, curled up in Cyclamen's pink eiderdown, buttressed by pink pillows, like an earwig in the heart of a rose.

At Dodo's step he opened one eye, immediately closed it again, and burrowed into the pinkness. Dodo knew what he was doing, he kept his false teeth in a box under the pillow, and she waited politely till he re-emerged.

"Rough night," said Treff.

"St. James's and Pall Mall," said Dodo. "Quite a nasty little blitz."

Treff worked himself partially out of his cocoon and clasped his skinny wrists behind his head.

"Well, I've been very snug," he remarked selfishly. "Seen Adelaide?"

"I haven't been in yet. Would you like a cup of tea?"

Without waiting for an answer (Treff was a little mean about his tea-ration) Dodo put on the electric ring and set out two cups—one *famille rose,* one utility. All the furnishings were now in this piebald state; Dodo sometimes thought it fortunate that Cyclamen was in Miami. They knew this because she had sent Adelaide a Christmas card with a line on the back asking if any one had happened to find her charm-bracelet. No one had, though the early days of Treff's occupation yielded a considerable harvest of minor pickings. Handkerchiefs, for example, turned up continually—five stuffed down one chair; Dodo sent them all to the wash and when clothes-rationing came in used them without compunction. Boxes of cigarettes abounded. The bureau yielded a quantity of note-paper, pink but high-grade: also a great number of telegrams bearing such messages as WITH YOU TO-NIGHT, or CAN'T MAKE IT DARLING, or THREE DAYS STARTING TUESDAY, all signed BIMBO. (Treff thought the preservation of these missives showed a tender nature; Dodo, untidy habits.) More important finds were two bottles of gin, half a bottle of French vermouth, and a decanter of whisky. They were long since consumed, but the character of a Tom Tiddler's Ground continued to hang faintly about the place, and indeed after four years Dodo still found an occasional and invaluable hairpin.

Treff was still deep in his cushions when she returned with the tea, but fully awake and ready for conversation. She said:—

"There's a journalist coming at eleven to interview Aunt Adelaide."

"Dear me," said Treff. "Addie *has* become a personage."

"She always was," said Dodo sharply. "But the point is she won't see him. She says she can't be bothered. So I'll have to instead—"

"Or I will," offered Treff.

But Dodo shook her head. Gentlemen of the Press were not rare visitors, for the dramatic critics who had turned to the Puppet when other theatres closed still came regularly; and Treff persisted in trying to sell them articles on Perugino. Adelaide paid for his services with a pound a week and his keep, so it was quite natural, and even praiseworthy, that he should thus try to turn an honest penny; only it sometimes annoyed the critics.

"No, thanks," said Dodo. "I'll see him myself. But I do need some facts about Aunt Adelaide's early life. For instance, when did she marry Uncle Gilbert?"

"If her memory hasn't failed altogether," said Treff cattily, "Adelaide can surely tell you that herself."

"I hate worrying her; she's got such a great sense of—of privacy." Dodo paused; her aunt's reluctance to talk about herself was so very marked, one felt almost disloyal in going to other sources of information. But a theatre, of all enterprises, couldn't afford to neglect the Press; and if the article were well done it would be valuable publicity. Moreover, what the Press wasn't told it would guess at: far better to give a few facts correctly, and ask to read the proofs. . . . "Come along, Uncle Treff," said Dodo briskly. "When did they get married?"

Treff, divided between the desire to obstruct and the desire to show off his own powers of memory, appeared to meditate.

"The year we moved to Farnham. Eighteen eighty-six."

"Didn't they elope? Oh, dear," said Dodo regretfully, "that's so romantic, but I don't think I dare use it. Anyway, Uncle Gilbert's time in France must have come before that, because they've lived here ever since; so he made the Molière puppets—good heavens!—nearly sixty years ago. Do you know anything else about him?"

"Only that he drank like a fish."

"Uncle Treff!"

"You asked me, my dear."

"No one would employ a drawing-master who drank!"

"I don't imagine," said Treff, beginning to enjoy himself, "that he habitually appeared in a state of intoxication. In fact I was away at school, I never even saw him; but it all came out afterwards. The twins apparently put in some detective work—they were your Uncles James and John, my dear; and there was a Mrs. Ocock whose daughter also took drawing-lessons: she came to Mamma with really hair-raising tales. He was dismissed from his post at a school—"

"You needn't go on," said Dodo. "If he did drink as a very young man, I'm sure he gave it up when he married Aunt Adelaide."

"I'm sure Adelaide could make any one give up anything. But I must say it amuses me when I see my brother-in-law being treated as a minor saint."

Dodo sighed. If she now saw why her aunt had been so uncommunicative, the knowledge was almost useless: merely silenced herself also. "I shall just say they were married in 1886," she reflected, "and that the Theatre started in 1905; and in between I suppose Uncle Gilbert simply reformed and went on giving drawing-lessons. But how uninteresting it sounds!"

She gathered up the tea-cups, washed them and put them away—Treff never did a thing for himself if he could help it—and went rather dejectedly up to her own room for a sleep.

3

It is said by the wise that one should be careful in one's youthful desires, because in age they may be granted. So it had come about with Adelaide. During the most vehement, most intensely lived period of her life, between the ages of twenty-one and twenty-six, prestige was what she had set her will on. At first she had called it fame; then, a proper position; then, respectability; dropped for a while to the mere negation of disaster; beat her way back to respectability; and there, as her life found its new focus in Gilbert, would have been content to remain. But the momentum had to expend itself, and gradually, inevitably, Adelaide's position was built up into what she herself considered a slightly ridiculous eminence. During the blitz the Puppet Theatre had acquired more than æsthetic news-value: the mere paradox of its survival caught a public imagination peculiarly susceptible to the charm of anything at once delicate and hardy. (The journalist who described it as "a cyclamen flowering amid ruins" gave Adelaide and Dodo more pleasure than he knew.) Adelaide herself, with her white hair and straight back, above all with her great age, could not escape popularity: she was so exactly right, so perfectly picturesque; her comments on every subject (till she learned not to give them) were so pungent and uninhibited: she was, in short, such a character. Thus Adelaide became a personage by force of circumstances—not exactly against her will, but indifferently. The success of the Puppet Theatre pleased her, because it pleased Gilbert; also she did not like to lose money; but all talk of cultural value, or half-centuries of brave endeavour, struck her as so much poppycock. When admirers praised her artistic achievement Adelaide still, at the bottom of her heart, felt she was being made a fool of.

"In any case, it isn't my achievement at all," she told Gilbert, almost angrily. "It's yours—and I dare say partly Mr. Bly's, or even Old Bert's. I had nothing to do with it!"

"My dear, you were our inspiration," said he.

Adelaide smiled.

"I know I fed you all on beefsteak pudding . . ."

"You were the centre of our lives," said Gilbert seriously. "You held us together and gave us a respect for ourselves, and made us able to do something with our talents. My dearest, what a scurvy set we were!"

But this Adelaide would never allow. In retrospect the figures of Mr. Bly and the Old 'Un appeared not disreputable, but picturesque, their eccentricities merely engaging, their way of life merely unconventional. To Adelaide's mind they compared favourably with almost every one she had met since. In fact she no longer wished to meet people at all—avoided all new faces whenever possible, and particularly avoided reporters.

That she did not altogether avoid Mr. Jamieson was a pure accident. Dodo, giving the interview by proxy, had struggled for half

an hour to satisfy him with photographs of sets, the puppets themselves, old handwritten programmes, autographs of Diaghilev and
Yvette Guilbert; Mr. Jamieson peered at them all through very
thick pebble-lenses and observed they were no doubt highly interesting to the specialist. "You've the matter there for a grand monograph," he added practically. "Get some clever body to handle it,
Miss Baker, and publish a wee illustrated book." But what he had
come to get was information about the Lamberts; Dodo's couple
of dates fell very flat, and he persisted in his desire to see Mrs.
Lambert herself. "Mr. Jamieson, my aunt is eighty," said Dodo
severely. "And from all I hear tell, wonderfully vigorous for her
age," said Mr. Jamieson. "And she would certainly refuse to answer
questions about her private life." "Very well," said Mr. Jamieson,
"I'll change my tack. I'll just take her views on the theatre in war-
time, or some such artistic trivia." It was a competition in Scottish
and Saxon stubbornness; and resolved in the end, as has been said,
only by accident. Adelaide thought the obnoxious visitor had left,
wanted Dodo, and came downstairs.

Dodo saw no alternative but to introduce Mr. Jamieson, with the
remark that he was just going. Adelaide merely bowed. But Mr.
Jamieson stood his ground.

"Mrs. Lambert," he said, very deferentially, "I'm not here to
trouble you with impertinent questions. But your great knowledge
of the theatre—"

"Fiddlesticks," said Adelaide.

"I beg your pardon?"

"Havers," translated Adelaide. "Mr. Jamieson, good day. Dodo,
bring the bookings to my room."

With that she turned and slowly re-ascended the stair. Dodo, in
spite of the severe look with which this last injunction was accompanied, felt pleased. Adelaide might not have given an interview; but she had certainly presented a nutshell sketch of her formidable character. Mr. Jamieson was evidently impressed.

"That's a very remarkable old lady," said he.

"Very," agreed Dodo.

"Am I right in thinking that she's but a poor opinion of the modern drama?"

"Yes," said Dodo. "But it's only fair to say she's no ground for it, because she never goes to the theatre. She's only been to one theatre since the war started."

"Shakespeare, no doubt," suggested Mr. Jamieson.

"No; the Windmill," said Dodo. "She went because they never closed—like us. Mind you put that in!"

Above them a door shut with a very dismissive sound.

"I would like very much," said Mr. Jamieson gravely, "to have seen your Auntie at yon nudes. Good day, Miss Baker, and thank you."

They parted on good terms, and when Dodo saw the article she was pleased with it. Behind the pebble-lenses Mr. Jamieson had evidently an artist's eye: his description of Adelaide, careful, sober, and accurate, had something of the quality of a Holbein drawing. It did not appear, however, in his paper, but in one of the monthlies; and this pleased Dodo too, as being more permanent. Something at least, some fragment of a remarkable character, had a chance of being saved from oblivion; and the two dates were correct.

Adelaide refused to read this article, but Iris O'Keefe saw it, and paid a special visit to the Mews in consequence. In these days Miss O'Keefe was very busy—indefatigable at charity matinées, a resolute entertainer of the troops, presenter of diamond stars to Red Cross sales. Candid friends said plainly that dear Iris was working up for a damehood. And why not? For years now she had never played below the rank of Grand Duchess; it gave her quite a shock to be addressed, in private life, as "Miss." But if such were indeed her ambition, she had the magnanimity to desire the same honour for her old friend.

"That article," said Miss O'Keefe to Dodo, "was just the thing. If you only keep it up—"

"But I can't," said Dodo. "It was only by chance Aunt Adelaide saw him at all. You know what she is."

Miss O'Keefe flung up her glittering hands. She always wore a great many diamonds, both on and off stage; she said they were the quickest way to impress fools.

"Do I not, my dear! It's positively heart-breaking! Your aunt could have such a position as many would give their ears for—but she simply won't take the trouble. She *ought* to be a Dame, it's due to her. Just add it up, dear," adjured Miss O'Keefe—"fifty years' service to the theatre, ditto perfect married life, hand in glove with the museums, and an appearance beyond praise. My dear, when I read the Honours Lists, I often wonder who's responsible for the casting."

She spoke in the happy confidence that her own appearance was positively regal; and Dodo willingly paid the required compliment.

"We'd make a handsome pair," agreed Miss O'Keefe—who had transferred something of her frankness with the aunt to the niece. "And what a feather for the old Mews! My word, what a transformation scene!"

"I always forget," said Dodo, "that you used to live here too."

"So I should hope, for it's not a thing to shout about—at least not for me. Your aunt of course could make a feature of it—but she won't. She won't lift a finger. And the reason is she's entirely wrapped up in Mr. Lambert, and always has been."

Ever since her conversation with Mr. Jamieson, Dodo had had a vague notion of putting together . . . not a monograph, but some brief account of her aunt's life . . . not to be published, of course, or not for many years . . . but another garnering against oblivion.

Now, remembering Treff's uncomfortable revelations, she asked tentatively, "Do you remember them, when you lived here?"

"Indeed I do," said Miss O'Keefe promptly. "It wasn't at all the sort of place it is to-day, and the Lamberts were the only nice people—except of course for my mamma and myself—who resided here. They were our *only* friends. And they were so attached to each other—really romantically, you know—it made a great impression. Never a harsh word! (My own papa died when I was too young to remember him.) And Mrs. Lambert's appearance was so aristocratic, when I played my first title—only an Honourable, to be sure, in *The Scent-Shop Girl*—I simply modelled myself upon *her*."

"That was when Uncle Gilbert gave drawing-lessons," prompted Dodo.

"Did he? I remember he was very distinguished too—as indeed he still is. In fact, I've sometimes wondered," added Miss O'Keefe casually, "whether he ever changed his name."

"Good heavens!" exclaimed Dodo. "Why on earth should he?"

"If he came of some really good family, members of our nobility in fact, who cut him off on account of his artistic proclivities, it would be only natural."

Dodo laughed. She always enjoyed Miss O'Keefe's excursions into romance, there was a naïveté about them that contrasted so oddly with the rest of that lady's character. As a rule Iris never used her imagination at all; when she did, it at once invented the plot of a musical comedy. But how easily, thought Dodo, the events of even the recent past could become distorted! How easy to go astray—on anything but dates!

One thing however could not be distorted: the tale of mutual devotion which still continued. Though Gilbert was now so old that a little food, a little sun, met all his physical requirements, his mind followed Adelaide through her busy day, he always knew where she was, what she was doing. On the rare occasions when she left the Mews he retreated into a semi-coma till she came back, dying as it were a little death in her absence. And Adelaide, so much more active, needed the perpetual refreshment of five-minute visits to his room, or mere glances through an open door: on fine days when Gilbert could sit well-wrapped-up on the balcony, and Adelaide had her desk under the window in the foyer, they carried on long conversations so desultory and allusive that strangers who overheard imagined them to be talking to themselves; as indeed they were.

Dodo Baker watched and listened with protective tenderness. But sometimes—"How old every one is!" thought Dodo. She was thinking of the people she habitually lived with: Adelaide, Gilbert, Treff; Gerhardi and the two assistants. . . . Britannia Mews had become a pocket of age: often, when Gerhardi and his ancients were out sunning themselves (while Gilbert snoozed on the balcony above) one got the impression of an alms-house. Dodo did not wish to analyze her discontent, but the fact was that twenty years earlier she had stepped out of her own generation into the preceding one, with the result that, apart from acquaintances at the Post, she now knew no one of her own age.

From this point of view she would have done better to go to Somerset, where Alice, in the bosom of the Bakers, was missing her daughter less than she would have believed possible. The Bakers were a prolific clan; though Freddy's own generation had thinned out, nephews and nieces flourished, all married, all with children and even grandchildren of their own; and it was among this youngest division of the family that Alice (her situation thus the very reverse of her daughter's) now dwelt. The young husbands indeed were mostly absent, scattered over Burma and Italy and Africa and the Low Countries; but the young wives drew together, bringing in their broods to the big old house near Taunton, where once they used to spend such dull Christmases, and which they were now so glad to fall back on; and those who couldn't pack in billeted themselves round about, and they all saw each other every day. It was exactly the sort of life Alice enjoyed, and she became quite rejuvenated. She was no longer active, and spent most of the day knitting, in a large chair set either by the hearth or out on the lawn, according to the weather; but from that vantage-point she effectively directed the economy of the household, the education of the children, and every-body's private affairs. Sometimes the young wives caballed against her, which added a spice to life, but over the children she reigned supreme—a permanent, a stationary, Grandma, swarmed over as the young Hambros once swarmed over the Redan, and occupying a very similar place in their affections. The great event of the week was when on Saturday afternoon she was packed into the pony-cart and taken for a drive, for then the whole tribe accompanied her, relays of two riding in the cart, the others at the pony's head, or hanging on behind when they went downhill. It became quite a local sight. The number of children varied between five (in term-time) and nine (in the holidays). But even nine children were not too many for Alice, and she looked forward with delight to the new baby expected in July.

Of this female and juvenile flock Freddy Baker was the patriarch. At the Sunday gatherings (immediately organized by Alice) he often sat down the only man among seven women—his wife, his sister-in-law Ellen, his own sister Amy, and four young mothers. Fortunately, he had the Major. This new friend was very old, almost as old as Freddy himself, and retired, and lived in a very neat villa surrounded by a very neat garden, and thither Freddy used to betake himself when the women got too much for him, to sit over a small fire and criticize the Home Guard and discuss the nine o'clock news. And as the Major was a comfort to Freddy, so was Freddy a comfort to the Major—a fresh audience for his stories of pig-sticking, a man who could remember the Boer War. They became close friends, even to sharing their whisky, and did the *Times* crossword together every afternoon.

It was a happy time for Alice, in Somerset; not quite so happy for Dodo, in Britannia Mews. The Theatre still absorbed her, but not completely; and that spring, in the lull between the last of the blitzes and the first of the flying-bombs, she began to spend more time than usual in Kensington Gardens.

CHAPTER II

ON A PARTICULARLY mild day some weeks later Dodo, by going without tea, reached the Gardens soon after four o'clock. The April grass was strewn with courting couples, and animated by courting pigeons: they minced round in pairs like clockwork toys, ruffled cock behind sleek hen. Dodo directed her steps with discretion until near the Round Pond she found a single chair with no one making love within ten yards. (She had not the least objection to the lovers, but perhaps attributed to them too much of her own sensibility.) There she sat down and took off her hat and shook out the thick waves of her still very pretty hair; it was a gesture as instinctive and natural, on that remarkably springlike day, as the ruffling of the cock-pigeon's feathers. Indeed, blonde, platinum-blonde, brunette and mid-brown heads dotted the landscape, some dressed in pompadours, some tied up with ribbons. "How prettily girls do their hair now!" thought Dodo, with genuine pleasure. A book and a paper lay unheeded in her lap, they weren't nearly so entertaining as the spectacle before her. Not all the girls had escorts—or not yet. Some walked in couples, alert of eye: a gang of fourteen-year-olds squealed and sky-larked, two Wrens, briskly conversing, circled the Pond like ocean passengers taking exercise. They were very trim; a group of reclining soldiery whistled appreciation each time they passed, but the Wrens took no notice. They walked round the Pond four times (Dodo thought this probably constituted a mile) and walked off.

A few minutes after they disappeared a corporal strolled past Dodo for the second time. She had vaguely noticed him before, thinking he looked older than most of the troops, and less at home in uniform; there was something incorrigibly civilian about him. This time he caught her eye, probably by accident, before strolling on to the edge of the Pond, where he turned and stood with his back to the water, probably admiring the view. Dodo opened her book and began to read. She read two pages, and became aware that the corporal had moved back on to the grass and was standing a short distance away. In turning over she glanced up, and again he caught her eye. His intention was now unmistakable. But this is absurd! thought Dodo, half-incredulous, half-amused—here I'm forty-seven! The corporal looked about ten years younger—but she couldn't tell whether the neatly clipped moustache, light against a tanned skin, were blonde or grey. As though in answer to her thought he removed his cap; he was fair, but going slightly bald. He sat down on the grass and began to fill a pipe; Dodo at once became conscious of the matches in her hand-bag. She looked down again and read the same paragraph twice over, and sure enough the classic phrase struck politely on her ear.

"I wonder if you could let me have a light?"

"Yes, I think so," said Dodo.

While she fumbled in her bag he moved a yard nearer; from the way he resettled himself Dodo perceived that they had yet another thought in common—that the grass was damp. To right and left younger warriors sprawled full-length in puppish confidence: the corporal kept his area of contact as small as possible.

Dodo said impulsively, "Would you like to sit on my newspaper?" He grinned.

"Thank you very much. I do suffer from rheumatism."

"Then you shouldn't sit on the grass at all," Dodo pointed out.

"There are a couple of chairs under that tree. Or I could bring one over here. . . ."

"As a matter of fact, I'm just going."

He looked thoroughly disappointed.

"I'm afraid that must be true, because I can't flatter myself that I've alarmed you."

"Of course not. Only—"

"Only what?"

Dodo looked at him squarely.

"I don't want you to waste your time. I mean, it's five now, and if you're looking for a date for this evening, which is perfectly natural, you'd have to start all over again about half-past, and if you want to have dinner anywhere you ought to be there by seven, or there won't be any food. I'm just telling you."

"You don't think an hour and a half would leave me enough time?" enquired the corporal seriously.

"Good heavens, how should *I* know?" cried Dodo.

"There's a chap on our site who says he can pick up a date in forty seconds flat."

"I dare say he can," agreed Dodo. "I've seen it done, in Piccadilly."

(334)

"Of course, no one ever offers Ginger a newspaper to sit on. On the contrary, Ginger singes the grass. If I'm going to tell you much more about Ginger, I'd better fetch that chair."

He did so, and returning gave Dodo many interesting particulars about his friend, life on an Ack-Ack site, and his own previous career as an architect in the cathedral city of Winchester. He talked with an odd detachment, as though he saw himself as a faintly humorous figure; and with great fluency, as though it were some time since he had let himself go.

"Do you like being in the forces?" asked Dodo curiously.

"Very much. In one way, of course, I don't like it at all. I dislike the washing arrangements and the interference with my personal habits. But I like the chaps, and I like doing a useful and warlike job which is within my powers. We're not glorious, but we're necessary."

"Like the A.R.P."

He laughed.

"I'll tell that to the chaps."

"No, you mustn't," said Dodo, very earnestly. "You don't know what a comfort it is to hear the barrage go up. We take a pride in it. You tell them that!"

"I will. It's nice to be appreciated. It's been nice of you to let me sit here and talk."

With some surprise, Dodo realized that it was six o'clock. He made no attempt to detain her, nor did he suggest another meeting; they parted as casually as they had met, without even a handshake. "Good shooting!" said Dodo. "Quiet night!" said the corporal; an exchange so formal that it might have come out of a book of etiquette for time of war.

2

WHEN Dodo got back to the Mews Adelaide immediately observed that the walk had done her good. Dodo, feeling rather acutely that there was nothing to conceal, replied that she had been picked up by a soldier.

"I'm surprised that it hasn't happened before," said Adelaide calmly. "Was it by the Serpentine?"

"No, by the Round Pond."

"What sort of soldier?"

"A full corporal, darling, in Ack-Ack. He just wanted someone to talk to."

"Humph," said Adelaide.

"He did really. I warned him."

"What precisely," enquired Adelaide, "did you warn him of?"

"You know perfectly well what I mean. Is Gerhardi off duty yet?"

"Gerhardi's back-stage: the lighting's gone wrong again."

Dodo groaned. Things were always going wrong, because everything was getting worn out, and it was almost impossible to procure the nuts and bolts, bits of wire, electrical fittings, needed for repairs. (Three-ply wood, for example, simply vanished; the last piece in the workshop had been found by Dodo lying in the road after a blitz—no doubt part of some one's blackout—and she brought it home in triumph.) Even the puppets were getting shabby, which was serious, for part of their charm had always lain in their immaculate miniature perfection. To them both Adelaide and Dodo made sacrifices: Leda's swan was replumaged from the latter's best pre-war hat, and a certain dark-blue velvet of Adelaide's cut up into the Madonna's cloak for the nativity play and a most useful midnight sky. But what work it all meant! What stitching and contriving! Treff was clever at touching up a head, but it was a pity, thought Dodo, he couldn't sew. . . .

Gerhardi had fixed the lights when she joined him and was arranging the puppets on their pegs ready for the evening performance. They were doing a ballet, *The Brave Tin Soldier,* and Music Hall.

"That uniform," he said at once, "should go to the cleaners. It is unspeakable."

"Well, it can't," said Dodo. "They take six weeks. Any news at the Post?"

Gerhardi paused, his fingers twitching on the strings so that the soldier appeared to shudder.

"They are saying if Hitler knows he is beaten, he may use gas. Gas will be his secret weapon. . . ."

Dodo, considering the red jacket, which was indeed very soiled, remarked that gas could hardly be called a secret.

"It will still be abominable. Will you look at these trousers? They should be white, and they are yellow like an old man's moustache."

"Rub chalk on. Or couldn't you Blanco them?"

"And where am I to get the Blanco? Also I need black enamel and some window cord. You know I never make difficulties, but this is too much!"

Dodo consoled him as well as she was able, but for once could not take his troubles seriously; which was odd, since they were all —from the shortage of Blanco to the prospect of gas—so eminently her own troubles too. She felt unreasonably cheerful; as Adelaide said, her walk had done her good.

3

As the weather continued fine Dodo formed the habit of slipping across to the Gardens before the evening performance. She usually walked twice round the Pond, once briskly and once more slowly, and was back in an hour. It was a sensible way of getting exercise, and one which her aunt warmly encouraged.

On the sixteenth of these promenades, or when she had circled the Pond thirty-one times, the corporal rose from a bench and politely saluted her. He said at once:—

"I couldn't get up last week. Were you here?"

Dodo felt annoyed; he seemed to have forgotten that no word had been said of a further meeting. She said rather coolly:—

"I always walk here in the evening."

"That's what I thought," said the corporal blandly. His manner was not exactly more confident, but more carefree, as though he were in possession of some private good news. "May I walk with you?"

"I'm just going as far as the Serpentine. . . ."

"That's no distance. Ginger recommends the back of Apsley House."

"Do you mean to tell me," cried Dodo, "you've been asking Ginger's advice?"

"Certainly not. But I evidently returned to duty in a noticeably cheerful mood, because he at once congratulated me on breaking my duck. I can't help Ginger, you know, he persists in behaving like a mother to me."

"I think he sounds nice," said Dodo.

"He is. You mustn't think I've been bandying your name among the brutal and licentious soldiery, because I haven't. In the first place I don't know your name, and in the second our sergeant is a Plymouth Brother. We are known in the regiment as 'Ernie's Choir.' Ginger regards your mere shadow with the greatest respect. In fact, he said the reason he advised Apsley House was so that we could converse about the Duke of Wellington."

"You know, it's very odd," said Dodo, "but you manage to give the impression of being rather strong and silent."

"I assure you I don't usually talk at this rate. It's the excitement of seeing you again. By the way, my name is Richard Tuke."

"Mine's Dodo—Dorothy—Baker."

He repeated the name appreciatively, and at once went on talking: it was remarkable how much an hour's concentrated discourse revealed. Dodo learned, for instance, that he had never married, and never would, for the simple reason that on an income (after paying taxes) of six hundred a year he supported three women already—his mother and two elder sisters. "My family is one of the last examples," he told Dodo wryly, "of the true shabby-genteel. We know all the nice people in Winchester, and eat too much farinaceous food. One thing I've enjoyed in the Army is meat." The possibility of marrying any one with money had apparently never occurred to him; he was conditioned to think of money as something one scraped up to spend on other people. From twenty years' work he had achieved only one personal satisfaction: he possessed a cottage, picked up cheap in a moment of self-indulgence, and thenceforward evidently the pride and preoccupation of his life. (It wasn't near Winchester; it was in Bucks.) He began to describe it in detail, but suddenly and unexpectedly paused; Dodo, wondering what had stopped him, could only think of a small boy who interrupts the account of his rabbits with a "Wait till you see them." . . . There was a slight hiatus, and when he went on it was to speak about Ginger.

Ginger was a great help to them. They had both by this time become very conscious not only of each other, but also of themselves, and particularly of their ages: the notion that they were falling in love was shaded by a doubt whether they might not be too old for it—they could not make the direct approach of boy and girl. In this state of emotional self-mistrust Ginger was invaluable, a sort of invisible go-between, whom Richard avowedly feared to disappoint. He could ask Dodo for her photograph with less embarrassment, because Ginger thought he ought to have one. "Ginger has six, all different," explained Richard, "and all signed with love and kisses. You needn't put anything like that, of course; if you wrote something rather ladylike and aloof—'Kind thoughts,' or 'Good wishes'— Ginger would consider it just the thing." Dodo laughed and promised to find one, whereupon Richard solemnly produced a snapshot of himself, rather faded, and inscribed "Best regards." They laughed again as Dodo put it in her bag; but the fact remained that she now possessed his likeness. . . .

She herself hadn't talked nearly so much, indeed she had no opportunity: Richard knew only that she lived with her aunt and ran a puppet theatre. This second item did not interest him very much, and Dodo, who was used to the curiosity and envy of the intelligentsia, at first wondered why. In time she came to understand that he had a dislike for all that part of her life which he had not shared: he wanted to think of her, not as an efficient business woman, or even as an efficient warden, but simply as the girl he walked with in Kensington Gardens.

That evening he took her back to Albion Alley, and there under the archway they found it surprisingly hard to separate; but he would not come in to the Theatre. The Alley was deserted; the houses in Albion Place stood empty, their back windows for the most part broken or boarded-up. A creeper drooped long straggling trails over the wall of Number 7; at Number 8 the paint of the back door still showed faintly green.

"My aunt used to live there," said Dodo.

"Did she?"

"About seventy years ago."

They looked seriously up at the solid brick wall, with the spikes still so firmly embedded on top: it looked ready to stand seventy years more, unless of course it got a bomb.

"Next week?" said Richard.

Dodo nodded. He hesitated a moment, and then (as though at the prompting of a distant voice) stooped quickly and kissed her on the cheek. They were both acutely aware that this was only their second meeting, but—who knew where the next bomb might not fall? Dodo kissed him back.

CHAPTER III

THE TEMPEST SHAKES the oak: the insects in its roots run about their business.

On D-Day Dodo managed to get some enamel. She and Treff and Gerhardi took the wireless into the workroom and spent the afternoon overhauling the entire set of Hans Andersen. But before that, immediately after lunch, she had hurried across the Park to Westminster Abbey, and said a prayer there, and hurried back. She did not know quite why she did this, but it appeared to be a common impulse: all around her as she knelt people dropped in for a moment and hurried away again. In the streets outside, except for the mobbing of newspaper-men, there was neither excitement nor bustle;

every face wore a look of extreme preoccupation—concentrated, sober, yet curiously absent, like the faces of sleepwalkers; as though a united will was being thrown into the struggle. Once more, after the long pause, history was on the move—but moving away from England, back to the old cockpits, and leaving only spectators behind.

For seven days all thought was fixed within the narrow limits of the Channel and the beaches; then a single plane over London was hit, it was assumed, by the first shot; and then as the rumours took shape the spectators found their new rôle to have been prematurely adopted. The new planes were not planes at all, but flying-bombs—pilotless, and therefore not to be turned back by the barrage.

Like every one else, Dodo said it didn't sound too nice.

So good were her spirits at this time, however, that her chief anxiety was lest her mother should take fresh alarm and renew her efforts to get her, Dodo, out of London. They could not succeed; but if they were made, and rejected, both mother and daughter must suffer by it. Alice's next letter, however, arrived no sooner than usual, and expressed no unusual solicitude. "Take care of yourself, my darling," she wrote—but that was what she always did write; and moreover she wrote from Somerset. Upon that less-tried area London's buzz-bombs could make little impact. They were no doubt very dreadful; Londoners, poor things, were having a terrible time again; but one had become used to saying such things, just as Alice had become used to telling Dodo to take care of herself. It was not exactly indifference, but rather the same useful instinct of self-defence which had refused, after Dunkirk, to envisage defeat, and which now refused to envisage the equally possible reduction of Southern England to a rubble-heap. (Evacuated Londoners found this attitude irritating and illogical, just as Continentals had found the British attitude irritating and illogical in 1940; but Londoners carried illogic one step further by returning to London.) In addition Alice had a particular reason for cultivating serenity, for the new baby was due next month, and its mother inclined to peak; when Ellen, who still missed Treff, tried to talk her into making another attack on Britannia Mews, she replied stoutly that Dodo was old enough to know her own mind.

"Treff would be another man for Freddy," suggested Ellen.

"My dear, Freddy didn't really care for him at all," said Alice rather pointedly; for she felt it slightly presumptuous that Ellen, unmarried, should talk thus knowledgeably about men. To be sure, she'd had Treff in her house for over eighteen years, but as Freddy once said, they were really a couple of old women together. "I've never been possessive," went on Alice. "Dodo knows she can come here the moment she likes—though I'm sure I don't know where we'd put her, especially with the monthly nurse—but I know she hates me to fret over her, and I shan't. I've decided to do all the layette knitting in white, and Joan can crochet a pink or blue edging afterwards; it will be a nice occupation till she's about again."

It was a pity Dodo could not overhear this conversation; it would have reminded her of the tale about the burdock-leaves.

2

THE BUZZ-BOMBS continued to arrive with annoying regularity—particularly between eight and nine in the morning, when people were going to work, and between five and seven, when they were going home; and every one complained about them far more than about the blitz. The old, almost forgotten feeling of defencelessness returned, and with it the old suspension of all nonessential activity. People stayed at home as much as possible, and for the first time since the big blitzes attendance at the Puppet Theatre fell off.

"It's ridiculous," said Adelaide impatiently. "What on earth are they afraid of?"

At that moment, with a noise like an express train, a bomb approached. As it passed overhead the swing-doors of the foyer were sucked open, hung a moment ajar, and clashed back.

"Of sudden death," said Dodo.

"But the chances are precisely the same"— The engine cut out.

Dodo pulled her aunt inside the Theatre, where there was less glass. "—here, as in their own homes. Who's that under the stage?"

It was Treff. He waited to hear the explosion and emerged unaffectedly brushing his knees. Adelaide sniffed and said:—

"Perhaps Treff has found the solution. We might invite our patrons to crawl under there too . . ."

"The point is, Aunt Adelaide, people don't want to get killed now the war's nearly over."

"People never do want to get killed that I know of. But one has to come to terms with death."

Dodo, who was not on duty, sat down in one of the back seats and regarded her aunt speculatively. It was very rarely that Mrs. Lambert fell into anything like an abstract mood, and she wanted to hear more. But Adelaide, after a moment's pause, merely remarked that the Theatre was looking very shabby, and that as soon as the war was over they would have to think about redecorating.

"Turn the Slade loose on it," advised Treff, coming down the aisle. (The Puppet was always used to draw on unpaid labour of this sort; it exercised a perennial fascination over generations of art students.) "Personally I'd like to try something baroque: cherubs, for instance, with plaster behinds."

He took the seat next to Dodo's; Adelaide had drawn up the old rocking-chair; they all three sat in a row before the empty stage as though waiting for a performance. Dodo said suddenly, "I don't believe most people think about death at all. They avoid it."

"Then they must have very slipshod minds. But you are quite possibly right," agreed Adelaide. "Treff is looking uncomfortable already."

"Not at all," said Treff. "I've thought about death a great deal more than you imagine. We go where the flame goes when the candle's blown out."

Adelaide looked at her brother dispassionately.

"It's wonderful how you make do, dear, with your words and phrases. Don't forget the bourne from whence no traveller returns."

"But that's true," protested Dodo. "We don't—"

Her words were drowned by the noise of a second express train rushing overhead. The swing-doors clashed; Adelaide observed pertinently that in a few moments they might understand more of what they were talking about; but again destruction passed over, the explosion was well to the north. A peculiar instinct, however, like a weather sense, told them all it was going to be a rough morning, and Adelaide, after making her pointed remark, went swiftly upstairs.

"If only she'd stay down here!" sighed Dodo. "Uncle Gilbert never even notices them . . ."

"They wish to die together," said Treff stiffly.

"Well, I know that. But I wish I knew more of—of what is in her mind. It might be so helpful."

"Nothing else is in her mind," said Treff, still in an oddly offended tone. "Adelaide is simply fortunate in having some one she wishes to die with."

Dodo looked at him and wondered. Was he yearning, after all these years, towards his abandoned Principessa? Was he being paid out, at long last, for his old heartlessness? A third time the doors clashed, and now the thunder overhead was louder and more menacing . . .

"Never mind, Uncle Treff," shouted Dodo. "*We*'ll die with each other!"

"Pah!" ejaculated Treff—and since the engine at that moment cut out, his shrill voice echoed through the Theatre, taking them both by surprise. In the silence that followed they stared at each other with instinctive repudiation, aversion almost: they didn't want to die together; they resented, each of them, having no one better with whom to share this supreme intimacy. Treff's thoughts flew to a very different figure from his niece's—a voluptuous magnolia shape, half mistress, half Madonna; as for Dodo, she knew only that whoever else might be her right companion, it wasn't Treff.

Death fell, but not on Britannia Mews.

"I believe it's Hampstead *again,*" groaned Dodo.

"You can't possibly tell," said Treff crossly. "*I* think it was south of the Park."

3

    IT WAS that same afternoon that Richard Tuke, after exchanging impressions of the morning's work, said abruptly:—

"I've got forty-eight hours from next Saturday. I'm going to my cottage. Will you come?"

At another period Dodo's immediate reaction would have seemed to lack sensibility. She said at once:—

"I can't be away Saturday night, I'm on call at the Post. And there's a matinée besides. I can't possibly get away on a Saturday."

"Then come down on Sunday morning."

"I'm on call Sunday night as well."

"Can't you find a substitute?"

Dodo reflected.

"I dare say I could ask Mr. Birch. I've taken his duty before now, and he lives in Bedford Street." She became aware of Richard regarding her with a rather quizzical expression. "Well, I have to think about it, don't I?" said Dodo defensively.

"Obviously, my darling. There's a war on. Now think about me."

Dodo looked at him and did so. Compared with the calls of the Theatre and the Post, his suggestion appeared fairly simple. He was asking her to spend the week end with him, and at his cottage, where they would be spared all the shabby contrivances incident to hotel registers; her mind still working on this practical level, Dodo saw how easy it would be; she could go on Sunday for a day in the country, and tell Adelaide that if she were late back she would go straight to the Post. Never were circumstances more propitious; and she knew that much the same thoughts had already passed through Richard's considerate mind. How nice he was!

How more than nice, how dear! "I do love him," thought Dodo. "I know I do!" The moral, or immoral, aspect of the thing did not trouble her in the least; had he asked her to marry him—and the fact that he did not was simply a tribute to her common sense— she would have been far more disturbed than she was. While she was thus trying to arrange her thoughts, he suddenly spoke again.

"Aren't we to have anything?" asked Richard abruptly.

The question touched her to the heart. All around them boys and girls were billing and cooing as frankly as the pigeons; nesting too, probably, like the pigeons, when and where they could; and in her heart Dodo suddenly echoed Richard's cry—"Am I never to have any share in this? Am I never to know love at all?" It was almost too late already, youth had slipped through her hands; if now, at the eleventh hour, love turned and called back to her, how could she not listen?

"Yes," said Dodo quickly. "I'll come down on Sunday. I'll stay. Yes, Dick."

CHAPTER IV

SATURDAY NIGHT was fortunately quiet: Dodo rose after seven hours' sleep in good looks and with energies equal to what-ever the day might bring. She dressed carefully, putting on a blue tweed suit made as recently as 1938; the big blue bag, which she so often slung from her shoulder, easily accommodated a night-dress and sponge-bag. Dodo put them in with a slight sense of unreality; but she put them in. Adelaide and Gilbert were still abed when she left, so that she had only to look round the door and say she was off. "Have a nice time, dear," said Adelaide casually. "If I'm back late, I may go straight to the Post," warned Dodo. "Anyway, don't worry about me." "I shan't," said Adelaide, with a faint air of surprise; and added, "You're old enough to look after yourself."

Running downstairs, it struck Dodo that her unprecedented action in taking a day off was arousing remarkably little interest; for some reason she found herself thinking of the spectacularly white wedding which Alice had once, and with such enthusiasm, designed. There were to have been six bridesmaids, and a possible page. "I wonder what's happened to Tommy?" thought Dodo, rather unbecomingly. She knew he was married; she would have bet that the wedding was white. In the train, however, she put these reflections out of her head to concentrate upon Richard; it was rather late in the day to examine her feelings towards him, and indeed she was not doing so, her feelings were fixed; she was rather recapitulating those qualities which had fixed them. His humour, for instance, his quiet sense of the absurd, so often directed at himself—never was a man less conceited; the closeness with which his mind followed her own, making all conversation intimate. "My dearest Richard," said Dodo, under her breath. The words sounded very natural. She repeated them with growing conviction as the train ran out into open country. It was a bright morning, promising a fine day.

2

RICHARD was waiting. This was the first time Dodo had seen him in civilian clothes, and though his flannel trousers and tweed jacket were very old, he looked considerably neater than he did in uniform. There was even an odd, lanky elegance about him as he came striding down the platform, not obviously hurrying, but moving with great rapidity; the instant of their meeting produced a heightening of emotion, a heightened awareness of each other, as sweet as it was new. It's going to be all right, thought Dodo; it's going to be perfect. . . .

He said:—

"You've come."

"Didn't you think I should?"

"I couldn't quite believe it."

He gave her a long, deep look; as they turned out of the station his fingers caught and twined in hers. Dodo returned the pressure gladly; a little shock of excitement sent the colour to her cheeks. They walked thus hand-in-hand past a few cottages, a few shops; the village was so small that it could have fitted into its own church-yard; the only modern building in sight was the Village Institute with a war memorial in the tidy front garden. One could see at a glance there were no evacuées; this wasn't a reception area; yet even so short a distance from London, peace, it seemed, still dwelt.

A bell chimed desultorily; only rooks answered; the congregation was still putting on its hats. But opposite the Institute Richard suddenly let his clasp loosen.

"Damn," he said softly. "Here's Mrs. Vicar. We won't stop."

But the Vicar's wife was not easily avoided: with a beaming face she hurried down the path, calling greetings as she came.

"Mr. Tuke—or do I say 'Corporal'—no, I won't! Mr. Tuke, how nice to see you again! Are you on leave? Are you coming in to see us?"

Richard mumbled that he had a forty-eight.

"And you're honouring the village! Isn't that nice!" The lady's kind eye turned upon Dodo, and found her a most suitable object to rest on. As might have been expected, Mr. Tuke's friend was a thoroughly nice person, thank heaven there was no need to be charitable or even discreet. "Have you come down from London?" asked Mrs. Vicar amiably. "You have? Do tell me, are these buzz-bombs very dreadful?"

"Pretty nasty," said Dodo.

Lightly as she spoke, however, she couldn't disguise her air of competence, and the other at once recognized it.

"You're not a warden, by any chance? You are? My dear, I can't tell you how I admire you. We feel so out of it here—at least, not that exactly, but we feel we're not doing our share. I think the London A.R.P. are perfect heroes—and what a blessing it must be to get out of it, even for the day! Mr. Tuke, if you want milk, or food of any sort, don't hesitate to come to the Vicarage."

Richard replied that he would not, and moved a step or two on.

But the Vicar's wife, besides having taken a fancy to his friend, was also (as all good vicars' wives must be) a great opportunist; she looked at Dodo longingly.

"I wonder if I could ask you—no, I can't! Only it just happens, Miss . . ."

"Baker," supplied Dodo.

". . . Miss Baker, that our A.R.P. actually has a practice this afternoon, and if you *could* just say a few words to them—we so rarely get any one with first-hand experience; in fact they get so little encouragement at all—I know they'd be thrilled to the core. Or is it asking too much?"

In the circumstances (unknown of course to Mrs. Vicar) it really was rather a lot: with cheerful amusement Dodo wondered whether any other young woman, embarking on an illicit week end, had ever been similarly waylaid. She glanced at Richard to share the joke, and found he wasn't looking amused, he was looking furious.

"I'm awfully sorry," said Dodo, "but this really is my first day off in years . . ."

"Oh, dear, and you must be so tired! Still, wouldn't you care just to have a peep at our control-room?" pleaded Mrs. Vicar. "Even that would be something."

Dodo shook her head. As a matter of fact, she wouldn't have disliked doing so at all; she took a professional interest in all A.R.P. work, and had never seen how a country post was run. But Richard's expression was becoming agonized.

"Then I won't keep you any longer," said the Vicar's wife regretfully. "I'll just say this: If you *should*—in the course of a walk, you know—be passing between three and four, just pop in."

They got away at last. As soon as they were out of earshot Richard began to apologize.

"My darling, I can't tell you how sorry I am, but it was just damned bad luck. That woman's intolerable."

"Oh, I don't know," said Dodo seriously. "It's awfully hard to keep a post on its toes when nothing ever happens. I wonder how they work their shifts?"

He stopped and stared at her.

"Good Lord, you don't mean you *want* to go and give a ruddy pep-talk?"

"No, of course not. I'd hate it."

She took his hand again, and with only a slight effort they recaptured their original mood in time for the great moment that was approaching. Their path now skirted a field, under a tall hedge; at a stile halfway along Richard stopped and, placing himself between Dodo and the gap, said rapidly, "The garden's not in proper order, and it needs planting," then stepped aside and let her look.

There was his cottage. It sat squarely between a small plot and a small orchard, the whole fenced about with white palings. Wide flower-beds flanked the path—one side weeded, one still a solid mass of green; the front door was painted white, with a brass knocker. Structurally the place wasn't interesting, it was an ordinary labourer's cottage, but the neatness and completeness of its details gave it a demure charm. Dodo exclaimed in honest admiration.

"My dear Dick, how perfectly adorable!"

"It's nothing much," said Richard, with ill-concealed pride.

"It's perfect. I want to see inside."

They climbed the stile and ran—Dodo started running—towards the white gate and up the path between the odd flower-beds: Richard pushed open the door, as one did in the country—as one did, of late, in Britannia Mews—and again stood back with his air of proprietorship. Within it was just as charming as without. Dodo found it touching as well: everything spoke of a lonely man's hobby, there was so much evidence of care and taste and economy, such meticulous groupings of china and brass. . . . Dodo pictured Richard standing now in the doorway, now by the fireplace, wondering whether the big blue bowl would look better here on the table or there on the window-sill; fiddling with the ginger jars, altering the furniture. . . .

"Look!" said Richard.

There were three blue cushions on the settle, a blue runner on the dresser: he whisked them all over, and on the other side they were red.

"That's for winter. And red curtains. It alters the whole room."

Dodo put her arms round his neck and kissed him. It was the first time she had ever done such a thing, and he turned to her with delight.

"My darling, my dear girl!" he repeated. "It's unbelievable! All these years I've been making this place, and I didn't know it was for you!"

"Show me everything!" commanded Dodo.

With the greatest delight he led her upstairs and down, into the tiny bedroom (with flowers on the bureau) into the tinier kitchen, into a minute bathroom where the water ran out but not in. "When I bought it," said Richard, "it was a pigsty. I've done everything myself." Dodo praised all she saw, feeling fonder of him every minute; when they sat down to lunch at the gate-leg table, "This," she thought, "is domestic bliss."

After lunch they took deck-chairs into the orchard. But the sun, though bright, had little warmth in it; very soon they both began to feel chilly. The obvious thing to do was to go for a walk; a walk was part of their programme. "The wood's on the other side of the village," explained Richard, "and we can't get round without trespassing. However, it's only half-past two." Dodo knew he was referring to the gathering at the Institute, and experienced a curious sense of playing truant; but she silently acknowledged that he was right: one didn't, in the circumstances, plunge headlong into local activities. As they recrossed the stile she spared a fleeting thought for Cyclamen, to whom such circumstances were no doubt the commonplaces of everyday life: Cyclamen would purr her way happily from one ambiguous situation to the next, spared all embarrassments by the fact that she was so obviously ambiguous herself. "I look too darned respectable," thought Dodo crossly. "Darn it, I look my age . . ."

What next occurred, however, was not her fault.

(351)

By an extraordinary chance all the members of the local A.R.P. had on this occasion arrived for their practice not only on time, but considerably before it: there they were in the Institute garden—four elderly ladies, the Vicar, the postman, two Boy Scouts, and of course the Vicar's wife.

Richard seized Dodo by the arm and dragged her into the nearest shop—or rather into its doorway, for the day being Sunday, it was naturally shut. Dodo found herself nose to nose with a Newfoundland dog on a calendar, while Richard fiercely regarded birthday cards.

"Darling, this is absurd!" protested Dodo. "They've seen us!"

"Wait till they've gone in."

Dodo stared at the dog for a full minute, feeling so much of a fool that it was rather a relief than otherwise when a now familiar voice sounded at her rear.

"Those are the ones I was telling you of, dear, the ones with the dogs on them. . . . Why, here's Miss Baker!"

"Don't look round," said Richard childishly.

But the situation was impossible. Dodo immediately turned and said rapidly that she had been admiring the calendars because they were so much more attractive than anything one could get in London. Her glance took in Mrs. Vicar's stooge: one of the elderly ladies, sixtyish, easily flurried, no earthly use in a blitz, but obstinately willing . . .

"Yes, aren't they nice?" said the Vicar's wife. "This is Miss Rose, who takes incoming messages."

God help you, thought Dodo. Aloud she said, "I'm on the telephone myself. It can be dreadfully boring."

"Not in London," murmured Miss Rose respectfully.

It was appalling. The two Boy Scouts had already joined the group, the postman hovered on its outskirts: expectancy hung over them almost visibly, like a cloud. Richard said briskly, "Come along, Dodo, if we want our walk." But the Vicar's wife held Dodo's eye and did not release it. She was apparently practising telepathy, for

(352)

the words "five minutes" formed themselves distinctly in Dodo's mind.

"Could I come in just for five minutes, just to see your control-room?"

At once a sort of sigh went up, the group parted, forming a lane. Feeling a traitor to Richard, a busybody, and a conceited impostor, Dodo allowed herself to be conducted into the Institute and shown the map of the district (water-mains traced in red, standing water coloured blue) the First Aid cupboard, the beds for firewatchers— "Though as it's so near," said Mrs. Vicar honestly, "we generally sleep at home"—all the modest paraphernalia of a least small link in the chain known as Air Defence Great Britain. Dodo voiced this metaphor aloud, producing universal pleasure; she also, without intending to, gave a description of one of the worst nights in Chester Street, and said a few smug words on the importance of being pre-pared. But these too went down well, and every one thanked her as though she had conferred some substantial benefit on them. A buzz of animated talk ensued; second-hand bomb stories, narrow escapes by near relatives, were eagerly retailed: in another moment (Dodo knew from experience) somebody would start making tea. With Mrs. Vicar abetting she made her escape, and in the little garden that lady thanked her again.

"But I was interested," protested Dodo. "We don't realize enough, in London, how much work's done outside."

The Vicar's wife laughed.

"The best butter, my dear. You know, and I know, there's very little we *can* do here, except put out incendiaries. If anything serious happens we have to telephone Wycombe, where they've an N.F.S. and rescue squads and things, to come to our aid. I'm on that telephone myself."

"Good," said Dodo.

The Vicar's wife laughed again.

"What a rag-tag and bob-tail we must seem to you! But the boys *have* put out incendiaries, and if I weren't there anyone except Miss

Rose could manage the telephone—there are *no* incoming calls—or at a pinch the postman could go off on his bicycle. We can look after ourselves, you see."

They shook hands with mutual respect, and Dodo invited her new friend, any time she was in London, to come and inspect the Post in Chester Street.

Richard had evidently spent the interval making good resolutions: he smiled at Dodo affectionately, and said he was an ass. "It's just that I grudge you even for twenty minutes, darling. What's the report?" "Highly favourable," said Dodo; and they walked on towards the woods.

3

BEECH WOODS in spring are made for lovers. Like lovers they wandered arm-in-arm, pausing now and then to kiss, rather seriously, recalling and re-examining (as lovers will) all the incidents of their brief acquaintance. "I'm glad we met in the Gardens," said Richard; "it matches this." Dodo said, "Anyway, I'm glad Piccadilly has a nice name," and as usual he followed her thought immediately. They were in a mood to be benevolent to all lovers; they were glad that the boys and girls who picked each other up on that pavement had at least one touch of prettiness offered them. How much more was given Richard and Dodo! They had a beech wood to walk in, when they were tired of walking they found a rustic seat, when they were thirsty they found a cottage whose garden, like a loose nosegay, was also a tea-garden. "Did you know this place was here?" asked Dodo, fishing honeysuckle from her cup. "I don't think it is, usually," said Richard.

On the homeward journey they more often fell silent. The very fact that they were going home, together, subtly altered the character of the day. Thitherto, whatever the underrunning currents, its actual events had been those of any holiday: now the time was come to leave this familiar ground and explore the unknown territory of passion. The cottage waited for them very quietly; though it was full daylight, the small-windowed rooms were already gath-ering dusk. Richard moved uncertainly towards the lamp, then changed his mind and came back to sit and look out beside Dodo in the window-seat.

"Happy, my darling?"

"Perfectly happy," said Dodo.

(Once, long ago, in a hansom cab, the same question and answer passed between Henry and Adelaide Lambert; and like Adelaide, Dodo was lying.)

4

AT WHAT MOMENT it happened she could not tell; but suddenly her thoughts, her heart, her very soul, were in Britannia Mews. Or rather, hovering between the Mews and the Post, where her substitute was on call. . . . No, not till seven, Dodo corrected herself; I'm not on till seven. . . . The substitute was perfectly reliable, and lived in Bedford Street. The whole arrangement was perfectly normal and above-board; no one, even if it turned out a bad night, would reproach her, Dodo, for being absent. She had too good a record.

"It's so peaceful here," said Richard softly. "I wanted to give you a little peace."

Dodo smiled, but could not speak. A sheerly physical uneasiness was coming over her, which she could only liken to the moment before fainting. There was the same struggle to keep a grasp on the present, the same effort to conceal one's distress, the same certainty of failure. For a moment or two she did not hear a word Richard was saying: she was facing the possibility of an incident in Britannia Mews. The odds against it were thousands, probably millions, to one. The night might be perfectly quiet. "And why do I worry about the night?" Dodo demanded. "It's not like the blitz. Something might have happened to-day—and I can't telephone."

Richard leaned towards her, and it was his movement that woke her to the fact that she had unconsciously drawn away from him.

She had, however briefly, forgotten him. Nor could she now quite remember him again. Richard, beside her, was farther away from her spirit than the Mews or the Post.

"Because this is not quite real," thought Dodo. "We are . . . making it up."

At once she was conscious of an immense relief, like the blood returning to the brain. She knew now what was wrong. And she said:—

"I'm sorry, Dick; but I'm not going to stay."

He drew back and looked at her; not really in surprise—not really in surprise!—but beseechingly. Dodo, as her vigour returned, felt a momentary impatience with his meekness; he should have laughed at her and kissed her, or kissed her and stormed at her, or in some way or other have kicked up the devil of a row. However, the fact that he did not strengthened her conviction that she was now right.

He said, very gently:—

"What is it, my dear? Getting mixed up with all these people?"

"No, no, no!"

"Are you worried about your aunt?"

"A little. I've a conscience about the Post."

"I thought you'd got some one to go instead."

"Naturally." Again—how unfairly, when she could see what an effort he was making to forget himself and think only of her!— Dodo felt that flash of impatience; she jumped up and began to pace about the room: she had a subconscious desire to get some life into the scene—if she'd been watching a rehearsal at the Puppet, she'd have said, "That scene's dead." Richard followed her with anxious eyes, waiting for her to explain.

She did her best.

"It's not only the Post, though that's cleared my mind. I have the feeling—Dick, I can't put it any better—I have the feeling that we're both trying to behave as though we were younger than we are. We're trying to be . . . reckless; and the truth is that we're simply very fond of each other in a nice quiet way. Don't you feel there's something unreal about this?"

(356)

He shook his head.

"Well, I'm sorry, but I do. It's my fault. Oh, dear!" cried Dodo ruefully, "I seem to leave everything too late! I left it too late to get married, and now I've left it too late to have a love-affair! Dick, I'm so fond of you!"

"I know you are, my dear, or you wouldn't have come here in the first place."

"But I can't keep my mind on you," went on Dodo, with perhaps unnecessary frankness. "I keep thinking suppose there's an incident and I'm not there. I *know* I've a substitute, but there it is. If this were the real thing—you and I, being lovers—I shouldn't care."

Richard stood up. Against the light his tall figure loomed enormous, dominating the tiny room. For a moment Dodo thought he would step between her and the door; for a moment she almost wished he would. Only, being Richard, he didn't.

"I can only tell you, my darling," he said unhappily, "that it's real to me. But you must choose."

He waited a moment, and when she did not speak went quietly upstairs. When he came back he had her hat and bag.

"I'll come with you to the station. There's a train quite soon."

"No, please don't," said Dodo. "Dear, please don't."

But he doggedly insisted. For the fourth time they walked down the village street, past the Institute, past the few cottages, past the few shops. Now and then they exchanged comments on the pleasantness of the evening, or the freshness of the country air. Dodo would have preferred an honest silence, but if such trivialities helped him she felt bound to play up. They had mercifully only a short while to wait, and the station was very gloomy, so that they could barely see each other's faces.

"Good-bye, my dear," said Dodo sadly.

"Good-bye, my love."

"Am I going to see you again?"

At that moment the train came in; he had not time, or did not wish for time, to answer, but opened the nearest carriage door and put her in. There was no other occupant, and so no need to keep up an appearance of composure; but Dodo, who used to cry quite easily, did not weep long. Her heart was heavy enough, but the day had been tiring; most of the way, she slept.

5

Adelaide, who was still up, showed no surprise at her niece's reappearance.

"I didn't go to the Post after all," said Dodo. "What's the day been like?"

"Quiet," said Adelaide. "Have you had any supper?"

"Yes, thanks. And I've had a lovely day in the country, and inspected a village A.R.P." Dodo began to laugh; the whole episode now seemed to her sad and funny in about equal parts; on the whole she was glad to be home again. She sat down by the hearth and cocked her toes on the fender and lit a cigarette, her mind already turning to next week's programmes in the Theatre, next week's duties at the Post, while from the other side of the fire Adelaide watched her very attentively for some minutes. At last Adelaide spoke. She said abruptly:—

"D'you want the Theatre?"

Dodo looked up in surprise.

"Want it? Want to go on running it? Of course."

"That's not exactly what I mean. Your uncle and I can't last much longer," went on Adelaide coolly. "If you want the Theatre, we'll give it you. I imagine it's chiefly a matter of licensing it in your name, and the puppets and fittings could be made over by deed of gift. Do you want it?"

Dodo threw her cigarette into the fire and gave the matter her full attention.

"You could leave it me," she pointed out, "in your will."

"Certainly. But I like to manage my affairs myself," said Adelaide. "Gilbert and I would of course go on living here; there's another five years' lease of the premises, and that should see our time; after that you'll have to renew, unless they pull the place down to build flats. But don't try to launch out. The reason this place has been a success," explained Adelaide dryly, "is not artistic merit, but the fact that we've never taken more than three pounds a week out of it. You won't make a fortune; but then your people are well off."

"I don't mind that," said Dodo slowly; "but you ought to think it over a bit longer."

"I've been thinking it over for some time. Lately I've simply been waiting in case you had other plans."

"I haven't."

"So I see."

Dodo laughed. As once before, twenty-two years ago, her aunt's complete awareness of a situation was extraordinarily grateful. There was no need to explain anything. Dodo, indeed, was now quite ready to give a serio-comic account of her whole romantic excursion, but it would have shown Richard as a bit of a muff. And he wasn't a muff—not at all; he was simply extremely nice, and an architect in a cathedral town. If he couldn't shake off the shadow of the Close, nor had Dodo been able to shake off the shadow of the A.R.P. . . .

"I believe," said Dodo suddenly, "I've just discovered the secret of life."

"And what is that?"

"Be your age."

"Humph," said Adelaide. "You've been long enough finding it out."

"Be your age," repeated Dodo peacefully. "Thank you very much, Aunt Adelaide, for the Theatre; it's just what I wanted."

CHAPTER V

ADELAIDE DID NOT now very often leave the Mews, but she was still capable of a good long walk when she felt like it, and on the first Sunday in August, soon after the Theatre had been officially made over to Dodo, announced her intention of spending the afternoon in Kensington Gardens. It was about three o'clock; Gilbert snoozed on the balcony; Dodo, Treff, and Gerhardi had all brought deck-chairs out into the Mews; the last had a sketch-book open on his knee, and as Adelaide walked by she rather pointedly refrained from glancing at it. The sketches were for a new *décor* for the Molière scenes, and she considered them unnecessary. "Don't walk too far, dear," murmured Dodo sleepily, "it's awfully hot . . ." "I shall walk as far as I see fit," replied Adelaide. The heat was simply agreeable to her, she was very completely clad, hatted, and gloved; her umbrella was not for use against the sun. Thus equipped she proceeded slowly out of the Mews, leaving a slight sense of discomfort behind her.

"You see?" said Gerhardi.

Dodo sighed. When the transfer of the Theatre was first bruited Gerhardi alone had seen any objection: he said Mrs. Lambert would not find it easy to give up the habits of almost forty years. And so it had turned out: Adelaide, pointedly disclaiming all authority, was nevertheless constant with advice, and so used to having her advice taken that another opinion could not fail to annoy her.

"In any case," said Treff—referring to the original backdrop—"it's not Gilbert's work. It's very bad. I dare say Addie copied it herself from a toy theatre."

His guess was partly correct, for the crude design of curtains and pillars had indeed been reproduced from a twopence coloured Cin-

derella; but not by Adelaide, and not even Adelaide could now remember by whom else. The Puppet Theatre, always attractive to
amateurs, had in the course of time accumulated a whole body of
such anonymous work, some good, some bad, most mediocre, and
it was Dodo's intention to sort everything out, scrap the worst, and
put the salvaged three-ply to fresh use. Adelaide disapproved. Disclaiming (as has been said) all authority, repeating that the Theatre
was Dodo's to do as she liked with, Adelaide, and not in silence, disapproved.

"If it makes her really unhappy—" began Dodo.

"Any change will make her unhappy." Gerhardi riffled the leaves
of his sketch-book impatiently. "Gilbert Lambert had genius, that I
admit—at least when he made the Molière figures. The rest are no
more than competent. And Jackson's are good too, though not so
good as Barty's. But only Barty had a feeling for the scene as a
whole. We need new *décors* for the Molière, and for Music Hall,
and for the Pastoral, and now we have the material, and it is for you
to say whether I am to create them—though it will make Mrs.
Lambert unhappy—or not."

Dodo sighed again. In one way her character strongly resembled her aunt's: they were neither of them artists, they were or-
ganizers. Dodo disliked the Molière set, for example, not so much
because it was unfitting as because it was shabby; her taste for the
immaculate, though it coincided so happily with the requirements of
puppet art, was merely an extension of her personal habits. An
almost equally strong habit was that of deference to her aunt; and
the result was to put her in something of a quandary.

"We'll see," she temporized. "Finish the designs, and then we'll
see."

Gerhardi shrugged. Treff, an ancient Panama hat tilted over his
eyes, leaned back and observed that though Addie had ceased to
pay the piper, she would evidently continue to call the tune. He
added maliciously:—

"Gerhardi should make a puppet of her; then it would be our
turn to pull the strings. . . ."

(361)

Neither Gerhardi nor Dodo answered, but the former took out a chalk and began to sketch. Out of the tail of her eye—the sun was making her sleepy—Dodo saw a figure take shape: long, thin, very straight, all black save for the profile and the crown of hair. . . . She meant to say, "No, don't do that, it's unlucky," but the sun was making her sleepy. Presently Gerhardi's hand slackened, the crayon rolled away; a light snore—was it from Treff, was it from Gerhardi?—roused Dodo for an instant, no more. A vague premonition of bad luck again crossed her mind; and then sleep took her too in the heat of the sun.

2

IN KENSINGTON GARDENS the grass had begun to brown, and there was a smell of autumn under the chestnuts; but Adelaide, who liked autumn, sniffed appreciatively. She was enjoying her walk extremely; it was in its small way an independent enterprise, such as circumstances now rarely permitted her; away from Dodo's fond solicitude, away, even, from Gilbert's fond affection, she felt peculiarly and enjoyably herself.

In this agreeable state of mind she reached the great central avenue, and there paused a moment: to her right lay the Pond, to her left the Serpentine; suddenly out of the past careered a big dog, an Airedale, running round and round in circles while three children stood transfixed with horror. *Mad dog, mad dog!* Of course, this is where we used to meet the Hambros, thought Adelaide, and Treff used to play with the Black Watch. The name of that famous regiment returned without the least difficulty: she could even remember a line or two of their rigmarole . . .

> The Black Watch will go night and day . . .
> The Black Watch never needs winding . . .

which she and Alice thought great nonsense, and so it was. What a nice little creature Alice had been—a trifle on the smug side, good as gold, but how loving and sweet-tempered! "Much nicer than I was," thought Adelaide dispassionately. "But even then I had more backbone. It's lucky Alice never had to stand on her own feet. . . ."

And something else had happened on the dog day: the visit to Belle Burnett. (Adelaide bounced gently down the Bayswater Road, wearing her best hat with the ermine's head on it.) And something had come of that visit, if not in the way Mrs. Culver expected: Belle Burnett's string of pearls was, in a sense, the foundation of the Puppet Theatre. And the spiny shell was still on the mantelpiece in the Mews, indestructible, having outlasted generations of china . . . having outlasted Belle Burnett. Adelaide had never seen or heard of her again; she was probably buried in Vienna, or perhaps in Italy, or somewhere on the Riviera, in one of the little Protestant graveyards made necessary by the nomadic habits of the English. It was strange to reflect that Mrs. Culver too lay in alien soil—that at long last the two women had something in common.

Walking slowly, at the pace of her thoughts, Adelaide came to the Serpentine. There were boats out, propelled chiefly by sailors; one would have thought they had enough of water, but perhaps not, perhaps they were novices, tadpoles, straining towards their natural element; or perhaps they merely wanted to show off an accomplishment before their female companions. A large swan, moving with far less effort, cruised slowly among the reflected branches of a chestnut-tree; and looking at the swan, and the tree, and the water, Adelaide remembered Henry.

"Dear me," said Adelaide.

It was a very long time since she had thought about him. He inhabited no Bluebeard's Chamber in her mind; Gilbert, in the early days of their being together, had seen to that. Henry was simply dead, like Belle Burnett and Mr. and Mrs. Culver, like Aunt and Uncle Ham, and though he had certainly caused her great misery, Adelaide bore no grudges. I should never have married him, she thought impartially. And he shouldn't have married me. But why I *wanted* to . . . !

The enigma, after nearly sixty years, was insoluble. It was all too far away: if the young Adelaide had suddenly appeared there on the path—eager, self-confident, her will-power driving like a dynamo, her very hands tingling with energy inside her muff—the old Adelaide would still have shaken her head and asked what it was all about. I was unhappy at home, she reflected, but there was that other young man—what was his name?—who proposed to me; why didn't I take him? Poor Henry wasn't even handsome, so far as I remember . . . Here she paused, for she was aware that the later, the rather dreadful image of Henry in decay, might have obliterated something better; unfortunately Henry in decay was much more distinct than Henry in his prime, who was not nearly so distinct as the Airedale. However, she gave him the benefit of the doubt; perhaps he had been handsome after all. But as for the emotion he must have inspired—she couldn't recapture a trace of it.

The swan sculled away; Adelaide moved on. Many heads turned to watch her progress, for she was a more remarkable figure than she knew; several young Americans were reminded of their grandmothers, and at the bridge into Hyde Park one wistfully attempted to see her across the road. (Adelaide, misunderstanding their respective rôles, kindly informed him that traffic in England took the left-hand side. "Yes, ma'am," said the American.)

At Hyde Park Corner there were flower-beds—red geraniums, huge ginger-coloured calceolarias, hydrangeas whose unopened buds matched the browning grass. Adelaide admired them without enthusiasm, as the sort of flowers one expected to see in public places; what she did admire was the evident pertinacity of the gardeners—after five years of war, it was a creditable display. A band also still played; the celebrated bomb-hole, now neatly fenced off, distracted no attention from the strains of a piccolo solo. Adelaide, who was beginning to feel tired, paid twopence for a chair and sat down to look and listen—for the eye was amused equally with the ear. It was as good as a play: never before, surely, or at least not since the Great Exhibition, had the park seen so motley a concourse. French, American, Norwegian; the Czechs and the Dutch; ambiguous refugees; the A.R.P. and the N.F.S.; British troops with their air of stolidity, Polish airmen with their despairing swagger; one Chelsea Pensioner, one New Zealander; the music giving all a theatrical unity. Also there were women; Adelaide was particularly struck by the extreme youth of some of the mothers, girls in brightly-coloured slacks, their hair lying on their shoulders, and also by the high standard of their offspring. They've done well, thought Adelaide. She was referring to the whole generation of the 'twenties—the "delinquent generation" about whom Jeremiads used to appear in the Press, over whose morals and lack of stamina two elder generations shook despairing heads. And here they were, conscripted, taxed, rationed, bombed, wearing orange trousers and flirting in the park . . . We didn't know we were born, thought Adelaide.

At that moment, as though to point her words, the familiar rumble overhead, the familiar silence heralding disaster, filled the high summer air. But disaster fell to the south; few heads so much as lifted. Like rabbits in a field, thought Adelaide, when the stoat's out; we go on nibbling. And why not? What else was there to do? The next moment she herself sat up, suddenly alert, her attention far more urgently caught by nothing more than a familiar tune: the band was playing Gilbert and Sullivan. Now, there was something that had lasted! Tunes might come and tunes might go—ragtime, jazz, boogie-woogie—but Gilbert and Sullivan went on for ever. Adelaide felt a personal gratification, for this was the music of the Victorians, and what body, what vitality, it still possessed! Looking round, she saw the same emotion reflected on the face of every person over fifty; and even the young listened with tolerance. "Who'll play Mairzy Doats fifty years from now?" demanded Adelaide—the name having lodged in her memory by reason of its sheer inanity. She made a mental note to ask Dodo this when she got home; and at the thought of going home suddenly realized that she was extremely tired. Moreover, it was nearly five o'clock; she would have to take a taxi.

The nearest exit was Stanhope Gate; Adelaide stood up, judged the distance carefully, and put herself in motion. The stiffness of her limbs annoyed her, and she forced herself to walk briskly; but each step became more and more a matter not of physical strength but of

(365)

will-power. Her will-power, however, had never failed her yet; Adelaide passed out between the stone pillars and took up her station on the curb—leaning indeed rather heavily on her umbrella, conscious of a curious weight about her neck and shoulders. For the first time in eighty years she was being forced to give all her attention to her body; the task of holding it decently erect demanded all her powers. She succeeded, or nearly; would have succeeded completely—but that just then a very strange thing happened. She thought she saw her mother. Mrs. Culver was on the opposite side of the road, smiling at her rather coldly; she raised her hand in a gesture of summons, and Adelaide looked quickly aside—just as she might have almost sixty years before, caught walking in Park Lane alone—in a foolish attempt to conceal her identity. The illusion lasted only an instant before she realized the truth: that a lady of rather old-fashioned appearance was waiting, like herself, to catch a taxi; but the shock had been great. Adelaide had to steady herself against a pillar; the constable on point-duty looked at her uneasily. "Taxi!" mouthed Adelaide; and forced herself back to the curb.

A minute later, she saw Belle Burnett.

A car had slowed down to turn in at the gate; Mrs. Burnett was in the back, very smartly made-up, in a hat gay with flowers; when she saw Adelaide she leaned forward and smiled. This time Adelaide was not deceived, she cut Belle Burnett dead; but her physical senses were bewildered, she turned sharply, clumsily, and blundered into the path of a gentleman who had just crossed the road. He stepped aside and courteously raised his hat; Adelaide, taken by surprise, bowed back before she remembered that Mr. Vaneck too must be long dead. The heavy figure passed on—massive, well-groomed, exuding the familiar air of power and possessions: a figure not uncommon in that place, at that hour. Adelaide took out her handkerchief and pressed it to her lips—and suddenly, at that gesture, smelt the sickening odour of new varnish. Had she cried out, or not, when the taxi drew alongside? She did not know, she thought perhaps the policeman had stopped it for her; thankfully she crept in. But taxis were scarce, and just as the flag went down a

(366)

hand was laid on the door, a face appeared in the window. Debonair, brown-eyed—of course, of course that was what Henry looked like! "Henry!" cried Adelaide. Though to her own ears her voice sounded shrill and piercing, neither Henry nor the driver appeared to hear it. She fumbled at the door-handle, but Henry turned away, only the driver's stolid face stared through the panel. Automatically—her brain working as it were on two levels at once—Adelaide gave the address, yet still, as the cab started, tried to open the door; till the lock, snapping back, caught her fingers in so sharp a pinch that pain blotted out all else.

3

WHEN Adelaide had not returned by five, and then by six o'clock, Dodo went across to the Gardens, walked as far as the Serpentine and back, and returned to find Gerhardi openly anxious. "She would not like to be away so long from her husband," said Gerhardi. Treff, who never liked to bother himself, thought Adelaide might have gone to see Iris O'Keefe. "I've rung her up," said Dodo. "There was no reply." She now rang again, and was answered by Miss O'Keefe's housekeeper: Madam was away for the week end, and there had been no callers; she, the housekeeper, had been out only between five and six. "Then that was when Adelaide called," said Treff comfortably. "She'll be on her way back now." Dodo looked at the time; it was nearly seven.

CHAPTER VI

AT SEVEN Dodo began ringing up the hospitals. They had no information. "We must try the police," said Gerhardi. "She would not like it, but we must try." At the Police Station the Inspector, to whom Adelaide's name was well known, promised to do what he could, and suggested ringing up the hospitals.

(367)

At eight, leaving Gerhardi at the phone and Treff upstairs, Dodo went back into the Gardens. This time she beat steadily from the Broad Walk to Hyde Park Corner, and enlisted the aid of two keepers. One of them had seen Adelaide, or a lady very like her, much earlier; walking slowly, he said, and attracting a good deal of notice. "What do you mean by that?" asked Dodo sharply. "Did she seem . . . lost?" The keeper hastened to reassure her: it was simply that the lady was generally striking-looking: people noticed her as she went by; if any of them were still about, no doubt they would recollect her. But the afternoon strollers were all gone, it was after sunset and the gardens were emptying rapidly. Dodo completed the circuit of the riding-track, returned past Albion Place, and at the corner of Chester Street encountered Treff. He had come to look for her with the news that the police had rung up again, to say one of their men had seen Adelaide at Stanhope Gate.

"What time?"

"About five. She took a taxi."

"A taxi!"

"Yes. So that's all right, isn't it?" said Treff persuasively.

For a moment Dodo was too angry to speak. *All right*—when it was then after nine! Only Treff, compact of selfishness, could so blind himself! She said curtly:—

"You needn't have come out to tell me that."

This time Treff kept silence. She had walked on so fast that he had almost to trot to keep up with her, and Dodo suddenly observed that he was shambling a little. She could not remember ever having noticed this before; and with better understanding her anger melted. For Treff was in fact shaken, and badly; he had come out not believing that his news could reassure her, but in the hope that she would reassure him—because there was no reassurance to be found with Gilbert and Gerhardi, or simply because he had grown despondent and tired of waiting in the company of those two old men. Even Dodo's curtness was welcome to him; he kept close to her side like an old dog.

"I thought you'd know what to do," explained Treff.

They reached the Mews. As Dodo hurried in Gerhardi called out to her from the stair, but she went straight to the foyer and rang up the police for herself. They could tell her no more: the constable on point-duty at Stanhope Gate had seen Mrs. Lambert, apparently waiting for a taxi. He managed to stop one for her, and she got in and the cab drove off in a perfectly normal manner. He knew Mrs. Lambert by sight, having once visited the Puppet Theatre. He thought she looked fatigued, but not ill, or likely to faint.

"And that was about five o'clock?"

"Five-ten, to be exact."

"If the taxi had been in an accident, would you know?"

"I've made enquiries, Miss Baker, and there's been nothing up to eight o'clock. And no incidents. We'll try to trace the cab for you, but that will take more time. Have you rung the hospitals?"

"Yes," said Dodo bleakly.

"If any further information comes in, I'll ring back."

"Thank you," said Dodo.

She hung up the receiver and for a moment sat with her head on her hands, trying to think clearly and reasonably, to weigh possibilities and judge what to do next. But the one fact so far to hand, that Adelaide had taken a taxi, simply bewildered her. From Stanhope Gate to Britannia Mews was a journey of ten minutes—fifteen at the very most; Adelaide should easily have been home by half-past five. What had happened, what could have happened, in that quarter of an hour? She became aware of Gerhardi calling her again, more urgently, and went out to find him still leaning from the iron steps.

"Dodo! Will you come up to Mr. Lambert?"

Reluctantly enough Dodo climbed the iron stair and went through to the bedroom. She knew how brief, when Adelaide was away, were Gilbert's periods of full consciousness: as she hoped, he had already dropped back into a half-sleep. But at her step he stirred, and opened his hand on the coverlet. Dodo laid her own within it: his fingers—dry and light as dead leaves—moved over her palm and at once withdrew. Without opening his eyes Gilbert said bitterly:—

"Where is Adelaide?"

"She's gone out, dear."

"That's what they tell me." The old hand moved helplessly, irritably, plucking at the quilt. "That fellow . . . and her brother . . . they've no sense. They said you'd know. Don't you?"

Mentally cursing both Treff and Gerhardi, Dodo nevertheless replied steadily,

"She's at Iris O'Keefe's. I think it's a big party . . ."

At once the hand, Gilbert's whole body, relaxed. For a moment he was silent, as though giving himself up to relief. Then he said crossly:—

"She shouldn't be so late. You'd better go and fetch her."

"Yes, dear."

"Take a cab."

"Of course."

For the next few minutes the small room was very still. Gilbert Lambert lay motionless, his short beard pointing at the ceiling; but his expression was once more troubled, and Dodo could not bring herself to leave him. She sat down on the end of Adelaide's bed— glad enough to rest; and presently, on a long sigh, Gilbert spoke again.

"Dodo?"

"Yes, dear, what is it?"

"If she's enjoying herself . . . don't hurry her."

Almost immediately, it seemed, he was asleep. The trouble had passed, leaving instead a look of peculiar childishness. Like a child, he was helpless; in the hands of others; and therefore the look was also innocent, and demanding of pity.

"If she is not found soon, I think he will die," said Gerhardi.

He had come quietly into the room and now stood at Dodo's elbow; she nodded without speaking. Breath, indeed, hardly stirred in Gilbert's frail body; the bed-linen, between the peak of his feet and his jutting beard, was hardly mounded; there was no more substance to him than his bones. Suddenly Dodo became aware that she was crying—and of Gerhardi's arm round her shoulders; and that the strangeness of this was only part of a general strangeness, as though the withdrawal of Adelaide had shattered a whole order of being and feeling in which they had all known their places and been content.

There was no comfort in Gerhardi's embrace: like Treff, it was he who sought comfort from her; they were all three, Treff, Gerhardi, Gilbert, instinctively turning to her, pathetically trusting, as Treff had said, that she would know what to do. She had to think for all of them; and now, though her head lay on Gerhardi's shoulder, her brain could not rest. Against all logic, the idea that Adelaide was still somewhere in the Gardens persisted: they were the only part of London, except the Mews, for which she had ever shown an attachment. Dodo knew she had played there as a child, walked there as a young woman; not only Adelaide had spoken of the Gardens, but Treff as well—and Alice Baker; so that from a hundred jig-saw pieces gathered over a number of years, Dodo could build up a very clear picture of young Culvers and young Hambros in the Gardens of seventy years before. If she could have formulated the thought that haunted her, it would have been this: that perhaps Adelaide had somehow slipped back in time, returned to her old playground, and might now be wandering there in search of the others. . . .

There was the taxi, of course; but by this time Dodo had ceased to think coherently; and indeed the business of the taxi was so thoroughly incomprehensible that she simply rejected it.

She said softly:—

"I'm going out again."

"What can you do?"

"I think she may be still in the Gardens."

"But this about the taxi—"

"It must be some mistake."

"Shall I come with you?"

"No. Stay by the telephone. Tell Treff to stay here, in case Uncle Gilbert wakes. Say—"

Dodo broke off. What was there to say? Nothing. She pulled herself to her feet and went out.

2

THERE WERE more people in the Gardens at night than she expected. When the railings were taken down a whole nocturnal population had moved in: tramps asleep, amorous couples who at her step blotted themselves against the grass; a couple of runners padded past, ghostlike in their white clothing. The silence, which was very noticeable, made them all slightly unreal; Dodo wondered whether she were as unreal to them—the ghost of a warden, in a coat of shadows. This idea of her own invisibility worried her; for it meant that Adelaide, all in black, could pass unseen at no more than a few yards; only blind chance could bring them together. It would have been reasonable to call out, but Dodo felt a reluctance to raise her voice in that stillness; her first attempt was answered by a half-mocking, half-inviting whistle, and she did not call again.

With the rising of the moon her search became easier: vacancy at least was apparent—the empty paths, the unoccupied hollows and breadths of grey untrodden grass; figures took on a sharper definition, declaring themselves at once man or woman, solitary or coupled; even the sleepers showed at a glance some characteristic unpromising shape. Only the deepest shadows, under the trees, now and then drew Dodo's steps; as often as not she found herself stooping over the cast outline of a branch, or a chair turned on its side.

She had turned for home, the search abandoned, when hope flickered for the last time: in the alcove at the head of the Serpentine lay a figure whose choice of bed—on a seat, not on the ground—and propriety of coverings—four or five newspapers—discovered an odd air of decorum. But at Dodo's approach the figure moved, raised from its shapeless wrappings a shapeless face—not Adelaide's clear profile, nor Adelaide's voice—as she whined out some plea or apology: a faint odour of decay was released on the night air. But Dodo pushed a coin into the dirty fingers and tried to question her: had she been there long, had she seen a lady with white hair? The creature only mumbled that she was doing no harm. Her nails, however, had found the milled edge of the shilling; with the vestige of a social manner (sketching as it were the caricature of all hostesses) she drew up her broken-booted feet in case Dodo wished to sit down. The latter did so, not expectant of more but simply because she was by now very tired; perhaps because of fatigue the situation did not even seem unusual to her; the silence, as neither spoke again for some minutes, became rather companionable. Then the old woman offered a remark.

"They don't cry the All Out any more. . . ."

"That's because the railings are down."

"They should cry the All Out," persisted the old woman, with some energy, "then we'd know where we were. I ain't afeard o' spirits."

"Aren't you?"

The old woman hawked.

"Why, what's spirits but tramps? They're the tramps o' the next world, same as we're tramps o' this. I told that to a clergyman once; and he couldn't answer me."

Dodo looked at her companion with more attention. There was a sort of patness about this reported speech, a touch of the *raconteur,* that reminded her of Treff. In very different circles both, perhaps, employed the same technique. They were of the same generation; which was also Adelaide's. Dodo said abruptly,

"If you were very tired, perhaps not well, and you took a cab, where would you tell it to go?"

"I'd tell it to go 'ome. If I 'ad a 'ome. If I 'adn't, why would I take a cab?"

"That's just it," said Dodo.

She got up, and turned for home.

It was pure chance, when she had crossed the Bayswater Road, whether she turned right or left, to Chester or to Bedford Street; she turned right, past the higher-numbered houses of Albion Place. It struck her how little damaged they looked: by night the boards across the windows might have been merely shutters, the shadows under the porticoes concealed their damaged front-doors—some boarded like the windows, some buttressed into place; one, neither buttressed nor boarded, stood an inch or two ajar, as though the owner had just gone in and forgotten to close it. Dodo paused. In spite of all fatigue her warden's instinct told her that that door ought to be secured. She flashed her torch over it, and the number leaped out above the lintel—a figure 8 in white enamel, hanging precariously by the lead of a glassless fanlight. . . .

Dodo mounted the shallow step and put her hand on the door. It moved fairly easily, scraping only a little dust and rubbish. From within came either an echo of the sound, or the sound of some other faint movement.

"Aunt Adelaide!" called Dodo.

She thought she heard the sound again; flashed her torch over the floor, over the walls, over two tall pillars; found at the foot of the stair a shadow that did not move; and the next moment was on her knees feeling for Adelaide's hands.

3

ADELAIDE opened her eyes. Her features were greyed with dust, on the left side a little drawn. Dodo turned the torchlight on her own face, and to her immense relief Adelaide's eyes focussed themselves; with an old gesture she drew herself up, straightening her back; the left shoulder a little higher than the right. She said:—

"Alice?"

"No, it's me, Dodo," implored Dodo. "Aunt Adelaide, are you all right?"

"Hold your light up a minute, dear. There, over your head."

Afraid to disobey, Dodo did so; and her aunt nodded.

"Those pillars were always shams: you can see now that the ceiling doesn't really rest on them. What time is it?"

"Nearly midnight. Darling, what *happened?*"

"I believe I must have over-tired myself, dear—just as you warned me." (This was the only expression of gratitude, of regret for causing so much distress, that Adelaide ever vouchsafed.) "Then I took a taxi—"

"We know that. But why didn't you tell the man to come home?"

"I did, dear. I suppose I forgot; but this is where we used to live. . . ."

It was as simple as that: no more than an odd, but not inexplicable, lapse of memory. And what happened afterwards Dodo could see plainly enough too: Adelaide, already shaken, entering that empty and broken hall, had either fainted or else, and more probably, suffered a slight stroke. She had been there, crouched on the stairs, throughout the whole search—not a stone's-throw from the Mews, within earshot (could she have heard) of Dodo's anxious steps . . .

"Gilbert will be worrying," said Adelaide, in her usual voice. "Help me up."

"Can you stand?"

"Of course I can stand."

Leaning on Dodo's shoulder, she rose stiffly to her feet; slowly they traversed the hall and reached the door, where Adelaide took her umbrella from the stand. (Describing this incident afterwards to Gerhardi, Dodo strove hard to convey the queerness of it: behind the door stood what looked like a length of drain-pipe, still painted, no doubt, under its grime, with birds and bullrushes—an old-fashioned umbrella-stand. Adelaide, entering, had instinctively put her umbrella in the proper place.) With this additional support she moved more certainly; they emerged under the portico and Dodo pulled the door to behind them; and a little shower of dust and plaster fell on their heads.

"It's time that house came down," said Adelaide. Whatever blind instinct, whatever old attachment had recalled her there, its power was ended; she did not look back. She said:—

"Who is with Gilbert?"

"Treff. Gerhardi's by the telephone in the foyer."

"At this time of night?"

There on the pavement of Albion Place, Dodo halted. Almost

her aunt's full weight was on her arm, but the old voice carried its familiar sardonic note—in the circumstances annoying.

"Yes, darling," said Dodo. "We've been ringing up the police about you. Also the hospitals. I've walked three times round the Park. We've been frantic. That is why Gerhardi is in the foyer, by the telephone."

Adelaide sniffed.

"As you don't mention Treff, I suppose he kept his head. And as you don't mention Gilbert—"

"I think we'd better get home as fast as we can," said Dodo.

4

It NEEDED all her efforts, and Gerhardi's to get Adelaide up the iron stair. Treff came out of the bedroom, nodded casually to his sister, and held open the door. With a sudden access of strength Adelaide walked in and sat down beside the bed and laid her hand in Gilbert's. This time his fingers tightened, clutched; he opened his eyes, his lips moved, and from the doorway Dodo caught a whispered phrase.

"But, soft! what light through yonder window breaks?
It is the east . . ."

"Old actor!" said Treff unkindly.

5

But Dodo, who had seen Adelaide's head drop suddenly down on the pillow, drew him away; they went downstairs to join Gerhardi, and eat the sandwiches he had cut for Dodo, and rest for a moment and relax after the long strain. (It only wanted the tinkle of broken glass, thought Dodo, to complete the after-an-incident atmosphere.) The two men had questions to ask, and when she answered them Treff at least showed less surprise than she expected. "Of course," he said; and—with rare self-depreciation—"I should have thought of it. She went home." "But it isn't her home!"

(376)

argued Dodo. "Here—or in Kensington, perhaps—but you've told me yourself you left Albion Place ages ago!" "It's where we were children," said Treff stubbornly. Gerhardi shrugged and said, "Because she had for a little lost herself, yes; but this is her real home, where her husband is, and where the Theatre is. But it is a curious thing, Dodo—you will think me superstitious—"

"We're all superstitious, these days."

"I had been thinking, while you were away, that if she did not come back, we should have a bomb. There could be no more Britannia Mews without her. And then when you did not come back either (do you know you have been away three hours?) I began to think the same about you. 'If Dodo does not come back, we shall have a bomb.' For by that time, you see, I did not expect Mrs. Lambert at all."

Dodo munched her sandwich and stared out at the houses opposite. (They were much less particular about the blackout since the doodle-bugs.) She said practically:—

"If we were bombed, they'd build again . . . probably put up blocks of flats. Albion Place is due for demolition anyhow. Could we have flats over the Theatre?"

"If it were an entirely new building," said Gerhardi. "And I tell you, Dodo, if they build, when our lease runs out, we shall need capital . . . At least some thousands, and a mortgage. . . ."

"Dodo can get it from her people," said Treff.

"I might." Dodo reached for the last sandwich. "After all, we're established. The Theatre's been a going concern for nearly forty years. I'd like to keep part of the Mews as a sort of forecourt—"

"With a café," said Gerhardi.

"We can't go all Glyndebourne."

"But a café is quite modest." Gerhardi pulled out a chalk and began sketching on Adelaide's blotter. "Have the theatre where it is, and a forecourt so, and the café opposite, with flats above if need be—make it something charming and original, and you will put up the rents of the flats. Treff talks of baroque—"

"Only for the Theatre," put in Treff.

"I would say, let us be quite modern. Dodo, look at my sketch, please, and say if it is not attractive . . ."

They bent together over the scribbled plan, and at once began to argue. For the first time Dodo's possession of the Puppet Theatre was a reality, its future firmly in her hands. All three of them felt it; the two men addressed their arguments to her, competing for her attention, while Dodo, knowing that hers was the last word, listened more than she talked. And they were right so to feel and speak and listen, and even to forget Adelaide; for the two old people in the room above were no longer concerned with the future.

THE END